For Marion

I

I spent three hours preparing the first words I dared speak to her. Victoria is not the kind of woman a stranger can approach without her feeling insulted. The first few seconds would be crucial: I would only have one phrase, one look in her eyes, to persuade her to forgive me, and to stop walking.

I'd just bought a cuddly toy so large that its long, bendy tail poked out of the plastic bag that the shopkeeper had put it in, and this appendage made it look as though I were carrying a fake-fur question mark. I regretted not having found out what kind of animal it was (because Vivienne would be bound to ask: 'What is it? Look how big its tail is! And what pretty whiskers! Here, touch it!'), but I had lacked the presence of mind to question the sales assistant. I took the escalator down to the ground floor, heading towards the car park where I'd left my car. Vivienne is the younger of my two daughters; we were supposed to be celebrating her fifth birthday that evening.

What is the name of this animal I'm carrying?

It's not a beaver, or a marmot, or a weasel, or a raccoon, but it's something along those lines – the sort of animal that you imagine lives on dry land, but without having given up the pleasures of bathing. Does it sleep buried in the ground like a mole, or nestled in the undergrowth like a rabbit, or gripping a tree branch like a squirrel?

I open the plastic bag to check whether the animal's paws are webbed or clawed. The escalator deposits me on the ground floor, and I am joining the main aisle when my attention is drawn to a woman's figure. She stands in front of a clothes shop with her back to me, looking at the items displayed in the window. I like this woman: her aura, the austerity of her clothes, the way she holds her head, the way she stands. I stop and watch her. She has a queenly radiance, an authority. It is a long time since I was so attracted to a woman encountered by chance. She moves along the window, then stops again. Prosperity and elegance. I have the feeling that her gaze lingers for a moment on the reflection of her face. Her hair is thick and wavy, her body voluptuous and full-chested. I watch her examine herself. She must be more or less the same height as me: just under six foot. She checks her wristwatch again. With meticulous indifference, she studies an evening dress worn by a headless mannequin; that, at least, is the attitude suggested by her expression, which alternates between irritation and dreaminess. Perhaps she was supposed to be meeting someone?

Much later, she told me the truth about her situation and why she was hanging around outside a clothes shop that day.

I like her calves, rounded and firm, held taut by the heels of her shoes. They eroticize her presence. Looking at them makes me want to make love to her.

She makes a phone call and moves away from the window. She listens more than she speaks. There are no clues as to whether this conversation is professional or personal, whether the words she is hearing are upsetting or pleasurable, whether the person with whom she seems to be in discussion is a man or a woman. Perhaps she's checking her voicemail? I watch as, pensive and absorbed, she drifts slowly towards me, and at the moment when we are about to bump into each other, she throws me a lively glance. In this glance I detect – in response to my face, my eyes, my fascinated and admiring gaze – a flash of surprise and discreet approval. I turn back, hoping she'll turn back too, and that she'll be smiling. But I see her wander on in silence, moving over the tiled floor with a tense concentration that has an air of finality.

I wondered what to do. I found it amazing that I could have sparked a look so indisputably complicit in a woman I had noticed only a few minutes earlier. I had sensed an instantaneous reaction to my presence, and in her eyes I had seen a start of astonishment or recognition – exactly as if this woman, bumping into me the day before a planned meeting, felt a thrill of surprise at seeing me, by chance, in public, sooner than she'd expected. But as I was sure that she didn't know me at all, I inferred from this that she recognized me as being to her taste, perhaps even corresponding to her most secret inclinations. Would I have followed this stranger if, upon seeing me, her face had not shown this almost unconscious flash of approval? There was a time when I wouldn't have hesitated to approach women I liked in the street, but I had lost the habit so long ago it seemed inconceivable to me that I could start again in these circumstances: with a woman who was out of my league and whom I presumed would not, as a matter of principle, allow herself to be chatted up by a stranger. So . . . what happened? Why did I decide to follow her? Because I had caught a glimpse of something beyond the here and now. I had seen her life reflecting mine. This flash gave me the feeling that I'd gone on a long, intimate journey with her, just the two of us. Nothing is more arousing than to glimpse the landscape of someone's soul when you look in their eyes.

I followed her into a café, where I spent an hour observing her. She slipped off her shoes. I saw her from behind and from three-quarters behind. The newspaper and the two books she had with her implied that she spoke English, French and German.

I contemplated her feet, which I thought magnificent. She kept leafing through her two books and she spread the *Frankfurter Allgemeine Zeitung* on the table. What could I say to her? She seemed nervous and impatient. Her eyes surveyed the shopping centre through the windows, and I feared that a third person would come in and destroy the intimacy of this private scene: a man would appear, she would signal to him with her hand, and he would sit next to her, apologizing for his lateness.

Her sandals had been knocked on to their sides, and she was trying to put them right with her toes. She was busy texting, absorbed by remote and doubtless important preoccupations, unaware that she had become the object of such anxious attention. I put a hand in my trouser pocket and stroked myself. I saw her in profile when she turned her head to scan the shopping centre through the windows.

I loved the dress she was wearing: long-sleeved, and fashioned in such light, floating muslin that the air conditioning made her outline quiver. I loved the gentle way her fingers hung suspended, as if in a drowse, each time a daydream immobilized her. I would have liked to have seen her face for longer than an instant, and to have memorized a reality more tangible than that unforgettable flash. Ankles, toes, wrists, fingers, fingernails, chin, hair . . . I familiarized myself with her body, piece by little piece, before I even knew who she was, before I had seen her smile or heard the texture of her voice. After this hour spent scrutinizing her, I could have pointed out her index finger from among a thousand others, or her earlobes, but without knowing the life of her face, its expressions and its routine. I hoped to be able to think one day, and to tell her with a smile, that I would always have one hour's head start on her.

She stood up abruptly, ready to leave, gathering her belongings. Then she led me on an endlessly wandering chase.

4

I'd told my colleagues that I had to leave earlier than usual, but that they could get hold of me in an emergency. As my job consists of solving problems at the very moment they occur, and as a construction site is constantly generating unforeseen complications, a state of emergency had become the habitual mood of my days: I feel time passing like the ticking of a thousand time bombs that I have to defuse. I didn't dare check my BlackBerry, which had been on silent mode in my pocket for the last hour, because I knew there would be a backlog of disputes to arbitrate, mysteries to unravel, colleagues to help and obstacles to remove. My assistant was the only one to whom I'd told the truth: that we were celebrating Vivienne's birthday that evening, and that I was in a desperate rush to find something spectacular to give her. 'Why spectacular?' she'd asked me. 'But you can contact me,' I'd added. 'Feel free to pass on all the calls you want.' 'Answer my question: why spectacular?' 'I don't know, just because. To make up for . . . you know I'm not home very much at the moment . . .' 'At the moment?' Caroline interrupted me. 'For months, you mean!' 'Exactly – for months.' 'And when they see your face, they hardly even recognize you because you're so tired. They probably imagine you've come to fix the washing machine!' 'You're absolutely right – come to fix the washing machine. And that's why tonight I'll arrive at the house at a time when families normally sit down for a meal together, carrying a spectacular present.' 'So get out of here, and have a great evening. I'll try not to let too many messages reach your BlackBerry, and I'll block anyone who might ruin your evening.' And then she added: 'Remember, your daughters don't need you to give them spectacular presents to know that you love them.' I looked tenderly at Caroline – 'Thank you, that's sweet of you. I hope you have a good evening too!' – and blew her a kiss from the office door.

Would I be brave enough to speak to such a distinguished woman? I was waiting for an opportunity to present itself that would allow me to approach her without seeming rude. 'Excuse me, madame, you've dropped your scarf.' 'Ah, thank you very much.' 'You're welcome.' 'Seriously, thank you. I like this scarf a lot.' 'I don't blame you. It's very beautiful.' She had to be able to forgive herself for listening to my opening words without slipping away, and then to succumb to the curiosity that my next words would undoubtedly provoke in her. 'All these horses on your scarf, do you like them? I mean, do you like horses? Do you ride?' I knew I had to offer her the chance to maintain her dignity, in her own eyes as well as mine.

But she didn't drop anything.

The most annoying thing was that she headed towards the bowling alley at the end of the shopping centre, where I watched her hire a pair of shoes and get ready to play. Afterwards, I went to the counter (where, pretending to be superstitious, I managed to persuade the ticket-seller to give me lane number eight, rather than thirteen, the one next to hers), then sat in an orange plastic seat from where I could watch this beautiful stranger throw her first bowls. How long would I have to wait before I could speak to her? Was I going to approach her in the bowling alley, or would it be better to be walking back through the shopping centre? It wouldn't have taken much to make me abandon my hunt when I dropped my shoes off at the counter; it wouldn't have taken much, in that moment of doubt, for me to exit quickly and remorsefully. Was I going to miss Vivienne's birthday because a woman I had never met before had responded to my glance with a flash of complicity? In spite of the alarm bells ringing in my head, I found myself incapable of escaping the enchantment I'd been drawn into by the vision of this woman.

I thought about what I could say to her.

'Madame, excuse me, this is not something I usually do, believe me, talking to strangers . . .'

'Madame. If I confess to you that I am sacrificing my daughter's fifth birthday, perhaps you will give my approach the indulgence it deserves . . .'

'Excuse me . . . madame . . . I'm sure you're going to turn me down . . . but I wanted to tell you . . .'

What time was it? I hadn't dared look at my watch for quite a while now.

I was aware of having put myself in a situation that no rational examination could justify. Circumstances had drawn me into a dazzling zone where I felt myself close to some kind of internal truth (which I will try to define a bit later). In spite of that, however, there was no doubt I was behaving absurdly. To lose two hours being taken in by the illusions of a single look could only be described as pathetic, especially to hear at the end of it all: 'You're kind . . . really . . . I'm touched . . . your compliments are flattering, but you know . . . I'm sorry I have to disappoint you . . . I'm married and I have two children . . . goodbye . . . have a good evening.' And that was a best-case scenario. Did the prospect of making love to a woman whose physical charms had captivated you justify becoming enslaved to the electrified naivety caused by this desire? In other words, would I have followed this woman for three hours if my attraction had been only sexual? I ended up persuading myself that something crucial awaited me: this feeling lit me up inside intensely, like a brilliant intuition. An event had occurred in her eyes – like words spoken, with a tone, a flavour, colours, a texture, an inflexion and a direction – and in that event I had begun to glimpse a new world. I could easily have given up on her body, her presence, the desire to make love with this woman and to kiss her lips: all I'd have to do was get up and head towards the exit. But not only did I refuse to turn away from that elsewhere that had sparkled in her eyes, but I was also afraid I would later regret such a decision and spend years thinking that this encounter might have changed my life. (I'm the type of man who has regrets that last decades.)

The players around me threw their bowls like illustrations of a particular mood or state of mind: grace, fear, pleasure, pride, humour or nonchalance. I noted in particular, in the aisle next to mine, a young girl whose technique was so lacking in skill that it was affected, almost artistic; her singularity was very attractive. I wondered which allegory my beautiful stranger was going to embody. And then she started playing – with astonishing ease. Her bowls seemed not to roll at all, but to advance so silently and motionlessly that it was almost meditative, and it was only when they hit the pins, with an unstoppably violent impact, that I sensed it would have been impossible to go faster, or in a straighter line, or to be more devastating. It was only when the bowl smashed into its target – not during the time when it had the appearance of a mysterious undertone – that the violence animating this woman at the moment when the black sphere left her hand was revealed. It was absolutely incredible. With my fingertips, I caressed a cool metal railing while admiring an allegory of, simultaneously, an orgasm, a thunderbolt, a passionate outburst, and dominance.

She returned to the seat where she'd left her belongings. I saw her almost face-on: her cheeks had reddened, her hard stare pierced the floor, she wiped her hands with a paper towel. I had the feeling that the violence had washed away the anger that inhabited her, in a deflagration of light, vengeance and irony.

But what was she doing there, a woman like her, dressed like a lawyer, in a bowling alley, surrounded by teenagers having fun?

I ventured a look at my watch: it was 9.30 p.m. I checked my BlackBerry: twenty-six missed calls, eighteen voice messages and nearly sixty emails. I was surprised that my wife had left only two messages, the first just after I left the construction site and the second when we had been supposed to sit down to eat.

I had to wait another hour before I could talk to her. What did I do during that time? I watched my beautiful stranger throw bowls and destroy perfect arrangements of pins. I hopped up and down to keep warm: it was cold in the bowling alley. I decided not to have a drink at the bar located a bit further off because I would have had a less clear view of the show she was giving me. A little girl sat close to me. I ended up phoning Sylvie to explain my absence and send a kiss to Vivienne and Salomé.

I pressed the 1 on my BlackBerry. The 1 speed-dialled my home number and the 6 Sylvie's mobile. She was the one who answered.

'It's me,' I told her.

'Ah, hello. Hang on a second.'

I could hear my two daughters arguing. Sylvie calmed them down by talking to them in a quiet, composed voice.

'OK, that's settled!' she told me, picking up the phone again. 'What are you doing? Why aren't you here?'

'I had to stay at the tower.'

'I called the site at six thirty. Caroline told me you'd left to buy a present for Vivienne.'

'I didn't see her after that. I haven't even listened to the two messages you left me.'

'I wanted to know if we should eat without you. We were hungry and Vivienne was getting impatient.'

'So did it go well? They sound a bit excited . . . are they fighting?'

'It went very well. They were sweet. You should have seen

how Salomé made us laugh! She's incredible when she gets going – she's so funny!'

'You seem in a very good mood, anyway.'

'I'm tipsy.'

'What did you drink?'

'When she started imitating her sister! Even Vivienne was in stitches . . . and Fréderic could hardly breathe!'

'Fréderic? Hang on, the Deneuves were there? Fuck, that's unbelievable! *They were at Vivienne's birthday dinner?*'

'I told you last night, David.'

'What? You told me last night that the Deneuves were coming to dinner, that Fréderic would be there, at Vivienne's birthday? Fuck . . .'

'I told you last night that I'd invited the Deneuves and their daughter to dinner. It was Vivienne who wanted Carla there for her birthday. I asked her parents if they wanted to come too. I told you last night that I'd had that idea, and that the Deneuves had said yes. Anyway, how would that have changed your problems with the site if you'd remembered that the Deneuves were coming to dinner?'

'You must have really had fun. Didn't they say anything?'

'About what?'

'About me cancelling.'

'You didn't cancel. We waited for you and you didn't turn up. Not quite the same thing.'

'OK, about me not turning up. They didn't say anything about that?'

'What do you want them to say? We waited for you. We tried to get hold of you, but there was no answer.'

'And Vivienne?'

'And Vivienne what?'

'Didn't she say anything? She didn't say anything about this birthday dinner happening without me, without my gift? Didn't she say anything? Didn't she ask for me?'

'Would you have wanted her to ask for you, to start crying?'

'Not at all. I'm just asking if everything went well, if she was happy with her birthday party.'

'Right, and I'm telling you: everything went very well. Vivienne was happy with her birthday party, and so was Salomé, and so were the Deneuves.'

'Were they arguing? I heard them screaming, earlier. Were they fighting?'

'They've had a long day, and they've got school tomorrow. Carla fell asleep on the sofa. I asked Vivienne to go to bed.'

'I'd like to say goodnight to her.'

'Hang on, she's in the kitchen with Christine. Vivienne, it's Daddy, he'd like to have a word with you. You don't want to talk to him? Just quickly, send him a kiss and say goodnight . . . No? You don't want to? Are you sure?' And then: 'She doesn't want to. She's exhausted. I'm going to put her to bed. Vivienne, it is Daddy, though, don't you want to blow him a big kiss? You want to send him a kiss on a flying carpet? And tell him that you love him? She's nodding, she says yes, she loves you and she's sending you big kisses on a flying carpet. She's here in front of me and she's sending you huge wet kisses.'

'Give her a kiss from me and tell her I love her.'

'He sends a kiss. Here's a kiss from Daddy. He says to tell you that he's sending you a kiss and he loves you.'

'Lots. Tell her I love her lots . . . lots and lots and lots!'

'David, what's up with you?'

'You couldn't care less, could you? It's all the same to you and them.'

'What is? What's all the same to us?'

'Whether I'm there or not.'

'David, what are you on about? What's the matter with you? You sound like you're going mad.'

'You hardly even notice my absence. I was thinking what a disaster it was, to miss Vivienne's birthday party! And what actually happens? Hardly anyone even notices I'm not there. You check by phone that David really isn't coming and then you move on to something else. You sit down and eat without me.'

'What time are you coming home? Are you going to be at the tower for much longer?'

'I don't know what time I'll get home.'

'You want us to cry for you, to stop living? You're never here! Obviously we have to cope with your absence. Why don't you come home and tuck in your two daughters?'

'I can't. I can't promise that. I don't know what time I'll be able to come home.'

'Well, that's a shame for you. I'm going to have to hang up, Vivienne's waiting for me. Shall we hang up?'

'If you want. Let's hang up.'

'I'm hanging up. I love you. I'm going to put Vivienne to bed.'

'I love you too. Say hello to the Deneuves for me.'

I hung up. I put my BlackBerry in my jacket pocket.

I saw my beautiful stranger, bent forward, getting her breath back. She gathered her belongings and started walking towards the exit.

We were queuing to pick up our shoes. Three American girls were standing behind me, talking noisily. They made loud remarks to a group of men who were waiting in the queue a few metres further up. My beautiful stranger turned around, visibly annoyed, and her eyes met mine. She froze for an instant, stupefied to find me behind her, and then a smile appeared on her lips to cover up the emotion that had gripped us both. That smile made it clear that she remembered having seen me in the shopping centre.

She did not go back to the position she'd occupied before turning round towards the shouting. Her body was slightly in profile, half turned towards mine, as if, by keeping my eyes on her face, and above all by her awareness of it (being unable to respond to it without demonstrating a boldness that she might one day have to justify), she wished to perpetuate the emotion that connected us, however tenuous. It seemed to me that she took pleasure in offering herself to my eyes and in knowing herself admired. She was tactful enough not to make me feel that I had broken the most basic rules of decorum by staring at her. (All it would have taken, to make this clear to me, was for her to look at me, even if only once.)

We advanced towards the counter. My heart was beating so fast in my chest that I could hardly stand up.

An elderly, grey-haired lady waiting in front of us wished to speak to the three American girls without having to shout. She offered to swap places with my beautiful stranger, who refused with stubborn courtesy – in fact, she fended off the same request four times in a row. Jubilantly, I guessed the reason why she was being so inflexible: she did not want to upset the harmonious order we had created between our bodies and our faces. I found this refusal astonishingly open and explicit, almost as if it were a declaration, and I was dizzied by the lack of care she took to conceal from me her attraction. No grey-haired old lady was going to make us give up the sensations our bodies had begun to feel in this enclosed space – that was what she was telling me. The queue moved forward, but the architecture of our intimacy was unaltered. Only a barely perceptible smile hinted at the complicity of our two bodies in their synchronized movements.

We picked up our shoes. I took care to keep away from her: I wanted her to know how she'd feel if I disappeared without trying to make contact with her. I imagined that, in the moment when I went up to her, this small fear she'd felt – a glimpse of the pain that seizes us in the face of something irreversible – might encourage her to break her own rules and allow a stranger to speak to her. I confess to this single instance of cold-blooded strategy.

I followed her into the shopping centre, but only for about thirty metres; if I left it too late, she might suspect that our second meeting was due not to a combination of circumstances but to an act of stalking all the more disturbing because it had lasted three hours. I walked behind her, moving slowly closer. I had the feeling that I was sending the sounds of my footsteps directly into her thoughts, where I feared they would make her panic. But perhaps she would be thrilled to sense me behind her? I sped up. I wanted to overtake her just enough to be able to speak to her sideways, without forcing her to turn her head and above all without approaching her head-on. It was the fear of committing errors that transmitted these subtleties to the small amount of clear-sightedness that remained to me in my panic. And at the moment when it would have taken only a slight turn of the head for her to listen to my first words, I saw her move her face towards mine.

If, at that precise instant, I had given up on the idea of speaking to her, intimidated by the possibility of letting such a woman into my life; if I had told her, 'Excuse me, I'm sorry, I thought you were someone else,' before drawing away and going home; if I could have known that approaching her would drag my existence in a direction I was not at all sure I wanted it to go, Victoria would not have died a little less than a year after our meeting. She would still be alive today. I would not be living like a hermit in a roadside hotel in Creuse, separated from Sylvie and the children, brooding over my guilt. I would not have been destroyed by the role I played in this drama, nor by the two days in police custody that followed from it. But it so happened that Victoria's face did turn towards mine and that I was felled by her astonishing gaze.

'Excuse me. Madame. I'm sure you're going to turn me down. But I wanted to tell you. And you would be right to do so. And I should point out that I am not in the habit of approaching strangers in shopping centres.'

An incoherent start. Did she slow down, almost to the point of immobility, in order to better follow my train of thought? I was surprised that such clumsy words could make her stop so quickly.

'But, you see, earlier, when I passed you in the shopping centre – do you remember?'

She smiled at me. It would have been crass of me to expect a more explicit response from her. I sensed that she was about to start walking again. We were both nervous.

'So anyway, in the three hours that followed, I thought about you several times. To be honest, I didn't stop thinking about you. I told myself I should have gone up to you. I was annoyed with myself because I hadn't dared. So, when I saw you again, I decided that this time I wouldn't let myself have any regrets. Who knows where regrets can lead you, the way they change over time . . .'

She looked at me indulgently. I noticed she had little freckles around her eyes. Unconsciously, her look hinted at the desire and disbelief she had felt when our bodies had brushed past each other, but I sensed she was trying to control her expression, fearful it might betray her thoughts. This deliberate reserve turned her into an attentive but neutral listener. I had the feeling she wanted to concentrate, to gather information, to check whether her first impression had been correct, to remain dignified and respectable; or, perhaps, to bring to our contact the same slightly cold seriousness she could see in me. Because of my fear, I wasn't sure I was putting much feeling into the way I looked at her.

'Basically, why should one refuse to tell a woman one finds beautiful – I mean a woman one doesn't know – that she's beautiful? I see you're smiling. You find me ridiculous.'

'Not at all. I'm listening to you with the greatest attentiveness.'

'It's the same kind of impact as when you walk past a painting and you're struck by its beauty. A single second may be all it takes for a person's face to leave an impression as lasting as, I don't know, five hours of an opera . . . Do you understand what I mean?'

'I think your praise is disproportionate. Either that, or you're practised in the art of approaching women. And obviously your technique is very effective – the proof being that I'm standing here listening to you, ready to hear more.'

'I don't have a technique. You are the first woman I've approached in years.'

She looks at me attentively. She is trying to interpret the expression on my face.

'Shall I tell you the truth? It wasn't in the queue that I saw you for the second time, but when you entered the bowling alley. I couldn't imagine talking to you in a place like that, where professional womanizers must proliferate. I have to confess my guilt: I've been watching you for quite a long time.'

I flash her a knowing smile. She looks at me suspiciously. I keep talking, without giving her the time to study my response more carefully.

'I watched you bowl for a reasonably long time.'

'Don't you have anything better to do than follow strange

women into bowling alleys?' she said in a hard voice. 'I hate knowing I was being watched.'

'I adored it. You were dazzling.'

'No one could accuse you of understatement.'

'This is the only way I could find the power to speak to you. Grandiloquence is a form of energy. You can't imagine how much courage it took me to approach you.'

'You haven't answered my question.'

'Which one?'

'What you usually do with your days.'

'Try to guess.'

'I don't know. You seem like an intellectual. I mean, as well as being grandiloquent and having lots of spare time. And you use the word *proliferate*. So . . . a journalist, perhaps? Or a philosophy lecturer? Or a psychoanalyst? Or you write plays. You're a screenwriter.'

'No, but you're not entirely wrong. There's some truth in your perception. But my job is not at all – or rather, I should say, no longer – artistic. Highly cerebral, on a human and on a material level, but no longer remotely artistic.'

'Do you regret that?'

'Regret what? That my job is no longer artistic? Occasionally, yes. But I don't have time for that kind of thing.'

'You still haven't told me what your job was.'

'Architect.'

'You're the first one I've ever met.'

'I'm a construction manager now. I plan and synchronize all the different activities. I conduct the orchestra. Can I invite you to have a drink with me?'

'Sorry, I'm expected somewhere. Another time.'

'Are you sure? Just one drink. Twenty minutes.'

'You can see me another time. I'm leaving tomorrow, but I'll be back in just under a month. Do you work in Paris?'

'Don't you?'

'No, in London. But I travel a lot.'

'You know, instead of wasting time talking here, we could go somewhere more agreeable. What do you think? My car isn't far.'

I felt her hesitate; her eyes devoured me. All I had to do was insist, and she would have come with me; all I had to do was look in her eyes a few seconds longer and the army of attraction would have conquered the empire of reason. She was about to agree, to say yes. Her face quivered; I could see she was willing, one way or another, to get out of her meeting. But it was late, and it was Vivienne's birthday, and the Deneuves would perhaps be awaiting my return, so I decided to postpone the time she was ready to offer me: 'I understand, don't worry,' I said. 'We'll see each other another time.' She deftly took a business card from an outside pocket of her bag and handed it to me. With care, I read the few words printed upon it: Victoria de Winter, Executive Vice President, with a company name and an ugly logo.

'I'm often in Paris.'

'What is it, this company?'

'It was originally one of the jewels of British industry. Nowadays, it's a multinational corporation, essentially American, with offices in about twenty countries.'

'Executive Vice President?'

'I'm global head of Human Resources. But I'm going to have to leave you. What's your name?'

'I don't have a card on me. David Kolski.'

'Call me. Or send me an email. I leave tomorrow, but as I told you, I'll be coming back soon.'

'I have to go to London in a couple of weeks, as it happens.'

'In a couple of weeks? So, around 10 September. I should be there. Send me your dates by email and I'll let you know. In any case, we'll see each other – in Paris or in London.'

She smiles at me. Looks deeply into my eyes. There is a long silence. And then she utters the incredible words: 'And we'll see if the spark is still there.'

2

It was my principle never to see the women with whom I'd had sexual relations – or any kind of physical intimacy – more than once. I acted in the strictest anonymity, discreet as a cat, surrounding myself with the most extreme precautions, as if I were contemplating burglary. I undressed these women with the same avid and wonder-filled fervour as a burglar venturing through the darkness of an unknown house, torch in hand, hoping to uncover a famous painting, precious jewels, a safe . . . then afterwards I slipped away soundlessly, careful to leave no trace of the break-in behind me. And each of these encounters was engraved in my memory as a unique moment that might never have happened. I told myself that an adulterous erotic experience could have no consequences as long as it remained strictly a one-off and ended up as nothing more than a memory in the minds of those who had lived through it. But a second rendezvous draws a line that connects these two points: it gives direction and meaning to what had previously been nothing more than poetry hanging in the air. And that is how a story begins, and with it a moral aspect – the idea of betrayal or cheating. I had never budged from this principle of prudence and moral integrity (yes, moral integrity, rectitude; I insist upon this point) since I had been living with Sylvie. I had experienced this kind of thing only with unknown women I'd approached in the street; I had always forbidden myself affairs with women from my professional milieu, my network of friends or the city where I live, in order to eradicate all risk of complex situations or dangerous entanglements.

None of the women with whom I shared such rendezvous during these years were more than moderately pretty, or at least none were considered more than moderately pretty by the majority of men. The speed with which they made up their minds depended to a large extent on the urgency of their desire, and they were more likely to act on a rash impulse if they were amazed at having been approached with tact and sensitivity by a man who seemed different. The consideration, the scruples, the courtesy with which I deployed my words acted on their imagination like a spell; they were not accustomed to being treated like princesses, unlike those more physically attractive young women who are used to being chatted up by men from the first days of their adolescence. (And anyway, I have never liked pretty women so much as ordinary women who have a particular detail or something about their presence with the power to excite me. Like a precious stone that starts to gleam, as if for me alone, amid the setting of their plainness. Pretty feet, for instance, or honeyed skin, or a look in the eyes . . . for me, those things constituted an unparalleled erotic experience. I don't know how to describe this, but it was as if these women's plainness vastly magnified the desire ignited by a single aspect of their person.) Often, their modest social extraction helped things along; they were never bourgeois women or women occupying positions of power, but students, secretaries, commercial attachés, sales assistants in perfume shops or department stores. Victoria was the first woman of that stature I had ever approached: intimidating, moving in the higher spheres of industry, with a spending power greatly superior to mine.

I must admit that in general these adventures turned out to be

21

disappointing, for the very reason that had made them conceivable from a moral viewpoint: there was no time for them to blossom and become interesting, and in particular no time for me to overcome my shyness. With most of these women, when I was about to penetrate them, I lost my erection – or it diminished markedly after a few minutes of promising intercourse. Why? Sometimes I felt unexpectedly repulsed by these bodies I had picked up in the street, carried away by an uncontrollable arousal. Or, sometimes, pernicious thoughts would rise up from the most ancient zones of my brain to dam the flow of my confidence and disturb the tranquillity into which the pleasure had begun to let me slide. I feared I would be unable to procure for these women the orgasm that the eloquence I had used to seduce them had allowed them to suppose they would enjoy with me – instead of which, they were given a performance I suddenly suspected they would find pathetic. Or, out of nowhere, I would see my situation as absurd, deathly, horribly sad; I would think that I must be in a seriously worrying state of emotional destitution to have been reduced to hurriedly begging like this, to this mediocre creature, beached naked on the mattress of a two-star hotel, for these crumbs of love and consolation. At that moment, the despair that had led me to this room, without me really being aware of it, spread through my brain while I tried to make love to a stranger's body. And I suddenly saw how lonely that stranger was, how terribly fragile and vulnerable and human. Lying on top of a not very attractive student, picked up in the street two hours earlier: isn't that the most pathetic thing that a married father of two – a construction manager for a hospital or a school – could possibly do? I felt sure that no kind of bliss could possibly flower in a young woman's lower abdomen from such an abrupt, arbitrary, mechanical coupling between two bodies that knew nothing of each other. I anticipated the disgust that would end up seeping into her shame; I guessed at the remorse that had begun to invade her thoughts; I hated myself for having been skilful enough to lure her into such a seedy hotel – against her interests, counter to her interior beauty – just to serve as an outlet for a lost and troubled man. I removed a flaccid, gluey bit of flesh from the young woman's vagina, I smiled, I gave her a brief kiss of apology on the lips, I rolled on the sheets and nuzzled against her body. I caressed her, and made her come with my tongue (each of these failures increased my skill in this area). She did her best to bring my cock back to life with her lips, but ended up getting dressed and exiting the room without saying a single word, leaving me abandoned on the bed, flooded with remorse. (I made her leave with an icy reserve intended to distance her from me as quickly as possible: I listened to her getting dressed with my eyes closed, and didn't open them again until I heard the door bang shut.) These moments left behind them an impression of having erred and an aftertaste of disgust, but they also left me feeling redeemed, as if I had managed to free myself from the baseness that had dominated my thoughts during the preceding days. I rushed to Sylvie, following the path of escape back the other way with my outlook reversed. I ran towards home with the haste of an amorous suitor. Now it was my wife who embodied desire, fullness and harmony, supplanting the illusory mysteries of the wide world and the transitory young women I passed, who were lit up like Christmas shop windows by the simple fact that they remained distant and unreachable. Most of these experiences revealed to me that it was not married life that represented the desolation of reality (as I was weak enough to suppose at regular intervals, imagining that such a circumscribed existence was depriving me of fantastic orgasms, incredible experiences, truly unique sensations), but these momentarily enchanting young girls I approached in the street.

I am exaggerating: sometimes I shared with them an over-whelmingly sweet complicity. These timeless moments are stars shining in the night sky of my mind, the light emanating from them so evocative that when I summon the memory of any of them, I am plunged back into a precise period of my life: a context, a season, a state of mind. (In most cases, the young women's names have been erased by forgetfulness, but I retain quite a sharp memory of their physical presence, whether it's a scent, a gesture, an attitude, the shape of their breasts, or the texture of their skin.) This one was a redhead, we had just made love: I didn't know if she'd come, but I had suddenly lost my hard-on in the full flow of intercourse, and I was furious with myself. 'Don't worry, it doesn't matter,' she told me. I was staggered by her humane forgiveness. We talked, curled up together, our fingers touching. November, 6 p.m.; I loved her fingernails; we heard raindrops against the windows in a deep black night full of wet lights, mist and damp softness and wind, dead leaves trampled on the pavements. I wished this moment would never end, that this enclave would shelter my madness and weakness for years and years, that I would never have to move or to leave these sheets. Her name was Aurélie. A bus passed in the street outside; car horns blared from traffic jams like birdsong from a rainforest. We hadn't switched the lights on when we entered the room two hours earlier, and now only the glow from the street-lamps made our bodies visible in the darkness. We fell asleep. The young woman woke me with kisses: 'It's gone nine, we fell asleep. Don't you have to get back home?' Gently stroking her breasts, I asked her to tell me about her life. We were no longer thinking about making love; we'd both understood that we were in this room for something else. 'It's nearly midnight, I have to go,' she sighed eventually. 'All right, go ahead, get out of here.' She leapt out of bed, and I watched with tenderness as she dressed. 'I adore your body, Aurélie.' She stopped what she was doing to aim an embarrassed but grateful smile at me. 'It's the first time a man has ever looked at me like that. It makes me feel strange.' 'I adore your body. I find you beautiful. I could watch you for months, for years, without interruption.' 'You're mad! I'm stuck with a lunatic.' 'You're not wrong.' 'And anyway, I'm too fat. Look at my bum, my thighs. I'm ugly.' 'No, you're not. You're not ugly at all.' She finished tying her laces, then came and leaned over my face – dressed in an anorak, with a red scarf wrapped around her neck – to share a long kiss with me. 'Here's my number,' she whispered in my ear. 'I'd like to see you again. Call me if you want.' Then she disappeared.

Without having made a decision, or really being able to explain why, I had now gone five years without persuading any unknown women to come to a hotel with me. My sex drive had calmed down; I no longer had time to hang around in the streets; and I think that, with age, I had lost the boldness, the courage, the determination required to begin most of these adventures. It's always said that, at the age of forty, men have an explosion of libido, but for me the desire to seduce had disappeared five years ago, at the age of thirty-seven, and had not reappeared. And Victoria? Beyond the fact that I liked her, what had led me, in this case, to approach Victoria, and what did I expect from such an encounter? Was I going to take her to a four-star hotel for a one-night stand? Had the prospect of falling in love crossed my mind, in spite of the fact that I was married and loved my wife? (To stop living with Sylvie seemed simply inconceivable to me.) I had no desire to keep a mistress or to complicate my existence with a passionate affair.

If I had been followed by a neutral observer during these last few hours, who had watched me carefully as I approached Victoria, and as we talked in the middle of the crowd; if this observer, having seen Victoria hand me her card and watched me examine it with wonder, had followed me to my car and asked if they could sit next to me; if this observer, sitting next to me while I drove home euphoric from this providential meeting – daydreaming, my cock hard, drumming the steering wheel with my thumbs – and watching the road through the windscreen, had asked me to explain why I had stalked and approached this woman, I would be at a loss to provide them with a rational response. 'This encounter seems to have made you very happy. Could you tell me what your happiness consists of?' I would have thought about this for several minutes, watching the A11 motorway through the windscreen. 'You want to know what my happiness consists of?' I would say to this observer sitting next to me. 'Absolutely. If this happiness were a safe that we could open, what would we find inside? Or, if we could send a miniature camera into a sick person's stomach . . .' – I was driving, relatively fast, in the left-hand lane, with my signal light flashing – 'But above all, I would like to know where this happiness is aimed – in which direction. I would like to know if you know where this happiness might lead your life.' The traffic was moving smoothly. At 11 p.m. this road is generally not too busy, and I was wondering if, with a little luck, the Deneuves might still be at the house when I got back. I would think for a long time before replying that I knew what it was like, this happiness that gripped me, but I would find it difficult to describe. 'But why do you want this happiness that I'm feeling to lead me somewhere? Can't happiness be simply a state, an atmosphere that permeates your thoughts, your body, your veins, and gives reality an unusual depth, as if, all of a sudden, the world were hailing you, inviting you to a huge party held in your honour, a party thrown by the sky, the trees, the night, even if it's raining a bit this evening and the landscape is hidden by enormous clouds?'

I would turn towards the observer sitting next to me and I would say please don't ask me any more questions, please don't dampen the bliss that this business card slipped inside my jacket pocket is making me feel – this card that contains a telephone number, a London address, a mysterious-sounding surname. I would ask the observer sitting next to me why they felt the need to quiz me about the purpose of my behaviour. 'You understand the risk in this kind of attitude, don't you?' they would respond. 'What do you mean? What risk are you talking about?' 'I'm talking about the risk of being led into a dangerous situation, of suddenly waking up in the lion's cage without having really wanted or anticipated it, because you've been extremely hypocritical; or, perhaps, because you refused, when it was still possible, to wonder where you were going.' I had just overtaken a truck; it had started raining more heavily; I switched the windscreen wipers on. 'Would it bother you if we listened to some music?' 'Not at all – go ahead.' I put the CD player on and skipped straight to track three: notes played on a piano came through the speakers. 'What is it?' the observer sitting next to me would ask. 'The last piano pieces written by Franz Liszt. I can't stop listening to them. I find them deeply moving.'

I listened to the music in silence for a few minutes. I was thinking that the only way I could make myself understood would be to describe how I'd been feeling since the end of August – only that feeling would explain why I felt obliged not to let Victoria vanish into thin air. What had happened could not be examined solely in terms of its purpose. Obviously, at some point or another, I would have to face this question of my intentions, and later, that of my actions, but, right now, I just wanted to delight in the enchantment which this magical, providential encounter had brought to my life. Amid the most depressing reality (in a shopping centre, coming out of a toy shop, near a car park, at the end of an exhausting day), an event had occurred that had set off vibrations in the farthest reaches of my imagination. For quite some time now, I'd had the feeling that I was walking beside a wall – a high, endless, austere wall that deprived me of all light – and it was as if the sudden appearance of Victoria had made a crack in the wall, and through this opening I could glimpse a space – very close, close enough to touch, on the other side of the wall – through which I might disappear. This longing that gripped me, I knew it by heart; I knew it was directed towards that indiscernible elsewhere that had shimmered since for ever in my dreams. 'For a few days I've been living in the hope that reality would open up to let me pass, and then seal shut behind me.' I had been dominated by the intuition that something *might* happen – and this hope had been enough to make me happy, circling my mind like a beautiful and unforgettable melody. The car would be filled by a gale of laughter, and I would turn my head to the observer sitting next to me. 'What are you talking about?' they would ask, struggling to keep a straight face. 'Seriously, that is hilarious. You're too old to believe in fairy tales! What exactly is this place like, this indiscernible elsewhere?' I would reply that it was all very hazy ('to me as well'), and that this elsewhere had no name. 'What I do know is that it has always sparkled in my dreams like a promise of fullness and consolation. Sometimes I think my only longing is to escape from reality, even if I don't know exactly what I mean by that.' This elsewhere had only ever existed in the feeling that perhaps, one day, some ultimate place would open up its arms for me, and in most of my daydreams this place was personified as a woman encountered by chance. The feeling came and went, and its intensity varied with my moods and the seasons, but it held such poetic power for me that since adolescence I had felt what was clearly an exaggerated attachment to it. True, the blissfulness that this state of expectation brought to my interior life sometimes made me wonder if the state of expectation was not, in itself, the mysterious place; if this hope of escape was perhaps nothing more than a spiritual anaesthetic, there to make existence bearable, to help me endure its stresses and tensions, its sadnesses and disappointments. What's more, on the rare occasions when I had stopped believing in it, when I lost my conviction that an event was about to happen that would allow me to escape the narrow confines of my existence, I found myself realizing (and telling a doctor) that I was going through a period of depression. (The doctor prescribed Prozac.) I should, however, make something clear: this expectation of an imminent, life-changing event meant that I had never thought of my existence as disastrous. 'Do you understand what I mean?' I would ask the observer sitting next to me. 'I can't say I don't like my life, but only inasmuch as nothing prevents me from hoping that something is going to happen that will change it profoundly – and make it a bit less abhorrent than it is. I love my life because of the dream that permeates it: that something will soon move or change it – a woman, a miracle, an encounter, an amazing job offer, an unexpected event, a brilliant idea germinating in my brain. When I love my life, it's this dream that I love. An amusing paradox, don't you think?' I am, no doubt, what people call a daydreamer, even if my job forces me to deal with the most uncompromising reality, meaning that I must, on a daily basis, be organized and pragmatic, completely focused on the practical and the material; the very opposite of what one thinks of as a daydreamer. I feel sure that there are many others like me: we would be surprised to discover the stratagems most of our contemporaries feel obliged to develop (and the fairy tales they need to nourish their imaginations, as well as their children's) in order not to crumble, in order to cheerfully obey the sound of their alarm clock, in order to endure all they endure without being defeated by the humiliation they feel – and, in this way, we end up convincing ourselves that existence is nothing more than a dismal exercise in survival. I would have to explain all of this to the observer sitting next to me in order for them to understand my behaviour in the shopping centre, and even then I would conclude with the words: 'I'm going to tell you a story about something that happened to me a long time ago. Perhaps it will help you understand why I approached that woman without any qualms or concerns.' I left the motorway at the Rambouillet exit. I was now only a few kilometres from home.

I was nineteen years old. I was studying architecture. I had been with Sylvie for a year, though she was still living with her parents. I was living in a twenty-square-foot attic room in Saint-Germain-des-Prés. One night, coming home from a dinner where I'd drunk quite a lot of alcohol – it must have been about one in the morning – I got into bed and was almost immediately seized with an urgent need to go to the toilet, probably due to the poor-quality Indian food we'd eaten. I have always found it crazy that such an important story could begin in such a ridiculous way. In those days, barely a year after leaving home, I still hadn't quite freed myself from certain maternal directives (I went to my parents' house every weekend to have a bath, get my laundry done, and receive my weekly allowance), which explains why I still slept in pyjamas. This is such an absurd thing for an adult – a student in Paris – to do, that I can hardly believe it was ever true, but the story I am about to tell bears the indelible stain of this anachronism. I put a pair of trousers on over my preposterous nocturnal outfit and went to the public toilets close to where I lived, on Boulevard Saint-Germain, near the corner of Rue du Bac. I had come to find it so unbearable to use the toilets on the attic floor of my building – relieving myself crouched over a concrete hole, crippled by cramps, holding on to the walls so I didn't fall backwards – that I had got into the habit of going outside to do my business, like a dog.

I was on my way back that evening when a young woman, passing me on Rue du Bac, murmured, 'What a handsome boy.' She did not stop, or even turn around. (I know this because I watched her mysterious outline, haloed with luxuriously thick brown hair, recede into the distance.) I was on the verge of adulthood, and the scars of my adolescence were slowly fading: I was beginning to understand that some women could find me attractive or to their taste. But still, I had never imagined I might be able to seduce such an incredible woman. I was dissuaded from running after her, in spite of the invitation she'd given me with those words, by three considerations: firstly, my shyness with women; secondly, the fact that this unknown woman had not turned around to seal her compliment with a smile; and, lastly, the grotesque lion-tamer's suit concealed beneath my clothes. Even supposing she let me approach her, and that she didn't object to me accompanying her, I would still have had to content myself with walking alongside her in the street, with the collar of my raincoat buttoned up to my throat. And if she insisted on going for a drink in one of the bars that was still open in Saint-Germain-des-Prés, how could I reply without making myself look ridiculous? And even if I had been dressed normally, would I really have dared catch her up? To say what? What do you say to a young woman who has just confided to you, in a murmur and a look, that she finds you a 'handsome boy'? How can you respond to such a phrase without it seeming like you are claiming your prize? Even now, battle-hardened by the experiences of the twenty-three years that have passed since that night, I don't know what attitude would be fitting in such circumstances, nor what words I should have spoken to her – all

I know is that an extreme awkwardness (manifested in a pile-up of rootless words, unfinished sentences, hesitations and sighs) would have been the most suitable behaviour for the situation. Perhaps, if she had gone further than the casual compliment she had paid me, and if, after a brief silence, she had said, 'Come on, I'm taking you with me' . . . perhaps. But she hadn't. She hadn't even bothered to turn around.

I crossed the threshold of my attic room, weighed down by regret at having chickened out (the narrow spiral of the staircase had set off insidious ruminations, magnified from step to step and from floor to floor), furious with myself for having such a lack of poetic flair. A beautiful woman calls me a 'handsome boy' in the street, and I let her slip away into the darkness without even attempting to reply? I was so angry with myself that I punched the wall (violently enough that I briefly feared I'd broken my fingers) before realizing that I could still try to find her: because of her high heels, she would be moving through the night as slowly as a procession. I took off my pyjamas and put on whatever clothes I could find, rushed down the spiral staircase, and ran to the place where we had brushed past each other. I wondered if the whole episode had been conjured from the Indian spirits I'd drunk in such quantity; if the unknown woman had never existed, if she had never spoken those words to me. But I went off in the direction she'd taken, moving up Boulevard Saint-Germain in long strides, the pavement speeding beneath me while my shoes flashed by on either side of my vision, right then left. I ran as if in a dream, ignoring the few people I passed, before stopping abruptly. I stood frozen for a few seconds, breathless and perplexed. What should I do? Maybe she'd turned into one of the side streets? If she'd stayed on this boulevard, I would already have caught her up by now, and been able to speak to her. What would I say? I had no idea. Seized by a sudden intuition, I decided to take Rue Saint-Guillaume and head towards the Seine. A woman like that – nocturnal, like a character from a novel – was bound to feel drawn by its black, metaphysical, slowly moving water, shimmering with reflections. I ran down the middle of Rue Saint-Guillaume until I turned right on Rue de l'Université, then joined Rue des Saints-Pères and kept going down to the river. There are times when I think that my memories of this pursuit are something I dreamed in my bed rather than actual experiences. Sometimes, on the verge of sleep, I start running in a dark place, and today I am unable to say with any certainty whether my pursuit of this woman took place in reality or in a dream city, within the illusions of a drowse. I ran for a long time without feeling even slightly tired. I felt like a ball thrown by a child in an apartment hallway: the street's grey walls rushed past on either side of my face. And at the very moment when I stopped at Rue des Saints-Pères to look around for any sign of her . . . there she was, in front of me. I had appeared at the corner of these two streets just before her, so I must have burst into her field of vision like a missile – a panic-stricken, dishevelled, very confused and red-faced missile. She had continued to move forward, and I had turned my head in her direction at the precise instant that she reached me. Her face came suddenly into focus – in extreme close-up – like a vision hatched by the night (or the most beautiful dream) in my eyes (or in my imagination). Her face hung before me like a portrait. She smiled at me. She was sublime. She shivered like a tree. I was panting like a madman. I felt embarrassed that she had surprised me hunting her like a barbarian; I would have preferred to be seen strolling thoughtfully, crossing her by chance for a second time: 'Hey, you again – what a coincidence . . .' But no, the state I was in could leave no doubt whatsoever that I had been seeking her through the night with the furious determination of a young woman rummaging through the contents of her handbag to find a lipstick. I stood silent. I couldn't think of a single thing to say. In any case, the fact that she had discovered me chasing after her freed me from the requirement to speak first; it was up to her to respond. She turned around just as a taxi appeared; she lifted her hand and the car stopped; we got in. 'Good evening,' she said to the driver, before giving him an address that I did not memorize (names of various streets came to my mind in the weeks that followed, each of which I felt sure was the one she had mentioned). On the other hand, I do remember that, in reply to a question posed by the taxi driver, she said that the building in which we would spend the night was located in the ninth arrondissement.

I found myself in a seemingly limitless apartment. She explained to me that the owner had cut off the electricity, but had failed to tell her where the circuit breaker was located, which was why we would have to rely on candlelight. 'Which, I'm sure you'll agree, is not without its charms,' she concluded, sliding the key into the lock. (I hadn't dared ask a single question about any of the information she'd given me, such as her relationship with the owner or the reasons she was staying there.) Having lit the candles of a candelabrum with a silver lighter that she took from a pocket in her handbag (without removing her summer coat), we began to walk. The apartment seemed to spread out like a forest as we moved through its twists and turns, the darkness making it feel endless. The hallways seemed not to lead from one side to the other, but rather to lead us ever more deeply into the heart of its night-time. She walked in front of me without saying a word, opening heavy doors as I followed her into new depths of darkness and immobility. Finally – 'Here we are' – we entered a room through which I moved carefully, protected from the night that encircled me by the intimate brightness of the candelabrum she held. After a few minutes, as the young woman lit the candles that were situated all over the room, I noted that it seemed to be first an office, then a living room, then a library, then a music room, and finally a bedroom, though in truth she probably used it for all these activities. 'Sit wherever you like,' she told me, pointing out various possibilities: two sofas, a *méridienne*, a wall seat, and a corner area containing several armchairs. I sat in a sofa on its own, calculating that the absence of other seating nearby would oblige her to sit next to me (on a piece of furniture large enough that we could talk without touching, if it turned out that this was how we were going to pass the night). 'I'm going to get something to drink. What would you like?'

'Gin or vodka or a white spirit like that, if you've got any,' I replied, calculating that, given my inebriated state, it was a better idea to keep drinking the kind of beverage that had already got me pretty well wrecked.

'I have Bombay Sapphire gin, tequila, vodka . . .'

'Let's go for the Bombay gin,' I smiled. 'That sounds perfect.' She returned a few moments later with a bottle and two glasses, and she sat next to me on the sofa. Having served us both, she lifted up the shining liquid to the level of her right eye and said, 'Cheers!'

'To our meeting,' I replied, imitating her. 'To this providential meeting.'

What happened next left some wonderfully enduring sensations in my memory, but every time I tried to mentally relive this confused and fragmentary night (which I did for many weeks afterwards), my attempts at reconstructing it were short-circuited by a sudden cut to that bitter moment the next day, about 6 p.m., when I woke fully dressed in my bed.

The details of this night come not from the memory I might

have kept (with its source in an awareness born prior to my leaving), but from the reminiscences that filled my mind when I woke in my attic room many hours later – with no idea what had happened, nor how I had managed to get home. I am almost certain that we didn't make love. We didn't talk either, which explains why I never knew this young woman's identity – first name, surname, occupation or home city. I think she kept her skirt on, and I did the same with my trousers (unless something much more graphic occurred during that period of time erased from my memory), but I do remember us rubbing against each other. I loved the soft coolness of her chest and stomach against my skin. I remember the taste of her lips, the touch of her toes between my teeth. The look in her eyes was like the proof of a theory: it was complex, but its fullness gave me the sensation that I was moving through a material of the most wonderful softness . . . smooth, almost like flesh . . . or like velvet, green velvet. I can see, again, her fixed, frantic smile, where glimmers of sadness shone now and then. She was, I think, several women at once: lively, serious, tragic, cheerful, powerful and childlike. But perhaps it was the alcohol, and the various states it must have put us through, that gave me this impression of different beings, later compressed by my memory. I loved the patterns she drew on my skin with her nails. I lost my fingers in the voluminous folds of her hair. It is unsettling to have lived through these moments in the darkness of an apartment without electricity, and then to have to vanquish the darkness of amnesia in order to remember them: the night seemed to grow ever denser, and in my memory these images are surrounded by that pervasive night. She stands up and walks away from me with a movement that drives me crazy: elegant and musical, a little intoxicated, with the grace of a perfectly balanced rider on a galloping mare. I remember marvelling at the way she moved through the room, barefoot, aware that her shoes counted for nothing in the dancing sensuality of her presence. I watch as, bare-chested, she plays the piano – a melancholy song. Her breasts tremble between her arms, and the whiteness of her body contrasts with the piano shrouded in night, but the gleams on the black lacquer reflect the sheen of her lips, the gleam in her eyes, and, perhaps, I hope, the wetness of her lower lip. She stares at me while she plays. The piano looks wet, her eyes look wet; I am streaming with happiness and emotion. Where are we? Who does this apartment belong to? I remember wondering that several times without thinking about asking the question out loud, unaware that, from the next day on, I would spend years trying to recollect the address she'd given to the taxi driver, trying to remember a church or a monument that I might have glimpsed through the taxi windows, trying to locate the streets where the taxi picked us up and where it dropped us off. Even today, when I walk around the lower part of the ninth arrondissement, I am seized by peculiar sensations – I feel a sudden retch of optimism, or I am consumed by insane happiness for a few seconds, or a strangely dense, historical atmosphere, like the air in an old, dim palace, spreads through my mind – as if, unconsciously, I detected the closeness of this building. In this way, I have, over the years, marked out a territory where I am convinced this lost night took place: around the Église de la Sainte-Trinité. And it is always to this area of Paris that I go for walks or to eat out, as if my imagination felt itself magnetically drawn there. I also identified – ten years later, at a friend's house – the music she was playing: the last piano pieces written by Franz Liszt (I have been listening to them again lately). But why did I drink so much? Because she was drinking? Because she wanted me to drink so I would lose track of her and this night spent together would remain like a mysterious island in the dark sea of the past? Did I drink to forget my fear (I had only made love two or three times before)? Leaning on the piano, I watch her play, looking down on her white fingers as they alight briefly, methodically, on the keyboard. I listen very carefully to these pieces she interprets, noting that they grow thinner, less substantial, that they are ever more tense and bare, disquietingly slow. After which everything crumbles, certain images fall apart. I see myself pushing her on to the bed, biting her nipples; I hear laughter in my ear, quite loud laughter; but these images are incomplete, as if they are blurred, mad, full of holes, burning with alcohol and drunkenness, and this disorder is suddenly interrupted by the brutal reality of my bedroom walls in that moment when I open my eyes, the next evening.

I have no idea what happened. Did I walk home? Did she put me in a taxi? Did I climb the seven steep flights of stairs on my own, before collapsing on the bed? Why didn't I stay in her bed, huddled close to her body? Did I act crudely or repulsively? Did I force her to throw me out? I tried telling myself that she was reluctant to fall asleep with a stranger, but that she arranged to meet me the next day at teatime – and that it was perhaps on my way home that I wiped myself out with alcohol. The empty bottle I discovered the next day on the carpet of my room would support this theory, and it is because of this bottle that I have often wondered whether the night was, in fact, nothing but a dream. The conclusion I have reached is that, even if I did truly experience it, what remains of this night makes it the exact equivalent of a dream: it has the same astonishing beauty, the same spark of idealism, the same miraculous simplicity, the same despair caused by the impossibility of ever rediscovering it. As with a dream, it is not my memory that recalls the details of this story, but my imagination (which has, I know, been irrevocably suffused by it), on a plane that is more essential than that of memory, more intimate and universal, with the power of a myth. That this somewhat strange story left such a spellbinding impression on me, at an age when I expected a light to appear, a direction to be revealed, probably explains the importance it ended up acquiring and the influence it would always exercise over my relationship with reality.

So that is the story I would tell to the observer sitting next to me in order for them to understand what made Victoria's appearance in my life resonate so deeply within me. I parked the car in front of my house, cut the engine, switched off the headlights, and saw Sylvie's silhouette through the French window. I would turn to the observer sitting next to me and tell them that the night I had just described had lived within me ever since, my imagination filled with the prospect of some kind of ending to it (through the occurrence of a similar event, like a contemporary echo of that miracle) and that every year, around its anniversary date – 12 September – its influence over me was intensified. Over a period extending from the end of August to the middle of October, this memory spreads a luminous sensation of imminence throughout my entire being. Out of nowhere, I feel tightenings in my stomach and my veins, and these tightenings send strange flashes through the inside of my body.

I heard a fingernail tapping gently against the windscreen. I turned in the direction of this sound and saw Sylvie bent towards me, smiling questioningly.

'What have you been doing alone in your car for the last ten minutes?' she asked me through a narrow opening after I'd lowered the electric window a little bit.

'Nothing. I was thinking,' I replied, kissing her on the lips.

'Oh, you were thinking? What about?'

'Nothing, just work stuff. I've had a difficult day.'

I got out of the car and we went into the house. I dumped my bag on an armchair and collapsed on the sofa.

'So, anyway, this birthday . . . was it nice?'

'Really nice. We had an excellent evening.'

'And the Deneuves – when did they leave?'

'I don't know. Maybe half an hour ago.'

'So, any news? How are they?'

'They seem fine. We had a really good time.'

'Back in a minute,' I said to Sylvie as I stood up. I locked myself in the toilet, where I started stroking myself while thinking about the body of the beautiful stranger I'd just met. I took off her blouse and kneaded her breasts through the black lace of her bra. I saw her walking in front of me in the shopping centre. She began touching my cock. I took off her bra and saw her naked breasts – they were perfect, heavy and dark – and started sucking her nipples. I made love to her. I felt her calves round my hips. She groaned. It turned me on. I came. I unloaded between my fingers. I was trying not to make too much noise, to keep my panting quiet. I heard Sylvie clearing the table: she passed the toilet door on her way to the kitchen. Victoria was lying on the bedsheets, happy and exhausted, my wet cock plastered to her thigh. I tore a piece of toilet paper from the roller on the wall. I wiped my cock. My gaze fell upon the cover of a weekly newspaper. House prices falling. I pulled my trousers back up, flushed, and opened the door. I went to the bathroom to wash my hands. My face was red. I passed Sylvie in the hallway as she was coming out of the dining room with a pile of dessert plates, the top one covered with the remains of a birthday cake; five candles were huddled together in one corner and little silver forks criss-crossed on a bed of cream and crushed strawberries.

'And the present you got for Vivienne in the end, what was it? You didn't tell me.'

This question hit me like a bolt of lightning. The bolt went through my body and down into the exact centre of the earth. I felt its heat rise up my spine.

I had left Vivienne's cuddly toy somewhere, but I had no idea when or where. Had I forgotten it in the bowling alley, in the café, in the shopping centre when I was talking to Victoria?

'A cuddly toy. A big one. An animal.'

'Oh, cool! What kind of animal?'

'I don't know. I forgot to ask. I didn't recognize it. An enormous animal with claws and a big tail, brown and black. Very cute.'

'And where is it?'

'In the car.'

'Go and get it. It'll be great for her to have her present when she wakes up. She was sad that you weren't there to give it to her. I promised her it would be by her bed in the morning.'

'I'll go tomorrow morning.'

'No – go now, please.'

'I told you, I'll go tomorrow.'

'I promised her it would be next to her bed when she woke up.'

We were in the kitchen. I filled a glass with tap water and drank it straight down.

'You're really annoying when you put your mind to it. Have I got to do it myself? Where are the car keys?'

'On the hallway table. But I'm wondering if I didn't leave the toy in my office.'

Sylvie had left the kitchen without having heard my final words. I opened the fridge, wondering what there was to eat.

3

I was surprised by how relaxed I felt. The glory of the approaching moment – when we could embrace, when dinner would be over – was accentuated by the large, square, solemn table between us. If I'd wanted to take her hand, I would have had to lean across and stretch out my arm, and our fingers would have just met over an arrangement of lifeless flowers, between two candles, in the middle of the table. Victoria seemed amused by this gulf between us, as if it were a challenge she had not anticipated in choosing such a high-class restaurant: that was what the glint in her eyes suggested to me, anyway, from far away over the tablecloth. I kept smiling, as if my lips were obeying an irresistible impulse, and these smiles were wider and more luminous than usual. I had the feeling that my face had changed.

As I've already said, I am not used to having dates with women of this standing. I had felt apprehensive about it, but that had not diminished the gladness that flowed through me when, coming out of the hotel lift, I saw her in the lobby. She stood with her back to me, near a marble pillar, looking in the direction of the windows. I had walked towards her, my heart pounding, already intoxicated by the coming evening, happy that her presence was having the same effect on me as it had done in front of the clothes shop, and when she offered me her hand, I took the initiative and kissed her on the cheek. She told me about a reservation she'd made in a well-known restaurant in the area – 'A chic, fashionable place. I've never been, but I've heard my friends talk about it' – and I replied that it sounded perfect. We walked slowly through the streets, leaning against each other, like a long-established couple out for a stroll. This intimacy seemed all the more fascinating to me as it was the fruit of a fifteen-minute conversation and a few emails – in other words, nothing of any substance. The acceleration we experienced during this start to our relationship was dizzying; we knew we were alone in a space where our desire was reverberating, but the atmosphere was one of uncertainty, sustained by a risky conversation and manners that betrayed a fear of making a mistake. We knew we would end up in the same bed, but in spite of that we pretended not to know it.

I had sent the first email the day after our meeting. As Victoria had mocked my grandiloquence, I had exaggerated it with lyricism and an escalation of sentimentality – a fault I readily admit. In that first email, I restated that our fifteen-minute conversation had been an 'enchantment'. I mentioned the three women I had seen that day, 'each as overpowering as the others': the beautiful stranger I passed in the shopping centre; the warrior throwing heavy black bowls; and the young woman with whom I spoke. I told her that my desire to know her was formed during my one-hour head start – 'and you can be sure that I needed all that time to gather the courage to approach you'. I was able to evaluate the third woman 'in the closeness of a tête-à-tête, with glances and smiles and little freckles around her eyes', and I liked her even more than the others. 'Why?' Firstly, because she decided to grant the wish that her predecessors had provoked twice over and in such different ways – 'that of getting to know you'. I added: 'The first two made me fear I would be dismissed, and the third did not dismiss me. How could I not be eternally grateful to her?' I hoped that she was not repenting her decision to let an unknown man approach her and that she had not already decided to 'put an end to the future possibilities raised by this audacity'. I confirmed the dates of my stay in London, asking her to let me know if she would be there then, or if we should plan to meet in Paris. I ended with a request that she recommend a hotel for me 'as the one I usually stay in – a bland three-star in a boring area – tends to depress me'.

Almost as soon as I had sent this email, I regretted having been so explicit. I had taken a thoughtless risk; even wrapped in the epistolary preciosity of another century, the clumsiness, the presumptuousness of this message could not fail to insult the delicacy she had shown in agreeing to give me her card. I had always dreamed of experiencing a moment like this one, and I had just compromised its consequences through my outrageously demonstrative behaviour; she could not possibly reply to my words without fearing she would appear overly adventurous or indulgent.

I was on the top floor of the tower when, the next day, I received her reply on my BlackBerry. I couldn't believe how bold she had been. Each time I reread her message, I felt even more amazed. No woman had ever responded to the expression of my desire with such a categorical affirmation of her own – meeting my gaze as an equal – and this attitude enthralled me.

First of all, she thanked me for 'taking the lead again' and allowing her to 'simply reply'. 'Repenting my decision? Not yet . . .' She believed the world belonged to the bold, and on the basis of this principle, she told me that I would have one part of it and she would have the other, because she was accepting my proposal to meet up with her again in London at the end of October – 'so we can take our time . . .' She was concerned, however, by this idea of the 'three women' whom I claimed to have observed. 'Who on earth did you think you saw? Or who do you think you imagined seeing?' She concluded: 'I am somewhat confused . . .' Then her message ended with a few lines that floored me: 'I permitted myself the liberty of asking my assistant to reserve a hotel room for you. We have a special "company fee" of €150 (please see the attached forms, particularly if you are aiming to arrive after 6 p.m.). This place is not far from my office, which would allow me to slip away easily without losing too much time in the crazy London traffic. Just reply to let me know what time you think you'll be free of your obligations . . . For me, 6.30/7 p.m. is OK.'

What joy! The idea that Victoria could react to my message with any kind of initiative was already enough to arouse me, but that she should act on a matter as intimate as my lodgings, as linked to my body as the bed in which I would sleep, and, finally, that the woman of power should identify herself with the potential mistress by asking her assistant to reserve the room in which I would stay . . . that is what stirred up in me such deep emotions. 'So we can take our time . . .': coming from someone I didn't know, I found it hard to imagine a more erotic phrase. Not to mention that electrifying allusion to the moment when she could 'slip away' from her office to meet me at the hotel 'without losing too much time', like a secret mistress. The detail that concluded this paragraph – 'For me, 6.30/7 p.m. is OK' – was unambiguous confirmation of this email's erotic power. Because the surprisingly early hour suggested that Victoria had to cut a fairly sizeable segment of time out of her day – this woman who, like all high-level executives, must normally share out her time with the greatest parsimony. Had the head of Human Resources in an industrial multinational employing 12,000 people ever left her office around 6 p.m. unless it was to accompany her son to the paediatrician? I deduced from this that it must have been just as important for Victoria to meet me as it was for a high-level executive mother to care for her progeny – except that in one case it was a duty to herself, her body and her erotic imagination, and in the other case to the maternal ideal.

'Why three women? Did I seem so different from the other two, when I started talking? I'm afraid you're deluding yourself about me. I assure you, you mustn't idealize me.'

We had ordered oysters accompanied by white wine. I took it as a good omen that Victoria should decide not to eat much ('I'm not hungry,' she told me, smiling, as she closed the menu): I imagined her guts being twisted by anxious desire. Half the bottle of wine had already disappeared and its effects were added to the two glasses of champagne we had drunk in the restaurant bar.

'You won't be able to stop me idealizing you. We're here together this evening precisely because I did. How can I make you see? For me, you represent something specific. The reason I followed you and went up to you isn't only physical – it's not only your face and your appearance that I liked. If a man chatted up every woman he found beautiful . . .'

Victoria frowns at me suspiciously. She asks: 'Why? Are you so sensitive to that many women's bodies when you walk in the street?'

'I was speaking generally. Personally, my tastes are so definite that very few women attract my attention. I have feelings for a surprisingly limited number of women.' Victoria's expression is tender and amused. I am pouring the liquid from an oyster shell between my lips when I hear her ask: 'And this something specific, if you don't mind me asking, what is it?' I put the oyster shell on the plate and wipe my mouth with my napkin. 'It's difficult to say. It would be simplistic if I said it was a woman of power. But let's say a liberated woman: ambitious, intelligent; a woman who knows what she wants, who knows how to win respect. I have always been attracted to women who refuse to let men dominate them. They fascinate me. I admire them. They inspire me.'

'They inspire you . . . Are you talking about women with butterflies in their stomachs, incapable of even swallowing a single oyster?' Having confided this, Victoria moves her glass to the level of her right eye as if she is making a punctuation mark – a sign invented through drunkenness, like an 'exclamation comma' – before bringing it to her lips. Would she have been so reckless if the large square table that separated us had not placed her so far from my face? I smile at her, then add: 'I've said too much about this, Victoria. Anyway, I know it's true – I talk too much. All the mystery of our meeting will soon have vanished. I think I've had too much to drink.'

'The reality is a lot less dazzling. Let me tell you that nobody sees me the way you do, or at least nobody takes so much pleasure in it. Just ask the unions if you don't believe me . . . Me too, I'm drunk.'

'Who's to say that their furious battles against you don't inspire feelings of admiration in them? Perhaps they fantasize about you as a woman of power, or simply as a woman? You have no idea.'

'I would be extremely surprised. But you're wrong about one crucial point: they are not battling furiously against me.'

One waiter had come to take away our plates and cutlery, and a second had just vacuumed the white tablecloth with a silver-coloured mechanical hoover. Now a third brings us the dessert menus. Victoria raises her right hand to prevent him leaving, and says in English: '*One minute*. What are you having?' she asks me, quickly reading the menu. 'Do you want to think about it or order straight away?'

'What are you going to have?'

'I think I'll try . . . the peach melba.'

'You have a sweet tooth. I think I'll have the chocolate mousse.'

'All right, let's order now then,' she says, closing the menu. And then in English: '*So, we'll have a peach melba and a chocolate mousse. Thank you.*'

'*And a half-bottle of sparkling water.*'

The waiter takes the two menus and moves away. Victoria poses her chin on her joined hands and looks at me seriously. I say: 'I wanted to tell you, or rather confirm to you – I think the moment has come – I am a man of the left. I have all the ideas and principles that you'd expect, all the hope and anger. And even a certain kind of gullibility.' I give Victoria a broad, complicit smile: she replies by faking a grimace of disgust. 'It won't have escaped you that I am right wing,' she replies in the same faux-serious tone. 'In favour of capitalist principles and the free-market economy . . . it goes without saying that I proclaim this loudly and clearly.' I bring the glass of white wine to my lips, place it back on the table, and look at Victoria with a heartbroken expression: 'This is what's going to cause a problem between us.'

'Unless I manage to make you switch sides, as I fully intend to.'

'Really? And how do you plan to do that?'

'Through the truthfulness of my arguments. Seriously, David, left wing? An intelligent man like you, in an age like ours? You disappoint me.'

'I am very unlikely to switch sides.'

'In that case, explain to me your attraction to powerful women. Explain what you're doing at this table, in a chic restaurant in London, with the head of Human Resources for an industrial multinational, founded mainly on American capital – pension funds, in fact! It would seem you've come to the wrong address.'

'It is a little strange, I agree. If we persist in this irrational desire to get to know each other, you will discover a few complexities of that kind in me.'

'Yes, you do seem quite complex. I can sense something sensitive and refined in you. Sorry, I hope I'm not embarrassing you.'

'Not in the slightest. I fully acknowledge my sensitivity.'

'Personally, I adore it. That mixture of strength and delicacy is what first struck me about you. You're speaking to a recruitment specialist, remember – I would advise you to value this assessment.'

'I do value it, Victoria.'

'It would be impossible to have a conversation like this with any of the men I come across in my working life – with the notable exception of my boss, who is a brilliant, cultivated man. An opera buff: you know the type. With the others, it's rare to get beyond cars, dirty jokes, football results and the latest electronic gadget. But I like them. I think they've ended up valuing me too. Fingers crossed, I've managed to get them in my pocket. But at what price?'

'What do you mean?'

'We were talking earlier about how you idealized me . . . if you happened to see me with them, that idealization wouldn't last three minutes. I have to make concessions to the masculine beast, be conciliating. It's essential if I want to stay in the good books of a number of men who could make my life difficult – site managers, for instance. So I am not too demanding about the quality of conversations; sometimes I'm as oafish as they are; I even go to watch football matches in old stadiums in Poland – it reassures them to see me at their level. That's what some of my trips to factories are about.'

'Do you travel a lot?'

'All the time.'

'But how . . . I was talking earlier about my admiration for women who have a fulfilling professional life. In other words, they position themselves as men's equals. It's about time, anyway . . .'

'Tell me about it!' Victoria interjects.

'Exactly. But how do they manage when they have children? Could women with children do your job in the same way, in the same conditions, without immediately being penalized? You, for example: could you do this job if you had children?'

Victoria looks at me in silence for a few moments.

'It's a question of organization. You just have to make suitable arrangements. I don't think family life is really the problem. Anyone who feels held back by having children doesn't really want to evolve. Personally, I believe that if we really desire something, we can always manage – and that includes working at a high level in a company. And that is the only thing I wish to say on this subject: that we can choose our own life. Anyway, I can see the desserts coming . . .'

I take advantage of the silence caused by the waiter's intrusion (as he places the plates in front of us with meticulous precision) to exchange some increasingly meaningful glances with Victoria. The waiter pours some sparkling water in our glasses, puts the bottle back on the tablecloth, and asks us if we would like anything else ('*No, thank you,*' Victoria replies, with a smile) before moving away.

'Your chocolate mousse looks pretty good.'

'So you could do this job and have children . . .'

'Oh yes, it's really delicious. Are there any women in architecture?'

'Architecture is no longer my job.'

'Why? What made you decide not to be an architect any more? I'm sorry, I've forgotten what your job is called.'

Victoria lifts the spoon to her lips.

'Construction manager.'

'What led you into that area?'

'You seem surprised. Does it disappoint you that I could give up a profession as chic as architect to get my hands dirty in the noise and dust of a building site?'

'Don't forget that I work in the industry, and that I'm involved in practical matters. My esteem is not limited to ideas people and white-collar workers.'

'Did I get carried away by my prejudices? Sorry, I thought I'd sensed . . .'

'You remind me of my friends the unionists, who always discern hints of irony in my questions, or dishonest ulterior motives. So . . . now I know how to get your back up!'

Victoria bursts out laughing. I give her a severe look.

'I can readily believe that. I imagine you have limitless experience in that area.'

'Oh, come on, laugh! I'm teasing you! It's typical of the left to have no sense of humour when it comes to politics.'

'It's easy to have a sense of humour when you dominate the world.'

Victoria gapes at me. I glance at the spoon suspended in front of her face. There is a large piece of peach melba inside it.

'Do you think you're part of the unwashed masses? David, seriously, look at me: *do you truly consider yourself to be an oppressed worker?*'

'Don't be fooled by appearances. My lot in life isn't as enviable as it seems. Having said that, I must admit that you're right: I have no sense of humour when it comes to politics. Even in a context as romantic as this one, in the company of a woman like you.'

'But I like that in you. I don't want you to change at all. It's so rare. I could tell as soon as I saw you that you were an idealist.'

'People are often amazed that I gave up architecture for construction sites. Some of them were disappointed by my choice.'

'Were you an architect for a long time? Tell me – I want to know everything about you.'

'For seven years. I started in a big agency.'

'Want to taste?'

'Absolutely.'

Arm outstretched, she offers me her spoon, and my lips close around it. I straighten up and savour the taste of the peach melba while staring at Victoria for a few seconds: I have the feeling that the look in Victoria's eyes is spreading through my mouth, permeating my palate.

'I love it,' I say to her, smiling.

'So I see,' she replies mischievously.

'Where was I? I'm a bit distracted . . .'

'You were telling me you'd started . . .'

'That's right. Afterwards I worked for a slightly smaller agency, where I supervised building work. I adored that: I enjoyed following my projects through to completion, testing them against reality.'

Victoria tastes her peach melba. I watch the spoon inserted gently between her lips.

'Architects don't generally know much about construction sites. By doing that, I was able to make myself something of an expert. It was around this time that I won a competition. Well, it's a bit more complicated than that. In fact, it was a conceptual competition that was supposed to lead to a commission. I worked on it in the evenings after I finished work at the agency.'

'And you won? Congratulations!'

'You see, I'm making great progress already: I only suspected you of being ironic for a very brief instant.'

'I like the way you smile when you enjoy admitting your

guilt,' Victoria told me in a way that made me shiver. 'So you ended up with a commission . . .'

'I handed in my resignation and created my own agency. But as I only had one project and my activity was reduced, I invented an occupation that consisted of proposing to architects that I would supervise the building work on their projects. I went to see them and I told them: "You leave the site supervision to me and then you can close your eyes. When you open them again, the building will be up." I was wearing two hats: architect and construction manager, a rare combination that inspired confidence. So I was subcontracted to work as a construction manager. This left me quite a lot of time for the architecture projects I was trying to develop.'

Victoria has finished her peach melba. I can see the spoon marks on the insides of her glass dish.

'And the competition you won . . . what kind of building was it?'

'Kinetic houses.'

'Kin-what? Sorry, what did you say?'

'Never mind, it doesn't matter. All that's in the past . . .'

'No, come on, what kind of houses? Please, I didn't mean it like that. I want to know everything about you!' If the table had not been so wide – a fact that Victoria's accusing glance at the expanse of tablecloth between us seemed to deplore – I am certain that she would have taken my hand.

She picks up one of the flowers scattered over the table by its stem and begins turning it like a propeller near my right hand. 'Come on, tell me, please: what were these houses that you created?' The flower's rotations show the same insistence as Victoria's eyes, staring deep into mine. The petals assault the tablecloth with a smooth, elastic fury. I stop the flower between my fingers and, with my thumb, caress the yellow velvet of its stamen. I hear Victoria ask me: 'Are you really not going to say anything?' We pull on the flower with exactly the same strength – her on the cut, pointed end, and me on the blooming, colourful end. We remain silent for a long moment, our eyes meeting; my cock has grown hard. I yield for a second to the pull she is applying to the stem, and my hand moves over the tablecloth towards the glasses. Finally, I say: 'Kinetic houses. I'd designed a revolutionary kind of housing.'

'What do you mean by revolutionary?' I look at Victoria without replying. She pulls sharply on the stem. I smile at her. She gives a little series of tugs on my hand that seem to implore me. 'David, does it bother you to talk about it? I feel like I'm forcing this out of you. Please tell me if you'd rather talk about something else.'

'Not at all. I like being quiet and watching you. I love watching you. I find you beautiful.' Hearing this, Victoria smiles at me and lowers her head a little. I let go of the flower and look into her eyes: there is a strange feeling in my stomach. 'All right, I'm going to tell you – but briefly. It involved a housing estate with a variable geometry. The houses – about thirty of them – were constructed on runners, on an oval-shaped circuit; a slightly irregular oval. The houses could move, like train carriages on rails. The first Friday of each month, at exactly midday, the movement began and the houses slid slowly for four hours until they had reached a new position . . .'

'What an incredible idea!'

'The inhabitants had different surroundings, faced a different direction. Instead of private gardens, there was a park divided into parcels of land that gave some sense of privacy. The community paid for the services of a landscape gardener and a team of gardeners to maintain it. The idea was to have a journey across a landscape in nine chapters, with nine different views.

The idea was to vary the orientation each time and to enjoy the specific sensations provided by each setting.'

'You mean that a sitting room, every six months, could be east-facing or west-facing?' Victoria asks me, the flower in her hand rotating interrogatively.

'Exactly. What's more, the gardens of the nine parcels of land were all completely different. The inhabitants would find themselves in the same landscape every nine months, but not in the same season, because of the time lapse.'

'That's a very beautiful idea. I love it. It's very you.'

'The project was very enthusiastically received. Architecture critics wrote that it was revolutionary. Engineers came up with incredibly sophisticated solutions for the problem of moving the houses. But it was never built.'

'Why? What a shame! What happened?'

'The mayor of the city happened to become a government minister. He was the one who'd supported us. He had to leave his post as mayor to take over an important ministry.' I pause for a moment. Victoria pushes the flower towards me tenderly: 'You were unlucky.'

'The vicissitudes of life . . . As soon as he became a minister, he lost interest in the project.' Victoria delicately withdraws the flower from between my fingers and caresses my hand with the petals. 'I kept looking for work supervising construction sites. Until the day when the boss of a Parisian agency said OK, we'll hire you as a construction manager, but only as a staff employee. And that meant liquidating my company. Giving up architecture, in other words.'

'So . . . did you hesitate for long?'

'I spent a week trying to work out what I wanted to do. It's a strange experience, finding yourself at a crossroads like that, and being aware of it.'

'You ended up saying yes.'

'Strange as it may seem, on the day of the meeting, I still hadn't decided – I couldn't. When I was seated opposite the architect who ran the agency, he asked me if I had made my decision, and I looked at him without saying anything . . . Victoria, I don't know if you can believe this or understand it, but I didn't know what I was going to say.'

Victoria lowers the flower to my wrist; with the petals, she sends light, calligraphic shivers all the way up my forearm.

In this moment, I almost tell Victoria that, at the time of that meeting, Sylvie was pregnant with our first child. As she was not able to work, or take on any kind of professional activity (for reasons that I will explain afterwards), it was up to me to provide for our family. We were about to become three, and the question was whether I would have enough confidence to take the risk of maintaining the company and waiting for it to make money. Had I been single, it is almost certain that I would have remained independent; I would have been mad enough to believe that I could make it on my own and become an architect.

But I wanted so desperately to spend the night with Victoria that I didn't risk telling her about Sylvie at this point in the evening – in contrast to my normal behaviour in such circumstances.

'What are you thinking about?' Victoria asks me.

'Nothing, sorry. I'll tell you another time. You know as well as I do that we don't always do what we want in life. You can take the left-hand path when you dream of taking the right, but the right-hand path scares you: it fuels your dreams but you know that it could put you in danger, that it will lead you into a forest of uncertainty . . . so you end up taking the left-hand path, which, despite everything, you find quite appealing. It's possible to discover charms in anything once you take the trouble to look at it closely. One second before you make this choice, you may not know – not even have the faintest idea – what decision you are going to make . . . That's what I was thinking about . . .'

'You took the left-hand path,' Victoria cuts in. 'You said yes to the agency boss when you dreamed of keeping your own agency.'

'I said yes, all right, I accept – and that acceptance took me by surprise. It seemed to burst out of my brain like a rocket. I felt like I was seeing myself from the outside: I saw myself leap out of my life and run towards this man. But, above all, I noticed that, having said yes, I didn't feel any regret. I remember a strange feeling in the pit of my stomach: a blissful feeling. Like in that moment in an important meeting that seals a relationship that will last a long time; when you discover that the person you're in love with is also in love with you; when you think *yes*.' Victoria is about to interject, but I start speaking again: 'This was not the only reason, but in some way you might say that I made my decision based on this man's face. When he asked me for my decision and waited for my response, I looked at his face. This face welcomed me: it was my new life. I saw it as a refuge. I understood that, with this man, nothing bad could happen to me . . . I would be protected. As for him, he felt sure he was welcoming a man of great talent to his agency, and as it happens the future proved him right . . . It's strange, and it's probably difficult to understand from the outside, but I'm not sure I would have made the same choice if I'd had to give my response on the phone. But maybe his voice would have played the same role as his face . . .'

'You seem to regret it.'

'Not at all. I never think about it. I love my job. It's our conversation this evening that . . .'

'Our conversation this evening that . . . what?'

'That makes me present myself in this light, in the light of this failure. But in reality, my professional life, even if it's hard and often violent, subject to increasingly unbearable pressures . . . I'm happy about the job I do. I don't want any more – I think I've had enough to eat,' I say to Victoria, laying the silver spoon on the tablecloth.

'And you left this agency ten years later?'

'But of course you're right, Victoria.'

'Right about what?'

'About bitterness and regrets. I never ever think about it, but if I consider the matter clearly and carefully, then yes, it's true there are regrets, and a little bitterness. I regret not being an architect, but I suppress that truth through work, I swallow it up, I suffocate it with twelve-hour days. But all it takes is a conversation like tonight's. Thank you for that, by the way: I learned something about myself.'

Victoria smiles at me tenderly: a smile that is not surreptitious but assured, intelligent, full of words and thoughts, as long as a speech of consolation.

'Would you like a coffee?' she asks.

'Very much. But decaf, please.'

'Coffee stops you sleeping? It stops me sleeping too, but tonight I'm going to have an espresso.'

I pretended not to have understood or heard this. But if any doubts remained about what Victoria wanted to do after this dinner, her bold remark swept them all away.

'Who do you work for now?'

'For a company that specializes in engineering and contract management. We act on behalf of the people who finance the buildings – the clients, in other words.'

Victoria turns around and looks for a waiter. Not seeing one, she turns back towards me.

'I've never managed to remember the difference between the contractor and the client!'

'The client is the one who finances the building – a property developer, for instance – and the contractor is the construction company that's been given the task of building it. Defined like that, I think the two roles are fairly easy to understand . . .'

'I forbid you to make fun of me.'

'I'm not making fun of you. I am situated between the two; my role is to ensure that the building is finished on time, at the agreed price, to the required standard. If the property developer needs a completed building on 12 October that should cost him €50 million, my task is do whatever it takes for the building to be of the necessary quality, for the job to be finished on 12 October, and for the bill not to be any higher than €50 million. It's rare that both deadline and budget are not exceeded. My job is about reining in those two wild horses – time and money – and I strive to master them through putting a huge amount of pressure on the construction site: on every head and every hand, on every floor and at every moment. Do you understand? I have to make sure that the painters are not going to be obstructed by the electricians, who haven't finished installing the wiring in the false ceiling. Sounds stupid when I say it like that, but it's essential – and that example is multiplied a hundredfold with every passing minute. I coordinate and I anticipate. I deal with all the different trades; I direct them on and off the construction site like a theatre director – or, rather, the director of a variety show. I have to understand the problems some of them may encounter and help them to resolve them, even when they refuse to be helped – because often when people are in the shit, they don't want you to help them get out of it; they'd rather try to swim on their own, even if that means sinking. So I provide them with engineers. I lock people in a room with other people they've been ignoring for months and force them to talk to each other.'

'Which building are you working on at the moment?'

A waiter arrives at our table to ask if we need anything else. We order two espressos along with the bill. Victoria says she would like hers very strong. Then she calls him back – '*In fact, I'm sorry, I would like a double espresso, strong, short, thank you*' – before returning to the intimacy of our discussion.

'I'm working on the Jupiter Tower. It's a tower in La Défense; you might have heard of it.' Victoria bows her head, a thought on her lips; the expression that hovers on her face is a mix of tenderness, surprise, gratitude and disbelief. An expression glitters in her eyes: it's like a daydream that she is turning over in her thoughts, the way you turn a boiled sweet on your tongue. I hear her murmur: 'I don't know, I don't think so, but that name reminds me of something . . .'

'There have been quite a few articles in the papers. It will be the highest tower in France . . . if we manage to construct it.'

'Why do you say that?'

'It's a figure of speech . . . Because it's a difficult building. We're on the thirty-second floor; there are another eighteen to build, and we're two months behind schedule. Two months is huge. It's absolutely unthinkable that the Jupiter Tower won't be finished on time. That's how it is: the system in which I work is one of total intransigence. I'll explain why another day. I have to somehow reduce this delay, while hoping that we don't encounter any new difficulties, while hoping that those two months don't become three months, four months, five months, because otherwise I risk getting trapped in the most trying situation a human being can imagine. I've already been through that kind of hell, for a shorter period and faced with less terrifying stakes. My life was about as pleasant as a war zone.'

I burst out laughing while lifting the glass of white wine to my lips.

'I don't understand. You're talking about hell, about terrifying stakes. What do you mean?'

'I'm talking about huge financial stakes. If the client tells the people he's sold it to that the Jupiter Tower won't be finished on time, I'll let you imagine the furore, the legal complications, the threats of financial penalties, the pressure that would be put on us . . . in other words, ultimately, on *me*. Because I am the only one who is capable of correcting the situation – in concrete terms, I mean. Not only in terms of registered letters and imprecations, but with tangible results, with a tower that will be built more quickly. The only person who has intimate knowledge of the building – all the companies that are working on it, their bosses, their economic situations, their ability to increase the numbers of workers and be more involved – is the person who's in charge of the site from half past six in the morning to nine in the evening. So I'm the one who will bear the brunt of this crushing pressure. *I alone have to carry the weight of the highest tower in France on my back.* I will become a bête noire for a number of very important people concealed in the anonymity of international finance; I will poison their nights and the lives of their advisers.'

'But who are you talking about?'

'About all those people who should take over the building at a particular time, and who had not planned to begin their operations six months late. Two thirds of the tower has been bought by a bank that will have its offices there. A bank is OK – they're institutional types; they're scarily demanding, but I know what they're like, and they behave correctly. But the other third has been bought by investors who wish to remain more or less anonymous. I don't even know who most of them are: their identities are mysterious. What's certain is that I don't want to have any contact with all those who are only in this for speculating. Now, if I succeed, nobody will think to congratulate me. Everyone will assume that the Jupiter Tower just shot up like a dandelion.' Victoria laughs and lashes my hand with the petals of her flower. The waiter places our coffees on the table and hands me the bill. She cries out: 'You're exaggerating! David, stop! I'm sure you're exaggerating!'

'You think they'd hand me an envelope stuffed with cash to thank me for all the twelve-hour days I worked over four years? On the other hand, if the tower is late, there'll be a swarm of people who will besiege the tower, wearing visitors' badges on their pinstriped jackets — people to whom I've never been introduced: Russians, Chinese, businessmen accompanied by interpreters, lawyers, advisers — and they'll close in on me to obtain official clarifications, first-hand explanations, discreetly, when my bosses have ordered me not to tell anyone the truth, to keep my personal predictions to myself . . . You see the kind of situation I mean?'

Victoria looks at me incredulously, cup in hand.

'And this delay you're talking about — what caused it?'

'Technical problems that we encountered. In structural terms, the Jupiter Tower is a complicated building, with overhangs that are difficult to construct.'

Victoria has just swallowed a mouthful of espresso. Instantly a grimace spreads across her face. She puts the cup back on the table, shivering slightly. I say: 'Is it strong? Perhaps it's not a good idea to drink something like that.'

'That's an understatement. You want to taste it? Don't move, I'll come to you. I've had enough of this big, formal table — and most of all, I've had enough of using this plant to communicate with you!'

Holding her cup, Victoria gets to her feet. I stand up in turn, to pull out the chair to my left so she can sit down. 'Ah, at last! That's better. Thank you very much. So . . . where were we? Do you want to taste this nectar, this magic potion?' I take the cup from her hand and swallow the black, bitter liquid, thick as ink, that shimmers between the porcelain walls. Victoria's right foot swings smoothly along the white tablecloth under my gaze. It is terribly arousing. We now find ourselves in a tête-à-tête of almost indecent intimacy, given the restaurant's atmosphere. I am tempted to caress her ankle, moving rhythmically like a pendulum in what seems to be a prayer of desire addressed to my fingers.

'It's much better, having you close to me like this,' she tells me with a big smile. 'You were talking about overhangs . . .'

'That's a very strong coffee,' I say to Victoria, handing her back her cup. 'Yes, I was going to explain to you . . . but it's difficult right now.'

'Concentrate. We need to finish this chapter.'

'Do you want us to leave now?'

'I want to know the end. I told you: I want to know everything about you.'

'I'll hurry up then. You should know that the Jupiter Tower looks a bit like a bolt of lightning.' With the handle of my spoon, I carve the building's outline into the white tablecloth. She says: 'Yes, that's quite aggressive.'

'You know that sign warning against the dangers of electrocution? It's like a gigantic, concrete, three-dimensional version of that, displayed for everyone to see. The Jupiter Tower will be like a warning sign and an allegory of this age in which we're smiting ourselves.'

'In which we're *doing what to ourselves*?' Victoria interrupts me, her face a picture of astonishment.

'We're smiting ourselves, in the true sense of the word. Try

to imagine the power of that impact, a 230-metre-high tower –
250 metres with the spire – visible from the Champs-Élysées and
the Tuileries, from the Place des Ternes, the Île de la Cité and the
banks of the Seine: a gigantic lightning bolt in the Paris sky. I'm
not talking about divine punishment. The Jupiter Tower is not a
religious tower, it's political – metaphysical at most . . . I can see
you smiling; you find me ridiculous. But I'm going to keep talking. The highest building in France will end up embodying the
commitments we will make – soon, I hope, collectively – stop
laughing, please – in order to . . .'

'Because we're smiting ourselves?' Victoria asks ironically.
'*And why are we smiting ourselves?*' she adds, scrunching her nose
in a grimace like the ones you see on the faces of American
actresses in TV series.

'Through the stupidity of our world, of this headlong rush
to . . .' Victoria lets loose the laughter that my words have been
building inside her: 'What an apocalyptic image! My God, it's
true, you really are left wing!' I reply with absolute seriousness:
'I knew you would disagree.'

'I'm with you as far as ecology and saving the planet. But, for
the rest, I can see all too clearly where you're going with this. I'm
so bored of this discussion about the dangers of the free market,
the damage it causes, how cynical or barbarian we capitalists are.
Until proved otherwise, capitalism is the only system capable of
producing wealth. Do you want to go back to the good old days
of Communism?'

'Don't pretend to misunderstand me. That's not what I think,
as you know perfectly well.' Victoria draws an enormous dollar
sign on the tablecloth before tossing away her spoon. She says:
'One thing is bothering me. How did your architects manage to
sell this project to the capitalists who are funding it?'

'It was an international competition. They presented their

building as an abstractly shaped object that might make you think of a lightning bolt on a summer night . . .'

'I think people will see your tower as a Christmas tree,' Victoria says, pointing to the faint remains of my drawing in the thick tablecloth. 'It's Christmas every day, thanks to the wealth produced by capitalism and the free market. Wonderful presents under the tree! Thank you, capitalism, for these beautiful gifts that you bring us in your sack!' Victoria draws a simplified fir tree on the tablecloth. She adds baubles and tinsel, and then attempts to draw, further off, a huge snowman. I ask her: 'So, these presents under the tree . . . I suppose you're talking about bonuses, stock options, golden handshakes, that kind of thing?'

'You really are very funny. I was talking about the jobs that have been created, thanks to which proles like you are able to feed their families, go on holidays, and pay for their children to go to university.'

'I don't know how to thank you. I like your snowman.'

'As a reward, dinner's on me. I don't see any reason, in this world where both of us want to live, and where women would have as much power as men, why I shouldn't be the one who pays the bill.'

Victoria paid, and we left. The air outside was cooler. We drifted through the night as if by chance, choosing streets as they struck our fancy – for a mysterious perspective, a stand of trees in a lamppost's glow (it has to be said that this was a very nice neighbourhood) – but in reality, I was leading us towards the area where I thought my hotel was located. Victoria said, 'Shall we go this way?' and I pretended to hesitate: 'Yes, why not? But then . . . no, let's take this street, shall we?' and Victoria agreed: 'If you like.' It came to me that she wanted us to get lost, and in this way to push back into the depths of the night the moment when she would have to make a decision. She had seemed more brazen at certain moments during the dinner, but now she appeared to be floating in an anguish of indecision. We didn't dare hold hands. We walked side by side, brushing against each other. I wondered if she feared the desire that she felt for me — if the ease with which she yielded to me went against her principles and her self-image — or if she misread the hesitant reserve that tensed my body, the fear of disappointing her that haunted my thoughts, as indifference, leaving the two of us as immaterial spirits, in suspension, incapable of becoming tangible for one another.

I was thinking that it would probably be more reasonable not to start anything. Did I really have to complicate my life by risking the pleasure of this night, and the probability that I would want others? Conversely, was I sure my desire for this woman was strong enough? Was I certain I would be able to cope with her ferocity, the demands of her pleasure? All evening, my gaze had kept straying to that long cleft revealed by her generously unbuttoned blouse, through the transparent material of which I could see the fine lace of her bra; I was in thrall to the depth of this furrow, to the way it kept opening and closing as Victoria leaned forward, tender and trusting, or straightened up vindictively. Nevertheless, the possibility that, once she was undressed, I might no longer fancy her, had been in my thoughts all evening. What would I do if Victoria seemed stripped of all her enchantment? She had one of those bodies that, revealed, could be overpowering or, on the contrary, could instantly blow away the illusion of voluptuousness that it had created.

One other thing had preoccupied me throughout our dinner: the provincial, conservative, Catholic-inspired atmosphere that permeated Victoria's body and her wealthy-neighbourhood face, her wide, child-bearing hips, her bourgeois shoes, clothes, hairstyle. Was I going to be able to bear it? Would this ideological exoticism prove arousing? When Victoria had stood up to visit the toilets, just before paying the bill, I had followed her magnificent hips as they crossed the restaurant – and I had known that I wanted to make love with this classical, sensuous woman, to abandon myself to the fascination she exercised on my imagination, to submit to her queenly desires, to surrender. Of course I fancied her: I admired her; her career in the higher echelons of industry impressed me; her femininity enthralled me; I was seduced by the knowledge of her wealth; she inspired me. And that old-fashioned flavour which had, to begin with, bothered me, ended up by exciting me: the prospect of profaning this ultra-respectable atmosphere with kisses electrified me; I wanted to strip away the codes and symbols with my fingers, to stroke them and smear them with sweat. I had never known such a complex erection, provoked by a desire that mixed so many contradictory sensations. Her green eyes flashing with intelligence, the attraction I felt for her breasts, the pleasures of her brown hair with red highlights . . . all of this gave a piquancy to the authority of her political convictions (which I loathed) or the arrogance on certain questions that her professional position conferred on her – things that, away from this context, would have filled me with revulsion. It was the combination of these different opinions that, for me, constituted Victoria's reality, and their contrasts fed the attraction I felt for this woman. It seemed to me, as I walked the streets of London beside her, that the erection that hobbled my movements would never die down.

'David, I'd like to know the reason for this silence. Are you having doubts?'

'Do I look like I'm having doubts?'

Victoria stops walking and looks at me. She says: 'I don't know. A little bit.'

'And you, Victoria? Are you having doubts?'

'Yes, I admit it. I'm having doubts.'

'Look how charming that street is. Come on, let's cross over, we're going to go that way.'

'Are you sure? Where are we going?'

'Wherever the streets take us. Wherever the night takes us. Watch out for that taxi!'

'Do you know what I'm thinking about?'

'I've got a vague idea. You're questioning yourself.'

'There are several things I'm wondering about. Perhaps you're wondering the same things, and we could help each other out by responding together.'

'You're right, we probably are wondering the same things. It's possible, anyway.'

'What do you mean? Why possible rather than probable?'

'Various questions are conceivable in this kind of circumstance.'

'Oh, right.'

'Victoria.'

'What?'

'What are you wondering?'

'I'm wondering what you're thinking about. I'm wondering what your intentions are. I'm wondering what we're going to do.'

I stopped suddenly. Victoria halted a moment later and turned around to listen to me. 'Is there any point . . . do you think it's a good idea to ask these questions out loud? Seriously, are you being sincere? You don't know how we're going to answer these questions?' I started walking again as I finished speaking. As I reached Victoria, I drew her towards me and held her close. She gripped my arm tenderly: 'I'm turning back into a little girl, a debutante. I feel stupid. This evening is intimidating me.

I don't know what we should do. I don't know where your hotel is any more.'

'So you think we're lost?' Victoria lets go of my arm and moves away. I look at her and say: 'I'll tell you what we're going to do. And above all, I'll tell you where our hotel is.'

'Our hotel?'

'Our hotel.'

'So? Where is it?'

'Behind you.' Victoria turns around and examines the building we're standing in front of. She starts to smile – a big, happy smile that lasts a long time. We move very close to each other.

I lean down to kiss her. Victoria turns her face away at the last moment, and my lips graze the corner of hers. 'Come on, what are you doing?' She takes me in her arms, and I press my erection against her hip.

We went upstairs to the room without speaking or kissing. I switched the light on as we entered: Victoria moved into the room, and I watched as she dropped her handbag at the foot of the bed. I put the key on the desk, along with a few coins and my BlackBerry. From behind, I saw Victoria examine the room's decor, as if distanced in the abstraction of an imminence. She looked at the furniture, the pictures on the walls, but in reality, it seemed to me, she was hiding in a waiting room of her mind. She was absorbing what the room was transmitting to her consciousness about the events that would happen there – from the place where she stood, near the curtains, where she sensed that I would join her, to the bed which stretched out to her left, large and white, with a rose on the pillow, where she knew our caresses would lead us. The thick, oatmeal-coloured curtains – drawn, opaque, lit intimately by a single lamp – accentuated the

dramatic effect. We were inside a cube of hushed silence, suspended in the night.

Finally, Victoria turned around, surprised not to hear anything, and she saw me observing her from the other end of the
room, a smile on my lips. Her face confirmed to me what her
body's tremblings had suggested: that same propriety which,
in the street, had diverted my kiss to the edge of her lips, now
led her gaze over the carpet and the furniture. She had that
oblique, indistinct, horizontal look that often accompanies a
vague fear, a dreamy wondering, the beginning of remorse. As
Victoria moved, each instant stretched out; her gaze lengthened
simultaneously in time and space; a smile that appeared suddenly
took ages to dissolve. We could hear cars passing in the street,
but it seemed like their murmur had been distanced by the same
kind of disturbance that was slowing down the flow of her
gestures, her thoughts, the words she wished to speak, and she
was silent.

I could scarcely believe that this hesitation of her entire being
was not deliberately designed to eroticize the waiting. I moved
towards her. Commandingly, I took her face in my hands and I
altered its angle as I would a projector or an adjustable lamp,
so that her eyes were fixed on mine. I felt again the spark that
her green eyes had provoked in me when I passed her in the
shopping centre. There was a seriousness, and a certain grandiloquence, to the way my fingers turned her face, telling her to
look straight at the truth. I forced Victoria to brave my gaze, and
forced myself to immerse my eyes in hers.

The spark that was consuming us did not die out. I felt Victoria's face struggling between my fingers. As our eyes bored
into each other, a pressure grew inside our bodies – a moment of
desire that kept repeating itself in a loop, like a stuck record –
and in the instant when this pressure was about to reach its

paroxysm, Victoria exploded. Her mouth pounced on mine. I heard seams bursting. She devoured my lips furiously while trying to undress me. She needed to slow down her fingers as they struggled with each buttonhole on my shirt: they suffered like insects striving to overcome obstacles; I could see them trembling with impatience. Having removed my shoes, thrown my shirt at the curtains, and yanked vertically at my trouser legs, she paused, radiant and breathless. I saw her squatting, pressing her hands on my torso and moving them slowly; shudders ignited the surface of my body. Suddenly she stopped, and I stared at her. Drops of sweat running down her temples shone through this incandescent lull like crystal ladybirds. I waited, tensed, tortured, for Victoria's palms to start descending once again towards the elastic of my underwear. The heavy seconds of this suspended moment, this unbearable pause, were counted down in the heartbeats of my desire. The movement began again. Victoria watched her hands move down my chest in the light of her gaze. I closed my eyes. Her hands descended faster towards my stomach. Then Victoria pulled away. I no longer felt anything. I found myself alone. I waited a few seconds in the black night of my closed eyelids, but she did not reappear. Suddenly it was cold; I thought of the next morning, and felt sad.

I opened my eyes again and saw Victoria in front of me, a smile upon her lips. She backed away from me – 'Look' – and started to undress, slowly and meticulously unbuttoning her blouse. She threw it on top of my shirt, rolled up in a ball at the foot of the curtains. The zip of her skirt sputtered between her fingernails like a motorboat on a waveless sea. We never took our eyes off each other. I had the impression that her lips were drawn into a faintly warlike smile. Her skirt joined my trousers near the bathroom door.

Victoria stood bare-legged in high heels, bra and knickers. Her body was absolutely gigantic, but harmonious in its proportions; her hips were like something an artist might have dreamed up for the phenomenal appearance of a goddess; she reminded me of a statue in the grounds of a chateau. I wanted to go to her, but she stopped me with a 'Wait' that brooked no argument. Now, in her eyes, I saw the same severity that I had seen on her lips a few moments before; it must have excited her for me to look at her body. My erection beat time in my underwear. I had never come close to a physique comparable to hers — soft and firm, fleshy and metallic, in full bloom but without the slightest hint of fat — its majestic fullness a contrast to the chamber music of most of the attractive bodies one encounters. 'Look,' she was saying, 'look at my breasts. I want to show them to you. I hope you like them. They're for you. I'm giving them to you.' And her chest appeared before my eyes like a slow-motion shot of a natural phenomenon in a television documentary.

I contemplated her sublimely heavy, pear-shaped breasts. I found them beautiful — ideally shaped. I didn't think I had ever seen such perfectly circular, coin-shaped areolae. Victoria's face was utterly serious. Her arms were held slightly away from her hips: she was inviting my eyes to journey over her body, to linger in her most intimate zones, to drink in the pleasure that my gaze produced in them. I sensed her shivering under this full-frontal assault. Like a pair of bellows blowing on embers, my probing gaze seemed to breathe red glowing waves on to her fervid body. I thought she was going to come just from being watched.

I removed my underwear, and Victoria did the same. Like me, she wavered, knocked off balance by the emotion she felt. When she threw her knickers on top of my underwear, I saw her beat back a smile that transgressed the gravity of her expression. I loved this little escaped smile, in which I found proof that both of us knew the exact proportion of playfulness and theatre, of mischief and fantasy, in this night's erotic equation. I lifted my eyes to Victoria's so I could respond with my own complicit smile, but hers had already disappeared. My cock, fully hard, stood straight in the dimness. Victoria looked at it for a long time, as I had done with her breasts, the great wall of her hips, her beautiful statuesque thighs. Her eyes, thick with desire, gave me the same pleasure her fingers and her lips had given me. It occurred to me that another woman, watching my cock from a distance with the same avidity, would probably have had this experience cut short as it turned flaccid almost instantly, shrivelling with shyness. But with Victoria, it was the opposite: fully concentrated on this most vulnerable part of my anatomy, she increased its confidence and boldness, even gave it a new pirate-like swagger. With this woman, something extraordinary was happening. I moved towards her and took her in my arms. I held her body against mine as tightly as I could, and I kissed her on the mouth.

We made love for five hours. Anxious by nature and always fearing that I will disappoint, I became a different man in this bed – freed of all worries, carried away by an irrational exhilaration.

For me, Victoria was like a deep nocturnal forest that I strode through without knowing where I was going, through woodland, amid ferns, under tall shivering trees, far from any path. There were noises, puddles, odours, dampness, shapes that vanished, treetops overhanging our bodies. I thought of nothing. I let our frolics lead where they would. I experienced moments of fulfilment and astonishment, euphoria and intimidation, and then episodes of grace when Victoria smiled at me, overcome with happiness, as if we were lying in a glade.

Naturally, undisturbed by any sense of modesty, our bodies

found themselves in one position after another. I was on top of Victoria, or she was on top of me. My heels pressed against the sides of the bed and I saw her breasts sway beneath my thrusts. I took her from behind and she bit the pillow. We did it on the desk. I had her in the bathroom, where she'd gone to pee. She led me to the base of a large mirror and told me to watch her lips as she sucked my cock. Victoria demanded that I take her doggy-style, then stared at me in the mirror and yelled: 'Look! Look at you making love to me . . . Look how much pleasure you're giving me . . . you're so hard . . . I'm going to come . . .'

Her expression changed in flashes: she begged me; she clung to my arms as though a wave was about to take her away. I heard her cry out, and saw her assaulted by the shocks that ran through her body: it bucked and reared, as if some powerful creature were biting it. Finally, Victoria remained tensed for several seconds, in a painful paroxysm, and her fingers, as if she were terrorized, tried to catch at something — something that must have hatched in the night — like the hand of someone drowning that reaches above the water and attempts to grasp an imaginary rope, before disappearing.

I couldn't believe my eyes. I had never been sure about my ability to make a woman come. Sylvie had always kept the results of our lovemaking secret, but Victoria — under my incredulous gaze — seemed to be engaged in a merciless battle, as if the orgasm were destroying her, or expelling her from herself, or dragging her to the bottom of the water.

Our bodies, thrown on the bed in the chaos of an explosive climax, groped blindly towards each other without altering their initial direction and, because of this, created some singular images: a face on an ankle; a kneecap on a torso; hair spread out over a spine. Victoria's body continued to sizzle and to emit brief, fading jolts for several minutes. She was exhausted, her eyes feverish. Locks of her wet hair were plastered to her face. A faintly demented smile lingered on her lips. 'Bastard,' she said, in an agonized sigh, 'you're going to kill me.' It took her a little time to calm down. Then she curled up against me, and we held one another tightly.

We told each other secrets. We examined ourselves with the most total objectivity, like a doctor analysing a symptom or checking a knee joint. As I hadn't come, all it took was a kiss before a new embrace interrupted this discussion. And we made love for a long time.

Victoria told me that she had been born in Barcelona to an English mother and a German father; she'd been brought up in France, which is why she spoke perfect French. Because of her family origins, she had always lived essentially like an expatriate: she had worked in China, Singapore, Germany and now in London. Had she ever lived in this city before working here? Never. How long had she been doing this job? Two years. Had she graduated from a business and management school? 'Not at all. I studied Philosophy at the Sorbonne. The woman you see before you is a doctor of philosophy,' she admitted with a smile. 'I could talk to you about Kierkegaard if you want.' I was lying on my back, my arms entwined around Victoria; her head was resting on my shoulder; one dreamy finger drew mysterious signs on my torso. We talked without being able to look each other in the eyes. There was a sleepy slowness to our murmurings. Victoria was examining the phalanxes of my fingers ('I love your hands,' she'd just confided to me) when she told me how handsome she had found me the two times she had seen me in the shopping centre. 'Why do you say two times? Had you already seen me before that moment when our eyes met?'

'Yes, but your face wasn't turned towards mine. I noticed you straight away; you were like a slightly injured angel, separated from the other people in the crowd. I was struck by your resemblance to the actor Joaquin Phoenix – I don't know if anyone's ever told you that . . .'

'People say it all the time.'

'I adore that actor.'

'Me too. *The Yards* is one of my favourite films.'

'And mine. Anyway, I was sad that day – really sad – and seeing you, glimpsing your face, made me suffer even more. I already felt like I was on the edge of a precipice, but then, when I saw you, that finished me. I thought: I've already tipped over into the abyss, now I'm going to crash to the ground!'

'Yeah, I'd sensed some kind of tension in you. I'd thought that someone must have hurt you, upset you.'

'I can't tell you why for the moment. It's a long story. But I'd started to fear getting older. I was going through a typically feminine period of panic!'

'For this reason that you prefer to keep to yourself.'

'Exactly. For this reason that I prefer to keep to myself. I was thinking that, at forty-two, I only had a few months left of being seductive. I'd lost my self-confidence. I'd started doubting my body and the effect it could have on men. When I saw you walking through the crowd, indifferent, I thought: it's over, men like that don't look at me any more. I felt like crying when you walked past me without even noticing my existence!' Victoria bursts out laughing. She squeezes my fingers, then kisses them tenderly. I tell her: 'When our eyes finally met, I don't think you saw indifference.'

'That's true, but it made me even more sad. I wondered why I never met men like you in any of the places I go to regularly. Why must it always be in the street, in trains, and never at the parties

I'm invited to? It's unbelievable: how can you explain this curse? I was in despair when I saw you disappear.'

'I thought the same thing.'

'It's not possible for women to approach the men they like. It's very unfair.'

'You should have turned around. I did. If you'd turned around, I would have gone to you.'

'Turning around would have been like approaching you.'

'I suppose.'

'That's precisely why I resisted the temptation to do it. A woman cannot turn around for a man, even if she's dying to . . .' I think she smiled as she spoke those last words. She continues: 'You can imagine how I felt when I realized you were standing behind me in the queue at the bowling alley. It was terrible: I had to fight against the desire to eat you up with my eyes; they kept flickering around your face without knowing where to settle. I was afraid you'd think I was mad!' One of Victoria's fingernails is drawing little circles on my chest, like buttons on an officer's tunic. I reply: 'I didn't notice anything.'

'It was far from pleasant. You were staring at me. I felt like a mongoose in front of a snake charmer. And when that elderly American woman asked to swap places with me . . .'

'I remember. That was the moment when I began to think that you liked me.'

'I sent her packing. I wanted to savour my emotion, to enjoy that surprise a bit longer. It's funny: I felt very strange – crazy and fragile. I didn't know how to get out of the situation. I managed not to meet your look: I still don't know how. I was afraid you'd discover what a state you'd put me into. I threw brief glances at your clothes, your hands, your shoes, and at your face when you turned your head. I liked your clothes a lot: you seemed refined. There was something sophisticated in your look, which is quite rare with men. I wondered if you weren't gay.'

'You thought I was gay?'

'I decided you were. Handsome and virile, but with a gentle aspect: I thought you must be. I felt reassured that you were gay. It was less dangerous. I didn't have to ask myself any difficult questions.' I turned my face to kiss Victoria on the forehead. She lifted her face for a kiss on the mouth, which I gave her. 'And afterwards? What did you think when I approached you?'

'I heard footsteps getting closer behind me. I saw a shadow level with me that was going to overtake me. You were talking to me. I stopped and listened to you. The way you spoke was beautiful. I loved your story of the opera that lasts five hours. My heart was pounding in my ears. I was having trouble suppressing the smile that I could feel growing inside me. I admired the courage that you must have needed to come and talk to me.'

'I was sure you were going to slaughter me.' A long silence. I close my eyes. I feel good. I have the impression I could fall asleep to the sound of her voice, rocked by this perfect narration. I hear Victoria murmur in my ear: 'You were right to be afraid. I could see you were terrified. If I hadn't felt that you were more or less certain to fail, I would never have let you speak to me, even if I did like you. However, when you told me that you'd followed me, that our meeting in the bowling alley had not been down to chance, I thought you were just a womanizer who spent his days hanging around in the streets to satisfy his needs. I was angry with you for duping me.'

'I did explain that I didn't have time . . .'

'I know, I listened to your explanation. And little by little, I felt a sort of rebellion in my brain: I wondered what right I had not to believe you and to be so negative in my judgement of you.

I realized I was constructing a defence mechanism. First of all, I thought you were gay, now I saw you as a sexual obsessive – what next? The truth is that you put me into a state I'd never experienced before.'

'Keep going. It's exciting to relive this scene through your eyes. I'm listening to you with my eyes closed and I feel as if I'm in your body, facing this stranger who's come up to me.'

'All these questions went through my mind while you talked to me. I knew I was trying, through fallacious arguments, to loosen the hold you had over me. Heat radiated from my solar plexus, and something was zooming about inside my chest. I felt like my skeleton was flesh. The heat spread through my lower abdomen. I was trembling and sweating, and I couldn't speak. I felt alive, and so damn pathetic.'

'I asked you if I could take you out for a drink. I don't remember what words I used. *Can I invite you to have a drink with me?*' Victoria laughs, gently and affectionately, when she hears me speak these words as shyly as I'd pronounced them in the shopping centre. I repeat: '*Can . . . can I invite you to have a drink with me?*'

'Something like that, spoken very cautiously – which gave me confidence. Apart from a very proper upbringing, which had taught me to reject this kind of invitation, I also had an important business meeting to attend. I hesitated. I was ready to let myself be twenty minutes late. I could feel I was on the point of surrendering. But I ended up controlling myself. I said no, and I appreciated the fact that you didn't insist.'

'I asked you if we could see each other soon, in London or Paris. You gave me your business card.'

'I looked at you. My cunt was burning with the desire to make love to you. We were speaking in a civilized and respectful way, but I could sense, behind those words, a more primitive, animal

79

language, that scared me – I found it too intense, especially with a stranger I'd just met in a public place! And so I accepted your invitation to see each other again: I said yes, then wondered out loud if the spark would still exist. Later it occurred to me that I must have been completely mad to have said those words: *We'll see if the spark is still there!* To a stranger! Such an explicit declaration, to a guy who'd just met me! I wasn't myself any more. I haven't been able to stop wondering what you must have thought of me when you heard me say those words.'

'For me, it was like a miracle. Generally, women don't say that kind of thing. I felt like you were propelling us into a fairy tale.'

'I was afraid you'd think me a slut.'

'Quite the opposite. I thought you were a magician. Only a woman who was out of reach, a truly extraordinary woman, could say such a thing to a man who'd just approached her.'

I am speaking with my eyes closed. Deep inside me is a feeling of infinity. I hear occasional cars pass in the street, a toilet flushing in a neighbouring room, a door gently closing once in a while, nocturnal and mysterious.

'I'm far from a slut.'

'I never doubted that, Victoria.'

'I bloody well hope you never doubted it!'

'So why worry about it?'

'Because of how easily I was persuaded to give you my card. The next morning, on the 7.13 Eurostar, still half-asleep despite the icy shower I'd taken, I felt mortified that I'd let myself be chatted up by a womanizer, and what's more – let me speak – don't interrupt me . . .'

'OK, I'll let you speak. I'll tell you later.'

'Thank you. What I have to say is important. I wouldn't want you to think that I feel this kind of attraction on a regular basis. You could have kissed me that day, in the shopping centre. We would have made love that evening, perhaps even an hour later if I'd gone with you to have a drink; I would have taken you to my room and leapt on you. I was horrified by that knowledge; it wasn't like me. I had only one desire – it was all I thought about after we spoke in the shopping centre. I wanted you to take me; I wanted to see your cock and suck it. I was shocked by the consequences that might follow from what had been nothing but a stupid hormonal fantasy. I told myself I was weak and vulnerable. You can't react like that to seeing a stranger – cancelling a business meeting – the idea is intolerable! But at the same time, deep inside me, a little voice whispered: "Why not?" The night before, none of the men at that dinner could have given me one hundredth of the feelings that you communicated to me – in less than ten minutes, standing there surrounded by onlookers – with your body, your words, your gestures, your eyes. I didn't know where I was any more. I found it agonizing and wondrous. David, do you understand? I told myself: "Admit it!" "Admit it, Victoria!" "Admit you like him, that he makes you melt, that he devastates you!" "Admit it!" "Admit the truth!" "Let's get it over with!" And I admitted it. I told myself: "I admit it." "Yes, I admit it – he devastates me." So where did this unease come from, this feeling of mortification? It's because I like to know where I'm going. I'm a rational woman. I like to organize things – not for nothing am I head of Human Resources! I like planning, organizing, anticipating. I hate leaving things to chance. I like things to be clear. I like events to be explained, discussed, justified.' A long silence. I stroke Victoria's arm with my thumb. Her head is still resting on my shoulder and the words she speaks flow, gentle and intimate, close to my ear. 'I thought that if I was in one of those romance novels that I pick up some-times from the seats on the Eurostar, I'd be able to tell myself it was a *coup de foudre*, but I'm too rational to accept that I could feel such a thing, that I could not be in control of events. I was angry, but at the same time, when I touched myself through my trousers, I was soaking wet. I stared through the Eurostar win-dow at the passing landscape, repeating to myself that my attitude made no sense . . . and yet I was able to make myself come just by gently touching my crotch for a few seconds. This wasn't me. I didn't recognize myself.'

'I know that. I believe you. I'm experienced enough to have detected it.'

'Are you talking about your experience as a womanizer?' Vic-toria sounds serious when she asks me this. I open my eyes and shift to the right so I can look at her face. I say: 'I'm talking about my experience with women. I'm forty-two. I do have some experience with women!'

'Sorry, but I'm haunted by this fear. I'm afraid that, for you, I'm just a woman you've hunted. You did the right thing by approaching me, and I did the right thing by letting you capture me. If one thing is certain, it's that we were right, both of us, to yield to our urges. What time is it?'

'Ten past five.'

'I have to go. I need to go home.'

'*At ten past five in the morning?* Why? Don't you want to stay with me? We could try to sleep for a few hours.'

'I need to go home and get changed. I didn't bring a change of clothes.'

'So? Just go and buy a pair of knickers tomorrow morning in the first supermarket you see! Stay with me. I want to sleep in your arms.'

'I can't, David. Really. I can't go back to the office in the same clothes I wore yesterday. I can't go to the office two days running in exactly the same outfit.'

'Oh, really? And why is that? What a strange rule!'

'I never do it. Someone in my position cannot go to the office two days running in the same clothes – don't ask me to explain why, that's just how it is.' Victoria plants a kiss on my lips and jumps out of bed laughing – 'If there's one thing I'm sure of, it's that my staff, my assistants, would immediately know that I'd spent the night with a man!' – and then she locks herself in the bathroom.

From the other side of the door, I hear water running.

I look around in the darkness: our belongings are scattered all over the room, and the sheets have been torn off the bed. I see a pillow on the desk, left there by Victoria; three small bottles of champagne (which we drank from while kissing) lie abandoned on the carpet, surrounded by damp stains; the quilt that matches the oatmeal-coloured curtains has been thrown near a wall.

I begin to feel sleepy.

My modern-day goddess soaps herself under the roar of water while singing operatic arias.

My eyes seek out her high heels, her business suit, her lace bra. This night makes me feel incredulous, wildly grateful, gently happy.

And suddenly I understand everything: it's absolutely clear. I grasp the reason why I'm here, providentially, in this hotel.

The ease with which Victoria was persuaded to hand me her card; her sadness which, she told me, was caused by an upsetting event, the day we met; her long speech about how this was not the kind of thing she did, how I should not misjudge her; her habit of organizing everything, planning events; and the panic attack she'd felt at being forty-two; these different pieces of the puzzle suddenly fit together to reveal to me the crystal-clear truth: Victoria wanted a baby.

This idea did not seem so abhorrent to me. I even imagined granting her this surprising gift, coming inside her. Unfortunately for Victoria, not only had no semen spurted from my cock during the hours we'd spent in each other's arms, but I was never going to see her again. My principles meant I would disappear for ever the next day.

4

When I moved to Paris to study architecture at eighteen years old, I had not managed to seduce any of the three girls I'd fallen in love with during the previous five years. Only one fairly plain Alsatian girl had thrown herself into my arms a couple of summers earlier, driven by some inexplicable urge. (That she, rather than someone else, should have been the only one to show any interest in me has always remained a mystery to me; she had short blonde hair and we spent a whole August kissing every evening on the beach, though I never dared touch her breasts or slide my fingers under her knicker elastic.) In spite of the progress that this fling allowed me to think I'd made, however, my isolation was not diminished. I had felt for a long time that I needed to get away from the suburbs, to escape that prison of discipline and work where my father kept me sequestered, in order to meet people who would appreciate me. I told myself that the girls I met elsewhere would be more open-minded and interesting than those I had known for years, and above all that they would discover a less withdrawn and anxious boy than the one who lived with his parents. This prospect had always soothed me and given me long sentimental daydreams.

The house where we lived, located on a roadside at the edge of an ordinary village, had been built by my father: for four years, he had devoted most of his free time to the construction of this detached house, at a time when we were living in a two-bedroom apartment in a dilapidated tower block. Born in Poland and having moved to France with his parents at the age of eight, my father had, like most of the men in his family, become a builder. For years, he had worked as a labourer (often for temp agencies), before joining a medium-sized construction company where his personality, his professional skills and his leadership abilities had been noticed. He was distinguished from common mortals by a face like Burt Lancaster's, and the severity of his temperament gave him an instant authority over everyone he met (he is demanding to the point of being pathological, even verging on harassment and violence). Clearly, his boss saw the uses these qualities could be put to. My father moved up the hierarchy until he was the team leader, and then he set up his own business.

My parents met in the early sixties at a dance held on Bastille Day in a village in south-west France, where my father – working on the building site of a school in Toulouse – had gone to rest for a couple of days (staying with the parents of a co-worker who was originally from that area). He had been captivated by the beauty of my mother's face. Her resemblance to Grace Kelly is substantiated by most of the photographs from this time (and I hope you'll forgive me for poeticizing what was, perhaps, just a very pretty face), and according to family legend, a thrill rippled through the crowd when, as the slow dances began, this stranger – who had magnetized the curiosity of all the young girls – summoned the courage to approach the prettiest of them all (sitting on a chair under a plane tree) and ask her to dance with him. Everyone had known he would ask her for this dance. A round of applause rang out when the third slow dance ended and my mother explained to her partner that three dances was enough, and she returned to her seat under the plane tree. My father quickly joined her, bringing a glass of white wine that he'd bought for her at the bar, and they all lifted their glasses in a toast. (My father's friend, who later became my godfather, was with them, as was my mother's best friend, now my sister's godmother.) Burt Lancaster walked Grace Kelly back to her door (she lived with her parents, of course), where a kiss that I imagine as being as flamboyant as something from a Hollywood film brought this fateful night to its conclusion. The next morning, he was introduced to the girl's parents, and they saw each other every weekend until their wedding eleven months later.

It would be impossible to count the number of times the children of this union had begged their parents to tell them the details of that night. My father, as if delivering a lecture on astronomy, always emphasized the exactness with which the events seemed to follow each other in order to grant the wish that my mother's radiant presence had hatched in his mind (their bodies, thrown by chance under the plane trees that beautiful summer night, had been drawn to each other by an unquestionably precise mechanism), but also the fastidiousness with which he had conducted himself. I find it amusing that the birth of their love should obey that principle which my father always placed above all others (even if the principle is, by its nature, so foreign to love affairs) – namely, the importance of well-made, stable, tangible things, stripped of all guessing and moods. 'Everybody went silent. It was crazy. Nobody spoke a word. Everybody had sensed that something incredible was happening,' my godfather said, before my father stoically resumed his story. 'And when I heard them applauding us, after the last dance, I knew for certain that I was going to marry her. There's nothing more to say, children. Except that I understood, when I saw her face, why my destiny had led me to this godforsaken place. And so . . . and so I did what I usually do – like I do at work, like on a building site. I worked hard, applying myself and using my brain.' So said this authoritarian man who, in contrast to his son, was not romantic or emotional, not prone to sensitivity or introspection. My sister and I – reassured to know that we were the result of a mathematical night devoid of chance; happy to have it confirmed that, with such a methodical man, our parents' story could not have happened any differently (we learned at this time that we could not *not* have been born: a pleasant truth to hear, provoking gently amazed, gap-toothed smiles in both of us) – asked for this story to be told to us again and again throughout our childhood, in spite of the small number of variations that its repetition entailed.

The one thing that undoubtedly most fascinated us was the established fact of the two protagonists' beauty. Over his steaming plate, my father made an almost perfect circle with the middle fingers and thumbs of both his hands, and said: 'Your mother's waist was so narrow, I could put my hands around it like that!' 'You're joking!' I said. 'Mum was so thin, she could go through that hole?' 'But that's impossible, it's rubbish,' my sister moaned. 'How could a woman's waist . . .' 'Obviously you couldn't get through that hole, even at five years old, because you're so fat!' 'But I swear it's true!' my father exclaimed. 'Queer!' my sister shouted at me. 'Stupid twat!' 'Yes, it's true, he's right – I was very thin at the time,' murmured my mother. 'Not thin – slim,' my father corrected her. 'Slim, perfect, like a mannequin! She was easily the most beautiful girl in the village.' Unfortunately, even if there remained echoes of her early beauty in her Greek nose and oval blue eyes, my mother's face had ended up deteriorating. By the end of my childhood, nobody who had not known her as a young girl could have suspected that she had once been sublime. Even I had to verify it by digging out a beautiful album full of enormous photographs of their wedding. As a schoolboy, consumed by a full-blown Oedipus complex, I repeated this verification process many times: under the crackling glassine paper that covered each page hid a dazzlingly beautiful young woman. I prostrated myself before a few of these sacred photographs, in particular the one where – leaning over a table, smiling, pen in hand – she signs the town hall register. She looks like she's been struck by a lightning bolt of surprise, lighting up her mind and inspiring that unearthly smile which gives her presence a gracious, light-headed look. Wide-eyed, my mother awaits the future: she is opening herself up to welcome the anticipated delight which, at that moment in time, is dazzling her. She's happy, in other words. Which is also to say: she doesn't know where she's going. Though she is certain of one thing: her life from now on will be different from the one she has known. A man has come, and he is going to take her far away from here. I have never failed to glimpse, in that suspended smile, the thought of a child: my own presence. What I see in these pictures is the first light of her love for me. My mother is seeking me out in her thoughts. That uncertain smile is intended for me alone.

But all of that faded with time, giving way to a face weary with resignation. The clear water of her beauty became cloudy, as if the heavy mudfish that circled her mind had stirred up a mess of particles that never resettled; or like the water in that blue bucket where she wrung out her floorcloth, turning greyish-brown. I created these two images in order to explain my mother's very particular decline, following a strange combination of discipline and dereliction, rigour and neglect, constancy and withdrawal. The dying of her spark was the result of her confinement, of the lack of prospects and enchantment, of the disappearance of all dreamlike thought. The words 'pleasure', 'desire' and 'plan' no longer existed for her. All thoughts of attractiveness having been removed, my mother went out only to shop in a nearby hypermarket where the checkout girls who said thank you were the only people she saw. My father hated the idea of having close relationships with anybody. I saw my mother sink into an existence devoid of any horizon, conditioned solely by the duties attendant on her status as a housewife (and God knows that my father included self-sacrifice in his intransigent definition of that status) – hence the slimy mudfish that I mentioned earlier, undulating gloomily through her mind. From this period, we can date the anguish I feel regarding the idea of the housewife. My mother no longer smiled. Any unexpected situation or cheerful suggestion that we might make would be met with an unconquerable resistance (she said no – invariably) or triggered tearful protestations. It seemed to us that, having given up on the pleasures of life for so long, she had lost all taste and desire for them. Eating an ice cream on the terrace of a café one sweltering afternoon? She saw no point in agreeing to this brief extravagance. 'We're going home.' Hardly anything did not seem superfluous to her. She ended up physically resembling these tattered thoughts.

The beauty of my father's face, by contrast, was of a kind that increases with the years of work and insomnia, that intensifies with the vexations and the bad moods, to such an extent that it had lost none of its impact.

It amazed me that such striking parents could have given birth to such ordinary-looking adolescents. My sister was so unattractive that I spent years denigrating her appearance. I told her that, in giving her our father's most spectacular attributes – nose, ears, shoulders, hairiness – the gene pool was demonstrating a brilliant sense of irony. She replied with some remarkably violent insults – 'Queer! Faggot! Cocksucker! You've got a girl's face!', that kind of thing – while throwing forks at me. I wasn't as ugly as her, just plain, with a face as unstriking as my introverted personality. Just as I found it difficult to make my presence exist for others, my face remained as if hidden within itself, buried in its own features. In spite of this, I spent hours in front of my parents' mirror cabinet trying to convince myself that my appearance was not as irredeemably ordinary as I might imagine. I searched my face for some secret aspect that might contain the seed of an implicit and late-flowering beauty. As an adolescent, I believed that my salvation would only arrive when I met a divine woman who would take me under her wing and protect me – but how could I attract such a woman (even were I to become the greatest architect of modern times) if my face continued to remain wrapped in itself without emitting the faintest flicker of light? On certain days, from a certain angle, in certain circumstances, my appearance did not make me sad: I managed to find myself attractive. This happened when I'd been transfigured by someone smiling at me shyly in a corridor, or a twenty out of twenty in my maths homework had procured my teacher's congratulations. I remember those glorious days when my face seemed to light up with a majestic arrogance. But this pleasure that my features managed to communicate to me when I examined them closely was not proof of any genuine beauty: they were fictitious qualities, latent and unfinished, which – in their fugitive splendour – I alone could perceive. I examined my reflection as a painter studies the picture he's working on, and just as the painter's look produces the paintbrush's touch, so this desire to improve my appearance led to the modification of the parameters that I was able to identify as requiring further improvement. It was through looking at my face, monitoring its vibrations, following its metamorphoses with judgements and analyses . . . it was through this mental investment in my face that I ended up achieving the goal I had set myself: the way others looked at me began to change.

At around eighteen – through wishing them into being, urging them on, demanding that they flower – I managed to make the feminine aspects of my face expand, to make them spread through infiltrations of grace what my father had ungenerously passed on to me in a watered-down, hesitant form. To begin with, this inheritance had given me a puppet's face, grotesque and idiotic. After that, it conferred upon my presence the characterless look of an office equipment salesman – I entered my adult years with the ideal physical appearance for filling out purchase orders. It is amusing how my father's working-class harshness had mutated in me towards the compromises of the tertiary sector, illustrating the degeneration of the masculine ideal in society that accompanied the development of the service industries. (Then again, to judge from the night I lived through at nineteen, with that unknown woman on the street who had enchanted me with the words 'What a handsome boy', some glimmer of attractiveness must already have been perceptible in my face, even if only in the darkness of a Parisian street.) So, between eighteen and forty-two, through sheer mental power, my features had flowered into something more feminine. The balance of my face altered; some details were accentuated, overshadowed others, became adornments. My mother's youthful beauty began to shine brightly in my face; certain subtleties that I'd been able to discern now bloomed; the impact of my presence grew stronger; a kind of music began that seduced those who heard it. The more refined my face became, the more women liked it, were lured by it, and let me know it.

So, as I neared forty, my dearest wish was granted: women liked me. In other words, it was now possible that they would turn around in the street. I had wanted this, I had worked for it, and now I had it. It was incredible. (I should point out that all of this disappeared after the tragedy. These days, whenever I glimpse my face in one of the mirrors of my hotel room, I am horrified by the scale of its devastation.) It is true that, thanks to the impact I now had on women, I committed misdemeanours with bodies encountered in the street (I mentioned this aspect of my love life a little earlier), but I never took advantage of these sparks of attraction when they emanated from women who impressed me. I flashed them brief complicit smiles (as if to say: I'm married, but you're lovely), and the hope inspired by these reactions reinforced my belief that one fine day an extraordinary woman would turn my life into a novel. So that is how, after going through various stages of transformation, my face reached the stage where, for the first time, I dared to approach Victoria. That was the first time, and it will be the last. She has been fatal for me – as if the path I took when I began this work on my features had, all along, been a gloomy one, leading only to death.

I apologize for having devoted so much time to the biography of my face (I who have no time to lose; on the other hand, it seems to me that the tragedy in which I became entangled has its roots in so many factors that I have trouble removing them from my path without first submitting them to a detailed examination, even the most pathetic among them), but this narcissism is the central narrative of my adolescence. While I don't wish to seek out any excuses, it is certain that my father's demonic demands encouraged me to turn towards my face in this way. I saw my face as both a wound to be healed and a promise to be fulfilled, just as – during that time – I lived life simultaneously as though it were an obstacle to be overcome and a plan to be carried out: I dreamed of becoming an architect while knowing how difficult it would be. My father's extreme severity left me no choice but to try to like myself as much as possible (and in a manner proportionate to the madness with which he besieged me), particularly by seeking peace in the conflict between me and my self-image. Basically, I didn't want both of us to be looking at me in a sharp-eyed, perpetually critical way; I at least wished to be able to tend the wounds he inflicted on me by thinking reassuring thoughts. But I suppose that this narcissism was also the corollary of the painful rejections I received from girls, for reasons undoubtedly linked to my physical appearance, my shyness, and the various complexes that gnawed at me – and also to the isolation caused by my reputation as a goody-two-shoes. On the subject of this last point (and to conclude this topic), I did sometimes discern a favourable attitude towards me; some girls might have thought that, after all, maybe I wasn't as bad as all that and they could probably have a good time in my company (particularly those who rejected the usual male opinions), but these feelings never got past the ambiguous stage: my unpopularity meant that being too close to me was always a problem.

My father's authoritarianism was at its most intransigent with regard to me. He demanded absolute obedience from me, unflagging rigour, exemplary behaviour, exceptional results. He couldn't bear the slightest deviation from these standards – the tiniest slip, the briefest dip – so I found myself under constant pressure, even on Sundays and during holidays. I had to increase my general knowledge (French history, science, literature, history of art, etc.) on my own initiative, by borrowing a vast number of library books – and my father would check that I had digested the contents of these books through the most severe questioning. This idea that recurred constantly in his speeches – 'on your own initiative' – was the cornerstone of the regime of self-improvement I was supposed to force myself to follow: 'You won't amount to anything if it doesn't come from you, if it's not on your own initiative! Nobody ever amounts to anything in life if all they do is obey orders!' he yelled at the kitchen table, when it was hardly even possible for my marks to improve. So, it was not only my marks that had to show proof of my determination to undertake years of study, but also my attitude: the intitatives I took to improve my performances, the words I spoke, my facial expressions. When it came to me, he had developed a kind of disease, in a fairly vile part of his brain, that got worse from month to month, making his demands about my future ever more unreasonable. I thought he was going mad. I might have been able to find some appeal to the situation (all the more so as it was based on a positive assessment of my abilities: even if my father was chronically disappointed in me, at least he held a high opinion of my potential) were it not for a certain psychological violence that formed part of our daily regime. Sometimes there were even physical abuses inflicted with a belt, though these left him so upset each time that he ended up apologizing.

In order to justify the sacrifices he expected of me, my father would tell me the history of the Polish proletariat, the monumental efforts he and his parents had made in order to better themselves, and finally the duties that he imagined this line of descent gave me a moral obligation to carry out. Men had suffered for centuries, working hard under the dominion of the powerful. My grandparents had suffered for decades, working hard under the dominion of the powerful. He himself, my father, had suffered for years, working hard under the dominion of the powerful. True, he had become a bit more powerful than any of his ancestors, but in spite of that he had still come up against innumerable difficulties. 'You see how difficult it is? Do you want to end up with a life as shitty as that, full of problems? Eh? Answer me! Stop pretending you're deaf and staring at your plate and answer me, for fuck's sake!' he would yell at me when I brought home a mark of sixteen out of twenty. Thus, in memory of the vast sufferings endured by my family for centuries, I owed it to them to continue this process of liberation to its conclusion. In fact, as far as my father was concerned, it was a question of taking my place alongside the powerful. We suffered, we worked, we battled hard to get to this point; it would be indecent if, in your turn, you did not use all your strength – and I mean ALL of it – in this struggle, so that we can finally take our place alongside those in authority. That, in a nut-shell, was what I heard practically every day for the whole of my adolescence. And to convince my father that I had fully under-stood, in all its finest points, this ultimate requirement, I had to want the most extreme form of solitude and take pride in it as being proof of my superiority. At some point, I would have to break away from the masses in order to be able to dominate them – so you may as well do it now, he told me. 'You'll have plenty of time to have friends when you're an adult. You're wasting your time with these morons. You're going to throw away your strength and your energy on them, you're going to fall in love with these jerks! Like with that other one, what was her name again? . . . you know, the other one, shit, help me out here . . . brown hair, spots, looked a bit stupid . . . she came here twice on Saturdays, damn it!' my father frothed. 'Stop it, leave him alone. Anyway, he's not see-ing her any more,' my mother told him, placing her hand on mine. 'Véronique!' my sister shouted, to piss me off. 'You're talking about Véronique! He really wanted to fuck her, but you can imagine – she's not that stupid – she didn't want to get screwed by this queer!' 'Stupid bitch – shut your mouth! You look like a lorry driver!' 'Véronique – that's it!' my father leapt up. 'But, you stupid boy, there'll be thousands and thousands of Véroniques when you're older – you'll have to scrape them off you! But only if you work your arse off now! Ohhhh yes! Only if you devote your time – today, not tomorrow; now, not another time; straight away, and not when it will be too late – to your studies, to working, concentrating, succeeding! Véroniques! And more Véroniques! You poor dumb fool, you'll have millions of them when you're a success! It's worth the wait! Let me tell you, my boy, it's well worth giving up your turn now!'

I loved Isabelle when I was eleven. I loved Dominique when I was thirteen. I tried to go out with Véronique when I was fifteen. I loved Marie when I was seventeen. As far as I'm aware, none of these girls loved or wanted me.

The prospect of distancing myself from this suburb had always soothed me (she was so sweet, the wavy-haired girl who danced beneath my eyelids every night before I fell asleep) – so much so that, as soon as I had passed my baccalaureate, raring to enter the complex and wondrous palace of adult life, I moved to Paris, exhilarated by the idea that I was going off to conquer my own destiny. I believed that time would transform my hopes into happiness, bring out my qualities, make me a successful man. It's strange: throughout my adolescence, I had hated time – because it passed so slowly. Time has since become my worst enemy (on construction sites, time is a legal and financial element, a source of conflict, a burning issue). When I get nearer to sixty, time will undoubtedly seem to move horribly fast. Anyway, having generally thought of time from the sole perspective of the damage it could cause, when I arrived in Paris I saw it as something beneficial, like a river that flows and gives life to the land that surrounds it. I was going to use it. The years would turn lead into gold. I was happy to wake up every morning: through the skylight of my attic room, I breathed in the city's vast sky. This space that stretched out over the roofs (sometimes cloudy and turbulent; sometimes impassive, like a concrete pavement; sometimes pink, unreal, as light as a silk scarf flying in the wind, etc.) gave me the feeling that I was going to build myself – but also surprise myself, digress, contradict myself, let the winds of chance bring random changes to the overly scrupulous order of my life, just like this skyline with its changeless setting, its identical context, with the same TV aerials and the same chimneys, appeared to me each morning as a different mood, a different experience, a different temptation or state of mind. I will never forget this period of my life, filled with anguish and ambition, dreams and fears, determination and curiosity. I had emerged from a prisonlike environment – that of my childhood – and entered a place of freedom, a glimmering palace, a paradise of anticipation: the exact opposite of paradise lost. I hoped with all my heart that a paradise would open itself up to me to reward me for my merits (what sublime naivety to believe in merit!), just as people had been deprived of paradise for their sins. As I became fulfilled, the world around me would be transformed, piece by piece, into paradise. For the moment, it seemed somewhat indifferent to my presence, except when I perceived occasional sparkles – and it was these sparkles that I would avidly seek out through all those years (and which, in some way, I still avidly seek out) so I could tell if the world had begun to take note of my existence. I remember feeling this when I went to bed for the first time in the attic room I'd rented: that I now belonged to this absolutely immense reality that surrounded me, nocturnal and unfathomable, humming with life and mystery, with beautiful women and secrets, with intensity and love affairs, with letters slipped under doors and silhouettes gliding along streets . . . Eyes closed, on the borders of sleep, I thought of all these things.

Through the dividing wall across from my bed, I sometimes heard my neighbour taking a shower, having a drink with a man, and listening to symphonies at low volume. Her name was Anne-Sophie. Her great-grandfather had paid for the construction of the building at the end of the nineteenth century, but her family now owned only a large apartment on the fourth floor (where her grandmother lived with a housekeeper), the studio apartment where she lived and an attic room that she looked after in return for the rental payment. It was through Anne-Sophie that I had been able to move into this room, and it was also through her that I got to know Sylvie. My father had finally agreed that I could live in Paris (rather than commuting by train, which would have exhausted me) on the condition that the rent cost no more than 300 francs. 'It's up to you to find something at that price,' he told me. So I went to Paris at the beginning of July to check out the information boards in a few places, of which I'd made a list, for flats to rent. I had decided to begin my search close to the architecture school where I was registered, on Rue Jacques-Callot in the sixth arrondissement. I had just arrived in front of the noticeboard when a thumb with a red-painted nail stuck a drawing pin on it at my eye level. As I had glimpsed the words URGENT and ATTIC ROOM TO RENT before the thumbnail could pull away from the pink notepaper, I rushed after its owner: 'Wait, I'll take it!' The young woman put her hand to her chest – the hand was suntanned, and its red-painted thumbnail had just decided one of the most crucial directions of my life – to indicate the fright I had just given her. 'You scared me!' she said, backing away. The young woman standing in front of me was more or less my age, tall and heavy, with a big nose and thick blonde hair. She was dressed in that preppy uniform that I have always seen her wear: moccasins, a man's shirt with the collar turned up, pearl necklace, Hermès scarf and navy blue cardigan. She looked me up and down. I sensed that my modest suburban appearance would make her think unfavourably of me, but that, on the other hand, the way I looked at her – the gentleness of my face, the care with which I expressed myself – would make an excellent impression on her. 'What do you mean, you'll take it?' she repeated incredulously. 'Don't you want to see it? Don't you want to know more about it? You didn't even read the whole notice.' She frowned; her palms were turned upwards.

At that point, I had not noticed the young woman who was with her, standing behind her and staring at me. 'I don't need to know any more. I need an attic room, and this one suits me fine.' A brief silence. 'It's important for me to live in Paris,' I added. The young woman to whom I was speaking gave me a puzzled look for a few seconds, before saying: 'What are you studying?' We had begun by calling each other *vous*, but she then pointed out that, as we were the same age, we should perhaps call each other *tu*. 'All right,' I said, blushing, 'we can call each other *tu*. I don't see any problem with that.' 'So what are you studying? Are you in this school?' That was when I noticed the shy face of her friend, standing further back and absorbed in an examination of my own. I felt a searing sensation in my stomach, as if it had been sucked into a vertiginous spiral. It was the first time a woman had looked at me like that: with benevolent intensity, without reserve. During the hours that followed, I felt a point of light in the deepest darkness of my body, like a radiant star. 'I begin my first year of architecture in October,' I stammered (my face was now scarlet). 'I want to be an architect.' The young woman who owned the apartment seemed to think aloud – 'Well, all right, perfect, that's excellent' – and began correcting the angle of the pink notice, which had been pinned at a slant. This mechanical movement must have been intended to grant her a brief moment to think over what was, for her, a commercial transaction to be conducted carefully, rather than awarded impulsively to the firstcomer; I would understand later that she was choosing not only a tenant (whom she wished to be solvent and punctual) but also her closest neighbour (calm and studious). At that moment, a young female student approached her: 'Excuse me, I see that you . . . is that your notice?' The apartment owner withdrew her fingers from the notice as if it had suddenly become burning hot. 'Indeed,' she replied in an unpleasant tone.

'That's perfect!' the student laughed, linking her hands in front of her throat. 'I'm interested in that attic room! I was just about to write down your phone number!' 'I'm afraid it's no longer available. I've just rented it out.' 'Can I still take your number? You never know.' 'I don't think that will be necessary,' the owner said in a decisive tone. 'I told you it's already rented.' And she abruptly tore off the notice, leaving a forlorn drawing pin adorned with an uneven pink ruff.

We walked for about ten minutes (I barely opened my mouth during that time, replying briefly to two basic questions that the young woman asked me; her friend didn't say anything either), and it was only when we got to the room that I found out the price. I was enchanted by the room: I loved the view over the rooftops and the odour exhaled by the walls, which seemed to me profoundly Parisian, historical, as sacred and spellbinding as the scent of a church. But while I paced the room and dreamily caressed the mahogany chest of drawers, it occurred to me that I still didn't know how much the rent was. My exaltation became poisoned with anxiety: every time I was about to ask the question, I held back, tormented by a premonition of bad news. I was afraid of bursting into tears if the deal fell through. Finally, I asked – 'And the rent?' – and I was gripped by an irrational dread. 'Sorry?' the young woman queried, not having understood my sentence because I was mumbling. 'The rent,' I repeated. 'How much is it?' 'Four hundred francs per month,' she replied, surprised. 'Ah, damn . . . sorry, it's my fault, I should have . . .' I muttered, avoiding her gaze (I feared I would see hatred in it; I thought she would feel the bitterest contempt for me). 'Should have *what*?' she said. 'What should you have done?' 'Asked you the price beforehand. But it's . . . I was so happy . . . I was so thrilled, I'm sorry . . . and the female student . . . you had someone who could . . . you should have . . .' I saw the two young women standing side by side, staring at me impotently. The friend's expression was notably more tender; it seemed to contain many manifestations of sensitivity on my behalf. 'What, is it too expensive?' the owner finally demanded. 'What's your budget?' 'Three hundred francs. Maybe I can raise it to 350 if I cut down on my pocket money. But I don't think so, that will be . . . no, never mind, I'm sorry . . .' The young woman turned to her friend, then to me, then back to her friend again. 'I'm really sorry, I don't know what to do . . . I'll write you a new notice, I can pin it up myself, don't worry . . . you'll find a new tenant easily . . .' While I uttered these broken phrases, muffled by shame, the two young women exchanged meaningful looks. I had the feeling that thoughts were passing between them. It seemed to me that the first was saying to the second that, if it were up to her, she would say yes, that the owner ought to offer me a discount on the rent. Out of discretion (given the intimacy of this exchange), I moved over to the worm-eaten bull's eye window. I opened one of its half-moon sections so I could look out at the vast sky – blue that day – that hung above the sea of rooftops. The two young women had begun whispering while moving towards the still-open front door. A French flag hung atop a monument decorated with statues. I found it beautiful, this curve of grey roofs decorated with thousands of aerials and chimneys. I could hear the cries of seagulls flying above the building; we were not far from the river. The whisperings behind me soon quietened down. I felt sure the response would be in my favour. I sensed, as I closed the half-moon section ('Leave it open,' I heard someone say behind me, 'we need to air the room a bit – it smells musty in here'), that I had just won an attic room – and also something like the possibility of a love affair. I forgot to say that it was hot that day, extremely hot; I was sweating under my nylon shirt. I went up to the young woman (also glancing gratefully at her friend, who lowered her eyes in a smile of admission) and she told me: 'Three hundred francs is all right. I'd rather have a good tenant for 300 francs than a bad one for 400!' 'She didn't seem like a bad tenant, the young woman we saw before. Are you sure you can give up . . .' I ventured. 'What? That vicious bitch!' This phrase had spurted from the friend's mouth, as if inadvertently. We turned towards her: she put her hand over the laugh that was disfiguring her lips, and, through the openings between her fingers, said, 'Sorry . . . excuse me, I don't know what came over me.' 'This is Sylvie,' the young woman told me, laughing. 'We've known each other since nursery school. You can thank her: she was very insistent that I give you this room . . .' 'What are you talking about? No, I never! All I said was . . .' 'Relax, Sylvie. I'm happy with the choice I made – you were right to chip in and convince me,' she told her gently. 'My name is Anne-Sophie,' she added, turning back to me. 'I live next door. Just behind the dividing wall, I mean.'

If I had to choose two words to describe Sylvie in that period when we met, or to explain what it was about her that most touched me, the words that come to mind are 'Stendhalian' and 'hussar'. Not that her body was particularly masculine: she was a woman in the shape that many women wish they weren't, with wide hips and quite large breasts; she would have preferred her thighs to be thinner, her bottom smaller. But, like those heroines in Marivaux who are forced to dress as men, and who seem all the more gentle because they must deepen their voices and strut around like pretentious birds, Sylvie seemed to be delivering a mischievous imitation of the male attitude. I felt this way even when she dressed in women's clothes, but Sylvie liked nothing more than items of men's clothing (not to mention military colours) such as black boots, tailored coats, riding breeches, wide-brimmed hats, a satchel slung over the shoulder, and a sky-blue rollneck sweater that made her look like an authoritarian general with a neck brace. Her natural mischievousness; her looks full of cunning; her mock-serious expressions that collapsed into helpless laughter; the habit she had of saying, as if by accident, the one thing she mustn't say (I could imagine her committing social suicide at a party); the attacks she made on conventional good taste through behaviour that she knew to be unsettling but which she pretended was inadvertent (I sometimes judged her very severely for this behaviour because, wishing to be part of conventional society and liked by the largest number of people possible, I was extremely annoyed by it) . . . this recklessness, this loud, uncontrollable aspect of her character was a significant reason why I saw her as a woman who was betraying her frailty through the outrages she committed as a male impersonator. And this effect was accentuated by her face, which could be interpreted as a fruitless attempt – a natural attempt, one might say – to mask a pleasant woman's face with a man's. Sylvie might have been truly pretty were it not that a number of distortions (which seemed to have been made after her physiognomy was created) gave her a slightly unattractive and hard look that contributed to this masculine appearance. Her ears, which stuck out and were disproportionately large, made her appear courageous or stubborn. Her short, thick, black hair increased the size of her head, and a lock of hair that fell down over her eyebrows concealed a prominent forehead. Her eyes were a bit too close together, giving her the intense, preoccupied look of someone about to face up to a great peril. Her narrow nose seemed to have been pinched at the end, as though she had taken offence at something that might well end up as a duel. Her upper lip, shaped like a seagull in flight, had the same decorative impact as a pencil moustache. Finally, the black looks she gave –

where, behind a transparent froth of light-heartedness, loomed the thick darkness of an occasionally tragic seriousness – gave rise at times to an intimidatingly harsh tone. I truly saw Sylvie as a childlike Stendhalian hussar, but a woman whose face looks a bit like Fabrice del Dongo is not the type whose charm and physical assets are praised by men – she didn't have much luck in love. Personally, I found that, because of this combination of different qualities, her presence radiated something which moved me, and that very quickly seduced me – in spite of the fact that she bore no resemblance whatsoever to the idea I had developed about the woman of my dreams. But it was because of these slight flaws in her beauty, her most personal idiosyncrasies, that Sylvie was able to win my heart. And then, of course, she was the first woman I'd met who had shown any real interest in me. She was the first woman to fall in love with me – and that, by contrast, was something I had long dreamed about.

It seems to me that a few phrases in this portrait give a clue to the illness that was going to strike Sylvie. Reading these words, with no other knowledge of my wife's story, is it possible to sense what would happen to her two years later? If, at the time I'd met her, I had wanted to describe her, would I have used these same words, these same sentences? If I think about it for a few minutes (as I have just done while looking at the scenery from my hotel-room window), I would assert that this is exactly how, at eighteen years old, I would have chosen to describe her look, her mind and her social behaviour. Even then, I had a feeling – without being able to know what it consisted of – that there was something divergent in her that drew my attention. There is no disputing the peculiar impact of her presence: at times it was vaguely unsettling, and on some people it produced feelings of embarrassment, distaste or exasperation. As for me, I understood two years later that, among many things about Sylvie that annoyed me, it was her illness – even before I was aware of its existence – that magnetized me: her black looks, her disturbing fantasies, like the rumblings of a battle that rages far off in the night (excuse the cliché, but I find it eloquent) in the background of a suspicious and irritating euphoria. Aspects of her behaviour that I had found mysterious and attractive – counterbalancing a certain banality and an unoriginal sense of humour – now appear to me for what they really were: symptoms of an illness.

Sylvie was the daughter of a lieutenant-colonel in the army and the sister of a boy who had just enlisted as a soldier (he was about to go to Chad, where France had decided to send troops). For me, on an ethical and ideological (and also a political) level, there was no horror so unfading, there was nothing so terrible and repulsive as being a soldier: that single fact put me into a state of indignation that I found it difficult to contain, and anyway, I had no desire to keep these feelings of hostility to myself, even if their enunciation could hurt Sylvie. Through an effort of self-will, I was able to control my sectarianism and to tolerate certain disagreements with the people I knew (thus, for example, I could always look past a classmate's contempt for Le Corbusier's philosophies), but the reality of a soldier – sitting opposite a soldier, hearing a soldier praise a soldier's life – that was something unbearable. The diplomacy required by life in society meant that I endured it, but only partially, not for long, and at the cost of an immense effort.

For the first two years, whenever I was invited to dinner at Sylvie's parents', the effort required to control my repugnance plunged me into a state of mute prostration, the hostility behind which could not possibly escape a mind as learned in matters of belligerence as an army officer, no matter how stupid. Being an idealist and a sensitive man who hated authority, I found it complicated to love the daughter of an army officer – and even more so a daughter who adored her army-officer father. When, after two glasses of Saint-Emilion, I cast aside my diplomatic reserve, I was capable of telling Sylvie's father that frailty was one of the greatest human qualities. Both of us had gone to considerable lengths, throughout the meal, not to start an argument; instead of the cutting phrases that we might have used on many occasions to eviscerate each other, we exchanged tense looks filled with mutual loathing. By the time the apple tart arrived, we both felt the necessity to assert our identities – and to annihilate our opponent's. As soon as my words were out ('Contrary to what you seem to think, I believe that frailty is one of the greatest human qualities'), I saw joy, irony, impatience and relish spread across this man's face, along with his confidence that he was going to tear me to pieces. His nostrils began to quiver, his lips glistened; he looked like a greedy man before a feast. His neck lengthened and lifted up his birdlike head; it turned sideways from his daughter's face to his wife's to make sure that they were not going to miss his crushing victory over this incongruous young man who had washed up at their dinner table. Meanwhile I, stirred up by the repulsion he provoked in my entire being, felt the same manly desire to fight him with my bare hands, to surrender myself to the most primitive urges, to wallow – muscle against muscle – in the most brutish struggle. 'A bit more tart?' Sylvie's mother asked me, in an attempt at diversion. (I thought her just as stupid as her husband. But she protected me when he needled me; she rounded his sharp edges and toned down any conflicts. Only up to a point, though: as soon as the battle erupted – always juicily, with barbed remarks – and each allowed himself the pleasure of insinuating to the other how ridiculous he found him, Sylvie's mother stiffened and, outraged, went over to the side of the established order.) Sylvie's father, his lips drooling, made jerky movements with his head. He couldn't wait to pulverize me. 'I'd love some. It's very good. What did you do with the shortcrust pastry?' I replied to Sylvie's mother, holding out my plate. 'Hang on a minute,' interrupted Sylvie's father, one hand raised. 'Hang on, dear. What our friend here said is very interesting. Tell me, young man,' he continued, attempting to suppress the horrible laughter that had already begun to moisten his expression. 'If I understood you correctly . . .' His birdlike head kept turning from his daughter's face to his wife's, expecting them to share his hilarity. 'But if, by any chance, I misunderstood . . . these things happen . . . please don't hesitate to tell me,' he added, struggling mightily not to let a huge and monstrous laugh erupt in my face. 'Seriously, you must tell me if I've misunderstood something . . .' 'Stop, leave him alone,' Sylvie's mother intervened. 'You are telling me that frailty . . . that frailty is what?' he asked, grimacing. '*That frailty is one of the greatest human qualities?* That is what you just told me?' 'So you like my shortcrust pastry?' the mother continued, not paying the least attention to what her husband was saying. 'I made it myself. It's my speciality. I'll teach Sylvie to make it if you like. Like that, when you're married . . .' 'Mum! Stop right there, please!' 'Yes, that's what I said,' I replied to Sylvie's father. 'Frailty allows us to see through reality, to go beyond appearances, to see details that no one else can see: truths that all those who boast of being in a position of authority and dominance cannot even . . . If you'll allow me to say what I really think . . .' 'Absolutely, go ahead. I'm listening,' Sylvie's father replied, waving his hand in front of him. 'Well, then, I think that, because of dominance and authority, which in my opinion characterize your relationship with reality . . . obviously, as you're in the army . . .' 'Yes . . . so?' Sylvie's father prompted me impatiently. 'Where are you going with this?' 'Well, I think you're ignorant of half of this reality. But, inevitably, you can't even begin to apprehend that,' I dared say to Sylvie's father, concluding my argument. An explosion of silence: you could feel Sunday wobbling on its pedestal. 'It's all right, never mind, leave him be. Go and smoke your cigar on the balcony,' Sylvie's mother interposed, anticipating the splenetic riposte that her husband was on the verge of unleashing on me. He swivelled towards his wife: 'What do you mean, leave him alone? This is unbelievable! I would remind you, dear, that we live in a democracy. And if this delicious young man has the right to tell us what is going on in my head, I have the right to respond.' Each time he used the expression 'delicious young man', with its horrible connotation, I saw the vilest irony spread across his face. 'No, but come on! Keep quiet, don't say a word, let him say what he wants! That's how societies degenerate, and our values, our values! No, seriously!' he raged, throwing a balled-up napkin on the tablecloth. All hints of hilarity had now disappeared from his face; his expression was grave. We had gone well beyond the limits of family joshing and entered the arena of politics. 'You cannot seriously ask me – *me*,' he insisted, jabbing a manly finger at his tie, 'to let a sentence like that pass without comment, at my table, under my roof?' 'But what's the big deal with that sentence?' asked Sylvie, slightly embarrassed by this turn of events. 'It's just an opinion like any other. We don't have to turn it into a drama!' 'Um, it's not exactly what I would call an opinion,' I ventured, striving to make myself heard. 'For my part, I think . . .' 'Well, exactly!' Sylvie's father continued. 'What our friend just said is not a truth, but an opinion. Therefore, I have the right to express the opposite opinion. As you know very well, both of you, ganging up on me . . .' 'Nobody is ganging up on you,' Sylvie's mother corrected. 'Let me say in passing that I'm not overly surprised to see you supporting our friend here. Because the opinion expressed by this delicious young man is an opinion that we might describe as . . . how can I say this? . . . how can I say this without sounding disrespectful . . .' he wondered aloud, as though in intense thought (when in reality he wished to belittle me in the most outrageous way by implying that it was difficult to describe my words without doing so in a way that he regarded as insulting). 'An opinion that we might describe as *feminine*? There you go, perhaps we can phrase it like that: the opinion expressed by this charming young man is remarkably *feminine*.' His expression had grown scathing and sardonic. 'Therefore it is entirely logical that you women should be on his side. But personally, I think that if men have started praising frailty – *we men*, who have fought for millennia! Since the Stone Age! Against the scourge! The terrifying scourge! – if *we* have started praising bleeding hearts! And so-called feminine delicacy! We are not out of the woods yet, children! If men start praising frailty, WE ARE NOT OUT OF THE WOODS YET!' And with this definitive phrase – with which Sylvie's father felt he had won the battle – he left to smoke his cigar alone on the balcony. Sylvie's mother rested her hand on mine tenderly for a moment (as if to say: fathers and their daughters . . . letting his daughter go with a stranger is difficult for him) before getting up to clear the table – 'Would you like coffee, David?' – while Sylvie stood behind my chair to hug me round the chest. We could see Sylvie's father, his back to us, through the closed French window, leaning on the balcony's wrought-iron railing, pensively watching the street while smoking his cigar.

The mistake I made, without a doubt, was to have besieged Sylvie until she hated what her parents represented for me. After all, nobody was asking me to share my life with them. I could have taken all this stuff with a pinch of salt, or looked elsewhere, but I demanded that her love for me should be opposed to her love for her parents. I rejected the idea that she could reconcile feelings that seemed to me utterly antagonistic; that she should manage to do so struck me as being degrading for me, and representative of a massive misunderstanding, as if Sylvie had no idea who I was or what I was going to become. Naively, I wanted her to acknowledge that her existence had been constructed on disastrous values; I wanted her to thank me for having opened her eyes, to say to me: yes, you're right, how could I? Thank God I met you! 'Your father is only a lieutenant-colonel! If he was a general, I might understand him blowing his own trumpet and swaggering around like he'd just come out of a meeting with Napoleon! But this pathetic jerk is only a lieutenant-colonel! Christ, am I dreaming? This failure . . . think about it, Sylvie! *This failure is nothing but a lieutenant-colonel!*' 'You're right – they're presumptious and ridiculous. I swear, having to talk to these idiots! Having to see their ugly faces when I wake up in the morning! Can you imagine what torture it is? It's terrible, I can't bear it any more. How did I put up with them? How did I put up with their ugly faces – their double chins, their plump superior airs – for eighteen years? David, take me away from this stinking cesspit, the medals, the golden epaulettes, the mouldy old fur!' As you might imagine, Sylvie never said this kind of thing about her parents. But she did hear me utter similar phrases, in varying degrees of subtlety, and the only effect of these sallies was to hurt her; to make the disagreements that consumed her mind – all caused by me – unbearable for her.

When I met Sylvie, her father was working in an office at the Ministry of Defence. Two years later, he would leave Paris to take command of the military camp of M., about three hours' drive away. They lived in an apartment rented to them by the ministry, behind the Châtelet theatre on Rue Bertin-Poirée, not far from the river: when you went out on the balcony, you could see the riverboats moving past. I went there to see Sylvie several times a week, mostly to work in her room – me on the bed and her at the desk. Her mother brought us 'collations' (that was what she called what, at my parents' house, were only snacks) and, on some evenings, in order that our work would not be interrupted by dinner, she obligingly brought us meals on trays.

Sylvie was doing a preparatory year for the HEC business school at the Lycée Hélène-Boucher in the twentieth arrondissement. The difficulty of her course, the huge amount of knowledge she had to absorb, and the worries provoked by her competitive exams were not really ideal for a love affair that was just beginning (even if Sylvie had decided on a philosophical approach to these two years, refusing to let herself be overcome with anxiety), all the more so as her parents kept a careful watch over our activities. So we loved each other like two inmates in the same prison: there was an unspoken agreement that our relationship would blossom fully a bit later, particularly on a sexual level, if only because we would then be liberated from all outside jurisdiction. For the first two years, the three times when we were invited to join Sylvie's parents at their family home in Brittany, I had to sleep in a room located on a different floor from hers. Sylvie, too, would have preferred to sleep with me, but she had warned me not to break her parents' rules by sneaking into her room in the middle of the night and leaving before the first glimmers of dawn, as I'd told her was the usual custom in eighteenth-century novels. 'Because your family lives in the eighteenth century! Honestly, the idea that, *in 1984*, they cannot tolerate their eighteen-year-old daughter sleeping in the same bed as a boy like me . . . fuck me, it's unbelievable! I'm not some thug! *But your father seems to think I'm going to rape you.*' Sylvie did not laugh: she looked terrified. 'What?' I asked. 'What's the matter?' She replied that if her father found her wandering around in the corridors in the middle of the night, he would take it very badly. 'I'm asking you now,' she said to me seriously.

(She had her Stendhalian hussar face, frowning like that. And it was her frailty that I saw struggling through these grimaces; struggling out in drops, like invisible tears.) 'I'm serious. Please don't try to come to my room tonight. There would be a big scene.'

Thanks to this man's extreme protectiveness towards his daughter (and not forgetting his demonstrations of all-consuming love for her, the purpose of which was to put into perspective, for me, the feelings I naively imagined she had for me; he would hold Sylvie tightly in his arms and stare at me as if to say, 'You see? The day she loves you as powerfully and undyingly as she loves me, we'll talk again'), I was given the perfect excuse to keep my distance from any circumstances likely to lead to the act itself. The prospect of making love to Sylvie didn't only fill me with dread, it took me to a part of my mind where I no longer existed. I had spent years dreaming of the vagina. I considered it as the supreme objective of my adolescence. The more desperate my desire for it, the more sacred and iconic it became to me. The problem was that, because I had spent years considering it as unthinkable, once I imagined myself in its presence, I myself instantly became something unthinkable – I vanished from my own consciousness each time I imagined myself penetrating my girlfriend's most intimate part. Of course, I had seen dozens of women showing their genitals in magazines, but the idea of seeing, for real, an actual, specific vagina gave me the same feeling of absolute incredulity as the idea of seeing, for real, François Mitterand's face in a private tête-à-tête while admiring Vitruvius's engravings – the same effects of utter impossibility and anticipated speechlessness, due in particular to the transcendental and incommensurable nature of the two objects in question: Sylvie's vagina and the President's face. In any case, as may be judged from the absurdity of this analogy (though I can guarantee that it perfectly fulfils its function: to faithfully reproduce the absurdity of my state of mind during that period), I was light years away from any kind of lucid, natural sexuality. But, as I have already said, there was no point in me thinking very deeply about this subject, as her parents' ceaseless vigilance gave me the perfect excuse for our relationship to remain comfortably platonic.

These few months took place on the misty border between childhood and adulthood. We exhibited all the signs of a love affair without consummating it sexually, nor even being naked with each other. For most people nowadays, this age is probably located at around fourteen years old; I was eighteen.

When we were together in my room, we were dissuaded from taking off our clothes by the presence of her childhood friend on the other side of the dividing wall – a preposterous excuse not to do anything. The moment when we would make love was constantly postponed: our relationship was like a wave that moves towards the shore but never breaks. This is, probably, an experience characteristic of extreme youth that can be quite beautiful in the constant giddiness it provokes. Since then, I have come to understand that the urge to postpone is the main failing of my temperament. Postponement is an idealist's reflex, and I have had to struggle against it for a long time in order to remove it from my daily habits. Putting it off until tomorrow, thinking that there's plenty of time, believing that conditions are not yet ideal, imagining that it would be better to wait a bit longer in order to begin this or that thing, face up to this obstacle, wonder about this or that subject, tackle that intimidating challenge . . . I lived like this for a long time, in a mode of perpetual projection towards the future. This implies a strange absence in oneself of everything active and substantial, and at the same time a heightened relationship with the outside world on an emotional and sensory level, short of any decision-making. This attitude can be described as essentially cerebral and consists in believing that life is not so much what we live each day upon waking, but the thoughts that we have. Anyone who dreams their life loves seeing it radiate through their mind like an absolute; and, naturally, the moment of conquering the absolute can only be postponed, because it is, by definition, located beyond all circumstance. Only by demythologizing life, by downgrading yourself in your representation of it (rather than sanctifying reality and expecting it to provide events that reflect this sacredness); only by considering existence as a locus of chance, work, accidents, will, deals, compromises, betrayals and power struggles can you decide not to postpone any more and to begin to live, to throw yourself into the lion's den with the others, and to fight there. This is something it took me years and years and years to understand.

Because of their density and because of the vividness of the events I was living through, this period seems to have lasted years. Everything was new for me – truly everything. Not only living in Paris in an attic room, but having a girlfriend, taking architecture classes in a lively school, watching the seasons change in a big city, feeling new desires being born within me. We delighted in the sensations that our relationship gave us: no longer being alone, feeling reassured, having someone to think about, to talk to, to confide our doubts or our sadness to; inhaling the scent of the other's skin, thrilling at the idea of the other's naked body and future caresses . . . When I worked in Sylvie's bedroom, we rewarded ourselves for our efforts with regular kisses (I got up from the bed to stand behind her chair, holding her shoulders, and Sylvie turned her face to press her lips to mine before I went back to lie down). We met each other in cafés, where we talked with our fingers brushing. We walked hand in hand through Paris. I told her how Charles Garnier had ended up winning the competition to design the Opéra (when the commentators of the day had been sure he would lose) by going to see the Emperor with a sycophantic design reworked at the last minute. In fact, as everyone who pays sufficient attention will be able to remark, the cupola reproduces the shape of an imperial crown (I told Sylvie, pointing at the building's summit from Avenue de l'Opéra), visually inscribing the sponsor's identity in the Parisian skyline. So it was that Charles Garnier, by being more politically astute than his competitors ('even if he was architecturally inferior') had won the competition. And we continued our descent of Avenue de l'Opéra in the biting cold of February. Sylvie, who clearly enjoyed listening to me recount these anecdotes, constantly repeated that I was going to become, in her words, an 'immense architect'. She told me she had sensed it the first second she saw me, that she had seen it in my eyes, where, at each moment, complex worlds were being designed. She found this fascinating. 'I could spend hours looking at your eyes, immersing myself in your gaze,' she told me, gently touching her fingertips to the arches of my brows. 'Something is always happening in there: thoughts merging with feelings, sensations with calculations, dreams with forms, structures, desires, visions . . .' Sylvie did sometimes express herself like that: this young woman was undoubtedly unique, even if I often found her speeches, her romantic fancies, her slightly facile jokes to be disappointingly sloppy and incredibly naive.

We had been together for about eight months when Sylvie revealed her body to me during a week-long holiday in a house in Provence belonging to Anne-Sophie's parents. We did not make love. We caressed each other shyly for six days. I remember the devastating moment when Sylvie's fingers closed around my erection; I felt, during that brief moment, that I had touched the absolute.

On the other hand, I have no memory whatsoever of the day

when we finally made love (it is curious that such a crucial event has vanished from my memory). But I think I waited several months before risking ridicule by trying to penetrate Sylvie. When, around 12 September – two months after this week in Provence – I saw the unknown woman in the street who murmured, 'What a handsome boy,' I remember that I considered myself to be relatively inexperienced.

Sylvie was not really my type, but no one was asking me to share my life with her or take any irrevocable decisions about our future together. We were happy with each other. She was perfectly suited to the man I was at that moment. We enjoyed our relationship unquestioningly.

I used to dream of a great destiny for myself. Perhaps I would become a famous architect, or one day something decisive would happen that would give a radical new direction to my existence. This hope was a bit like the scent left in its wake by an event that overtook me and that I had to catch up with. But I must admit that in this dream, I was accompanied by another woman (or perhaps this other woman *was* the event I had to catch up with). I also knew that, to catch this event, I must walk quickly, and that I must not waste time or get lost.

A few weeks before her illness manifested itself, Sylvie said to me one evening – after I'd come inside her – that she couldn't stop thinking about her father while we were making love. He was in the bedroom watching us. His presence gave her a mental block. She couldn't get away from those staring eyes that prevented her abandoning herself completely. 'Your father?' I demanded. 'Your father is watching us make love?' 'I can't manage to stop thinking about him, to stop wondering what he thinks of me when he sees me making love with you. I don't know what to do any more . . .' Sylvie began to cry. I was dumbfounded. I held her tightly in my arms for a few minutes.

Not only would Sylvie not protect me, I thought, but she would actually make me more vulnerable. She admired me, and she expected me to accomplish something amazing. But she never stopped to wonder if her own development, if the professional success she might achieve, could help me to feel freer, more confident, more secure. Despite the fact that she was in business school, she was not particularly ambitious. This imbalance between us implied that I would have to be responsible for the financial viability of any family we had together; everything would rest on my shoulders. Assuming I had the strength (although after what I had been through with my father, I felt able to deal with any situation), did I have the desire to squander my energy on the anxieties of a family man's responsibilities? Every time I asked myself this question, the answer was no.

Life scared me so much that, since adolescence, I had been obsessed by the desire to meet a woman of such calibre that she would make me feel protected and sheltered as if by harbour walls. I felt a strange intermingling of faith and terror, of fervour and defeatism. I could imagine myself as an acclaimed architect, or equally as an unsatisfied employee consumed with bitterness at having failed in life. I knew that certain circumstances could propel me towards the peaks of a dazzling career, but I could also end up in a morose, zestless, ordinary existence. Furthermore, my instinct told me that the question of whether I would share my life with Sylvie was not unconnected to the different directions my destiny could take. I walked the streets for hours brooding over these thoughts, attempting to analyse my situation and to identify my desires. I remember I visualized my youth as a junction of different corridors: looked at from outside, these corridors all appeared the same; no colours even seemed visible, only a wide-open space. Except that the colours did actually exist, and each corridor led to a different life; the important thing was not to choose the wrong one.

I was in this state of mind – in limbo, at a crossroads of different destinies – when Sylvie suddenly fell ill. It was just over two years after we met, near the middle of September.

I have a strange impression of seeing myself move through the darkness of my memory to the border of this event. Walking steadily towards the core of my youth, I feel like an actor, watched by the audience for several minutes as he disappears into the shadowy depths of the stage. This man who remembers carries only an electric torch, which barely illuminates the darkness that surrounds him. The audience watches him move away into this dense blackness, never encountering a wall or entirely disappearing, as if he were walking on a beach at low tide in the middle of the night. Little by little, each spectator understands – with the disturbed sensation that accompanies such discoveries – that the stage is an infinite space; that the theatre in which they sit is the actor's brain; that the actor is nothing but their consciousness, and the night into which the spectator is watching him move is in fact their own memory. And what's more, the spectator realizes that for the past few minutes they have been thinking about their past. Sitting in my spectator's chair, motionless before the black, rain-lashed windows of my hotel room, I watch myself move away into the darkness of this theatre while in the foreground, under spotlights, painted in flashes by blue police lights, Victoria's body is lying on the dry ground of a summer forest.

I tell myself that Victoria's body can only be explained by that of Sylvie lying in the foreground of this same stage twenty-two years earlier.

I tell myself that a blind, straight path, thought-out and obscurely logical, led me from that moment when Sylvie collapsed on the floor tiles of her attic room to the moment when Victoria was discovered in the forest of Sénart by a rambler's German shepherd.

What happened? What does my life consist of? I wish I could catch a glimpse of my own thoughts at the precise moment when the event I am thinking about occurred. I would like to know who I was just before my existence suddenly took the direction it did. I would like to be able to guess what I might have become had the incident I am about to describe not taken place.

It was around the middle of September, two years after our first kiss. Sylvie had been accepted in a modest business school and had started a four-week internship at the head office of an insurance company. Sylvie's parents had left Paris that summer (her father taking command of the military camp of M.), and she had taken over an attic room previously occupied by a boy she'd met in preparatory classes (he had left it for another one – a bit more spacious, and with its own shower – on the same floor). Sylvie's room was in a building at the corner of Rue d'Assas and Rue Vaugirard, in the sixth arrondissement, just across from the Catholic University. The fact that her friend lived close by was one of the factors that had attracted Sylvie to this attic room; she had confessed to me that she was afraid to live away from her parents in a building where she knew no one.

That day, we had agreed to meet at her place around 6 p.m. When I arrived, Sylvie told me that she felt like buying clothes. 'What, now?' I asked, surprised. 'Yes, straight away, before the shops close. Come on, let's go.' 'And where are we going?' 'To Stock Cacharel on Rue d'Alésia. Hurry up – it's already ten past six. We'll have to take the metro.' I found it odd that Sylvie would give in to such a sudden desire (she was not capricious or conceited), but all the more so that this desire should overcome her less than an hour before the shops closed. 'But are you sure? You really want to go today? It's too late! We'll never make it.' She insisted. I found her radiant. We rushed to the metro.

As we were running half the time in order to get to the shop as soon as possible, and as her imagination was electrified by her over-excitement about the shopping she was going to do, it took me a while to realize how strange her behaviour was. 'I want a red dress!' she sang while running. 'Checked trousers! A black hat to match my coat!' Sylvie revolved like a record around trees, holding on to their trunks with one hand, and I heard her singing the song found on this 45rpm single. She suddenly started sprinting in the middle of a sentence, and she finished most of her races with a scene in which, turned into a little girl, she played hopscotch on an imaginary course. 'What's up with you tonight, Sylvie? Why are you so excited? What happened today to put you in this state?' I watched her hopping from box to box. 'What do you mean, what's up with me? I'm perfectly normal!' she replied. 'Can't you see I'm in a good mood? I'm allowed to be in a good mood, aren't I?' I tried to see her unusual behaviour as the result of an ordinary, late-afternoon excitement, but some aspects of it struck me as so crazy that I came to wonder if Sylvie was not under the influence of some internal power beyond her control, hence the feeling I had in certain moments of having lost contact with her; it seemed to me that I was talking to a little girl.

As soon as we were in the shop, Sylvie locked herself in a cubicle to hang up the clothes she had chosen and I gave her my opinion on each of them. I could sense that, due to the restricted time she had to do her shopping, she was becoming increasingly fevered. She hesitated, dissatisfied with her choices; each outfit she put together had something wrong with it. A salesman came to inform me that the shop would close in barely ten minutes, and that we needed to hurry up. 'Yes, fine, hang on a minute, I'm making myself look pretty,' she shouted from inside the cubicle. I could tell that she was in a flutter. 'It's important to be pretty!

The body needs decoration!' She was yelling. We heard angry laughter. I smiled. The salesman moved away without saying anything.

The curtain kept opening and closing upon increasingly confused scenes. Sylvie had put on a pair of trousers without taking off the pair she'd just tried on. She appeared wearing a jumper over the dress she had donned a few minutes earlier over the trousers. 'Sylvie, what are you doing? What are you playing at?' She started walking around the shop in this outfit before returning to the cubicle carrying a dozen bits of clothing she seemed to have picked up at random, without even looking at them. The young man came back to see me, sent by two saleswomen who were observing the scene in silence, paralysed by the very thing that dissuaded them from insulting Sylvie for the chaos she was creating: fear of the unknown. The two young women stood aside and stared at her, in withdrawn poses (one of them was biting her nails), like people at the scene of a motorway accident. In fact, it was when I saw how the two saleswomen were observing us that I began to convince myself that something abnormal was happening. 'Sir,' the salesman said to me, 'it does not seem possible to me that your friend can try on all these clothes in the time that remains before the shop closes. Perhaps you should come back another day and make your choice more calmly, in better conditions. Don't you think so?' There was steel in his smile: I had to convince Sylvie to follow me meekly into the street.

We heard the clicking of the curtain rings on the rail. Sylvie had added new items to all those she was wearing before. Her face appeared to us through the oval of a pink jumper pulled over her head like a religious veil. A pair of trousers fitting tightly round her waist had been knotted over her stomach (a nervous quadruple knot that looked like it was choking with pain). She posed motionless before us, awaiting our verdict on this strange assemblage. 'Sylvie,' I said to her. She seemed not to see me, nor even to exist except through the exhibition of this textile sculpture. 'So?' she asked me, looking over my shoulder at part of the shop. 'What do you think?' 'Sylvie, what do I think of what?' 'Sir . . .' the salesman began; I could sense him twitching beside me. 'You know very well what!' she said, annoyed, bringing her gaze to my face and stamping her foot on the floor. 'Are you blind or something?' 'It's absolutely beautiful. But they're asking us to leave. The shop is about to close.' 'In four minutes,' the salesman confirmed, looking at his watch. The curtain rings clicked violently on the rail in response to the shopkeeper's sour remark. Sylvie disappeared from view.

I convinced Sylvie to buy only a pair of trousers and a dress. 'Don't you like the coat?' 'Yes, but . . . I don't know, let's come back another day. Come on, hurry up, they're waiting for us.' Leaving behind an unbelievable mess of clothes in the cubicle, we went to the checkout. 'Two hundred and seventy-six francs,' the young woman said.

It took Sylvie eight attempts to give the cashier a cheque that was correctly made out: the other seven finished up as confetti on the counter. Four of us stood there watching her struggle with her biro, scrawling clumsily on the paper. Either she got the amount wrong, or the figures she wrote did not correspond to the words ('Excuse me, miss,' the cashier said, 'but you've mixed up the six and the seven: you've written 267 instead of 276 . . .'), or she messed up the beneficiary's name, or she wrote the date in the wrong space. Sylvie became angry and annoyed with herself each time she noticed she had made a mistake, but when she apologized to the cashier, it was with great calmness, serenity and elegance, as if her personality kept splitting in two. 'Pardon me! My word, what was I thinking of?' she said in the slightly exaggerated tone of a scatterbrained bourgeois lady. In this way, Sylvie's manners were divided between the intense febrility of an enraged schoolgirl (meticulously tearing up all these failed cheques) and an imitation of civility dating from another age. It was this balance of extremes, alternating from one second to the next (with the same brutal suddenness of a switch being flicked) that was especially agonizing: it exerted an unhealthy fascination on all three salespeople.

Back in her room, Sylvie told me she had spent the afternoon making love with a boy she had met in the street. 'You made love with a boy? Today? What are you on about?' 'It's true. This afternoon. He's called Christophe. We talked in the street. I told him I felt like making love with him. He came here. It was very good.' 'When?' 'This afternoon.' 'You weren't at your work experience?' 'I didn't go back after lunch. I came here. About three o'clock. He left again at five o'clock. His name is Christophe.' 'Are you going to see him again? Did you like it?' 'I'm supposed to see him tomorrow. I hope he doesn't forget me. I loved it.' 'Are you going to leave me?' 'Why would I leave you, my love?' 'I don't know . . . You just told me you're going out with another boy . . . That's kind of unusual, you know.' 'You think so? I don't. He's very cute. I'm seeing him tomorrow afternoon. He's called Christophe.'

I could not believe this story – unless Sylvie had been in an even more distressed state than she had been in the shop. In any case, beyond the hurt that this confession caused me, thinking that she had made love with a stranger also made me feel surprisingly aroused – I got a hard-on, and I even thought about coming back to spy on them the next day so I could listen to Sylvie taking her pleasure with someone else. But this shocking thought was so intermingled with the abnormality of the whole evening that I took it to be some sort of collateral consequence of events.

When everything had gone back to normal, my thoughts would go back to normal too.

Sylvie was now expressing herself with a precision that I found even more disturbing than her spectacular agitation earlier in the afternoon, so much so that I overcame my reluctance and phoned her parents to inform them that something strange was happening to their daughter. 'What do you mean?' her mother asked me. 'I don't know. She's being strange. I don't recognize her. You should come.' 'At eleven o'clock at night? Pass her to me.' 'She doesn't want to.' 'What do you mean, she doesn't want to?' 'She says she doesn't want to speak to anybody.' 'You're asking us to come to Paris in the middle of the night because my daughter doesn't want to speak to you any more?' 'Do what you like, but I'm telling you that she's not being normal . . .' 'I'm putting my husband on,' she interrupted.

A bit later, Sylvie collapsed on the floor, as if some resistance inside her had broken. I lay her on the bed. She smiled at me and I took her hand. 'Do you want me to call somebody?' She nodded. I called the emergency doctor.

'Have you warned my parents? Have you told them that I fainted?' 'They're going to come. I had your dad on the phone. They'll be here in two or three hours.' 'He hadn't really changed since nursery school,' said Sylvie after a few minutes of silence. 'Who are you talking about?' 'Christophe.' 'You knew him?' 'Of course I knew him!' she laughed. 'Did you think I'd hook up with some stranger in the street and make love to him in my bedroom?' Sylvie laughed mechanically, a bit like a slowing engine, without being able to stop. I had switched off all the lights except for a little lamp on the mantelpiece, so it was dark in the room. 'You didn't tell me that you knew him.' 'I thought I did. I recognized him. He told me I was mixed up, that he wasn't who I thought he was, but I know he was lying,' she murmured, with a frown. 'He even said he wasn't called Christophe. But I know it's him. If it hadn't been, he wouldn't have agreed to make love with me all afternoon.' Some of the things she said to me were spoken conspiratorially. Then: 'I don't know why he didn't want to admit it was him. We were in the same class at nursery school in Paimpol. Why would I have slept with him if it wasn't Christophe, the boy I loved when I was four years old?'

There were two possibilities: either Sylvie imagined that she had spent the afternoon with a boy she'd met in the street, in which case she was delirious; or she really had spent the afternoon with a Christophe that she was convinced she knew in nursery school in spite of his denials, in which case she had lost control of her actions. In either case, the situation was difficult and worrying. I tried to find out more while I was waiting for the doctor to arrive, but none of Sylvie's replies helped me decide which of these two hypotheses was more likely. She just repeated that she was supposed to see the same boy again tomorrow at three o'clock, but I couldn't work out if this was real or if Sylvie had imagined this rendezvous.

Sylvie told the doctor she hadn't slept for a week, and that she'd managed to conceal this from me even though we'd shared the same bed for the two previous nights. She didn't stop talking during the entire consultation. She insisted on downplaying the seriousness of the symptoms I had mentioned. 'It's fine, it's over. It was nothing – I was just messing around. I'm telling you, I feel perfectly fine. Do we really have to keep going on about this? There's absolutely no point.' She kept repeating this, and I sensed that this uninterrupted flow of words was a way of keeping us at a distance from her mind, of avoiding any questions. 'What a gorgeous bag! I adore old doctors' bags. My grandfather had the same kind, full of cracks, with brass clasps. Could you buy me one for my birthday? You can find them in flea markets. Where did you find your bag? Oh, but I'm so stupid, you're a doctor – they must have given it to you when you graduated! My grandfather wasn't a doctor at all – he was a colonel in the army.' While Sylvie said this, she put her hand to her temple in a military salute and laughed. 'I don't know how he got it, nor what became of it. I'll have to ask my mother. Anyway, we're getting distracted. You're a doctor and you came to check that everything was fine. I imagine you must be reassured!' Sylvie did not realize that this logorrhoea, far from seeming like ordinary chattiness (which is apparently how she wanted it to appear: she was trying to adopt a casual, carefree tone), came across as a worrying form of behaviour. Having given up on his attempts to break through this syntactical armour, the doctor ended up prescribing Lexomil. 'You're exhausted after your sleepless nights. You must sleep. You need rest.' 'Yes, general. Your wishes are my commands!' 'Goodbye, miss,' he said, then signalled me to follow him into the corridor. I accompanied him to the top of the stairs. He asked me to go into more detail about what happened that afternoon; he did not seem to be taking his consultation with Sylvie lightly. 'You look worried,' I said. 'Is it serious?' 'First, tell me exactly what happened,' he replied. I recounted what I had experienced with Sylvie in the clothes shop and what she had told me about the boy she'd met in the street. 'She told me they made love all afternoon. I don't know if that's true. But it's unbelievable in any case, so it worries me.' 'I recommend the greatest vigilance during the next few days.' 'Why?' 'It's possible this is an onset of schizophrenia. Do you know if she's had episodes like this in the past?' 'No, I don't think so – she's never mentioned it.' 'It's always difficult to make a diagnosis in these conditions. But we must make sure that it's not schizophrenia. She has some of the symptoms, and she's at the age when this kind of illness can develop,' he added, writing a name on a business card. I was trembling all over. Even this doctor admitted he was baffled by the night's events. He had placed one foot on a higher step in order to rest the card on his knee while he wrote. I was overcome with a dreadful feeling of terror and solitude. 'Call this doctor on my behalf,' he said, handing me the card. 'He's a psychiatrist. All I can do this evening is prescribe medicine that will enable her to sleep. But she really needs to see him. I'm counting on you. Don't leave her in this state without doing anything, even if she seems perfectly normal tomorrow.' And with those words, he began walking down the spiral staircase.

The night, absolute and impenetrable, closed in around that figure engulfed in the spiralling gloom of the stairs. I felt crushed. I didn't dare shout out to him not to abandon me. I heard the glass door bang shut on the ground floor. I went back to Sylvie and persuaded her to get into bed.

By the time her parents arrived (it must have been around two in the morning), Sylvie had finally managed to fall asleep. I didn't want them to wake her up, in spite of her father's determination to verify for himself the state I had told him his daughter was in. 'She has to sleep. She's exhausted. You'll see her tomorrow morning.' 'This whole story makes no sense,' he grumbled. 'What do you mean by strange?' 'A state of extreme agitation. Irrational behaviour. For instance, we went . . .' 'I don't want to hear any more. It's bullshit. You're imagining it all. She needs her parents. She's not used to living away from us yet, you see – she's just a bit anxious, unsettled. We'll sleep here: my wife on the bed and me on this armchair.' I tried to share with them the doctor's concerns about their daughter's mental health (without using the word 'schizophrenia', of course); I told them he had recommended the greatest vigilance. 'He gave me the details of a specialist,' I said, showing them the card. 'You mean a *psychiatrist*! You want my daughter to see a *psychiatrist*?' he sneered. 'All because some idiot recommended it? Doctors who work at night are only fit for whores and junkies!'

I went back the next morning, twenty minutes before Sylvie left for work, and I could tell that she'd gathered what little strength remained to her in order to reassure her parents. She was affectionate, lively and cheerful. Her mother admitted that her face showed signs of tiredness – 'You look a bit off-colour, my love. You should come and rest at home next weekend: the country air will do you good' – but she did not even notice the armour of indifference into which her daughter had withdrawn. I could clearly see that the woman in front of us was a picture under glass; during the night, Sylvie had become absolutely numb. She responded to the questions her mother asked her, she took part in the brief conversations that her parents made, she submitted to her father's rituals of affection (he wanted me to understand just how well he knew how to deal with his daughter), but in such a smooth way that her behaviour seemed to me as void of human presence as a room that Sylvie had just left. If I was sure of one thing, it was that she was no longer there. 'Shall I go with you to your work experience?' I asked her. 'Don't worry, I'm going now. I've got to run. See you soon, Daddy. See you soon, Mummy. See you tonight, my love!' And Sylvie fled. It was obvious that this rushed goodbye had surprised her parents, for the first time since their arrival, but their reluctance to linger on such a disturbing feeling made them ignore this clue. Having gathered their belongings, they left the room as if nothing were wrong.

It seemed clear to me that there was no point going with Sylvie: you can't force yourself on someone who is no longer herself, and this situation would have turned me into a lapdog. I intended phoning her at work during the morning to make sure that everything was fine. Moreover, the idea of coming back at three o'clock to check whether Sylvie was in her room with this stranger she claimed she was going to meet had not left my thoughts. When I called her office, around 11 a.m., from a public phone in Rue Jacques-Callot, the young woman who answered told me that Sylvie had not come to work. 'What? Sylvie didn't come to work?' I repeated in a panic. 'Did she tell you she wasn't coming? Have you had her on the phone?' 'Why all these questions? Who are you? Is this personal?' 'I'm her boyfriend. She left me about quarter to nine, and she was supposed to go to work. Are you sure she didn't call anyone?' To myself, I muttered, '*Fuck, I can't believe it!*' 'Not to my knowledge. Listen, you sound upset, and I don't know what this is about,' the young woman said in a hesitant voice. 'But . . . I mean . . .' 'What? What do you mean?' 'I mean, your girlfriend . . .' 'Yes? What?' 'No, never mind, I didn't say anything,' she said, seeming embarrassed. 'Please, speak – tell me what you meant!' 'I don't know how to say this, and I don't know what to do. It's tricky.' 'I'm her boyfriend. I'm worried. Sylvie is not well. It may be serious. If you have something to tell me about this, please do – it's important.' 'Listen, how can I put this? These last few days – yesterday in particular – Sylvie has seemed . . . she's done some slightly odd things . . .' 'Like what?' 'Like, for example, in the canteen, she took about ten desserts, and nothing else, and she picked at all of them. And she spent all morning making hundreds of photocopies.' 'Making hundreds of photocopies?' 'I asked her to photocopy three contracts. I was in a meeting, so I couldn't stop her: there were piles of photocopies on my desk, all over the floor. There were towers of photocopies. She used up all our stock of paper.' 'I see,' I replied, half-choking. I found it almost impossible to express myself. I feared I would burst into tears at each word. I tried to keep my sentences short: 'If Sylvie . . . if she comes into work . . . please . . . tell her I called . . . that I'll come and pick her up this evening . . . I'll call you back to find out if you've heard anything.' The young woman showed great delicacy: she did not ask me a single intrusive question. She said a few kind things, to which I replied with a pulsing silence. She assured me I could call her as often as I considered necessary.

I used the same public phone to call my mother, to tell her what had happened during the night. It turned out she'd been trying to get hold of me to tell me about a conversation she'd had an hour earlier with Sylvie, who had been incoherent and mysterious. 'What happened? Have you had a fight? I hardly recognized her.' 'I'll tell you afterwards. What did she say to you? Do you know where she was?' 'She told me that *she loved me*, that I was the person *she loved most in the world*. She kept repeating the same words in a loop. She wanted to tell me how much she loved me before she went on a trip. I replied that I didn't know she was going on a trip. I asked her where she was going, and she said she was going on a very long trip. I remember that expression: *a very long trip* . . . So I said, but what trip? Where are you going? When? *Where are you going?*' 'And? What did she say?' 'It wasn't very clear. She talked about the colour red. She kept repeating, *the colour red, the colour red*. I thought she was saying that she had to find something – something she'd lost, perhaps . . . a bird.' 'A bird?' 'It wasn't very clear.' 'She was talking about a bird? Christ . . . I don't believe this . . . And afterwards?' 'She was telling me about a space she had to cross, I didn't really understand. *A space that she had to get over*. It was all confused. She didn't know if she was going to come back from this trip. That was why she was calling me: to tell me she'd always adored me, that she was happy she'd known me.' 'She was talking in the past tense? Are you sure she said "had adored", "had known", and so on?' 'Listen, I'm not sure. I think so. It was really strange. But what's going on with Sylvie?' I was crying, my forehead against the telephone. The glass door made a noise: I turned around. A man who was waiting impatiently, seeing the tears pouring down my cheeks, made an apologetic gesture to let me know that I could continue my conversation, and moved away from the phone box. So I told my mother what had happened the previous evening, and what the doctor had told me. 'What should I do now, Mum? Where is Sylvie now? Why did I let her go this morning? Fuck! And her parents . . . those morons . . . they didn't notice a thing! How stupid can they be? It's unbelievable. It was obvious she wasn't well. It was obvious she was going to die! She had already gone completely when I saw her this morning. We should have reacted! Held her back by force! Called a doctor! Called an ambulance! We killed her! Her parents — *my love, my darling, you look a bit off-colour, you should go and rest in the countryside* . . . fuck, no!' I couldn't speak any more. My saliva was so thick, I felt like I had mashed potato in my mouth. Words wet with tears and saliva were catapulted on to the windows of the phone box by my sobs; I wept while smashing my forehead against the metal part of the telephone. 'Don't worry,' my mother told me. 'It'll be all right. What do you think is going to happen to her? I'm going to wait for her to call me back, and then, I promise, I'll tell her to stay where she is and I'll tell you where to find her. Go to your room and don't move. I'll call you back. Hurry.' I was crying. I didn't say a word. I held myself motionless, eyes closed, against the telephone. All I wanted to do was listen to my mother's voice. 'David, what are you doing? Why aren't you speaking any more? Hurry up, go to your room. Perhaps she's called you too? Maybe she's left you a message? You never know. Go on, I'll call you back as soon as I have any news. Go on, my son, go ahead, I'll call you in twenty minutes.'

I went to my attic room. My mother called me every hour to find out if I'd had any news. Having disturbed her three times, I left my number with the young woman I'd talked to that morning so that she could call to let me know if Sylvie turned up.

The few hours I spent waiting for Sylvie to reappear were among the cruellest I had ever lived through. I had no idea that the worst was yet to come, caused by events that were taking place while I nervously paced the seven square metres of my attic room.

My mother gave me the news, in the middle of the afternoon. Sylvie had been found at the Porte de Clignancourt station, at the end of the metro line, in a state of extreme confusion. She had stepped down on to the platform and had disappeared into the darkness of the tunnel until she reached the place where the metro trains were parked at night. She walked like a ghost between the carriages. She picked up stones from the ballast and stored them in her pockets before throwing them at an oil can: it was this noise that led to her being found. Noticing the stupefied way in which this young woman was babbling, the employee who found her decided it was a good idea to call an ambulance while he led her towards the exit. She fainted in his arms before the emergency services arrived. The ambulance took her to the emergency room of the Fernand-Widal hospital, which is, I learned later, where drug addicts picked up in the street are taken; they suspected she was under the influence of a narcotic. We never knew what Sylvie did between the time when she left me and the time when – walking on the rails of the metro, drunk on the images and mantras rushing through her mind – she was picked up by an RATP mechanic. Now here is something strange: when she was admitted to hospital, Sylvie had given the police my mother's name and contact details. This convinced me that I was at the centre of Sylvie's thoughts, and it is also why

I blamed myself for provoking this crisis, particularly because of my behaviour, the arrogance of my ambitions, and the reservations I had unconsciously shown about our future. I asked the police to give Sylvie's parents the news as soon as possible – they had already gone back to M., and I didn't have the strength to call them myself – and then I went to the Fernand-Widal hospital, where I had to wait for ever before a nurse brought me to Sylvie.

I saw her at the end of a long corridor, in front of the door to her room. During the time it took me to reach her, I was able to notice that she did not seem weighed down by the experience. In fact, as I got closer, it seemed to me that she was in a triumphant mood. Hearing the sound of the nurse's shoes on the tiles, Sylvie turned towards us: 'Ah, there he is at last – my Prince Charming! It's high time he looked after his little Sylvie. How are you, my friend?' She came to meet me, and took hold of my chin, turning my face from side to side and laughing: 'You look sad, my friend. What are you so worried about? *Is it me you're so worried about, my friend?*' 'I was a little bit worried about you today, Sylvie,' I said, as she tapped me gently on the cheek. 'Why did you vanish like that? Where did you go?' 'It would take too long, and be a bit tedious, to tell you what I did today. But it was amazing – yes, I can say that what I went through . . . because, imagine . . . come on, let's go into this room and sit down on the bed . . .' Thus began Sylvie's enticing monologue, told with a scope and energy that was far from the way she had spoken the previous night, when she had tried to distract the doctor who had come to examine her. I found her sublime. Her beauty dazzled me as she moved along the corridor, not with the ease of an actress (because she wasn't pretending or faking), but with the radiance of someone who is naturally extraordinary. It was incredible: in most ways, she seemed exactly the same as she had the day before –

the same physiognomy, the same intelligence, the same temperament and experience – but, as if she had undergone some kind of meticulous brain surgery, Sylvie, unfettered, had gained access to the fullness of her own potential. This young woman who, the night before, still hadn't found her true face, seemed this evening to have cast off the pollutants that usually prevented more than 30 per cent of her interior light from shining out to the world – *as they do for all of us*. And that is why I was so fascinated by her astonishing metamorphosis. She had become another person – she had become herself. I discovered that, in liberating her entire self, Sylvie was possessed of a staggering erotic power.

I tried to question her about her internal state. Did she feel well? Did she feel capable of going home this evening?

It worried me, though, that her monologue had not stopped for a second during the twenty minutes I had spent in her company. And, despite the rapture into which her presence had sent me, I had begun to feel a vague anxiety. Sylvie did not respond to my questions. She seemed to flee my words the way a sailor tries to escape the zone of a hurricane. She started reciting poetry: I recognized Arthur Rimbaud's 'Le Bateau Ivre' in her deep voice that echoed the length of the corridor. Sylvie moved constantly, and with the grace of a princess. Most astonishingly, about ten minutes later, she started declaiming something in German. It was, she told me, by Goethe. 'You know Goethe off by heart?!' 'It's *The Sorrows of Young Werther*.' '*You know parts of* The Sorrows of Young Werther *in German off by heart?*' 'The Sorrows of Young Sylvie!' 'That's pretty surprising. I thought you were supposed to be rubbish at German?' 'But, my friend,' she said in a gentle, melodic voice, 'you imagine that you know me. You have me pigeonholed as a *good girl*. But let me tell you something: you're fooling yourself if you think you've plumbed my depths.' She said this with an affectionate laugh, and without the slightest hint of aggression. 'There are many things you don't know, and that you would probably enjoy discovering, if only you took the trouble to do so. If only you want me to surprise you – as I'm doing this evening, it appears. But you're starting out with the assumption that there's nothing more inside me that could attract you. You're ashamed of me. You always prevent me from speaking in front of other people. You're always afraid that I'll embarrass you by saying something stupid, or by committing a gaffe, or by making some coarse remark when I'm feeling cheerful, or by my inability to resist provoking people.' I couldn't believe my ears: what Sylvie was saying was absolutely accurate, but I was surprised that she should express these truths in a playful tone, without the slightest bitterness or reproach. 'I love you. I adore you. I want to live with you. *If I am certain of one thing, it is that you will be the only love of my life.*' Sylvie looked at me. From the heights of this pedestal of intelligence and beauty, she overwhelmed me. And then she moved away from me, a stream of German pouring from her mouth.

The doctor I saw described Sylvie's breakdown as an extremely serious case of manic depression, and said that they were not going to be able to keep her. He said they would send her to the Sainte-Anne hospital. 'You're going to put her in Sainte-Anne?' I muttered. 'But . . . that's a psychiatric hospital! You're going to put Sylvie in a psychiatric hospital?' 'I can't keep her. There's no point in her being here. But at the same time, it would be unreasonable to let her go home.'

I was still with the doctor (I was questioning him about manic depression, as this was the first time I had ever heard of it) when Sylvie's parents arrived. Having heard the doctor say a few words, Sylvie's mother interrupted by banging her hand on the desk. 'Stop right there! There are no mad people in our family, and there never have been. This is not from us.' The doctor looked surprised. I heard him say: 'First of all, madame, who is talking about madness?' 'You want to put my daughter in Sainte-Anne! I repeat: there are no mad people in our family!' 'Next,' the doctor continued, talking over Sylvie's mother, 'the problem cannot be addressed in those terms. Nobody is accusing you, or seeking to blame anyone.' '*And yet you should,*' said Sylvie's father, nodding knowingly. The doctor turned towards him. 'What do you mean by that?' 'I mean that my wife is right: there are no mad people in our family. We are perfectly sane. No doubt you are unaware that I am a lieutenant-colonel in the army, and that I am head of the military camp . . .' 'I don't doubt that you and your wife are . . .' 'And you are right not to doubt it. I have responsibilities to the Ministry of Defence . . .' 'I don't quite see the connection. What are you trying to say?' 'If you keep interrupting me, it will be difficult to understand.' 'All right then, I'm listening,' the doctor replied, with a glance at me. 'As there are, I repeat, and as there have never been, in our family, any mad people or weirdos or any mental illness . . . as there has not even been any unusual behaviour – never; I insist upon this point . . . And furthermore,' Sylvie's father continued, after a short pause (he wiped his forehead with a white handkerchief drawn from a pocket of his jacket), 'as our daughter has, in the past, never suffered any incident of this kind . . . as our daughter has always been sane, reasonable, balanced . . . as our daughter is well-educated, with thoughts that one could describe as . . . *normal* – not exceptional in any way, and certainly not *unusual* – there is no point seeking the cause of the illness with us, or with her . . .' 'Not even with her?' the doctor interjected. 'Not even with her. Exactly. You have understood me perfectly.' 'But in that case, where do you think we should seek the cause of your daughter's illness?' the doctor asked, glancing at me again, as if he wished to protect me from an imminent blow.

'You won't have to look very far, trust me,' Sylvie's father continued, casually gesturing at me with his chin. 'What do you mean by that, my dear sir?' the doctor asked him again. 'I hope we'll have the chance to have a private conversation on this subject, in which I may be allowed to elaborate on my thoughts. But to put it briefly, he is driving her mad; he is destroying her. My daughter has no need of a psychiatrist. She does not need to spend the night at Sainte-Anne, despite what you seem to think. Let's be logical and rational – although I know that isn't easy for people of your kind, nor for people like this boy. But perhaps this evening you might agree, as an exception, to make an effort. My daughter doesn't need any psychiatric help because she's not mad.' 'Or if she is, it's because she has become so, and not through any fault of ours,' Sylvie's mother broke in peremptorily, banging the desk with her wedding ring. 'Absolutely,' her husband agreed. 'Consequently, the most efficient way of resolving this problem is not to commit our daughter . . .' 'You could get in serious trouble with my husband, who has connections with the Ministry,' Sylvie's mother interjected. 'Because you do want to have her committed, don't you, if I've understood correctly?' 'We are going to take our daughter home this evening.'

When I visited Sylvie at the hospital the next day, I was led to a room where – sitting despondently on a stool, zombiefied by neuroleptics, devastated by the mental conflagration from which her mind had just escaped – she gave the impression that she was seeing me after months apart, as if she had just returned from the 'very long trip' she had told my mother about the day before.

She seemed to be carrying a huge weight on her shoulders. She spoke like a little girl, and the naive way she looked at us required us to address her in the gentle, simplified way you might speak to a child. She frowned and shook her head each time she heard a sentence that she couldn't understand, her look seeming to pass the phrase back to me like a nut I was to crack open for her. I was even afraid at one point that she was about to start playing on the tiles, but in fact she got down from the stool in order to pick up a slipper that had fallen off her foot.

Sylvie was unaware of our whereabouts. She retained no memory of what had happened the day before, or why she had ended up in the Sainte-Anne hospital. Shouts rang out in the room; people constantly repeated the same mysterious sequence of words and wandered in the light from the large windows with the docility of animals born in captivity. A wrinkled old woman, the edges of her lips whitened by dried milk, kept coming up to us and whispering the same secret. Others did not move at all, their empty gazes mixing with the brightness of the dining hall the way air mixes with air, or water with water, endless regret with endless regret. I was disturbed that my girlfriend seemed no different from any of these people slumped sadly on their seats, most of them elderly, as if it were already understood that she was going to spend her life in this place intended for reckless people, judged by society to be incapable of using the metro without being swallowed up by the powerful attraction of the tunnels. I was chilled by her shrivelled presence. A dreadful anxiety spread through me. Seeing Sylvie in this state was devastating. I saw her reduced to almost nothing, vulnerable and degraded, turned stupid by the neuroleptics, hunched in a hideous and ridiculous cotton dressing gown. She didn't ask me a single question about how long she would be there or why she was there. She seemed content to smile mechanically, a bit like the old lady who kept repeating the same meaningless phrase. I almost felt surprised that Sylvie still had all her teeth. From the few things she attempted to say to me, I gathered that she found it difficult to speak, that the medicine she was taking stopped the words forming in her mouth, and perhaps even in her thoughts.

I tried to introduce as many images as possible to her imagination (I told her we would go for a rest at her family home in Brittany; I talked to her about the walks we would go on together along the banks of the canal), but she responded only with occasional head movements and disconnected smiles. At times I noticed a complete indifference to my presence, to the existence of any kind of relationship between us. When I said goodbye, she barely responded; when I left, she did not even turn her head towards the door. She was like a sculpture, buried in cheap pyjamas that had started going fluffy as soon as they left the factory.

The psychiatrist I saw told me that manic-depressives always had relapses; that, if Sylvie was going to come out of the state in which I saw her, I had to know that she would inevitably return to it. 'When?' I asked him. 'Often?' 'At one time or another. Perhaps it will be in six months, perhaps in ten years; nobody can know how often the illness will recur, nor how serious it will be each time. The relapses may be mild, and they may also be more serious . . . like the one your girlfriend has just suffered, which was particularly strong.' This same psychiatrist told me that Sylvie's father had also got the military hospital in Val-de-Grâce to agree to look after Sylvie once they had a room free – 'Tomorrow afternoon at the latest.' I learned that her parents had refused to linger in Sainte-Anne; they had been content to drop off a few things (the slippers and the checked dressing gown that I had seen her wearing) and had seen their daughter only for a short time before retreating in shame.

Very soon after she was moved to the Val-de-Grâce hospital, Sylvie suffered such a violently allergic reaction to the neuroleptics she'd been prescribed that she went into a coma.

It was once again my mother who gave me the news, phoning the secretary of my university after she had been informed of this tragic incident by Sylvie's mother. I was handed a note in class that read: 'David Kolski, please phone your mother URGENTLY' with the word 'urgently' roughly underlined. From the same telephone box in Rue Jacques-Callot that I had used the time before, I heard my mother – emotional but strong, her voice trembling but determined to give me her full support for this coming trial – tell me: 'Listen, David, I have to tell you . . . it's bad news . . .' Instantly I panicked, hitting the glass with my fist as I stared at the school's facade. 'You'll have to . . . you mustn't panic. This is very hard, but you mustn't worry.' 'What? Tell me what's happened! They've realized she's mad? They're going to send her back to Sainte-Anne? *She's going to be committed? She's never going to come out?*' 'Nothing like that. Calm down and listen to me. She had an allergic reaction to the medicine. Something very rare.' 'And? What happened?' 'She's been in a coma since this morning.' 'What? *What did you say?* In a coma? But what do you . . . a coma . . . but, fucking hell, that's really serious!' 'If all goes well, she should come out of it. That's what the doctors say.' 'But a coma . . . a coma! People in comas turn into vegetables! What are you talking about?' 'Not always. People can be in a coma for a single day, and come out without any consequences,' my mother said in her gentlest, most tranquillizing voice. 'There are lots of people who go into a coma and come out of it very quickly; it happens all the time. Remember Mr Morandini, when he was knocked over by a car: he was in a coma for two days, and when he came out, he was just like before. He still does his cycling races.' 'Often, yes, but fucking hell . . . And you said *if all goes well – if all goes well* she should come out of it! *IF all goes well!*' 'They'll know a bit more later today. She might wake up before evening. Don't worry. In any case, you can go and see her: Sylvie's mother told me that you can go and see her, but only at the end of the afternoon – about five o'clock. They've left your name at the entrance. You'll have to give your name. It's a military hospital, so they can't just let you in like that. Apparently it's very closely watched.' 'Fuck, I can't believe this! What's been going on for the last two days?' 'Don't worry. Sylvie will come out of it. Call me if you need me to come and support you. I'll go to the hospital with you if you like.'

As if the situation itself were not already frightening enough, we had to go through the emergency department at the back of the building to reach the intensive care unit of the Val-de-Grâce hospital. I took the pavement that skirts it (and purely for this reason, I sensed that the emergency department led into a hell of pain and smashed bodies) and entered the hospital through the garage where the ambulances are parked in order to drop off the patients they've brought. I was constantly afraid that I would inadvertently see some horrible detail that I should not have seen. This neon-lit space was not part of the hospital itself, but it was not entirely part of the outside world either. I crossed this bare entrance with the feeling that I was passing through an intermediary zone between life and death, happiness and sadness, good luck and bad luck, the world where the thing had not yet happened and the world where it had just happened. It was as shrill and alarming as the noise of a helicopter. I pictured this dazzling entrance as the materialization of that instant when my mother told me that Sylvie was in a coma. Each time I passed through this area, I had the feeling not only of entering the hospital where Sylvie lay, but of moving inside my own misfortune: I myself resembled this tragic entrance located at the back of the building. Not only that, but during the five days that Sylvie remained in a coma, my arrival coincided several times with the arrival of an accident victim, brought by an ambulance in cautious haste. And the insistent urgency of this scene mirrored the seriousness of my situation: I felt I was, all at once, the ambulance, the victim, the trauma and the doctor. The movement around the stretcher was so frenzied as to suggest that the victim might pass away in the middle of the corridor. While I waited for a nurse to fetch me and lead me to the small room where I had to dress in a sterilized outfit, this wounded person who might die was wheeled away into the whiteness of the building's innards. I felt alone: no friend could help me through this trial, nor could they soothe the terror I felt. I was burning in a personal hell, surrounded by all these people bustling about, unconcerned by my pain, wearing white shoes, dressed in shirts with biro marks near the pockets. In the little room where I'd been left, I put on the protective gear they gave me, and a nurse appeared from the electronic world of the unconscious ('Hello. Are you ready? May I accompany you?') and took me into a room where sleepers lay in a line separated by screens. The atmosphere here was religious. The beeps emitted by the equipment (connected to the white bodies that I glimpsed between the screens) were like the tempo of an unheard requiem. It seemed to me that there were nothing but dead people in this room, dead people who had been mourned for a long time. I myself was dressed like a sort of sacristan (green slippers, green trousers, green shirt, green gloves, green mask), and even if Sylvie had not been sleeping, she would only have been able to recognize me from my eyes.

I learned that the allergy she had suffered was called neuroleptic malignant syndrome, and that because of the seriousness with which it had occurred, there was a risk she would never come out of her coma. Sylvie had a two-in-three chance of pulling through (her survival statistics were valued at 65 per cent), but it was the obverse figure that stabbed through me: for every moment of those five days of uncertainty, in each part of this scream-filled, sleep-deprived space, all I understood was that huge 35 per cent chance of her dying. If you think about it, that percentage is absolutely colossal. Three women aged twenty drink tea; after drinking the tea, one of the three must die – that was the kind of arithmetic that clarified my suffering. So, waiting in front of one of the three doors behind which she would wake up (or not wake up), I knew there was a chance that, in a few days, I might hold my girlfriend's icy hand in mine and caress the corpse of the only woman with whom I'd had an intimate, loving relationship.

I spent ages talking to her, trying to find words that, like diamonds, could shine brightly enough to scintillate in her imagination and wake her thoughts with a start – a bit like those mornings in Anne-Sophie's parents' house when the sun pulled me from sleep with its heat spread over my face and its brightness piercing my eyelids. Would I be capable of believing, truly and wholly, in the words I whispered to her, believing in them so fiercely that the images they conjured would pierce her recluse's eyelids? I was determined to reinvent my relationship with Sylvie. From now on, *my life had to be generous to hers* (I repeated, squeezing her fingers) and I had to stop protecting myself on principle from the visions that her words sometimes put in my mind (for example, every time the word 'baby' was pronounced, mirroring the word 'marriage'; every time she mentioned the idea of a rented studio flat for two, or a trip we could take together – 'In a few years,' she was always careful to specify – I turned away from her, I bristled, I refused to let myself be limited by any project that did not emanate from my own desires or long-term interest). I held her hand and begged her solemnly to forgive me. I told her that my reluctance demonstrated nothing more than my fears of the world and the failings I saw in myself – *and not in her*. I thought this so strongly that I imagined it would perhaps penetrate her brain: *and not in her*. I kissed her fingers.

The light of my love already flowed freely in this dark prison cell where I could just make out her closed eyes and mouth, surrounded by thick blackness. The sunlight of my words shone into her ears. For her alone, I created, through the syntax of my whispers, the equivalent of a beautiful countryside atmosphere: birds sang amid my words, the sound of a summer morning full of promise. 'We're only twenty. We've got our whole lives in front of us. Why should we worry? Sylvie, listen to me. I'm talking to you. Why do we put ourselves in this state? Aren't we going to spend our lives together? I'm telling you this tonight: I firmly intend to hang on to you. So why remain in this useless sleep?' But these birds that I invented to delight her, this sunlight that I shone at her face . . . would they be enough to penetrate the skin of her sleeper's eyelids? 'Can you hear me? Sylvie, can you hear me?' I whispered in her ear. 'It's me. It's David. I'm here. Come back to me: I'm waiting for you.' Sylvie did not move. Tubes came out of her nose and throat. A drip was attached to a vein in her forearm. Because of this equipment, I couldn't decide if she looked like she would have done were she sleeping normally (she was breathing peacefully) or if the coma gave the withdrawal of her consciousness some specific aspect that would explain why her face disturbed me so much. Her expression seemed slightly annoyed, as if Sylvie were preoccupied with a recurring thought; she was like a sleeper locked in a place in a dream that would suddenly be interrupted, like a metro train stopped in a tunnel. (To be honest, I felt a kind of repulsion for her face, altered as it was by the illness. That Sylvie was possibly dying made her seem as distant as a stranger to me. The shamelessness with which she maintained this state of tension under my gaze made me uneasy, as if she were showing me something a lover should not see: the hidden face of the crudest intimacy, like shit excreted from an anus. All of this filled my mind with thoughts of the finiteness of human life. It seemed impossible I would ever be able to kiss her again or have any intimate relations with her without thinking about death and remembering her face in this hospital bed – all the more so as it was not dissimilar to the expression one might have at the moment of orgasm. But these dark thoughts – necessary, no doubt, as an outlet for my anguish – went away as quickly as they had appeared, and my love for Sylvie won out.) I talked to her about the children we would have, about the house with a garden we would buy. (Sylvie couldn't stand living in an apartment – she'd told me this on various occasions – while I loved the chaos of big cities and dreamed of living in New York one day.) 'How many kids do you want? Tell me, my love, how many kids do you want? Two, three, four? I'm OK with five.' No response. The pulsing of breathing apparatus. The inescapable tempo of the requiem. I heard the clank of utensils on metal plates, trolley wheels on tiles, the footsteps of a nurse from Martinique in her flip-flops. There was nothing I found more agonizing than these background hospital noises (linked to the hospital's smell: a nauseating odour permeated the air around us, intensified by the room's uncomfortable warmth). Just as the atmosphere that fills your head when you lie on a beach with your eyes closed is made up of the roar of waves, the cries of seagulls and the laughter of children having fun, so these hospital noises constituted the quintessence of the atmosphere that spilled out around my agony. But, beyond the beeps emitted by the regulators (as regularly and indifferently as the ocean produces waves), the frequency and intensity of the various noises I perceived were as nothing to the enduring silence. 'Sylvie, can you hear me? I'm OK with five children: three girls and two boys! Unless . . . I know you, oh yes, I know you!' I said quietly, trying to laugh. (I had not, up to this moment, thought laughter possible, but perhaps, in the end, laughing loud and long, without meaning to, shaking in my chair, would turn out to be the most effective way of waking Sylvie and a few of her unfortunate neighbours?) 'Oh yes, I know you – you'd be perfectly capable of that! Oh yes, you'd be capable of doing that!' I continued, trying to start the engine of false laughter as if it were an old car on a winter morning. 'If I said I was OK with five children, you'd be perfectly capable of saying you wanted five boys! I say yes to five children and your response is: I'd like five boys! My romantic officer, you'd be perfectly capable of wanting to make a whole company. Five boys – six men in the house, all for you!' I squeezed her fingers while I described the face of the first hussar baby we would have. For each part of his face, I listed what he would inherit from his father and what he would be proud to receive from his mother: 'The most important thing is that he has your small nose. He should have my eyes that you love so much, but on the other hand he should have your ears. You know I love your ears. Nothing bad can possibly happen to someone with ears like that! I'd like him to have your forehead – your large, intelligent forehead. There'd be plenty of space on that forehead to tidy things away,' I said, while gently touching her wide, bulging forehead with my fingers. 'Things like dreams and desires, thoughts and ideas, memories and love and ambition . . . You'll help me to become an architect. We'll do it together! You know I'd have trouble succeeding if you didn't help me out a bit. With you, with this forehead, with all the beautiful things you've always tidied away here, we'll be a huge hit!' I leaned my head on her stomach. 'Don't you believe me? Sylvie, tell me – don't you believe me?'

Sylvie did not respond. I watched her breathing without listening, indifferent, undecided.

I came back every day at the end of the afternoon. I was no

longer sleeping. Anxiety burned in my stomach and chest. Bouts of diarrhoea forced me to visit many different toilets. I felt like my brain was being slowly eaten.

The idea that Sylvie might die, though devastating, also eliminated all my other fears. My resistance seemed boundless, and I felt an absolute indifference towards my own safety. I remember, some evenings, crossing roads almost without looking.

Each time I left the intensive care unit, I had no idea where to go or what to do. I felt lost in my own life, as if it were a foreign city; I had no landmarks by which to orient myself, and no desire except for Sylvie's awakening and the forgiveness that she might grant me. I could sit on a bench and stay there for a long time without really being aware of it. I hardly ate at all any more.

The clocks changed during Sylvie's second night in the Val-de-Grâce hospital. When I found myself outside at the end of my third visit, not only was it darker than it had been the previous day, but it was almost nightfall. I remember walking on the street and being grateful for this change of lighting; I was happy with the new atmosphere that was spreading through reality – dimmer, less cheerful, more poetic and contemplative. An atmosphere in which, I sensed, something mysterious existed that was protecting me. That evening, for the first time, I saw autumn as a space where the gentleness of my inner life could console my sufferings and create, all around me, the floating sensation of an ideal elsewhere that might one day be reached. That evening, and in the evenings that followed, I had the feeling that I could see my future opening up before me. Walking for hours in these reborn nights, I felt almost happy.

I look at my watch. It is 4.20 a.m. The hotel is perfectly silent. I wonder if I am the only guest.

My face is reflected in the windows. My gaze sinks into darkness and it has the same effect on me as the darkness that masses around a theatre stage, a cosmic night surrounding the actors who pace it and the stories they tell us.

I look at my reflection in this mirror of thoughts and darkness. One lamp is lit behind me. I keep drinking whisky and lighting cigarettes. I don't know how long I have been moving through this dense nocturnal matter, trying to recall the precise state that consumed me when Sylvie was trapped in her prison cell of sleep. But it seems to me that I have managed to capture the exact timbre of a few of the sensations that, during those five days, accompanied my prayers and the unfolding of my terror. Sylvie's face is within reach now; it merges with the pale reflection of mine in the window. I see her breathing, and the image is perhaps sharper than when I saw her in reality, between two screens in the Val-de-Grâce hospital, twenty-two years ago.

The pain I feel today is no less strong, no less unspeakably horrible than the pain that crushed me when I was afraid that Sylvie would not come out of her coma. It is the same kind of pain, full of death and guilt, terror and sadness, solitude and an inescapable alienation from others, the world, my life before this nightmare. The difference between these two states is that, today, there is no hope to diminish the pain that overwhelms me. Victoria will never emerge from the darkness that has swallowed her, because of me; and my two daughters will never be able to forgive me for wronging them, nor forget what they know their father did. Whereas during those five days I was able to remind myself that Sylvie's absence would perhaps be temporary.

I light a cigarette and let my thoughts drift in this darkness that has banked up at the windows. Sylvie is connected to beeping machines with screens that display the outlines of mountains. Looking closely at her face, you might think she was concentrating on some kind of research, terrified by its fruitlessness – as if Sylvie had reason to fear the imminent arrival of a disaster and was attempting to discover what it was, when and where it would occur. An intuition fills her mind, urging her to remember an event that has not yet happened. The grimace that lingers on her face shows her powerlessness to overcome this challenge. Or perhaps she feels as though she is imprisoned in a metro train stopped in a tunnel, locked in a single image – abstract and dazzling – that she must understand before she can escape, in order to avert the disaster which this image seems to prefigure.

I now know what that event was – the one whose future existence I glimpsed on Sylvie's face.

The mysterious image she was trying to locate in her sleep was revealed to her consciousness twenty-two years later when it burst into her life with a violence that none of us really recovered from. The policemen invaded our house one morning at 6 a.m. to brutally search it in front of my daughters (their room included), before bundling me, handcuffed, into an unmarked car in front of my neighbours, who had gathered in the street to watch. Sylvie's unchanging face is superimposed on the state of painful immobility in which our lives have been frozen for the last three months. This hotel in La Creuse; this small room drowned in twilight; this man sure he will never dare face his daughters again . . . I'm sure Sylvie would have appreciated a glimpse of this in the darkness of her coma before deciding that brilliant young David Kolski truly was the man with whom she wanted to spend her life. Nevertheless, she did possess a few hints to suggest that this man's love would not be as lasting as she imagined her own to be. 'Why doesn't he love me as much as I love him?': this worry ended up becoming obsessive. I realized this despite the care she took to conceal it. As the clues she discovered increased her certainty that she would end up being abandoned, Sylvie edged towards her outbreak of manic depression (this is, in fact, what I think happened) – all the more so as we were always a couple undermined by a kind of basic disharmony. Sylvie knew that she lacked the sophisticated fuel she needed in order to power my feelings through life's long journey – the same fuel that powered my imagination, my thirst for poetry, my desire for a life of radiance and triumph. I am sure Sylvie was intuitively aware of all this. Perhaps she even perceived that our love would be a disaster if she somehow managed to keep me close to her. So, had I been able to enter her mind during those five days, had I been able to shine a torch beam in there, would this have been what I discovered: a hotel room filled with twilight, and – in an armchair in front of black windows – a broken man, drunk on pain and whisky? *Am I, even now, still in the nocturnal gloom of the coma Sylvie fell into twenty-one years ago?* All of this feels unreal to me: this room looks like a place of the mind, with its isolation, its limitless darkness surrounding me, the rain falling on the countryside, that forest like a dark mass at the edge of the landscape, these raindrops falling on the windows and leaving sinuous traces on the face of my wife glimpsed in the transparency of my own . . . Perhaps I am nothing but a thought born in 1985 in the mind of a young woman in a coma, connected to machines by tubes and electric wires? I swallow a large glass of whisky. If only I didn't exist; if only I was nothing more than the vision of a young woman horrified at not being loved enough; if only Sylvie could awake and her nightmare dissolve; if only I could dissolve when this young woman awoke; if only I could return to my existence before this tragedy, before Victoria's death, before I was held in custody, before Christophe Keller, before my picture appeared in the newspapers . . .

Is there a worse torture imaginable than your wife and children, your parents and colleagues, finding out from the television news of the existence of your 'regular' mistress – because she has been murdered? Seeing her face, discovering her identity and biography, and finally being informed about the far from heroic role you played in her death?

Is there anything worse than being held responsible for a person's death, even if, in a strictly legal sense, society considers you not guilty and frees you, sending you home with a look that is impossible to forget (I am thinking of Christophe Keller's face when I was released from custody: 'You're free to go. Goodbye, and good luck for the future'), a look like a secret guilty verdict, as sharp as the point of a needle in your forearm?

I throw my glass of whisky against the wall. It smashes, leaving a picture of an explosion on the wallpaper's floral patterns.

I go to the bathroom. I switch on the ceiling light and look at myself closely in the mirror for a long time while I wash my hands.

I have never allowed myself to imagine what my life might have become had Sylvie not fallen into that coma. My entire existence was decided during those five days when I came to see her, when I found myself in a situation that required something like a sacred promise. When you think about it, there are very few situations when the words you can say are priceless. But it is certainly the case when — through these words, through the promises they articulate, through the offerings they represent — you buy the life of a loved one. You guarantee their value in exchange for a human life. Sylvie's emergence from the coma led to the creation of a sanctified mental zone, where all speculation is forbidden, where no thoughts venture except by chance or trailing shame — in the same way that you refuse to imagine the death of a child. In this zone, as in a safe, can be found the secret to the link that unites us. I have never betrayed what I said to Sylvie during the five days of her coma.

One night, as I was going to bed, Sylvie's father phoned me to say that he wanted to see me urgently. Hearing the way he spoke,

I thought he must have spent hours getting drunk on the hatred he felt for me. I sensed his repugnance at giving me anything, even if it was only the sound of his voice, as well as at listening to a single word pronounced by my voice. 'You want to see me?' I replied suspiciously. 'Do you have something in particular to tell me?' 'I don't have anything in particular to tell you. It is not up to me to say what really happened and why my daughter is in a coma now.' Sylvie's father was struggling with an indescribable state of pain, and the effort it cost him not to collapse made his words as taut as piano wires: I could hear them vibrate in his voice in a curious mix of tension and trembling, of aggression and sadness, of violence and frailty. 'I don't understand what you're after. I think perhaps it'd be better to . . .' 'You don't know what I'm after!' he interjected in a voice that was half hate-filled laughter and half insane whisper. 'It seems to me it is high time that the two of us had a real, man-to-man talk.' 'I don't understand what you're talking about. I don't know what you mean by a man-to-man talk.' 'A conversation between men,' he said in the same restrained tone, but with a greatly increased power, as if the volume level of his voice had suddenly been turned up as high as it would go. I began to feel frightened. It seemed to me that this man was going mad. He had opened the doors to his mind and the words he spoke echoed as if in a cathedral. 'I want us to stop the hypocrisy. To finally tell the truth. To talk like two men with balls.'

I met Sylvie's father half an hour later in a café in the Saint-Placide district. We sat on either side of a small table near the window. He ordered a beer, I had a glass of Côtes-du-Rhône. Our conversation was chaotic. It seemed obvious that it would not lead us anywhere and that it would have been more reasonable to put an end to it after the first few minutes, but I suppose we needed to prolong this confrontation, if only to avoid for as long as possible the torture of our sleepless nights. The few other customers in this café (mostly drunks at the bar) must have watched us like two wrestlers whose fight ends up in dense, heavy hand-to-hand combat. I couldn't detach myself from this man and the pleasure his insults gave me; I couldn't put an end to the ignominy of our respective attacks. Our comments were so despicable that whoever spoke humiliated himself in wounding the other. Our words tore each other to pieces, rather than examining the external reality to which they referred. Our discussions consumed themselves. We kept going back to insults delivered a few minutes earlier and drawing from them material for another, intensified attack. In this way, our meeting, which stretched itself out as it stomped on itself, became one more aspect of this endless waiting with which we'd been exhausting ourselves for three days: the madness of undiluted waiting that coils around itself.

Most of the questions that Sylvie's father asked me were like long daggers that he pushed into his own stomach. He demanded of this young man whom he hated that he tell him the most unbearable secrets about his daughter, as if he felt he had to die before experiencing the death of that child, and to die in the name of his love for her, and to succumb to wounds inflicted in his assumptions about her purity. 'We have to talk about sex. We have to talk man to man,' he told me. 'What's she like in bed, Sylvie? I mean sexually. I demand you respond to this question. Does Sylvie like sex, or is she shy and reserved, which, personally, I would tend to believe? If you want to know the truth, I'm convinced that you're corrupting my daughter, that you're degrading her, that you fuck her like a whore,' Sylvie's father told me, his face bright red and sweating, his hands trembling. 'Do you take her from behind? What are your favourite positions? You look shocked. Come on, stop pretending to be innocent – I'm sure this isn't the first time you've talked about this stuff with another man. I repeat my question: what are your favourite positions? What are her favourite positions? Has she ever asked you to do special things? Like what? I feel obliged, given the seriousness of recent events, to ask you this in the most direct way, and to demand that you respond,' Sylvie's father told me. 'Does she enjoy it? Have you made her come?' Sylvie's father asked me. (He was shaking with tics: his face produced brief, instantaneous sculptures that appeared when he said certain words, such as the word 'come'.) 'Tell me. I want to know. Be precise. Does she suck your cock? It's important that I know the truth, to understand what happened. Do you do it doggy-style? I imagine you know what that means,' he said, laughing. 'You fuck my daughter like a whore. I'm sure you take her from behind like a whore. I feel certain that you humiliate her by fucking her like a bitch. I can see it on your face. You're the one who made her ill. She went mad because of you. It's your fault that my daughter lost her marbles. You destroyed her. You destroyed her because you fuck her like a slut. I'm certain that the only way my daughter could escape from having to keep submitting to all your filth was to blow a fuse,' Sylvie's father told me. 'You must be wondering how I know this. You must really be wondering how I know that you're nothing but a pervert and a mental case. You're thinking, fuck, this guy is good. No wonder he's lieutenant-colonel,' Sylvie's father told me. 'It's because I found porn magazines in my daughter's room, under her bed. Got you there, didn't I? You show my daughter porn magazines? In order to get turned on, you have to show my daughter – before you fuck her – you have to show her pornography?' Sylvie's father said, choking on his pain and hatred. 'My wife found a suspender belt in a drawer in her room. Do you make my daughter wear suspenders? You dress her like a whore, you give her whorish things, you show her pornographic crap to get yourself hard, and afterwards you fuck her?' Sylvie's father asked me. 'And sodomy . . . let's talk about sodomy. Do you sodomize my daughter? Go ahead, man to man, look me in the eyes. I'm sure you fuck her up the arse. I am certain you fuck her up the arse. I'm sure you put your dick up her arse. I am certain things like that have happened. It was my wife who first came up with this theory. That pervert is perfectly capable of it – no doubt it's something like that which happened. That's what my wife said one morning, and I'm sure she's right. You sodomized her. You brutalized her. You fucked her like you'd fuck a whore. Go on, man to man, tell me the truth. My daughter, my little daughter, did you fuck her up the arse? Tell me or I'll smash your teeth in,' Sylvie's father told me. 'Fucking hell, at least have the balls to admit it, to acknowledge that you're nothing but a repressed queer,' Sylvie's father told me with frightening control (as if I were faced with an entire army ready to fight; something hostile and impassive, restrained and potentially devastating). 'Do you agree with me that you're a repressed queer? My wife and I have been sure of this since the day we met you: that you're nothing but a queer pervert who doesn't dare admit it, who defiles young girls with his vices, who leads them astray and harms them. You filthy queer, you bastard, I don't know what's stopping me from smashing your face in and knocking your teeth out,' Sylvie's father told me.

We paid the bill and went outside, but we couldn't manage to detach ourselves from each other and return to the solitude that awaited us. Insulting each other was easier than facing up to the pain of silence. I responded methodically to each of his remarks against me. I replied with meticulous observations, pronounced in a calm voice, on the values, mentality and ideology of soldiers and bourgeois conservatives.

'Always this crap about poetry, architecture and philosophy,' Sylvie's father told me as a parting shot as he was walking away (although barely had he spoken these words than he was coming back towards me to say something else or to respond to the words that had just burst from my mouth in response to his words, etc.). 'All these complicated books that you're constantly carting around with you! Which book are you carting around with you tonight, even in these tragic circumstances? I summon you to a café, and you, you turn up with a book in your hand. Show me, show me the cover . . . Gérard de Nerval, *Les Filles du feu* . . . fucking hell, you're off your head! Reading sick shit like that. Nerval! Reading Nerval on a day like this! My daughter's in a coma; she might die tonight; we meet in a café so I can get an explanation from you, man to man, and you turn up with a Gérard de Nerval book under your arm,' Sylvie's father told me. (I really thought he was going to hit me then, because of Gérard de Nerval; he'd raised his hand behind his head as if to smash me in the cheek with it.) 'You made my daughter completely mad. You turned her head. She doesn't know where she is any more. Because of you, she doesn't know the difference between reality and dream, fantasy, illusion. You've blurred her perception of reality with this crap about poetry, artistic ambition, becoming an architect! Architect, architecture, art, poetry!' Sylvie's father told me, moving away. 'Look what all this stuff has done to my daughter, look where it got her – the Sainte-Anne hospital! My daughter needs a solid, real, reassuring environment, where things have names that don't change, where events are clear, where life doesn't alter from one minute to the next like in a poem. You can't live in a life that's always moving and changing like clouds in the sky, where reality changes name and form and substance at every moment!' Sylvie's father told me, twenty metres away from me, shouting so that I would hear him.

'Before she knew you, my daughter – before she got into this stuff – she had her feet on the ground. The world where she lived was stable, rational, unchanging. She knew where she was. Nobody had turned her head. Nobody had messed up her values!'

He moved away from me. I watched his silhouette cross Rue de Rennes.

I yelled: 'Stupid twat!'

Sylvie's father turned around. He took his hands out of his jacket pockets. I saw him start to come back towards me. I ran through the night to the refuge of my attic room.

5

If I had stuck to my principles, I would never have seen Victoria again.

It must have been about 10.30 a.m. when I awoke, the morning after the night we spent making love. I opened the curtains: the sun was out, and to judge from the languorous way people were strolling along the pavement, the temperature must have been pleasantly warm. A man carrying his jacket under his arm was crossing the street. I got washed, then went downstairs to pay for the room. It was nearly noon by the time I was able to sit down at a table in front of the hotel.

The wonderful night I'd just experienced had left a happiness in my body that was increased by the pleasure of knowing I could venture out on the streets long after everyone else's working day had already started. Physical intoxication can trigger some very curious phenomena in the brain – enough to give a slave like me the illusion that he is an aristocrat freed from all constraints, or a person of incredibly rare abilities, even if he has always led the same tedious existence as everyone else. I am the kind of man who gets up with the sun to make sure that reality is not going to triumph over logic and order (as I've noticed it has a tendency to do when I'm not there; this is, in fact, the essence of my job – not allowing reality to ruin my plans), so I savoured the sweetness of getting up so late, when everyone who had to work was already absorbed by their tasks. I saw my contemporaries walking down the street, briefcases in hand; I saw them in the backs of taxis or behind the wheels of cars. Two young women moved behind the windows of the building opposite, phones to their ears. I felt a vague pity for all these people. I pitied their indifference to the world's beauty, and the fact that – at that moment – nothing sublime had just happened to them. I forgot that, the next day, I would once again be exactly like them: just as servile, or perhaps even more so.

The fact that I had spent the night giving pleasure to a woman – an incredible pleasure, many times over (and for the first time, I think, in my entire life – at over forty years old) – was not, as you can imagine, unconnected to the intoxication I felt. The euphoria that filled me had destroyed the parasites that had recently been undermining my self-esteem, never very solid at the best of times. I saw myself objectively as someone of value, whereas often I feel bogged down in myself as in a soft and spongy substance, absurdly repetitive and monotonous, flat and bland in my own eyes. I was happy, that morning, to be able to think of myself as something as important as the construction manager of the highest tower in France (clearly, if you think about it for a few minutes, I have a job that puts me at the fore-front of my profession), which, because of the oppressive complexity of each day's work, I had not thought about in such an ego-boosting light for a long time. Waking that morning in the room of my Mayfair hotel, I felt I had rediscovered a signifi-cant part of my freshness and my truth.

Who said cheating on your wife was reprehensible? Could something considered immoral have such beneficial effects on your morale? That morning, it seemed to me that, in certain cir-cumstances, it should be regarded as a duty to yourself to take little breaks of this kind, so beautiful and precious that they become sacred – the very opposite of all preconceived ideas of indignity or baseness. I had not felt so good for a long time. Sitting on this chair and letting my body relive the last few hours made me feel I was looking at a sunlit landscape after months of rain and cloud (whereas recently, if you'd asked me, I would have said I was feeling fine – 'Not too bad at all. I've been a lot worse,' I would even have specified). What I had experienced with Victoria was already, for me, surrounded by a magnetic aura. It had not yet been sanctified by time or perspective, but I knew that this night would remain one of the most memorable of my life. I knew I would regularly return to these images as a source of strength or a reminder of who I was. All the more so as I would never see this woman again: she would have to content herself with a place in my memory as an icon of sex and voraciousness, an ideal conception of blistering, passionate womanhood.

I saw dark green lampposts, brick facades with white windows, a telephone box, sparse traffic and lots of people on the pavements. On the other side of the street, there was an antique shop of the kind I love, full of furniture, statues, paintings and mirrors. I decided I would go and have a look after I'd eaten.

The waiter who came to serve me said he was sorry, but – as it was already too late for breakfast, yet still a bit too early for lunch – he would not be able to provide me with the scrambled eggs I was dreaming about. I had to make do with a very bad coffee, sweetened by a few sugar cubes. Physically, I felt a bit weak. Not only had I slept for barely three hours (it had taken me a while to fall asleep after Victoria left), but all I'd eaten the previous evening was a dozen oysters and part of a chocolate mousse.

The light in London that day – golden and metaphorical – seemed like the city's reflection of my happiness. This strange blaze gave a peculiar charge to the people I saw walking past, as if each of them were at the very edge of their self, on the verge of discovering a truth of the greatest importance about their destiny. But all those people filing past my eyes in the imminence of their resurrection did not know it yet. Only my bliss allowed me to glimpse it for them. I wanted to leap on to the pavement and tell each of them about the depth of feeling in existence, to tell them how certain I was that what had just happened in my life could happen to them too – if only they could stop withdrawing into themselves, being blind and fearful; if only they could decide to look around and open themselves up to others. 'Look! Can't you see this light?' I wanted to whisper to every woman I saw. 'The world is magical – make the most of it. Wake up! It's possible to be happy and give each other happiness. I experienced it myself last night. I spent an unforgettable night with one of you, one of the most important nights in the history of humanity. Live! It is essential that you start living again!' I kept pinching my cock, which felt both tender and titillated. Because I hadn't come, the pleasure I had experienced had not been transformed into an orgasm; everything was still inside me, begging to be released. I decided I would have to go and masturbate in the hotel toilets before leaving: if I didn't, there was a good chance I wouldn't be able to concentrate on anything – particularly on the works of art I would see in the museum.

That was when I received a text from Victoria, asking if I'd woken up. She told me that the night we'd spent together had been unforgettable.

Another text arrived a few seconds later, saying that this beautiful autumn light had put her in a wonderful mood: she was thrilled at the prospect of the lunchtime walk she was going to take.

I removed Victoria's second message from the screen and asked the waiter for a second very bad coffee. (I'd asked for a double espresso, but was informed that, at this time of day, there was no one around who knew how to make the coffee machine work.)

Hesitant, I wondered what I should do. My Eurostar left London late afternoon. I no longer felt like going to the British Museum; perhaps I would walk in the park or visit the Tate Modern building, converted by Herzog & de Meuron. I picked up my phone and began replying to Victoria's two messages.

And that is how, in life, you can choose a path without realizing it. You take a few seemingly harmless steps without noticing that they are the beginning of a path, without understanding that the first step you take always leads you in one particular direction. While you tap out texts on the keyboard of your smartphone, producing words and replies and pensive smileys, you see before you only the emptiness of the unknown, the blank space of what has not yet happened. You perceive nothing but your own energy. Yet all you need do is turn around and you can measure the distance you have travelled – and realize that you are, already, a long way from your starting point. At the same time, you understand that it would be difficult to return to your initial situation without an uncompromising effort, a drastic decision, or a brutal retraction.

When I was a child, I would sometimes let the mistral blow my inflatable dinghy far from the beach. I would watch the vast sky and listen to the waves lap against the rubber sides. I was absorbed by this blue expanse that seemed to erase the very concept of human time and make of me a tiny piece of eternity, gently rocked by the chance movements of the sea. The randomness of these undulations made clear our planet's solitude amid the infinity of the cosmos; the waves that rocked me made me feel certain that man has nothing to do with the physical laws governing matter. There was nothing human in this sky through which I spread. I was alone. The very principle of human life had vanished from my thoughts. It was the machinery of the universe that I could hear lapping against the rubber hull – *plock, plock, plock* – like an icy, random, ironic, unpredictable ticking. When I had to lift my head again (after, I imagine now, the passing of quite some time), I saw that the wind had created an astounding distance between the shore and my boat – a fact unrevealed by a single clue during that long dialogue with the motionless sky. If I looked carefully at the beach (the holiday-makers were now no larger than insects), I could just make out the figure of my mother standing at the water's edge. I saw her making wild, despairing gestures urging me to return. Watching her child being sucked towards an indifferent horizon, she panicked.

A lookout gesticulating on the shore: that is the image that comes to mind when I think about what can happen to us when we drift far from our lives, losing our thoughts in a space as boundless and featureless as an empty sky. Lying in a gentle, carefree daydream, rocked by the laws of lovers' movements, you feel like forgetting the world; you feel like listening only to the tick-tick-tick of your destiny lapping against the hull of a situation as beautiful as it is timeless: boy meets girl, they desire each other, they seduce each other, they wish to make love . . . little waves that creep under our boat and lift our hearts.

So it was that at the end of a chance exchange of texts in which we discussed a café, kisses, snacks and a lunchtime walk in London, I was sent this command: 'Stay where you are – I'll be there in fifteen minutes.' Not that I felt the slightest desire to dissuade Victoria from meeting me. 'OK, I won't move. See you very soon,' I replied, surprising myself with this snap response (I knew that 'OK' had utterly broken every resolution I'd made, including my most precious principle). And then it was done: I saw the envelope containing my message fly on wings away from the screen. The thing I had wished to avoid had now happened: I was moving away from the shore while staring at the vastness of the sky. Had I come back to myself at that moment, I would have seen myself on the shore, disapproving and panic-stricken, making wild gestures urging myself to return. But I refused to accept that I was entering into a new situation – just like, as a child, I had loved the dizzying unconcern I felt when I kept postponing the moment I had to check my position with regard to the coast. I had a hard-on again. I wanted to feel Victoria's ample breasts in my hands; I wanted to see her legs in daylight; I wanted to want her, seeing her calves amid other legs. I wanted to feel the impact of her face on my consciousness again. I wanted to remember the way her muscles contracted around my cock. I wanted to tell her that our night was the most beautiful I had ever known; I wanted to see a film of tears in her eyes as she stared at my face and thought about those words. I had already begun to need her.

Victoria arrived, radiant and overwhelming, her feet shod in black high heels, her legs sheathed in flesh-coloured stockings. She sat opposite me and beamed. She didn't kiss me, but placed her hand on mine. We tried to make conversation but our bodies were already communicating secrets beyond the comprehension of any language. Everything we said made us sound like travellers who have missed their train and are staring around wearily at the deserted platform: 'Excuse me, I'm sorry, what did you . . . ? You asked me something . . .'

'Me? You're asking me if I asked you something?' I replied, smiling.

'Yes, if you asked me something, just now. I think I did. What did you say to me?' We lost ourselves in the other's gaze. We were like two figures, one traced from the other. She was a mental vision that consumed me. I lost myself in this image as in a boundless thought. 'What I said to you . . . when?'

'Just now. Just a second ago!' she said. 'Stop it! Have you forgotten?' I felt Victoria's knee moving under the table, pressing against mine; it confessed to me the desire she felt to be in my arms again. The expression in her eyes translated this into a more articulate language than her knee (or our brains) was able to master. 'Let's go. I can't stand this any longer. I have to kiss you,' she told me. 'We absolutely have to make love.'

'Where do you want us to go? To your place?'

'No, there's no time.' She looked at her watch while she thought. 'I've got a meeting in forty-five minutes. I could probably turn up a bit late; I'd just have to warn my assistant . . .' She lifted her face to reveal a smile that slowly faded after she finished this sentence. 'I think I'm going to get a hotel room. We can make love in a hotel room – now, straight away. Come on, get your things. You're coming with me.'

Victoria went to the reception desk. I waited for her a bit further away in the lobby, though my eyes never left her. In that moment, I was aware that I was living through a situation of exhilarating beauty. I could not believe that such a thing could happen to me, particularly with the woman who was leaning on the counter, hips gently swaying, taking back her credit card and putting it away in her handbag. I wanted to plunge my cock between her buttocks, holding her firmly by the hips – standing up, behind her, against a wall, in the scent of her loosened hair . . . I practically had to repeat it to myself in order to believe it: I know a woman who can obey the urgings of her desire by renting a four-star hotel room for thirty minutes. I could see the authority of her impact reflected for an instant in the receptionist's face as he handed her some papers; she must have looked at him with an erotic gleam in her eyes – a gleam of impatience.

(I could see Victoria only from behind and afar, my eyes dazzled by this extraordinary scene.) A young blonde woman was moving towards the reception accompanied by a heavily built man, but Victoria easily overshadowed the seduction of this superficial sylph. Not even in my wildest dreams had I ever imagined that such a scene could actually happen one day. Victoria turns away from the counter and, just avoiding the fat man who is about to bump into her, I see her lips form the phrase, 'Excuse me.' She comes towards me, looking embarrassed. I can tell she's nervous: I suppose this is the first time she has rented a room at lunchtime, without any luggage, for a very brief duration – without being able to conceal the purpose of this room from the receptionist. 'The hotel was full. I had to explain to him that I only needed it for a short while . . . I think I blushed when he understood why I absolutely needed this room,' Victoria told me as she took my arm. We walked towards the lifts. All I heard now were whispers mixed with cheerful laughter: 'My God, what is happening to me? You see what I'm capable of, because of you . . .'

'I think it's wonderful. Believe me, Victoria, I find it wonderful,' I tell her, pressing the call button. 'But if the hotel was full, how did you . . . ?'

'I booked a suite.'

'A suite? We've got a suite?'

'What can I say? We only live once! It was the only room available, and only if we leave it before evening. I didn't know where to look when I agreed that we'd be out by this evening – and even by three o'clock if they needed.' Victoria puts her head on my shoulder and starts laughing – 'If you'd seen his face when I told him that . . .' – and we get into the lift. 'Fifth floor, quickly!' she tells me, looking at the room number on the card. The lift doors close as I slide my tongue between Victoria's lips, and she is caressing my balls when, five floors later, the lift doors open again, as softly and silently as her fingers on my trousers.

I was hungry and my head was spinning, and I couldn't get a hard-on. Victoria had rained minibar snacks over my body – we'd eaten chocolate bars and biscuits with cheese – and she'd attempted to revive my erection with her mouth, but without success. In any case, now that my weakness had reappeared, the fear of failure it brought with it meant that my prospects of resurrection seemed unlikely. I began to think that I should have contented myself with the memory of our night together. I made Victoria come with my tongue (her pubic hairs were silky, with blonde highlights; she had pale pink lips and a bulging clitoris that she loved me to take between my teeth; she choked and gasped while holding tight to my wrists; she yelled at the climax, burying her face in the pillow) and then we got dressed. Our thirty minutes had elapsed long ago; we were surely closer to sixty now.

'Will we see each other again?' she asked me.

'Do you really think there's any need to ask that question?' I said, surprised. Victoria smiled at me while she put her stockings on. 'Yes, you're right,' she replied. I watched her slide the opening of her skirt up over the impressive mass of her hips, fasten it over her flat stomach, and twist it in order to ensure it was symmetrical. 'I wish you could forget . . . I'm really . . .' I said to Victoria while showing her the snack wrappers on the sheets.

'I adore you,' she replied, touching my shoulder with her hand. 'It's normal: we made love all night, and you told me you didn't eat anything. To be honest, I'd have thought you were a machine if you could . . .'

'When are you coming to Paris?' I interrupted her. We were leaving the room. I closed the door behind me and we walked through the corridor.

'I don't know. Soon. I'll let you know. I leave for Hong Kong in a week, and while I'm there I'll hop over to Vietnam, maybe to Bombay too, and then I come back to London.'

'You seem to spend your life travelling.'

'I'll definitely be in Paris on 4 November. Maybe before, but definitely on the 4th.' I pressed the lift's call button. I watched Victoria as she spoke to me: she looked like a businesswoman again; I could sense that she was thinking more about her meeting than my presence beside her.

'The 4th of November? I'll write that down.'

'Maybe before – I'll let you know. But I know I'll be at a hugely important meeting with the unions on 4 November. It's about the closure of a plant in Lorraine – a bit controversial. What's wrong with this lift?' Victoria said irritably, jabbing a finger at the flashing call button. 'I'll have a pretty tough day – it's maybe not ideal for seeing you, as I might be shattered. But I'm not sure I could resist the chance to spend an evening with you,' she concluded, with a mischievous look.

We exited the lift, and Victoria told the porter that she needed a taxi. Caressing my cheek, she said, 'Take care.' Then, after a brief kiss, she got in the taxi. I glimpsed her face as she gave the driver an address, and then she turned to smile and wave at me through the window's reflections as the car's engine came to life.

I saw a stranger wave goodbye in a conventional way before going to a business meeting. I felt hurt by the speed at which the taxi pulled into the street. At that moment, I noticed, Victoria was looking away from me to check the traffic.

As soon as the taxi had vanished amid the mass of other cars, I was gripped by an intense feeling of anxiety and loneliness. I went to eat lunch on the terrace of the hotel.

Victoria's departure brought my morning's happiness to

a brutal end. The glorious London light now seemed to reach me as if through lattice shutters.

I missed her bitterly. It was unbearable, being separated from her just as I was beginning to live. I wanted to start all over again with the same intensity.

I could taste Victoria's cunt in my mouth. Her body's scent floated in the air. I felt the tip of her clitoris at the end of my tongue. Her face kept invading my thoughts.

I couldn't stop thinking of Victoria leaning on the reception desk. I couldn't stop thinking of her on her hands and knees in front of the large mirror, her brown hair glued to her face. I couldn't stop thinking of her playing with the flower stem on the other side of the white tablecloth at the restaurant the previous evening, and how she smiled each time I touched a petal. I couldn't stop thinking about the square bed with the wrappers of the snacks she'd fed me (naked, kneeling on the mattress) scattered over it like butterflies. I couldn't stop feeling enthralled by the beauty of these images; I was suffering, now that I was outside their radiance, forced to savour them from afar, the way you look at an island from the deck of a boat. I didn't want to go back to my life – I wanted to call Victoria and ask her for another evening together, one more night. I wanted to remain beyond reality for a little longer, to linger in this land I had discovered when I slipped through the opening Victoria made in the shell of my life. I wanted to secretly sneak through that opening again and remain there until tomorrow. But such a thing seemed impossible, without doing something truly stupid. But, then again, why not?

I didn't know what kind of feelings inspired me. I barely knew her; our ways of life were at odds with each other; I disliked certain aspects of her personality. The only thing I was sure about was that this woman had taken me to a place that now yawned like a void in my life.

A waiter came to my table to ask if I was ready to order. I turned my face to him – it must have looked terribly sad – and asked for chicken with mashed potato. 'Something to drink?'

'*Water. Sparkling water. And a beer.*' I looked at the ground in silence. The waiter didn't move. Finally, I asked him: '*What kind of beer do you have?*'

'Carlsberg, Kronenberg . . .'

'Carlsberg,' I interjected. The waiter removed the second plate and the cutlery that went with it, as if I had become a widower between the moment when I sat down and the moment when he came to take my order. He removed the deceased's belongings with great solemnity and delicacy. 'Very well, sir,' he said, bowing gravely, before going to another table and asking the man (who was finishing his meal) if everything was to his satisfaction.

I thought I was going to start crying. A tear appeared – one only – and I let it roll down to my lips, where I licked it away with my tongue.

I had not expected to suffer like this. I had even imagined that the benefits of this stay in London would last for several weeks, that they would give me strength.

The painful situation in which I found myself had sprung up as suddenly as a car accident – Victoria's taxi had run me over.

I spent lunch trying to order my thoughts in such a way that my anxiety would subside. How could I look at my situation to make it seem less like a problem and more beneficial and encouraging? It was a bit like being given an ornament and trying to find the right spot to put it in my apartment; I needed to find whereabouts in my thoughts, and in my imagination, the night I had spent with Victoria would find its place.

I decided I ought to keep texting Victoria until I got back to Paris. Perhaps all I needed was to return to my ordinary life a little less abruptly than was possible in this silent indifference. London has always seemed a hostile city to me – too sprawling and incomprehensible. I didn't know it very well. The sensation of being abandoned here was not good for my anxiety; it aggravated its effects. Once I reached the Gare du Nord, I would have no further need for Victoria; I would return to my usual life without any sadness.

But this new way of thinking spread only a thin, weak light in the gloom of my mood.

I thought perhaps I needed to open these shutters that Victoria had closed so suddenly on my London happiness. I could decree that there was no limit to my desire, no enclosed space darkened by anxiety, but – on the contrary – a wide-open future in which to throw myself; a situation to master; a relationship that was just beginning.

I was removing the bone from my chicken leg when this second idea came to me. A joyful feeling spread through my mind, only to vanish almost immediately under a storm of calamitous thoughts.

There was no way I was going to abandon myself to a romance with this woman. I had to resist: that was essential, and I knew it. I lifted the glass of beer to my lips. The businessman who had been sitting at the table next to mine smiled at me as he walked away from the terrace.

So perhaps, without going so far as to remove all limitations, I could reopen those shutters once in a while to let a little seduction and unpredictability into my life, a little flavour of romance and mystery? Would I be able to do that without ending up in the horrors of a double life, without letting my feelings for Victoria become all-consuming?

I realized that the only way I could bring some joy back to my mind was to plan a final rendezvous with her. I felt a thrill at the idea of meeting Victoria in early November in a Parisian hotel, secretly, in the evening, with an autumn rain falling on the passers-by. Heavy curtains, moody lighting, a mirror hanging over a mantelpiece, our bodies on a large bed . . . I would part the curtains to look down at the shell-like umbrellas in the night's illumination: there would be traces of raindrops creeping sideways across the window, glimmering in the light from the streetlamps. We would make love in secret, separated from the world, suspended in the desire to become unreachable; we would be concealed in an unsuspected corner of the great city, unbeknown to our respective real lives, professional and familial. I saw us as two burglars, hidden in a palatial apartment after we had robbed a safe, caressing amid the sparkle of diamonds and precious stones. Those hours would be all the more beautiful for their rarity, transience, danger, their concealment from authorities who hate being cheated: spouses and bosses. Victoria contained within her, like a kernel, this fantasy of the sorceress who appears as if by magic to fulfil her passionate desire to be looked at, to be celebrated, to be consoled and glorified, before disappearing again for an unforeseeable length of time. So it was that she had allowed me to admire her when we saw each other in the shopping centre. It was also in this dazzling fantasy world that she had shown herself to me during the last few hours.

A pretty woman in lace-up boots walked past on the pavement, her beauty diaphanous and typically British.

I was having trouble imagining myself in this role of regular lover; it presupposes a constant connection with the woman you are in love with, ongoing discussions, the need to make up elaborate lies; I couldn't see myself carrying the weight of this extra life on my shoulders. But, above all, would Victoria agree to subject herself to an arrangement of this kind – secret and sporadic, with a man who (she would soon find out) was not available?

How would she react when she learned that she had made love with a married man? A woman like Victoria would never agree to restrict our relationship to a series of discreet meetings in hotels.

I was lifting the glass of beer to my lips when I remembered the suspicion I'd had early that morning: she wanted a baby. This thought had left my mind earlier when we went up to the room. I smiled at the realization that the idea of my fertility had already cost her an expensive dinner and a suite in a four-star hotel – with not a drop of semen in return. She must hate me. At the very least, she must be questioning the advisability of choosing me as her stud.

I raised my hand to get the waiter's attention. I wanted a strong double espresso.

I hung about all afternoon. I didn't feel like doing anything, so I just killed time.

I started sending emails, even though I'd told all my colleagues that I was going to stay in London for an extra day. 'I'm taking the day off, so don't expect any news from me,' I'd told my assistant in the euphoria of my departure. 'Thank God – it's about time!' Caroline replied, returning my smile. 'Finally, we'll be able to breathe for twenty-four hours.' And now I was asking her questions about problems I'd left hanging. Sensing a human presence at the other end of my smartphone was a bit like clinging to a lifebuoy while swimming far from the shore; for a few minutes, I stroked the soft wet plastic that floated on the waves. Then the conversation ended with a pleasant text from Caroline: 'See you tomorrow. Have a nice day in London.'

I lay down in the middle of Hyde Park. I had stomach cramps.

I was upset that I hadn't heard from Victoria. She must have forgotten me amid all her professional tasks. I tried to reason with myself: I knew she had a meeting, that she had to work, but

I couldn't get over the suspicion that thinking about me now filled her with doubts.

I began to think again about the objective my bosses had set me a few weeks earlier at a special meeting. I had to find a way to reduce the delay – to reduce it as quickly as possible, and ideally to end up ahead of schedule. 'If you're well ahead of schedule, that could be very useful for us afterwards, if you see what I mean, David,' said the director of the property development firm (ranked third in the world). The memory of this phrase made me shudder. During my relatively brief time with Victoria, she had been enough to overshadow this, but now she had left my life again, the memory returned in all its cruelty: of the terrifying difficulties of achieving this objective. That same man had told me to use all possible means to overcome the difficulties I would encounter – as long as it didn't affect the budget: 'I want things to be clear between us. It's essential that you reduce this two-month delay. But don't come to me afterwards and say that it's going to cost us God knows how many thousand euros . . . Understood? Are we agreed? Until next time, then. Good luck. I'll let you sort out the details with Daniel and Jean-François,' he said while standing up (he'd put his hand to his ear to imitate a telephone while he looked at Jean-François, and the latter had nodded briefly, while closing his eyes, in a reassuring and determined way), and then he left. Daniel and Jean-François are my direct superiors; they are the real bosses, but I'm the one on the ground, so I am the one who is informed of the (theoretically sound) decisions that have been taken in the comfort of a large office in Avenue Montaigne. Which means, of course, that the 'means' mentioned by this man will be my own means – and nothing but my own means. In other words, my energy, my convictions, my imagination, my tenacity, my persuasive abilities, the teams I have to motivate, my life force and my drive – the thing inside a man that makes his heart beat, and that would soon have to be increased in order to maintain the industrial pulse of an immense machine: the construction site of a fifty-storey tower that is well behind schedule. I tore off a blade of grass with my teeth and chewed it, grinding its fibres with my molars. My eyes were closed. The taste of the grass mixed with the taste of Victoria's cunt that lingered on my breath, acrid and intense, medicinal in its bitterness.

The next day, as I had anticipated, I felt absolutely fine. My memories of that stay in London were dreamlike and sublime. Images of pleasure moved through my entire body like a brood of rare birds; soft-feathered, their wingbeats caressed my stomach. Now that I was back in Paris, I understood that the anguish I had felt the day before had been the consequence of an unbearable wrench: barely had I met Victoria when I'd had to relinquish her.

This day back at work began with a somewhat stormy meeting, during which I spoke with an eloquence beyond my usual capabilities. Dominique came up to me afterwards and told me how impressed he'd been by my contribution; he asked me where this sudden mix of authority and diplomacy had come from. 'You were hitting them and stroking them at the same time. Jesus! How did you do it?' I smiled at him. I'd just put a fifty-centime coin in the coffee machine; that morning, I wanted work on the Jupiter Tower to progress so quickly that everyone in the business would have to consider David Kolski, from this moment on, as the greatest construction manager in Europe – such was my state of mind at that moment. 'I have my secrets,' I replied, taking my espresso from the machine. 'Do you want a coffee?'

'No thanks, I'm fine. But before the meeting, I was thinking that we'd never manage to reconcile the two sides, that this conflict would ruin our lives. But . . . fuck me, how did you do it?'

'I'll tell you my secret one day, in exchange for something else.'

'You fucker – that's you all over! In exchange for something else . . .'

'What I do know is that I feel great.'

I knew perfectly well where this strength had come from: it had come from thoughts of Victoria, and in particular from the pleasure that ran through me every time I let myself think about the possibility that we would see each other again on 4 November, from the pure intoxication that illuminated my mind in flashes at the most unexpected moments. So it was that – sitting on the steps of the outside stairs that cover the three storeys of the prefabricated building that houses the contractors' offices (on a vacant lot surrounded by a hotel, a concrete car park and office buildings, about 100 metres from the Jupiter Tower) – I felt the desire to thank Victoria for these shoots of happiness that she had given me. Buttocks numbed by the coldness of the galvanized metal in these shortening October days, I impulsively wrote a few lines on my laptop: 'What banal, disciplined, submissive failures they seemed to me – like slaves to luxury – all those people around me yesterday evening on the Eurostar! You can see that they're not really living, that they're letting their lives drain away in reality like a tap leaking water into a sink. They were all working, reading documents, sending emails, checking notes, highlighting words with marker pens, calculating commissions . . . I saw them absorbed in the Excel tables on their screens, leafing through business documents illustrated with photographs of unknown things (a man sitting next to me was looking at images on his computer of abstractly shaped metal objects that I thought must have been parts from a nuclear power station) while I felt incapable of doing anything other than thinking about you, your pussy, your eyes, your breasts, your hands, your lips, your ears, your wrists – all these bits of flesh and blood that now feed my desire. I had to fight against the urge to stroke my cock, which was hard . . . Images of our night together flashed through my mind with the same endless intensity as the landscape on the other side of the windows. I've just remembered that the clock is ticking: I'm writing this somewhat lyrical message on my laptop and hoping that it is not ridiculous to express, unedited, these feelings inspired by the memory of a woman I'm missing. You are able to make me forget the existence of this construction site: I have a meeting in three minutes and I have to hurry . . . I'll finish by telling you that I am stunned by what your body has done to mine.'

That same evening, just before midnight, as I was about to get into bed, I received the following reply from Victoria. I sat on the sofa in the sitting room to read it: 'Finally I have a little time, in this completely insane day, to surrender myself to the effects your email had on me. Until Friday, I will be leading a seminar for my whole worldwide Human Resources team. The schedule is intense. Imagine the shock I got when I found your email – so utterly unrelated to what I was doing – on my BlackBerry. I read it avidly during the first break in the meeting, and I could hardly stand up for the sudden desire I felt, like an intense necessity. It all swam together in my head: our night together, the glasses of champagne, the pleasures of making love with you and still wanting to so much, again and again, again and again, each time I think about it.

'It is 10.30 p.m. and I am nestled comfortably in bed with all my pillows. I spent the day, which seemed to go on for ever, fighting back my desire to reply to your words; I felt like I was a hostage to my professional position. Imagine – I have to look after more than twenty heads of Human Resources who have travelled from all over the world for this three-day seminar that I'm running. My thoughts are jumbled, barely organized. You must see, in that disorder, the strength of my desire, the panic in my senses, the pleasure I feel at having finally had the time to tell you: again, again, again . . .'

I wrote a fairly long message to Victoria, ending with the words: 'I adored what you revealed of yourself in our intimacy, and the way in which this unknown woman offered me her body and took mine. The way we feel about each other . . . I find it pretty staggering that we sensed that immediately, instinctively, in a shopping centre, in the middle of a crowd. I'll continue this email a bit later because I still have many things to tell you. With tender kisses . . .'

Victoria replied fairly briefly the next day. I told myself that her Friday must be madly busy because of her seminar. I went home quite late. In my car, I heard the weather forecast on the radio: the weekend was meant to be sunny. It was raining now, however, so I switched the windscreen wipers on. I was looking forward to the time I was about to spend with my daughters.

On Saturday we went to the Fontainebleau forest to climb rocks and pick up chestnuts. We wore wellies. I love walking in the dead leaves and damp grass of autumn. At one point Vivienne disappeared into ferns so huge that their leaves hid her completely; she moved around inside this space, as if in a crypt, and I had no idea where she was; Sylvie and I pretended we were worried until, unable to contain herself any longer, Vivienne burst into hysterical laughter.

Salomé wanted to come with me to the video store that afternoon. Sylvie wanted a comedy we'd be able to watch the beginning of with the girls. I couldn't choose. We looked over the shelf displays, and from time to time we picked up a DVD, examined the illustration and read the blurb on the back.

'I'm sure this is a good film,' I told Salomé.

'But, Daddy, we already decided that we were going to get *The Wizard of Oz*. You're not going to do the same thing Mummy does!'

'What do you mean by that?'

'You know what I'm talking about. Not being able to choose . . . spending twenty minutes hesitating between two things . . .'

'No, don't worry, there's no chance I'll become like her — otherwise my job would be a nightmare. Hey, look at this, it's a cinematic masterpiece.' I give Salomé the DVD: she takes it, looks at it, gives it back to me. 'Why would your life be a nightmare if you had the same thing as Mummy?'

'Because my job consists of making quick decisions. So, if I didn't know what to do, or what to choose, each time a problem . . . and if I had to spend twenty minutes . . . you can imagine! Often I have to make a decision before the question is even put to me: that's called anticipating. So, ideally, I would answer the questions twenty minutes before they've been asked.'

'Oh, really? Well, not tonight, apparently,' says Salomé ironically.

'I am a bit better on the building site. Anyway, why are you talking about that?'

'About what?'

'About Mummy — about her taking twenty minutes to . . .'

'Because it's getting worse and worse.'

'I really don't think so.'

'I'm telling you it's getting worse and worse. I don't know, but I think she's going to end up . . .' I wait for Salomé to finish her sentence while watching her from the side — but she never finishes her sentence. While we are talking, she distractedly runs a finger over the DVD boxes displayed on the walls. I watch her fingernail following the contours of faces and the letters of the titles written on the boxes, filling them with thoughts, drawing mysterious patterns. 'That she's going to end up doing what?'

'I don't know.'

'Stop doing that with your finger. Look at me.' Salomé turns her face to mine. 'What do you mean, you don't know?'

'I don't know how it's going to end, but she's driving me crazy.'

We continue to let our eyes drift over the DVDs on the wall. For a few minutes, we don't speak.

'What about that?' I ask Salomé. 'Do you think it's any good?' I show her the DVD; she shakes her head. 'All right, I'll take your word for it. It sounded good to me.' I put the box back on the shelf. 'What makes you say that it's going to end badly? She's always had trouble choosing, sure. She often tends to hesitate – I agree. But . . . that's part of who she is, it's part of her charm . . .'

'Her charm? You're kidding . . .' Salomé says, tapping rhythmically with two fingers on Nicole Kidman's forehead. 'It's obvious you've never been to the supermarket with her. It's a nightmare. It kills me, seriously – I can't stand it any more . . .'

'You're worrying about nothing, Salomé.'

'It's like going shopping with a madwoman. She's constantly picking things up and then changing her mind, turning back and putting them back on the shelf . . .'

'You're exaggerating a bit, aren't you?'

'Not at all. The other day . . .'

'Mummy's fine. I'm telling you, she's fine. Look, we're going to take this film.'

'You're crazy – it's not fine!'

'Why, you don't like it?'

'Not that! Yes, it's fine – it's not bad. But I've seen it loads of times, like . . . I don't know . . . 20 million other French people!'

'But I haven't seen it. I'm the only French person who's never seen it. This evening, I would like to see it. This is the film I was looking for. But you clearly don't agree . . .'

All four of us were sitting in the bedroom after dinner to watch *The Wizard of Oz*. Vivienne was in the middle as usual – she had wanted to nuzzle against a man's body and a woman's body, to feel the hairiness of my thighs on one side and the softness of her mother on the other – while Salomé was stretched out at our feet across the bed, lying on her stomach and her elbows. Sylvie was surprised that we came back with the DVD of *The Wizard of Oz* when she had asked for a straightforward comedy; I pointed out that it had been Salomé's idea, and that it had seemed a good one to me – a film that the children could watch in its entirety rather than just the first twenty minutes. My post-London euphoria had not left me, and my two daughters had quickly understood how they could take advantage of it: as soon as I started negotiating with their mother, they ran towards me so I could take them in my arms, crying out, 'Daddy! Daddy! Thank you, Daddy!' Sylvie's initial reaction, however, was to say no – 'They're tired. They've had a tough week. They need to rest' – a verdict met with a breaking wave of hops and jumps either side of me. I'd had to hold Sylvie tightly, pressing my joy-filled body against her, before we could all reach agreement. 'All right, all right,' she capitulated to our happy mood, 'but only because it's you.' And so, snug in the feel-good comfort of the pillows around our heads (except for Salomé, whose face, in profile, flickered in the darkness under the lights of the TV screen), we watched *The Wizard of Oz*, and Vivienne's sighs of wonder were like white birds flying up from a lake in the moonlight. I spent the evening imagining Victoria's body superimposed on the film's images. It was a bit like drawing inspiration from two sources at the same time – one of them constant, fluid, developed, the other fragmentary, repetitive, obsessive. The second source, with its bursts of desire and memory, resembled more closely what can be achieved with cinema than the first one – that forties classic that chugged through our evening at the same steady speed as a train.

I didn't hear from Victoria until the next day. I had woken late, mowed the lawn, changed the plug on a lamp, and begun reading a book that was getting a lot of press attention. Vivienne was so desperate to go to the park – where she hoped to see a boy (on whom, I presumed, she'd developed a crush) – that I ended up agreeing; I was not really in a position to deny her on that particular subject. Sitting on a bench, I watched her whizzing down the metal slope of a slide, over and over again, while surveying the park entrance – because the boy she wanted to see was not there. I talked for a few minutes with the father of a little girl that Vivienne knew: he worked in IT, and he was asking me about my job as construction manager. He knew about the existence of the Jupiter Tower through his daughter (Vivienne told anyone who would listen that her father was building the highest, most complex and strangest-shaped skyscraper in the world: a concrete lightning bolt), but also through a television report that many other people had seen – quite a few had told me about it during the days that followed its showing on the eight o'clock news on France 2 (because during this report, there was a brief shot of my face, as I talked about the difficulties of overhangs: 'If we manage to construct this tower . . . we'll be able to say that, ultimately, we did well, even if it was a close shave . . . but quite often I wonder if we're really up to the task,' I had concluded, laughing; back then, I had enjoyed emphasizing the building's complexity, because I thought we would easily overcome our difficulties. Now that we're in the shit, this phrase resonates gloomily in my memory). 'It's a beautiful building, but from what I've heard, not easy to build – not easy at all!' said this affable man who was standing next to me. And it was at that moment, about 6 p.m., that my BlackBerry vibrated. I took it out of my coat pocket and saw that Victoria had just sent me an email with an attachment. All the message said was: 'Some Sunday thoughts from Victoria.' I turned towards the man I'd been talking to (he'd just said something about the Jupiter Tower's overhangs) and asked him to excuse me for a minute ('An emergency. You see, even on Sundays.' 'Of course, go ahead, that's no problem. I'll see you later,' he replied) and I sat on another bench. 'Vivienne!' I called out. 'I'm here, on this bench – don't worry!' My daughter smiled at me briefly, then got back to building her castle: the only castle in the sandpit to be higher than it was wide. She was crouching, feet on the ground. I found her utterly gorgeous. She was trying to smooth the surface of an oblong construction with her hands; the castle might have resembled a sex toy, but it was probably intended to be what her father the hero spent most of his time doing, far from her.

It was nice here in this park. The weather was good, the light soft. I opened the attachment and it appeared on the screen.

I noticed that it was entitled 'Meeting Minutes'.

I should point out now that this heading would be on most of the pieces of writing I would receive after this (because Victoria would soon get into the habit of spontaneously sending me long extracts from her private diary), which means she was using the template of her job as head of Human Resources to write about her personal life: the template 'Meeting Minutes'. She was probably doing this out of convenience, or because she wished to conceal her most secret thoughts behind the facade of a professional document, but it made a strange impression on me: reading these pages, I was never able to get away from the thought that they had been written by an executive of a large industrial group with offices in twenty countries – and I quickly understood that Victoria couldn't get away from this thought either. She lived this way, constantly and intensely, and that is perhaps why she proved so determined when it came to romantic relations: she knew exactly what she wanted, and had trouble understanding why she shouldn't treat her desires as a woman in the same radical way as her professional projects. The title 'Meeting Minutes' would, for me, always signify this: that her private life was irresistibly mixed up with her professional life. The times and places assigned to each of these two spheres were wholly interchangeable, and even she found it extremely difficult to separate the private woman from the woman of power. The performance of her job necessitated such an intermingling of mind and technique, sincerity and calculation, the truth of her being with the lies of the company, that these two extremes, united in her, ended up forming a single entity – the entity Victoria de Winter. I felt it at each of our meetings. There was the private woman on one side, the Kiloffer executive on the other, and the concept Victoria de Winter that resulted from the fusion of the two – powerful, determined, mobile, complex, sexual and passionate. It was this fusion that had struck me in the shopping centre; it was this fusion with whom I'd eaten dinner and spent the night; it was this fusion who negotiated with the unions; it was this fusion whom I held in my arms each time she came to see me in Paris.

'Meeting Minutes

'Subject: Sunday 16 October

'Author: Me

'Recipients: You, perhaps

'Sunday – a wonderful sunny October day. I've just finished my homework, and the sunlight is streaming into the kitchen where I'm sitting.

'I am deliciously exhausted. I swam this morning for more

than an hour, and my muscles are still warm and twitching. I love this feeling.

'A cup of coffee in my hand, a bar of chocolate in my mouth (I admit it: I do have a sweet tooth), *The Marriage of Figaro* in the background. I'm getting ready for the opera, which I'll go to see on Saturday in Paris.'

I stopped reading for a moment to check where Vivienne was.

I was surprised that Victoria was telling me about an opera she was going to see in Paris a few days from now: she'd told me before that she wouldn't be back in France until 4 November.

'I enjoy the music more when I have soaked up the libretto, the melodies, the twists and turns of the plot. I know some of these arias almost by heart: I have listened to Mozart since I was a little girl – he is an old friend – and I have been listening to this opera non-stop since last week.'

Having finished her tower, Vivienne was climbing the bars of an iron cage.

So, Victoria listened to Mozart operas on Sundays in her apartment, after exercising in an ultra-posh sports club, filled with London's high society.

I have never been to the opera. For me, if there is one method for separating people according to their social extraction and cultural background, it is classical music. In that sense, it was not irrelevant that Victoria had chosen to begin the first piece of writing she sent me with a description of her pursuits as a music-lover. Whether or not she was aware of the meanings this could have for a man like me, she was nonetheless asserting a territory, a difference and an identity – and, indeed, nothing was more suggestive of Victoria's actual power than the fact that she listened to *The Marriage of Figaro* at home. Not only was she from the upper bourgeoisie, but she enjoyed the privilege of belonging to the administration council of a publicly listed industrial multinational (which, as she had already explained to me, was not the case for all heads of Human Resources), and – quite naturally – she delighted in learning by heart the arias she had listened to since childhood. All of this was logical; it seemed to me to have an indisputable coherence and even a kind of artistic perfection. I might have felt belittled by this demonstration of superiority (and, indeed, my initial reaction was to feel excluded by the naturalness of this idyllic image, so distant from what my cultural background allows me to appreciate), but there was something incredibly sweet in Victoria's efforts to express her intimacy. I felt that she wanted to welcome me into it, that she was opening up her world to me as she had opened up her body – and the intoxication this caused me was all the more profound because the world in which she moved seemed so distant from mine; as unreachable and mysterious as a mountain glimpsed through mist.

I imagined Victoria in sweatpants – or in a negligee – padding through her apartment, coffee in hand. I imagined a vast and light-filled space, with contemporary furniture mixed up with antiques and eighteenth-century paintings; a loft in a factory renovated by an architect, on the banks of the Thames. She nibbled on her chocolate bar while singing the arias she had just learned by heart. She collapsed on a leather sofa and sent her slippers flying on the polished cement floor.

Vivienne was trying to get her spade back from a little boy who'd borrowed it when she was in the iron cage. Each of them was holding on to an end of it with unwavering determination and pulling hard. I sensed that the little boy was about to start crying. 'Vivienne!' I called out. 'Let him have the spade. You've got the rake. He'll give it back to you later!'

'But, Daddy, it's not his spade! It's mine! I need it!'

'He'll give it back to you in a minute – use the rake.

Be nice . . . please.' And I saw my Vivienne surrender her spade to the little boy.

I turned my eyes back to the screen and began reading where I'd left off:

'I'm going to go to my office soon and prepare a few files so that my team can keep working while I'm away next week. I know that I'm going to send you this while I'm there. I've worked out the reason for your silence this weekend. That's fine with me, and further underlines what a stranger you are to me. I know absolutely nothing about you.'

I stopped reading, and lifted my head. My gaze fell upon Vivienne, crouching in the middle of the sandpit. She was flattening the top of the sandcastle she'd just made with her bucket.

I could still feel the shock wave caused by the words I'd just read. It lit up each of my organs with a specific and delicious sensation, each one distinguished by the subtlest nuances of happiness and pleasure.

Victoria had guessed that I was married; she had guessed that I had children. Perhaps she had even guessed that I was reading her words in a park while tenderly watching my youngest daughter crouching in a sandpit. And Victoria calmly told me – with a naturalness as staggering as that with which she had undressed in front of me on our first night in London – that this reality she had 'worked out' was not a problem for her. She accepted it.

That was the meaning of this message she had written for me and posted under the strange title 'Meeting Minutes': she accepted me as I was.

I finished reading her letter: 'It is always intimidating to get to know someone new and to discover an unknown world, with things you can love and understand, and things you cannot accept.' I lifted my head, deflated: there were things she could not accept . . . but what? What could she be incapable of accepting if she was capable of accepting that I was married? 'Likewise, I wonder how far I will let you go, how much of myself I can reveal. It's a bit comical to talk of "revealing" when we were naked in front of each other a few days ago . . . But that nudity was physical, and took place between two lovers passionately attracted to each other. What about the other nudity – of our beings?'

That was how Victoria's letter ended. I saved it in a newly created file that I named 'Spark.doc' – this is the file I have open now, as I reread the messages I received over ten months. I got up from the bench and walked towards Vivienne. I get up from my chair and walk towards the window to look out at the land-scape: it is no longer raining; night will fall soon; I'm starting to feel a bit hungry. Vivienne looked up at me. 'Shall we go?' I asked her.

'OK, Daddy,' she replied. 'Can we come back?'

'If you want, my darling.'

'I love coming to the park with you,' she added sweetly.

'Me too. I really love coming here with you. I had a wonderful time. We'll come back whenever you want,' I said, crouching down to hug her. Vivienne gathered her belongings. I helped her get her spade back. The little boy had left it on the bench where his mother was sitting (but they had gone while I was reading Victoria's letter: I didn't see them go). We left the park. My car was parked nearby. I put Vivienne in her child seat in the back, and we went home – where, I remember, the smell of a *pot-au-feu* cooked by Sylvie awaited us. I am crying. It is no longer raining outside, but the raindrops that have been streaming down the windows of my hotel room all day have been replaced by tear-drops. I am crying because I have not seen Vivienne for three months and I don't know when I will find the courage to go and see her again – I who have become a monster, I who feel so ugly.

I move away from the window, pick up my coat, leave the room, close the door behind me and walk downstairs. I ask the hotel owner if she knows where I might be able to eat a *pot-au-feu*. My hands are on the edge of the counter. She sits behind it on a chair, below me, in front of a computer. 'A *pot-au-feu*?' she asks me, surprised.

'That's right, a *pot-au-feu*.'

'A *pot-au-feu*, a *pot-au-feu*, a *pot-au-feu*,' she repeats to herself while thinking, one hand on the lower part of her face. 'Er, no, I don't know – I can't think of anywhere. Maybe in Guéret? Or in Aubusson? Yes, more likely at the Lion d'Or in Aubusson.'

'I'll try in Aubusson. You're right – that's a very good idea.'

She looks at me intently for a few seconds.

'Is everything all right? I mean . . . excuse me for saying so, but I get the feeling that . . .'

'That what?' I ask. She doesn't reply. She smiles gently during a long embarrassed silence. 'Why do you ask me that? Do I look like there's something wrong with me?'

'I didn't say that,' she replies kindly, coming out from behind the counter.

We stand before each other with nothing else to say. She watches me affectionately in silence. I have been in her hotel for three months; I pay her at the end of each week with €500 notes that I take from a briefcase hidden under clothes in the wardrobe of my room; it's only natural that she is intrigued by this inexplicable behaviour. The place she runs is a tastefully decorated inn, and most of its clients come for relaxing weekends. So my presence is even more unusual because I am staying here so long, because I am on my own, and because I spend most of my days locked up in my room. On the first evening, when the owner asked me how long I planned to stay, I replied, 'We'll see. Probably a few days. I'll let you know,' before retreating into an icy reserve that warded off all thoughts of attempting a conversation. Only recently had we begun to exchange a few brief words; this is the first time the owner has spoken to me so directly, on a topic as private as my psychological state. In fact, as my face had been shown on television and in certain tabloid newspapers (when Victoria's body was discovered and this heinous crime became a perfect human-interest news story, delighting the journalists who covered it), I was terrified by the idea that someone might suddenly recognize me and, misremembering the story, suspect me of having done something worse than I actually had (or tar me with the sick aura that this story exuded) – so much so that I did everything I could to avoid any situation where I would have to explain to the owners why I had entrenched myself in one of their rooms, locked by a key on a wooden fob with a picture of a wild boar on it.

'Your eyes are red,' the owner says softly. 'It looks like . . .' I see her hesitate.

'Like I've been crying?' She smiles affirmatively. 'I have been crying, it's true. But I feel better now – that's why I'd like a *pot-au-feu*. I'm sure everything will be fine. Everything gets better with time – don't worry,' I say to her as I move away. 'Anyway,' she says, as I walk towards the door. I turn around. 'Anyway, if you need anything, anything at all, really, I . . .' she says without finishing her sentence. Her eyes are as black as night: deep and bright, like a wolf's fur in an old painting, black fur with flashes of light. 'You're very kind, thank you,' I reply.

Beginning with that Sunday in October, we wrote to each other regularly by email and text. One morning, I received a message from Victoria announcing that she had to be in Paris the next day to take part in a conference on Human Resources; she had just decided she would stay the night, rather than returning to London in the evening, so would I like to see her? Perhaps we could plan to eat dinner, have a drink, meet somewhere?

My reply was annoyed, but nevertheless left the door open for a possible meeting ('That's very short notice! I'm an important man, you know – I'm in great demand! Seriously, though, I can't get out of the commitments I've made for tomorrow night: I'm invited to the inauguration of an office building on Avenue Kléber. The architect is counting on my presence – my firm supervised the construction – so it's important that I go. I'm going to try to leave work a bit earlier than normal, so I can see you before this inauguration . . .'). My attitude can be explained by the importance of appearing at this ceremony, but above all by the indecisiveness that Victoria's arrival had suddenly and strangely produced in me. The desire to see her again had haunted my thoughts for days, but now it was an imminent possibility, I no longer knew if I wanted it to happen the next day. I no longer knew if I was ready for this affair to become real; the idea of it gave me the feeling of closing myself in with a lid. When the prospective rendezvous had been in the distant future, I had found delight in the pleasures it promised. The thought of that evening had made me happy, in certain circumstances had even inspired in me a healthy pugnacity; a few incidents had taken place on the construction site that I would not have dealt with so bravely were it not for the feeling that Victoria was beside me. But now that her arrival had become imminent and I had to decide if we were going to meet or not, I panicked. My desire to see her again lost its certainty. I would have liked this evening to be postponed for a week so I could go back to dreaming about it, go back to waiting for it, go back to exchanging messages about how much I was looking forward to it.

Nevertheless, the next day, knowing that all it would take was an 'OK' sent by phone and I would be able to hold her body again, to see her smile close gloriously over my cock again while she looked me in the eyes (I couldn't concentrate on my work. My colleagues talked to me and I had to make them repeat most of what they said. The site was noisy, and I yelled: 'Eh? What? What did you say?' 'I'm saying . . . I said . . . the panel . . . the panel is rotten! We can't keep it! We need to do it again!' 'OK, that's fine! Ask Dominique to order a new panel!'), I decided I could meet Victoria before going to the inauguration, as it went on quite late. At worst, I could even miss it and join my small group of friends for the dinner, which would take place in a local restaurant. I really liked the person who had been the construction manager on this restructuring job, and I also knew the architect – he was well known, and I had worked on his buildings from time to time. I had been flattered when his assistant had called me two days earlier to tell me that he was counting on my presence. My awareness of the desire that my presence could inspire, that same evening, in such important people, gave this day a special value – it seemed like a good omen and put me in an excellent mood. So I sent Victoria a text telling her that we could meet early in the evening. She asked me where I'd like us to meet, and I replied that I didn't know. She said, 'Give me some idea . . .' and I sent her a text written like a nursery rhyme in which I gave her the choice between a café, a park, the Louvre museum, or her hotel – it was up to her.

The few hours that we spent in her room at the Concorde Saint-Lazare passed in an atmosphere of enchantment that I rarely encountered afterwards. Victoria was so insatiable, and her body was so alluring to me (I was incredibly aroused by its reactions to the pleasure I gave her) that hardly had we stopped making love before we felt like starting again – and we would start again.

Time passed, reining in its speed. I felt it shining all around me like something made of precious stones and gold coins that would fill the chest where our two bodies were hidden. Each second gave me the feeling that I was an emerald, a pearl, a flash of gold in the precious womb of time that protected us from the outside world. Time was the atmosphere of this room – an incandescent and almost unmoving time. It contained a greater number of physical, mental and sensory phenomena than would normally be possible.

People were expecting me. It was inconceivable that I should not turn up to the party – I had been lucky enough to be invited by a world-famous architect who was counting on my presence at the inauguration of his building – yet instead of rushing there, I found I could not stop making love. As the seconds ticked past on our watch faces, it became ever less imaginable that I would make it to the inauguration, or even to the dinner that would take place afterwards. Yet, strangely, the way I perceived this seemed to be inverted by my mind: the importance of what I was giving up transferred itself to the thing for which I was giving it up. I was not anxious at the idea of missing that party, because what I was experiencing in its stead was of such beauty that the exchange was justified. I did spare a thought for the people I was supposed to be with at that exact moment, and it seemed to me that they would undoubtedly wish they could be making passionate love in a Parisian hotel. While I heard the shrieks and screams that escaped Victoria's lips, I imagined that the famous architect would be happy that I was living such a glorious moment; he would be proud that I had managed to discover, amid our unmagical reality, such a rare and enchanted enclave. The thought of his aesthete's gaze watching me accentuated the density of this unique moment.

Because of the double-glazed windows, the room was absolutely silent. Each time I parted the curtains, I was surprised to discover so much life outside: a whole city below us, soundless. Pedestrians walked towards the station to catch their trains; cars were imprisoned in traffic jams; people went out to eat, entered the restaurants in front of the hotel; a mass of illuminated signs shone on the buildings. When I'd seen enough of the street, I turned around, letting the curtains fall closed again, and saw Victoria lying on the bed. She was luscious and immense, as stunning as a classical masterpiece. She gave me her hand and said, 'You're beautiful. I almost want to sodomize you when I see you like that.'

'Come on, Victoria . . .'

'Am I starting to scare you? Ha, don't worry – I'm not really going to sodomize you! Come on, make love to me. I want you so much . . .'

After we'd made love in various ways for quite a long time, Victoria suggested we eat dinner in the room. By this point, I had given up on the idea of going to the inauguration ceremony, so I said yes.

It must have been about 10 p.m. We were both naked, the sheets were messed up, and our clothes were scattered all over the room. We'd just ordered dinner from room service. 'Victoria, I wanted to tell you something. It's important for me. I'm sorry that I'm only telling you this now. It's not a good time, but there is never a good time to admit this kind of thing, so I may as well get it over with now.' Victoria watched me, breath held, as if begging me to continue. 'I wanted to tell you that I'm married, that I'm not free. I have two children – two daughters – a five-year-old and a thirteen-year-old. I've been married to this woman, my wife, for twenty-one years.'

'I thought so.'

'You did?'

'Men like you are never free.'

'I might have been divorced. I might have been free temporarily, after a divorce.'

'But you're not. Anyway, I was convinced that you had children. Whether you were free or not, I knew there would be children.'

'You suspected it that first weekend, because of my silence?'

'I thought you were with your family – with your wife and children – and that it was difficult for you, if only as a matter of principle, to communicate with me.'

'You were right.'

'Then again, those same principles didn't stop you communicating with me the weekend after that.'

'You're not going to criticize me for that!'

'Not at all. You should keep cheating on your wife with me – I agree completely.'

'I am not cheating on my wife.'

'You're not cheating on your wife? What are you doing, then?'

'I don't know, but I'm not cheating on her. I'm experiencing something else, something more, but I'm still faithful to her. I hate the word "cheat". The expression "cheating on one's wife", I find it horrible.'

'And not only because it's horrible to cheat on your wife? It's the expression itself that you dislike?'

'Do you think it's horrible to cheat on one's wife?'

'I imagine it's horrible to discover that you're being cheated on – that the man you live with has a mistress. I trust you not to let your wife ever discover that you have a mistress.'

'I don't have a mistress, Victoria. You're wrong if you think I do.'

'So what am I, if I'm not your mistress, lying naked on this bed with you?'

'We're seeing each other. We're together on this bed. We make love, we send each other messages. We decide if we're going to see each other or not. We meet so we can touch each other, see each other. Since tonight was so perfect, perhaps we'll decide to stop everything, and make do with the memory of it. That's what I've been thinking all evening, and that's why I wanted it to be so beautiful, and why I've done everything I could to make you enjoy it – because it's the last one. Tonight is the last night we will spend together. I am not the kind of man who cheats on his wife, to use your expression, and I am even less keen to cheat on her when the woman I'm doing it with uses that expression.'

'All right, then, I take it back. I'm usually too proud to take back anything I say. But tonight, if you want, I will take back that expression – "cheating on your wife".'

'Thank you. But I don't know if that will change anything about this probably being the last night we spend together.'

'I can't make out if you're being serious.'

'I don't know that myself. Maybe I am being serious? I think I am.'

'It's up to you. I can't force you to, no matter what. I understand what you mean. I'm happy that I've spent all this time with a man who says this kind of thing. You're a beautiful person. What's inside you is very beautiful. But you have to know that I would like to continue.'

'I would like to continue as well. But I don't want you to become my mistress. I want it to be something else.'

'What kind of something else?'

'Something else like tonight. Something uncertain. Something sensual and physical, but which doesn't belong to reality – something that takes place in our minds, in our imagination. I want each meeting to be like a dream we're having: we wake up from this dream and we go back to our lives. And the dream we had should have no further effect on our real life than the memory we retain of it, which enriches us with something more — something precious, that we wouldn't give up for anything in the world. I'm talking crap. It's pathetic, saying stuff like that — I'm sorry. That's precisely why I should avoid having a mistress.'

'I like you. You're a strange boy, but I like you.'

'I like you too. Since I met you, I've gained at least 40 per cent in strength and confidence.'

'If only I could have the same effect on the 12,000 people who work under me. If each of them could, because of me, gain at least 40 per cent in strength and confidence, imagine how Kiloffer shares would rocket!'

'As would your stock options . . .'

'I'd shower you with gifts.'

'You are the most wonderful gift.'

'I have a question to ask you. I'm a bit afraid of the answer, but I'm going to ask you anyway. Am I the first woman you've seen . . .'

'It's the first time. I know that must seem implausible, on the face of it, but I can promise you . . .'

'That it's true,' Victoria interjects.

'That it's true. Exactly. I'm not going to try to make you believe that I've been faithful for twenty-one years. I've had a number of adventures . . .'

'I hope you used protection, at least!' Victoria blenches.

'Of course I used protection.'

'But how can I be sure when you didn't use protection with me?'

'I'm telling you, Victoria, I always used protection. You don't have to trust me, in which case let's call room service so that, as well as your sea bream and my rib steak, which should be here any minute . . . Speaking of which, maybe we should get dressed?'

'You're right. I can't let room service in when I'm completely naked!'

'Anyway, you'd just have to ask them for a packet of condoms. When I fuck you again, after dinner, you'll be protected.'

'Maybe you'd come then.'

'Yes, maybe I'd come then.'

'Is that why you haven't come?'

'I don't think so. It would be convenient for me to say that that's why, but it's not.'

'So why haven't you come?'

'I don't know.'

'Do you come normally?'

'Not very often. With strangers, I mean.'

'Don't I turn you on enough for you to come?'

'How can you even ask me that when I've been making love with you all evening?'

'I'm going to make you come. You'll come with me – you'll see.'

'I'm sure I will. I'm not worried at all, personally. This is only the second time we've made love, Victoria.'

'You can come in me, David. I would love it if you came in me.'

'How do I know you're on the pill?'

'Do you really think I'd want you to get me pregnant at my age? Without your knowledge?'

'I was kidding. Having said that, if you did want a child – I mean, a child on your own – now would be the time. And you'd do it without my knowledge.'

'And once you'd fertilized me, I'd disappear?'

'I usually disappear, once I've got what I want from women.'

As I was saying this, there was a knock at the door. Victoria stood up and went to the bathroom. I pulled the sheets round my body to cover it completely. I saw Victoria, in a fluffy white dressing gown, walk barefoot on the deep-pile, flower-patterned red carpet. She headed towards the door and held it wide open. A man dressed in livery entered the room, pushing an impressive trolley on which – under silver domed lids – sat our two plates. There was also a bottle of fine wine, chosen by Victoria, our glasses and our cutlery, all arranged on a white tablecloth. The man lifted up two drop leaves, creating a nice table, and we sat either side of it. I had dressed, but Victoria was still in her dressing gown.

Over dinner, Victoria revealed to me that the day we met, a man had stood her up: she'd waited for him for a while in the place where I first saw her. She couldn't get hold of him. She'd left him several messages, and the last one said that she would wait until 8 p.m. in a café in the shopping centre. Having given up on him, she went to the bowling alley to release the anger that had welled up inside her. 'I was really in a strange state. But going bowling did me a lot of good.'

'Where did you learn to play? You were really good. I was impressed.'

'With a girlfriend, when I was young – about twenty-two. We'd go looking for men at the bowling alley on Friday nights. I like it. I'm quite talented.'

'And this man – who was he? What was special about that rendezvous?'

'Do you really want to talk about that tonight?'

'Why not? I've already told you I'm married.'

'True. But I'm more prudish than you.'

'I don't think so. A bit less brave, maybe.'

'We'd split up a few days earlier. Or, to be more precise, we'd had a discussion about our future. He'd imposed conditions that I didn't like. I'd told him that. He'd replied that, if that was the case, we ought to split up. I'd said OK, let's separate: I don't agree with these conditions you're trying to force on me, so let's separate. And we split up.'

'And what were these conditions, if you don't mind me asking?'

'I don't mind you asking any questions you like, but I'm not necessarily going to reply. I'm happy to tell you this story, because you asked me to, but certain details are going to have to remain a secret for a while longer.'

'This wine is wonderful. Have you tasted it?'

'Not yet,' Victoria replied, picking up her glass. She moved it towards my face. I lifted mine, and the two glasses touched with a gentle clink as our smiling eyes met. 'To tonight. To our meeting. To the magic of these moments,' I said to Victoria.

'To chance. To the benefits of chance and providence,' she replied lyrically. 'You're right – it is wonderful,' she agreed a few seconds later after she'd rolled the wine around her mouth. 'I chose a Château Haut-Brion 1995.'

'You're completely mad.'

'I thought the first of our Parisian nights together deserved a great wine. Especially if it's going to be the last.'

'I think this wine goes perfectly with your body, with the smell of your skin, with your voice when you come, with the silence of this room, with the atmosphere of the October darkness that I see outside when I look through the curtains and see all those lights. It's strong and complex.'

Victoria watches me with a smile on her lips, her fork suspended just above her sea bream. The whiteness of her dressing gown brings out her golden skin and her freckles. Protecting her naked body, and with her hair falling immaculately on to her shoulders, this dressing gown seems to provide a striking connection between the private woman and the woman of power. I cut my rib steak and ask her: 'If you split up, why did you arrange to meet in that shopping centre? And why in that shopping centre, in front of that clothes shop? It's quite a strange place to meet someone . . .'

'He was in the area at the time we'd arranged to meet. There's a clothes shop in that shopping centre where I buy quite a lot of things. He liked going shopping with me, giving me his opinions . . . He loved buying lingerie for me.'

'I like shopping with women too. I couldn't care less about lingerie, but I like clothes.'

'We'll go, then. You have taste – you're always very elegant. Which is quite strange, actually, for a man who works on a building site.'

'I don't see the connection. Quite a few of my colleagues are like me.'

'You're right. What I said was stupid,' Victoria says. 'I apologize. He, on the other hand, was a nightmare. He wore all sorts of rubbish and believed he was super chic.'

'What's his job?'

'Mathematician. He's quite well known in his field.'

'And why did you have to see each other again?'

'I was waiting for that question.'

'Well, obviously! How could you imagine we'd have this conversation without me asking you the reason for this new rendezvous – arranged by you, as well – when you'd split up just a few days earlier? It's the only question to be asked, in fact . . .'

'To tell him that I agreed.'

'Agreed to what? To accept his conditions?'

'Yes. To accept his conditions.'

'But why did you change your mind and decide to . . .'

'So I didn't lose him, obviously. So he'd come back to me. So he'd agree to stay with me. I didn't want to be alone.'

'Which means that the conditions he imposed on you were acceptable after all.'

'They weren't. But I ended up thinking that they could be, because my sadness won out over my aversion to them – or rather over the reluctance I felt at having to submit to them in the long term. The conditions were not just occasional, but the principle of our relationship. That was what he wanted.'

'I gather from that rather complex description that your boyfriend was imposing something that you were able to accept – and perhaps you were able to accept it because you liked it, at least in certain circumstances – but that you refused to let it become a habit, to become the principle of your relationship.'

'You're very intelligent.'

'I still need to figure out what this man was imposing on you.'

'And what I wanted him to impose.'

'And what you wanted him to impose.'

'I'll tell you another day, I promise. Anyway, he didn't turn up. I left him four or five messages while I was waiting, and then afterwards you approached me. You gave me your telephone number, and I realized we were going to become lovers. So, three hours later, when he called me back to apologize for not having come to our meeting, he asked me what the good news was that I wanted to tell him (because I'd left him a final message saying that I had something good to tell him, that he would undoubtedly be happy to hear), and I replied that I'd met another man. He seemed surprised. Another man – what are you talking about? Another man – I fell for another man – so it's over between you and me. But when? When did you meet this man? While I was waiting for you, I told him. I was waiting for you and another man saw me waiting. He liked me. He was appalled that someone would stand up a woman like me. He asked me out. I don't want to see you any more. He told me that he didn't believe me, that I was being a bit obvious. I insisted so much that in the end he believed me. He told me that he would see me again when this crude womanizer had abandoned me. I told him that if there was one thing I was sure of, it was that the relationship I was beginning with this man would last. Oh really, and what makes you say that? he asked, laughing. The look in his eyes, I replied. What's so special about the look in his eyes? he asked me. They are gentle, sincere, profound, I replied. I can see that he is impressed by me and that he wants to please me. It's the first time anyone has looked at me like that in fifteen years, I told him. Maybe I went a bit far – I'd spent several years of my life with Laurent, after all – but I believed what I was saying.'

'Don't you live together?'

'We were in separate places. Since then, he hasn't stopped calling me. He leaves me tons of messages. He's trying to seduce me again. He wants the three of us to go out together.'

'And what do you do with these messages?'

'I don't reply.'

'It is a pretty incredible story. You replaced one lover with another almost instantaneously – without a minute's interruption. You arrange to meet your ex to tell him you want to get back with him: he stands you up and while you're waiting for him, you meet the man who's going to replace him. That sequence of events makes me wonder.'

'You're right – it's crazy. Life can be miraculous when it wants to.'

'On that point, I agree completely,' I told Victoria, touching my glass to hers. We toasted again. 'To our love,' Victoria said.

'To our last night together.'

'Bastard,' Victoria replied, with a smile that was intended to be sarcastic.

*

The next day, I got an email from Victoria telling me about how she'd spent the afternoon before our evening – and then the happiness she'd felt with me. I wrote in reply:

'My very dear Victoria.

'I loved what you wrote to me. It was so spontaneous. You were right to send it to me as it was without reworking it. I love its style – dishevelled, a bit crumpled, happy and quick-tempered. In that way, it bore a slight resemblance to the Victoria I left on the threshold of her room after this interlude of love, intelligence and complicity. I told you this morning by text that I adored our evening together yesterday at the Concorde Saint-Lazare. What I didn't tell you was that, the day before, I had decided not to see you in Paris, and that it was only yesterday morning (perhaps even a bit later) that I yielded to my desire to see you again. I really love your description of the moments that preceded our meeting, which match perfectly what I went through myself. How I wish I could always lead you from rendezvous to rendezvous, from stolen evening to stolen evening, in this state of exaltation and anxiety, impatience and emotion, and how I would love it if these physical, cerebral, sensitive and sensual meetings could always make you feel the way they made you feel last night. I love imagining you abandoning your conference, wandering through the boulevards, preparing yourself mentally, doubting me, looking in the windows of Galeries Lafayette, being afraid of your body, delighting in this dreamlike autumn, thinking, trembling, losing your desire, fearing disappointment, waiting for me to call you. You can't know how much, and why, the description of these wanderings resonated in my mind. That day, you were like a woman I might have dreamed up entirely, a figment of my imagination. Do you truly understand what I'm saying? I never get tired of penetrating you, kissing you, licking your pussy . . . it's incredible that your face and body continue to have this effect on me. I don't remember ever having made love for that long without feeling the slightest desire to stop. There's something so natural about the way my cock grows whenever I touch you, the way it fits perfectly inside you. I don't know how to explain this naturalness, so free of doubts, fears, pretence, misplaced ambitions . . . And today, Victoria, I can't wait to see you again in Paris on 4 November, and then – if everything works out – on the 17th, and to love you, again and again, to love you as passionately as we did in our first two meetings, each one allowing me to get to know you a little better, and to want you even more. I am exhilarated at the idea that you belong to me, that you are mine, that you are my Victoria. And here, as a post-scriptum, is a wonderful paradox: to be possessed by another takes us back to ourselves.'

6

From now on, it was as if the few days that preceded that evening would act as a matrix for the first months of our relationship. My strength was massively increased by the Victoria effect; in my imagination, she had become an ideal of enchantment. In fact, it seemed to me I'd never been as happy as I had been since we met. But it was from a distance that I felt this most intensely, in the tension of absence and longing, when our contact was generally limited to phone conversations and compulsively sending messages. And, exactly as had happened the day before our meeting at the Concorde Saint-Lazare, I sometimes found it difficult to think serenely about the meetings that punctuated our relationship. Not only because of the guilt they could cause (and which, strangely, I never felt about our texts, emails and phone calls, even though – through their contents and their frequency – they brought us ever deeper into an emotional commitment bordering on addiction), but because of a reluctance that it would be difficult for me to explain except by comparing it to the mechanics of a sort of internal resistance: something undefined rubbed against the wheel of my desire, or pressed a mysterious brake whenever I tried to feel excited about a meeting that would take place a few hours later. Even the day before, I was thrilled at the idea of the next evening, as at this point the prospect of seeing Victoria again was mixed with our daily conversations. Reading her messages, filled with impatience at the thought of seeing me again, I felt as cheerful as she seemed. The morning before we met, the imminence stood out more clearly from the background of our normal daily relations, and in the hours that led up to the meeting, it came to seem increasingly threatening. It scared off desire the way a forest fire makes wild animals flee. Sometimes I would turn up to our meetings and I wouldn't want to see her at all. To begin with, I was able to conquer this resistance within three minutes and feel the same intense attraction as if we had seen each other the night before, and the hours that we spent making love were magical. But as the months passed, it would become increasingly hard to overcome this, for reasons which grew ever more precise. The tragedy into which I would be drawn was formed in the crucible of this curious paradox.

But at the beginning, whenever she was in London or away travelling, this constant connection between us gave me the self-esteem of one of the chosen few. That was how, during the first few months, I was able to face the challenges of the construction site with a little more spontaneity and confidence, as if I had grown so that the outside world was more suited to my size. It was not that I was generally too small to cope with the difficulties of my job (I'd always had the reputation of being an excellent construction manager), but this particular site had shown itself to require a bit more madness, more rage, more detachment and recklessness than was habitually found in my temperament – and whatever the strange mental substance was that Victoria injected me with, those were precisely the qualities that it spread through my mind, along with a permanent euphoria.

According to the schedule, the building's shell had to be completed by 20 December, meaning that by this date the Jupiter Tower should have been constructed and its highest point should appear like a climax in the sky over La Défense, before we began working on the building's interior. During the early September meeting with the boss of the property development company, I had pointed out that because we were two months behind schedule, it would be difficult to meet this deadline of 20 December, but that we would do everything we could to complete the shell by a reasonable date. 'Reasonable – that's an interesting word,' the boss said ironically. 'What date do you think it would be reasonable to suggest to us now?'

'I don't know. It's difficult to say. At this point, I think we should accept that the issue is no longer to reduce the delay but to make sure it doesn't get any bigger. In which case, we could commit to finishing the shell by, I don't know, about 20 February. So . . .'

'I think you've known for a long time that that would be unacceptable,' he broke in.

'I know; it was a hypothesis. All I'm doing is listing the different hypotheses.'

'But that hypothesis was never considered,' said my direct superior Jean-François in a cold voice, as if to protect himself.

'Hopefully the teams working on the shell won't encounter any new difficulties, and that date of 20 February won't turn into 20 March,' I added, in order to make him understand how inappropriate his comment was. After a small pause, I continued: 'But I agree we shouldn't consider the hypothesis of an even longer delay, nor even the continuation of the delay we have now. Let's consider the situation optimistically.'

'At this crucial point in time, I am surprised to hear you talk in terms as vague as optimism,' the boss chimed in sarcastically. He was talking to me in a way that, while not wounding, was becoming increasingly sharp. Knowing my reputation for scrupulousness, he wanted me to give him, irrationally, the prospect of a utopian (and therefore lucrative) deadline. He was hoping that I would tell him, in the intoxication of some momentary madness, that we would finish the shell of the tower by 20 December. After pausing for a few moments to stare into my eyes, the boss had continued: 'It's not a question of being optimistic or pessimistic, nor of being tired or hesitant, or of crossing our fingers and hoping for the best. It's a question of being realistic, efficient, determined, of being part of a crucial process, of knowing how to anticipate problems. You know this list of qualities as well as I do. You have to improve the teams' productivity. You have to meet our objectives.'

'In that case, as it does not seem conceivable – and I hope we can all agree on this point – to finish on 20 December . . .'

'Absolutely,' Jean-François replied impatiently.

'In that case,' I continued, 'we could set ourselves the object-ive of reducing this two-month delay by two weeks – in other words, of completing the shell in early February. By the 5th, for example.'

'I propose that we try to reduce it by a month – that the delay should go down from two months to one.'

'We have to be realistic, though,' Jean-François replied. 'To be honest, I agree with David. To do it before early February . . .'

'Let's try anyway. Let's try to complete the shell by 20 January. Do you agree to commit yourselves to this date?' the boss asked.

Jean-François had looked at me – silently, questioningly – across the meeting-room table, and I had nodded.

'We'll try,' he told the boss.

'You agree that it's possible?' the boss asked, turning towards me.

'No matter what, you can count on me, and on my teams, to give it 200 per cent. We won't spare our time, our drive or our energy. We will fight. I can commit myself to that.'

I might have added: 'As for the rest, what will be will be.' But I didn't.

'I didn't expect any less from you,' he replied, rising from his seat. 'Reduce this delay for me. Even better, get ahead of schedule. If you're well ahead of schedule, that could be very useful for us afterwards, if you see what I mean, David. Use all the means at your disposal to succeed, including legal pressure and threats of penalties for the construction company. I'm counting on you to give it to them straight: send out registered letters, make them scared,' he added, turning towards Jean-François. Then, looking at me again: 'Don't let François Gall get away with it any more. You need to put him under constant pressure. Help him if you think he needs help to motivate his troops. Depending on the circumstances, you need to be behind him, beside him or against him. What I demand of you, David, is that François Gall completes the shell by 20 January. Don't let up. But be very careful: do not go over the budget. Do you hear me? Not a penny over the budget! I want things to be clear between us. It's essential that you reduce this two-month delay. But don't come to me afterwards and say that it's going to cost us God knows how many thousand euros . . . Understood? Are we agreed? Until next time, then. Good luck. I'll let you sort out the details with Daniel and Jean-François,' he said while standing up. And then he left.

These men of power understood that, when they imposed objectives on their employees that they knew to be outrageous, the employees would – the vast majority of the time – react with such servility that the targets became realistic. Not because they were. Not because those obedient employees thought they could be. But simply because they ended up meeting the targets – at the cost of their health, their sleep, their peace of mind and a host of sacrifices that it is difficult to quantify in the medium term, particularly in terms of family life. Just because an objective was unrealistic, that was no reason not to demand it: that philosophy had always disgusted me, and it disgusted me that day just as it had each time before.

This was the meeting that I had remembered – with a surge of anxiety and bitterness – that day lying in Hyde Park, chewing on a blade of grass. I recall that, the day the meeting took place, we had another twenty-two floors to construct. If we wanted to complete the shell by 20 January, that meant we would have to complete a new floor every eight days for four months – when the most likely tempo was one floor every ten days, which would have given the deadline of 5 February that I had suggested.

However, for a number of obvious reasons, we failed to take into account the difficulty, for this particular building, of accurately estimating the pace of construction. Because the Jupiter Tower was irregularly shaped, each new part of it offered up new problems. We couldn't draw on our experiences of the lower floors to help us plan for the future. For instance, the first two overhangs had caused us huge trouble, whereas the third had been built without any particular difficulty. Improved speed was as hard to predict as the delays. We were doomed to move constantly through unknown territory, like sailors in ancient times navigating in the mist, hoping they wouldn't crash against the rocks. That September day, leaving the meeting with my stomach in knots, I told myself that perhaps those twenty-two floors would be like the third overhang? Perhaps we would manage to build them extremely quickly? Perhaps we would succeed in keeping to this infernal speed of one floor every eight days? I tried to convince myself of this as I walked down the stairs of the underground car park on Avenue Montaigne, but in all honesty I doubted the possibility. I regretted having let myself agree to such a horribly urgent deadline, just because the property developer didn't want to see his profits reduced. Because if he didn't deliver the tower on time, he might have to pay penalties to the people he'd sold the building to: a major bank and a long list of investors. Those penalties could end up being enormous.

This, I remember, was my state of mind when I saw Victoria in the shopping centre. Twenty days had passed between the day of the meeting and the moment when my eyes met hers and kindled the spark that brought us together, and in that time we had constructed only two floors (it would take too long to explain why, at this point in the construction, it was so slow-going). It was an easy calculation to make: at this unbearable rhythm of two floors every twenty days, it would take us seven and a half months to complete the shell, leaving the developer in a state of nervous tension and psychological violence that I hardly dared imagine – and which would translate, for me, into recriminations from my enraged superiors.

In fact, the opposite happened: the nightmare arrived later on, when the shell was already completed and we had started working on the interior. The four months that followed my first meeting with Victoria, on the other hand, remain among the most intense of my career. I oversaw the shell's completion in a trance, the way composers are supposed to finish their symphonies – carried away by an insane burst of energy, inspiration and confidence, of physical power and creative fervour.

The construction site was so complex that the best way of dealing with it was to feel that you were permanently above all contingencies, and not to let any insidious worries snake their way into your brain. Not only was this what I had learned from observing Victoria's way of life (being at once within and beyond, everywhere and nowhere; in other words, not letting it get to you. I'll come back to this crucial aspect of her character a bit later), but the strength she gave me also allowed me to apply this lesson to my own life. It takes a special kind of faith not to let yourself be a prisoner to your troubles.

The simple fact that I had managed to make Victoria as dependent on me as I had become on her made me believe that everything was now possible in my life. Being wanted that much by this woman had rendered me invulnerable.

I don't think it would be correct to describe this as love. Or, if I believed that it was love, it was only briefly – in moments of ecstasy, when I was flooded with happiness or holding her body in my arms. But the feelings she inspired in me were similar to a passionate romance in that they transfigured me. I moved now in a sunnier place, located above the one where I had spent most of my life. And this slight increase in elevation significantly altered my relationship with reality: I was wiser, more detached than I had been when I trudged along in the mud with the others. But, above all, it was the sense of superiority, mixed with the elixir of my mood, that enabled a temperament as measured as mine to become capable of the madness necessary to run an operation on this scale – a madness qualified by prudence, exactness and lucidity, but a madness all the same, an undeniable madness.

During these first months, not only did the construction site seem more bearable to me, but I found it more exciting. Going out with Victoria increased my love of risk, of challenge, of combat and adversity – my love of victory, in other words, which is not the same thing as a love of success. I was energetic, passionate and cheerful, raring to sweep away all the obstacles, to make it through, to finish my race. I was always impatient for the next message from Victoria, for the next time I heard her smile on the telephone. I was voracious, euphoric, greedy for more. I had come back to life. When I went home, I drove faster than usual: I even got speeding tickets on the motorway. I felt myself pushing the envelope of my ordinary humanness like a chrysalis transforming into a butterfly. I wanted to fight, to prove I was capable of standing up to the most insurmountable crises. I was like a warrior who wants to show his fiancée that he has succeeded in conquering the neighbouring province. I forgot that butterflies live such short lives. But at the time there was no need for that kind of thought.

There was François Gall, who was in charge of the structure, the metal frame, the masonry and the earthwork – the building's shell, in other words. There was José Delacruz, the head supervisor, a rough and experienced Portuguese man, always unhappy and bad-tempered, who managed the team leaders and the labourers. There was Olivier Berger, shell foreman and one of the engineers who designed the self-climbing formwork and all its tools. And, lastly, there was my friend Dominique Mercador. And me. Together, the five of us formed a core that was more united than ever before: indivisible.

We pulled together to sweep away the obstacles and to progress relentlessly towards the image we had in mind: drinking champagne on 20 January at the top of the finished tower. Persuading our colleagues to accept this unbelievable deadline, however, was no easy matter.

Everyone who works in the building industry has encountered, at least once in their career, a situation in which despondency is the prevailing emotion, where the objectives are so arduous that the workers end up convinced that they will never meet them. They capitulate in silence. Little by little, they slide into a state of inertia and resignation. What is needed, in this climate of depression, is for one person who has never given up to inspire the others with the conviction that they must not throw in the towel – and that is how, motivated by the determination of one sole individual who becomes the guiding light, a construction site can rediscover its momentum and triumph over seemingly insurmountable difficulties.

After that September meeting, the one person who did not give in was François Gall. I have already said that I myself had taken a real blow – hence that afternoon spent crawling in Hyde Park. José Delacruz spent the whole day muttering that it was not possible to keep up such a pace: 'Those twats are pissing me off. They should put on overalls and see how easy it is to increase the pace. Increase the pace, increase the pace . . . they can stick their increased pace up their arses!' Like José Delacruz, most of François Gall's colleagues could not stop themselves pouring out their hatred, complaining that all these 'technocrats' were 'arseholes'; that it was 'disgusting' to have to submit to such nightmarish conditions when the 'capitalists' who imposed them couldn't give a shit as long as they were filling their pockets. They said it was impossible to meet such a tight deadline when obstacles kept suddenly appearing and slowing them down. Even François Gall's bosses no longer believed; they spent their time blaming François Gall for the penalties that, because of this delay, they feared they would have to pay – while he bent over backwards to show them that he could finish the building's shell as agreed on 20 January, 'Perhaps even the 18th,' he would sometimes add confidently. I could see the exasperation on his bosses' faces: 'François, you've been saying that since the beginning. For months and months, you've been saying that you were going to reduce the delay. But what now? Do you have a magic formula that will finally make that happen?' François Gall was not born yesterday. He was a fifty-year-old man who had spent his life pouring concrete and constructing buildings. Some of the best towers in La Défense were his. He was experienced and competent, and he was not to blame for the delay in the completion of the Jupiter Tower's shell (which was, in fact, mostly attributable to a problem in the design of the tools). And even though he had explained the reasons why, at various times, he had been slowed down; even though he had thoroughly justified each of his delays with irrefutable arguments; even though he had explained that there was no reason why any new obstacles should arise, his words all crashed against a wall of indifference. 'You'll have to explain it to us. Maybe there's something we haven't grasped. How do you expect to do it – by magic? What kind of miracle will it take for you to meet deadlines that are more difficult than ever, when for two years every forecast you've made to us has turned out wrong?' The top boss announced: 'François, not meeting the 20 January deadline is not an option. Let me explain it to you: if you meet this deadline, we'll be able to avoid the penalties – that's what I'm negotiating anyway. You understand? But if you miss that deadline – if the building is not finished by 20 January . . . if you finish on 14 March, for instance, or on 22 April, that will cost the firm hundreds of thousands of euros. You understand? It will cost the firm hundreds of thousands of euros. So let me tell you that, if that happens, we will have a really unpleasant fifteen minutes. You, me, us, everyone. A really unpleasant fifteen minutes.' And François Gall replied: 'But seriously, it's going to work. I'm sure of it. We're all totally motivated now.' And his boss replied: 'Don't make me laugh. All you have to do is walk round the site and you can see that no one believes that any more.' And, without weakening, François Gall replied: 'I know they're a bit demotivated – I've seen it – but I'm going to get them back on course.' The boss was silent for a few seconds. Then: 'OK, it's noted. Thank you. I have my doubts, but I take note of your determination. You'd better keep your word this time, though. Seriously, you'd better . . . fuck . . . this time, no pissing around . . .' And, untrembling, François Gall replied: 'I know what I'm talking about. We're going to make it.' And his bosses looked at him sceptically. And his teams on the site were idling. And if someone had appeared in the room and said, 'I've found the man who's going to get us out of this hole – he's an American and he's never missed a deadline in his life,' François Gall would have been fired on the spot.

I still wonder how it was that François Gall held firm. The pressure they put on him was extreme. On construction sites of this scale, human beings are severely tested; often, they lose their nerve, disintegrate, resign, fall suddenly ill or commit suicide. Sometimes a man is summoned one morning and asked to leave. He has no choice. One hour later, he is in his car, en route to the head office to discuss his reassignment with the head of Human Resources. I've seen it happen many times, particularly on sites where the financial stakes are extremely high. This, in fact, is how my friend Dominique Mercador ended up at the Jupiter Tower site, replacing a fragile, unstable man who was not up to the job.

When François Gall told his colleagues that now was the time to produce one last gargantuan effort, they replied: 'What's the point? It's over. We'll never make it.' And François Gall had to persuade them, contradict them, win them over through his arguments. He had to transmit his conviction to everyone who was working with him: the team leaders, the foremen, every single labourer on the site had to be brought back to life.

When you are alone to this degree – forced to carry a massive challenge on your shoulders, while being surrounded by mass inertia – believing is not enough; you need to have faith. It's hard to imagine how important it is, on a construction site, to have faith.

With François Gall, we staged meetings at which we talked for hours. I explained to those beaten men, slumped in their chairs, that the only way they could avoid being a victim of the building was to meet the 20 January deadline.

'Show them you can do it! Tell all those men who doubt you where they can shove it. But don't do it by putting yourselves at fault – that would just be stupid. Fuck, lads, think about it! Do you really want to screw yourselves over by finishing Jupiter on 12 May? Channel your rage! Show them what you're capable of! Because, contrary to what you seem to think, channelling your rage into finishing Jupiter on time does not mean you're obeying them. How can you even believe that? Fucking hell, lads, it's the opposite! We're going to do it to make ourselves proud, so we don't owe them anything. This is our tower – we're making it with our hands. With our hands, lads! Right now, it's October – the weather's pretty good. But in two months, it'll be late December, early January. Think about it: early January on this tower, 220 metres up. I'm on your side – I'm not trying to demoralize you. When we're on the forty-sixth floor – almost at the top, only four storeys to go – it'll be . . . what? . . . minus six? Up there, at six in the morning, 200 metres above ground, in early January . . . minus six, minus seven, minus ten sometimes. We'll be working through the night, under neon lights, and you are the ones who will finish this tower with your hands! With your hands, for fuck's sake, at night, when it's minus eight! And you will be the ones, one evening, to plant the flag. And then we'll call the clowns. We'll call their mobiles and we'll say: "It's done." Do you really want to steal that moment from yourselves? Do you want these fucking technocrats . . . are you going to let them steal that moment when you can say to them it's done, we've finished, we got there on time – which really means fuck you, we're the best, tell your wife I said hello? And yeah, it's true, they're not going to come up here and thank you. They're not going to throw €100 notes at you. If that's what you want to know, I'm telling you: it's not going to happen. You're not going to be showered with cash, or be toasted for your hard work. You're not going to get any thanks at all. If those are the reasons you might get back to work, then you may as well stay at home. Pull a sickie, and I'll replace you. That's how it is. That's the world we live in. They'll hardly even thank you. They'll hardly even look at you. They'll come up to the top – there'll be four or five of them – and they'll come to check that we really have finished, that it really is fifty storeys high, and then they'll congratulate themselves. Yep, they'll congratulate themselves on this extraordinary success, they'll go on about how beautiful their building is, and then they'll fuck off. Two days later, they'll come back with the CEO of the bank, accompanied by two or three sycophants – the communications manager, the property adviser – our bosses. Not one of you will get a handshake from the CEO of the bank or the property development firm. They're too high up. They're stars. They would dazzle you with their brilliance. But there you go . . . is that really a good enough reason not to work yourselves to death? Is that a good enough reason – their doubt and ingratitude – not to do everything we can, to work like crazy, in order to get the shell completed by 20 January? Is anyone going to answer yes to that question? Good, that's perfect. I'm glad. Because, lads, the truth is the exact opposite! This is my point. This is where I've been going for the last ten days. This is where all my speeches have been leading you – to this point where you will finally understand that the truth is the opposite of what you thought. It's *because*, no matter what we do, there will always be a barrier between people like that and us, their system and ours, the system and our daily realities, their lives and ours, their demands and our pride, the abstract theories of their projects and the physical realities of ours, their fucking bank accounts and our fucking overdrafts . . . it's *because* there will always be this barrier between us, this chasm, that I say to you: we must always be spotless, straight as an arrow, super-professional, rock solid; we should never give them anything to complain about. You understand? We should be proud of the victory we'll achieve – we should be proud of conquering ourselves, conquering time, conquering the materials and conquering their mentality! We shouldn't kill ourselves working for them, but for ourselves! This tower belongs to us! When you're old men and drive past on the Versailles motorway, and you see this incredible lightning bolt in the sky over La Défense, you'll tell your grandchildren: see that tower over there, the enormous lightning bolt? I built that, a long time ago. And I would love it if you could say to them, to your grandchildren, forty years from now, that it's one of the greatest memories of your career, maybe the most beautiful of all your memories. I'm here today for this reason only – so that you can say those words in forty years' time. And not: see that tower over there, Granddad built that – it was a living nightmare, it's the worst memory of my career . . . we finished a year late.'

So it was that, in the space of a few days, a miracle began to occur. Obstacles dissolved, the labourers took the strain, and as if by magic the tower began to rise.

Increasing the speed at which a building of this complexity is constructed requires the elimination of the very idea of failure. It requires the same determination as the elimination of an enemy. All I had to do was watch the labourers, and the team leaders who managed them, to understand: they were making the materials bend to their will, they were conquering time. They were fighting to keep their stranglehold over something that can seem imperceptible but which it is sometimes possible to see dying, when you dominate it: time, mocking and contemptuous, which evades the grip of action and drags it into a rut, slowing down the efforts of men and stretching out their schedules. The labourers managed to transform time into hurtling blocks of concrete, into rising walls, into mounting storeys. They managed to bring these two principles into perfect alignment, so that the amount of construction achieved matched the time that had passed, not letting any of it leak uselessly away. In their hands, time could not laugh at man's powerlessness; it could not dangle like a flag on a windless day. These men's actions pulled time as taut as possible, and from this tension, a building was constructed at maximum speed. Sometimes, it even seemed we could produce more matter than the time allowed. It is in circumstances like these that we talk of time expanding.

It can happen that individuals, united by the same desire, become one entity, one energy, one intelligence. That is how the improbable can occur; one moment it seemed impossible, and suddenly it works. You have to see this happen at least once in your life to understand its fabulous beauty. This was the osmosis that I witnessed. I walked around the construction site and thought: 'Jesus, how are they doing it? Conditions are terrible. It shouldn't work. What has brought the machine to life, increased its power, enabled it to overcome all these obstacles?' What these men, transformed by the indescribable effort they put in, created out of thin air was not only a building, but a dream, a reflection of their desire, a projection of their minds, an expression of deep feeling that linked them all. It was palpable: they were giving body to something that already existed in their brains, that seemed to spring not from their hands but their imaginations. Like a child drawing a house while lying on the floor of their bedroom, or building a tower out of cubes. They were concentrated on an image of the building rooted in their minds, and this image climbed up in reality, day after day, floor after floor, in iron and concrete, like a slow but magnificent reward.

I thought of Victoria during every moment of these days. I felt unique and important.

Despite being busy or in meetings, Victoria always did her best to reply to the texts I sent her, even if only briefly or in the form of laconic smileys. These simple expressions, sent by her, were enough to give me courage.

Me: 'I miss you. I wanted a word with you. Your phone just rings and rings. Where are you?' 8.32 a.m.

Her: 'Sorry, I'm already in a staff meeting with 20 people. I miss you too.' 8.34 a.m.

Me: 'I'm at the top of the tower. We're constructing the 44th floor. I'm 220 metres above the ground, on the edge of the void. It's a beautiful day – the sky is blue, it's sublime. We've been going like a train for three days now. It's miraculous. I can't believe it. I wish you could see it. I wanted to share my euphoria with you. I've never seen labourers work so fast and with such determination as in the last week. There's a strong wind behind us now, and for the first time I feel like we're going to do it.' 8.40 a.m.

Her: 'I can't write much now. But I just wanted to say: BRAVO! I ADORE YOU!' 8.41 a.m.

Me: 'It's because of YOU, Victoria. None of this would be happening if I hadn't met you.' 8.45 a.m.

Her: 'Really? What a strange thought! Why? : -))' 8.52 a.m.

Me: 'I have to go. Can we talk tonight?' 8.55 a.m.

Her: 'Not tonight. I'm going to Germany with my boss. I won't be alone until late. Tomorrow morning?' 8.58 a.m.

Me: 'Oh yeah, I'd forgotten that trip. OK. Sending you lots of kisses, Victoria . . .' 8.59 a.m.

Her: 'Me too.' 9.00 a.m.

At one point, when things really started to go well, it felt like we were the crew of a yacht that was leading the transatlantic race. The faster the construction went, the more we burned with energy. It was a virtuous spiral, and as we got closer to completing the building, we grew ever faster and more impatient.

That was how we came to finish the shell not on 20 January, but on 5 January – fifteen days ahead of schedule. So, with the shell completed, the delay on the Jupiter Tower had been reduced from two months to three weeks.

Sometimes I think that things would have happened in the same way even if the Jupiter Tower's orchestra conductor had not met Victoria, if he had not been shooting up pure heroin for four months. Sometimes I think that François Gall's determination would, on its own, have been enough to carry the teams along. Maybe that's true – it's difficult to say. But in a way it doesn't really matter, because it so happened that the construction's miracle period coincided with that enchantment in my private life. The two events were superimposed, as if each owed the other the beauty of its existence; as if Victoria owed part of her beauty to our success on the tower, and the tower part of its success to Victoria's beauty. As in a fairy tale, one wave of a magic wand caused all the difficulties to be smoothed away, and the tower to rise from the ground as easily as a mushroom one autumn night.

That was why, each time I wondered about our relationship, I decided it would be dangerous to alter a single aspect of this subtle balance between my private life, the energy of my teams on the site and the speed of construction. The process might still get jammed, and the speed of construction fall back to one floor every eight or ten days, instead of the seven demanded by the schedule and the six that we managed through our increased pace. What was happening was magical, wonderful and fragile. I was happy in my private life and in my professional life. If we could keep this mad rhythm up for four months, victory would be ours, and we would be able to begin the next phase with confidence: fitting the building's interiors, where this time I would be in the front line.

I had more or less decided that I would disappear when our affair reached its zenith: the top of the skyscraper that Victoria had allowed me to build beside her. We would go up there on the day the shell was finished, I would open a bottle of champagne, and we would kiss. Then maybe I would light a brazier and we would make love in the sky above La Défense, completely alone, on a platform open to the winds, and we would see the stars through rectangles gaping out into infinity, as at the top of a lighthouse. The next day, I would explain to Victoria that I wanted our affair to end, and I would vanish from her life. This was how I answered my own guilty self-questioning whenever it pierced my conscience, and for me this ending had become an unspoken assumption. (It was also a way of evading my responsibilities and postponing the decision – I was quite aware of that.) In the meantime, I had decided to live the few months that remained to us to the maximum, especially as they gave the construction site the appearance of a sublime epic: for perhaps the first time in my entire life, I was living like a hero, and Victoria knew what to do to magnify this impression. When we saw each other in the shopping centre, she wondered aloud if the spark kindled when our eyes met would still exist at our next meeting. But it had never disappeared; for several weeks, it had been surviving its imminent extinction. We were both lit up by the extraordinary intensity of that spark. And I like to tell myself that, at ninety-five years old – a worn-out old man in an armchair – I will undoubtedly remember those four incandescent months with great emotion, and perhaps even with the glimmer of an erection. A spark that perpetuates itself each second after it has, theoretically, been extinguished: that is, quite simply, a miracle.

When we had to see each other, we arranged to meet at the bar of her hotel, and we drank a glass or two of champagne before going up to her room. We talked about our lives (I told Victoria about the shell's progress and she told me about the exhausting battles with the unions she was fighting in Lorraine). She sat facing me in an armchair. Between us was a low table holding snacks in ramekins and our two glasses, in which bubbles rose to the surface and burst.

Victoria's face was the face of a forty-two-year-old woman with important responsibilities. From a distance, she looked very serious and slightly severe. When, entering the bar, I saw that she had already arrived (she was reading files, taking notes, talking on the phone), I had trouble accepting that she was the one I was meeting. There was always a gap between the memory of our latest lovemaking, the texts we sent each other and the strictness of this stiff-backed, respectable, almost technical figure, who had, you could tell, spent all day struggling with complicated issues. Her femininity was diluted by the globally standardized appearance – irrespective of gender – of a high-level manager. Watching her, unobserved, in the impersonal atmosphere of a hotel bar, the impact she made was exactly that of almost all executives (no matter what their sex, their country of origin or their sector of activity) – those people you can see in the first-class carriages of the Eurostar. That was what I saw when I looked at her tired face, before a smile grew upon it as she registered my sudden appearance.

I sat down – I was always a bit tense at this point – and we started to talk. It took me some time to acclimatize.

Sometimes I thought I wouldn't be able to go to her room, that the apparent distance between these two principles – the somewhat dour and efficient, not terribly sexy businesswoman, and the fevered mistress whose bed I'd shared – could no longer be bridged. We had to drink a glass or two of champagne before I could glimpse the second of these two women in the remnants of the first, who gradually faded away.

When we went up to her room and I kissed her, when she tore off my clothes and we were naked, when I penetrated her and hours passed in making love, another face appeared to me – the face of an adolescent girl.

It was partly our physical intimacy, but more than that it was the way her mind was stripped bare, that turned her features, her skin, her looks and the light of her face into those of a sixteen-year-old girl. Victoria always sweated copiously, and the drops of sweat I saw meandering on the skin of her radiant face made me think of dewdrops on a flower's petals. Because her skin was as velvety as a rose, and she was sweet and childlike, virginal, born anew. She looked as if she were filled with wonder at discovering love and men. There was something inexplicably original in this newly hatched face. As I made passionate love to this beautiful and luminously ingenuous adolescent, I felt sure I was making love to Victoria's memory of herself. There was, in her expression, something like the awareness of a perilous aban-don, and the trust that, at sixteen, a girl gives to the man who deflowers her: the look of a virgin who gives herself knowingly and willingly. And, each time this happened, I felt bad at having thought of Victoria as a bourgeois woman corrupted by money, moulded by poisonous ideas, spending her time satisfying the demands of insatiable shareholders. I don't think I have ever met a woman who was capable of seeming so different, depending on the angle or the distance or the context in which you saw her.

Victoria literally had several faces – faces that had nothing in common, faces of different ages and functions, different imaginations and territories – and I found this faculty of hers supernatural . . . supernatural and captivating.

I have never loved a face as much as the one I was able to kiss into being with Victoria: a face that looked like it had been washed by rain, radiant and strangely pure, as crystalline as a sunny spell after hours of greyness . . . like the momentary and illusory birth of a new age. It was this adolescent beauty that kept me moored to our bed for hours and made me go home in the middle of the night with no other excuse than improbable, time-consuming conversations with the site engineers, caused by urgent problems that I simply had to resolve.

One evening, sitting in my office, I sent Victoria a text: 'I would like to give you something that no other man has ever given you. You've already done that for me.' Everyone else had left a long time ago, and I was letting the day's tension die down in me softly like a fire burning down to its embers. Another way to put it would be that, just as an aeroplane on a long-haul flight begins its descent half an hour before its wheels touch the ground, my professional worries had begun their descent towards the runway of my family life. It took me a bit more time than the journey home provided to settle into the roles of father and husband that I had to assume again as soon as I crossed the threshold of my house, whereas curiously the role of lover was directly connected to that of construction manager, with the two seeming to mirror each other.

I switched off the lights in my office and walked towards my parked car. As I pressed on the electronic keyring to unlock the doors, I felt suddenly happy. I started the engine and, following an interchange overlooked by the dark, imposing shapes of buildings and towers, I left behind the grandiose skyline of La Défense. Then I drove home, listening to the Arctic Monkeys' first album. Stopped at a red light just outside the small town where I live, I checked to see if Victoria had replied with an email. Which was, conveniently, exactly what she'd done. This is what I read:

'Dearest David,

'Finally I am alone, lying on my bed, a pile of books and newspapers by my side. It is only 9.30 p.m.

'On my BlackBerry, I have your strange text: "I would like to give you something that no other man has ever given you. You've already done that for me."

'I don't understand – what have I done? I would really like to know, to savour it, to feel its full significance. I gave you something you'd never had before? The way I love you? I don't think so. My emails and the way I tell you my most intimate thoughts? As you can see, your little text has plunged me deep in thought.'

That was not what I'd meant by my enigmatic text. But it's true that, around that time, she'd begun sending me pages from her private diary, under the title 'Meeting Minutes', talking about our meetings, and those entries seemed all the more arousing to me because it seemed Victoria had not written them with the intention of sending them to me. They struck me as genuinely intimate, truthful and absolutely sincere. The proof of this was that Victoria questioned herself about me, and that she was sometimes critical of our relationship, even upset.

So, after the meeting that took place a few days later, I received this document:

'Meeting Minutes
'Subject: Monday 7 November
'Author: Me
'Recipients: You, perhaps
'When I left my room, he was already sitting in the bar, in the same place as last time. I felt a bit more relaxed and sure of myself

because we'd had a few phone conversations in the days before that had enabled us to get to know each other a bit better, to demystify each other. Anyway, I felt good. David, on the other hand, seemed annoyed and embarrassed to be there with me, as he has been several times before. He started telling me about his building site. He seemed nervous and ill at ease, as if he were wondering what he was doing there. When he's like that, he talks in monologues, following an idea on his own . . .

'We ordered two glasses of pink champagne, then two more. And then we were interrupted by a telephone call – I wasn't happy about this at all – from his wife! He then told me he couldn't stay with me all evening, as we'd agreed.

'Suddenly he gathered his things and, just like last time, I didn't understand what he wanted at first. For a brief moment, I thought he was leaving, but no – time was short and he wanted to make the most of it. I let him lead me on his arm to the lifts and we locked ourselves in the room.

'What is this primal power that thrusts me into his arms? The same power that made heat radiate from my solar plexus in the shopping centre when he first spoke to me.

'And then the separation. As he walks towards the car park to get his car, I decide not to turn around. We are moving away from each other, and I know perfectly well that he is waiting for me to make some last sign with my hand.

'He tells me he has to go and see his wife, that she is unwell. He says there is an emergency this evening, that he'll explain it to me later. I suspect he's making it up. I don't entirely believe this story . . . it's a gut feeling I have, irrational and without any justification.

'It's 8.40 p.m. If I hurry, I can still manage to see a film at the cinema in Opéra. But walking through the cold November darkness doesn't really calm me down. I am furious that I have had to organize my arrival one day earlier for nothing – to be dumped with an excuse that seems phoney and clumsy. But what is my problem? Am I a little girl or a grown woman?

'I calm down a bit in front of the magnificent shop windows of Printemps Haussmann and Galeries Lafayette. I can always count on my passion for fashion to console myself . . . And then I feel furious again when some guy hits on me by telling me I'm "beautiful and strange". Can't he see I'm furious? Where's the respect?

'Finally, feeling slightly ashamed of myself, I buy a ticket for some crap American film whose title I don't want to admit.'

Sylvie had sent me several messages during the day. They had worried me a little bit, and afterwards she had phoned to tell me she felt anxious. She asked me to come home as soon as my dinner was over (I'd told her that I had to spend the evening with a contractor to celebrate his birthday). I'd sensed her anxiety for several days by then – it was perceptible in her muffled voice, like a cloth soaked with water, or like a bell whose clapper has been trapped in two fingers. Like everyone, she sometimes felt worried for no apparent reason, but what alarmed me was that Sylvie had been showing signs of frailty that I hadn't noticed in her behaviour for many years. What was happening? When I got home, having left Victoria in front of the Gare Saint-Lazare, I discovered that she was merely anxious in an ordinary way, stressed by the annoyances of everyday life, depressed by an ominous feeling she had about November. It really did seem as though Sylvie had known I was seeing my mistress and that she had wanted to play a trick on me. I was relieved to find her in a less critical condition than her telephone call had led me to fear, but I got angry with her, saying that because of her, I'd had to cut short a dinner that was important for my job. 'But you work ten hours a day!' Sylvie replied. 'Isn't that enough to get what we need, working ten hours a day? How is it possible, when you spend your life on the building site, that you can be in a situation where a dinner can have such a huge importance for your job?' Sylvie was not speaking aggressively. She made this simple observation in a faint, barely audible voice, huddled in a thick tartan blanket on the sitting-room sofa, her gaze absorbed by the soundless images on the TV screen: a drab, cement-coloured city, covered in stones and dust and patrolled by equally dusty people with rifles slung over their shoulders; the next image showed children throwing stones at placid soldiers sheltering behind barbed wire; in all the images, there was the same dust, the same stones, the same unsurfaced ground; the same bare, desolate earth, with the same merciless sun beating down upon it, as in the Bible. I turned back to look at Sylvie, and said that it wasn't as simple as that, and that we ought to go to bed. 'Everything will be better tomorrow,' I told her. 'Well, for us anyway,' I added, gesturing to the images on the screen.

After receiving a few pages about this interrupted evening, I replied to Victoria, telling her that these meeting minutes were having an ever more vivid effect on my imagination. 'For me, it is incredibly moving, exciting, flattering, if also slightly unsettling. I promise I am going to try to rectify these faults that you've pointed out!' I wrote in reply. 'In particular, I am going to make an effort to cut down on my monologues. It's true that I do sometimes hide my shyness behind a wall of words – a wall that can sometimes grow too high – but I promise I'll improve on this, and that from now on we will spend less time talking and more time making love.' As for the suspicion she'd formed about being left in the lurch for a fake excuse, I promised Victoria that I would tell her the reason for my departure the next time I saw her. 'My wife was very ill in the past. Mentally ill, I mean. She isn't any more – she hasn't been for many years – but each time she sends me a signal, I worry more than I ought to, and above all more quickly than I ought to. As soon as she tells me she's anxious, or if I sense it in her, I become extremely vigilant and quite worried. That evening, when she called me, I panicked – I admit it. I ask your forgiveness. Especially as there wasn't really anything wrong with her. I had a real go at her, in fact, if you want to know the truth. I've been sulking with her for the past two days.' I ended this message by telling Victoria that she was precious to me, that I thought of her every moment of every day, and that I couldn't wait to see her again. That was how I ended most of the messages I sent her.

One evening, just after we had made love (it was our third meeting in Paris, I think – 14 November – though it may have been the one after that: I forget), I parted the thick curtains to look outside. I still hadn't come, and I had remembered the idea I'd had about Victoria possibly wanting to have a baby. The sign for the Brasserie Mollard displayed its cursive script on the facade of the building opposite. People pushed at the restaurant's doors, probably as starving as I was, and I could see others behind the windows eating shellfish. I was naked. I shivered, feeling the cool outside air. It must have been around 10 p.m., and apart from the green olives we'd nibbled with our glasses of champagne before going up to the room, we hadn't eaten anything. I turned back to the bed, where Victoria was staring at me. I knelt down in front of her, took her foot in my hands, and asked her if she was hungry. She said she was: the eight hours of talks she'd had with the unions had left her ravenous; all she'd had to eat was a small tuna sandwich. 'What do you want to do?' I asked her. 'Shall we go downstairs and eat at Mollard or have dinner in the room like we did last time?'

'I don't know. How long have you got?'

'I should leave around midnight, something like that. It's difficult for me to get home after 1 a.m.'

'Let's eat here, then. It's simpler and more private – and the food is good, too. I can't really be bothered to get dressed and go out – it's so cold. And like this, we can make love again,' she added, wiggling her foot playfully in my hands.

'You're insatiable, Victoria.'

'You make me insatiable. With you, I always want to. All I have to do is look at you, and I want you . . .'

Victoria smiled – a wide and lasting smile, at once certain and pensive, like a mirror reflecting her desire. I looked at her in silence for a few moments, before asking: 'Why don't you have any children? Was it a deliberate choice? Did you decide you wouldn't have children, or did it just happen like that?'

'Why do you ask me that now?'

'Sorry. Perhaps it was a bit abrupt. I should have asked more delicately . . .'

'No, not really. It's just that the question is strange, coming out of the blue like that.'

'I don't know. It came to me while I was looking outside. I wondered how it was possible that a woman like you could be single and childless. It's not a problem – it's perfect for me – but as it's fairly unusual . . .'

'Who says I don't have any children, or that I'm single?'

'What do you mean?'

'I mean, where did you get the idea that I don't have children, and that I'm single?'

'Sorry, I don't understand. What do you mean?'

'I mean that I never told you I didn't have children, nor that I was single.'

'I don't see what you're getting at. You never told me you had children, nor that you lived with a man.'

'You never asked me, David. You never asked if I had children, or if I was married . . .'

'What do you mean? What are you talking about? Of course I asked you! Maybe not explicitly, but it was obvious!' Then, after a brief silence: 'Are you saying you do have children and you are married?' Victoria smiles at me and starts wiggling her feet in my hands again – wiggling them frantically as if to console me, to make me laugh. 'You should see your face,' she says.

'Why? What's wrong with my face?'

'It's all screwed up. You look panic-stricken.'

'Well, I'm sorry, but you're basically telling me . . .' I pause and look at Victoria. A wide, mocking, radiant, provocative smile is displayed on her face like the Brasserie Mollard sign on the facade of the building opposite. I thought she was going to finish my sentence for me, but no: Victoria seems to have decided to make me extort each of her revelations, like a wily defendant. Finally, I say: 'Do you have children?'

'I've got four.'

'Four children?'

'Four girls. Four beauties, aged sixteen, fourteen and nine-year-old twins. All very pretty, lively, intelligent. They'll all outshine me.'

'You're pulling my leg . . .'

'Not at all.'

I wonder if she will perhaps start unpacking all her secrets in one go, but she maintains an obstinate silence. She doesn't seem worried that I will react badly. Rather, she seems amused by my wild groping in the dark, and makes no effort to help me find my way. My dismay makes her laugh, as if this conversation is making me look as bemused as a child.

Staring at her commandingly, I say: 'Victoria.' Those four syllables echo in the darkness like the name of something that is, for me, increasingly elusive – an idea, an organization whose complexity I am only just discovering.

'Victoria. Do you really have four daughters?'

'You look like you don't believe me.'

Time passes between each of our replies – time, accompanied by cautious thoughts, as if I am climbing a staircase and discovering a landscape that seems to extend ever further with each step.

'And the father?'

'The father what?'

'I don't know . . . What does the father . . . ?'

'You mean my husband?'

'So you're married?'

'Of course I'm married! What do you take me for? Do you really think that, in the world I move in, and even more so in the world my husband moves in – the de Winter family – we could have four children without being married?'

She had said 'the de Winter family' in a starchy, mocking voice: I presumed she was imitating someone she detested (perhaps an old, sententious mother-in-law). If Victoria had, on a whim, made up an improbable story, she wouldn't have spoken to me in a tone any less facetious; there would have been the same sparkle in her eyes; her foot would have made the same little, amused movements in my hands, movements that seemed to say, as in a nursery rhyme: 'So . . . is it true? Or is it not true? Is it a lie? Or is it not a lie? Is she married? Or is she not married?' I examined Victoria's face, trying to work out what this was all about.

'And where is he, your husband?'

'In Paris.'

'In Paris? You mean you're separated?'

'Not at all. We're married, and we live as a married couple.

Everything is wonderful, except that he works in Paris and me in London. We see each other every other weekend in London or Paris.'

'Your husband lives in Paris and we're . . . You rent a hotel room when you have an apartment in Paris with your husband?'

'As you can see.'

'But your husband . . . Sorry, there's something I'm missing here. Does he know you're in Paris tonight?' Victoria looks at me aghast, as if the question she has just heard is so stupid she can hardly believe it. 'Of course not,' she says. 'If he did, how could I . . .'

'Obviously. Sorry. If he did, how could you . . .'

'Obviously.'

'And you're not worried that he'll find out you're in Paris?'

'How could he?'

'I don't know. He could pass you in the street, call your assistant . . . say he couldn't get hold of you on your mobile, he might call your assistant, who'd tell him you were in Paris . . .'

'He never calls my assistant.'

'And if he calls your daughters?'

'He calls them every evening.'

'So what city are you supposed to be in this evening, as far as your husband and daughters are concerned?'

'I told them I was spending the night in Frankfurt. They all think I'm in Germany, mugging up on the files for a nightmarish merger. Frankly, we're a lot better off here,' Victoria says, struggling to contain her smile (I have a feeling that my growing seriousness is going to end up making her laugh hysterically).

'So everything's fine.'

'Yes, everything's fine.'

A long silence.

I try to imagine her situation, and the more I think about it, the less able I am not to find it disturbing – when, really, it doesn't amount to anything more than having rented a hotel room and spending the night there. It doesn't bother me that Victoria lies to her husband (what else am I doing with Sylvie?), but I am shocked by the idea that she is capable of sleeping in the city where he lives and making him believe that she's staying in Frankfurt. The geographical lie – and I couldn't really say why – strikes me as a transgression that is far from harmless. Or, to be more precise, I feel like it will take me some time to get my head round it, as if it is connected to her very identity. I have the feeling that living within such a complete falsehood must entail the breach of a major taboo, although at this moment I am incapable of identifying that taboo. All I know is that I would find it difficult to make Sylvie believe I was spending the night in London when I was actually staying in Paris. It's true that, at the end of the day, Victoria's lie is no more serious than most of the lies we are forced to tell as part of our daily existence (it is simply more audacious, and a little more risky). But I also feel it is something other than that – that, beyond its practical function, what it says, albeit vaguely, is that the person who tells this lie is, herself, a lie. In fact, the falsification that makes it possible for Victoria to be stretched out on the bed here in front of me without her husband knowing is evidence not only of the strategy she is employing in order to spend time with me; it is also evidence of the ease with which she takes liberties with the truth. This ease is a space, and this space is her life. Her life is a fiction in which she passionately embraces the real world, her desires inciting her to commit the most extreme falsifications because only those falsifications can bring the rewards that will satiate her desires. Victoria is in both Paris and Frankfurt. And she genuinely is in Frankfurt at the same time that she is in Paris (tomorrow morning she will have a long phone conversation with each of her four daughters, describing the sky over Germany and the dinner she ate the evening before in a noisy tavern). Victoria has the ability to transcend the truths that encumber her in order to invent other, higher truths in which she is metamorphosed – like a goddess with unlimited powers. I understand now: the ankles I am caressing belong to a woman for whom everything is possible. Suddenly I find this situation incredibly stimulating, intoxicating, liberating, as if, in her slip-stream, we are all freed – from now on, nothing will be forbidden us. But, at the same time, this fascination is accompanied in my mind by terror. It's like seeing the propellers of an aeroplane on the runway of an airport: this immaterial, suspended circle is a beautiful reality (and it is thanks to this propeller that we will be able to soar into the sky, just as it was thanks to Victoria's powers that I could soar into a long-desired happiness), but get too close and its blades will tear you to shreds. The same was true for Victoria, lying on the bed: I had the intuition that I must not insert my scepticism into the fiction that she embodied, the fluid illusion of which was a result of the high-speed circular movement, like a propeller, of a number of keen convictions.

'But it must be strange for you, isn't it, being in a hotel room when you live part-time in Paris?'

'Is it strange for you?'

'But I go home to sleep. I'll be leaving in an hour.'

'All that means is that I'm better at this than you. If you were more inventive, we'd be able to spend the night in each other's arms. I have a more poetic vision of existence, that's all,' she says teasingly.

It occurs to me that she's right. This arrangement she's made so that we can see each other in the best possible conditions is evidence of a propensity for the poetic – or, to be more precise, for living life like a novel – which it would be unfair to take away from her.

'But when we don't see each other and you come to Paris, where do you sleep?'

'At my husband's place. At home.'

'That's not clear. Your home or your husband's home?'

'Our real house, with all our things, is in London. We have a pied-à-terre in Paris, where my husband stays for his work. This is a temporary situation.'

'What does he do, your husband?'

'He's a cellist.'

'A cellist?'

'Yes, a cellist. He's made several CDs and has played as a soloist with major orchestras. He's not hugely famous, but he's highly thought of in the world of music.'

A slender sword pierces my body: during the brief moment when the point of this revelation penetrates my thoughts, I feel the intense sting of jealousy.

I would never have imagined that Victoria, if she was married, would be married to a cellist. I feel increasingly unable to make her out. It seems to me that, the more I see her, the less she conforms to my expectations. And, of course, the nature of her husband's job is upsetting to me, the fact that he is an acclaimed artist, when I have given up my architectural ambitions: I have done what this man would have done if – lacking faith in his abilities, or in the possibilities of life – he had become a cello teacher in some music academy. And in spite of being knocked backwards by this conflicting information – or perhaps because of it – I can feel, deep inside me, a sensation I know all too well: the burning point of attachment . . . or even love. I know this is where love is born, when it is born. This is where everything begins, usually. This star flashed for a few seconds, and then I felt it fade into dimness.

'What's the matter?' Victoria asks me.

I don't reply. Eyes closed, I stroke the inside of her thigh. I hear her say: 'I love it when you do that. It's good – keep doing it . . .'

I open my eyes and stare at her for a long time. I say: 'But is everything all right, with you and your husband?'

'And with you and your wife?' I burst out laughing and kiss Victoria's foot. I say: 'Touché. But . . . I mean . . . it's hard for me to gauge . . .'

'What is hard for you to gauge?'

'If you're . . . the two of you . . .'

'If we're in trouble? If we need some time away from each other, to take stock of our relationship? Is that what you want to know?'

I smile and briefly hide my face behind her thigh, out of shame, before admitting: 'Yeah, something like that.'

'All right, then, I can tell you this: I will never leave my husband. I love him. He's the father of my four daughters. He's an exceptional human being. I respect him and I'm proud of him. I admire him today just like I admired him when I met him twenty years ago.'

'It's the same for me. I will never leave my wife either. I don't know if I admire her – it's probably a different kind of feeling, but one that's just as important. The idea of leaving her is inconceivable.'

'So that's perfect. What are we complaining about?'

'Nobody's complaining . . .'

'Well, a little bit. You seem a bit upset by what you've learned.'

'No, I'm just upset that I only learned it now.'

'What difference does it make that you only learned it now?'

'I don't know. You should have told me before, shouldn't you? What was stopping you?'

Victoria does not reply. Finally, she says: 'What's the point of saying things, giving explanations, weighing down the present? We didn't need that kind of information the other evening, in order to be happy, so why would I risk damaging that balance by telling you the banal details of my life?'

'Last time, in this same hotel, I confessed to you in a slightly idiotic way that I was married and I had children. You let me say it. You could, at that moment, have told me that you too had . . .'

'What would that have changed?'

'Nothing at all. Except that, in a normal relationship – an honest relationship between two people – they tell each other things. I'll go further: there are some things that are so important that they have to be said.'

'There can also be very important things that you decide not to speak about.'

'Is that what happened?'

'No!' she laughs suddenly. 'It's not even that!'

I watch her laugh for a moment, then I ask: 'So? Why didn't you say anything?'

'But does it really bother you that I'm married?'

'And the man you told me about the other day – who was that? Are you collecting lovers?' Victoria looks at me in silence. Her face shows no emotion: no cheerfulness, no anxiety, no panic. She is waiting. The ball is in my court. 'Does your husband know about your collection of lovers?'

'I don't have a collection of lovers.'

'Didn't you have a lover, before you met me? The day we saw each other . . .'

'It just happened like that. I wasn't looking for a new lover to replace the old one.'

'Although I guess it did suit you not to have any downtime

between the end of your old affair and the beginning of your new one . . .'

'How perceptive of you. Why not? Yes, I admit it, I prefer not having any downtime.'

'Meaning that, for you, the idea of living with your husband, but not having a lover, is unbearable?'

'Not at all. If I was forced never to have another lover, I would resign myself to that.'

'That's not quite what you told me last time.'

Suddenly, Victoria looks lost: something flickers in her eyes. She says: 'What did I say last time?'

'That you'd decided to get back with your lover and to accept his conditions. In order not to be alone.'

Victoria looks away. She is starting to show signs of weariness. I can sense her growing cold.

'You didn't answer my question.'

'Which one?' she asks, sighing. 'This is like a police interrogation . . .'

'If you had some kind of agreement with your husband. You know, like an open relationship . . .'

'Not at all. There's no agreement.'

'Does he suspect you have lovers?'

'He has no idea!' Victoria replies, laughing. 'He'd fall over backwards if he knew! He sees me as the mother of his children: an honest, upstanding woman who has sworn to be faithful to him. He knows I admire him. He couldn't imagine that I might like another man. Which is why he is not at all jealous or possessive, meaning I have more freedom than if he was watching me all the time.'

'You say he sees you as the mother of his children . . .'

'He's never been very driven by sex.'

'You don't make love?'

'Of course we do. But I'm the one who initiates it. He likes sex, but he could live without it. That's perhaps another reason why he's not jealous.'

'What do you mean?'

'He doesn't really think about sex. He doesn't see me as a woman who could make men desire her. He knows I'm attractive, but he has no idea how sexual men's looks can be – how extreme, how bestial, completely unlike his – and the fires that these looks can sometimes spark in women . . .'

I have a hard-on.

'That makes me want to make love with you, when I hear you talk like that.'

'So let's do it . . .'

'No, hang on, I still have things to ask you.'

'What about you? Do you often make love with your wife?' Victoria asks with a smile.

'Not very often. But I like making love with her. It's good.'

'So why do you rarely make love?'

'I didn't say rarely. I said not very often.'

'All right, not very often . . .'

'Desire isn't measured only in the frequency of intercourse. I always want my wife. For instance, I sometimes masturbate while imagining us making love . . . and yet nothing sexual may happen between us for quite a long time. Sometimes it's good, and even beautiful, to internalize the desire you feel for your spouse, to keep it within you like treasure. I don't know how to explain this. For me, making love is not proof of anything – nor is not making love. I think what counts is the imaginary world connected to your wife, to your relationship. When that imaginary world is dead, then the relationship is dead. In that imaginary world, the erotic charge linked to your spouse can have an incredible radiance, without translating into acts. It doesn't matter. My wife continues to inspire me, to move me. Her body still speaks to me . . .'

'I think I understand.'

'It's also the fact that we spend our lives doing things. We are essentially obedient soldiers. So, in the evening, when you get home, sometimes you don't feel like obeying – whether your desire or the appeal of your wife's body. Sometimes you just want to let go – to look at the person you live with, to think that she's beautiful or that you love her, to cuddle up with her.'

'You see making love as a chore? That's an original idea . . .'

'I don't see it as a chore. It's just that, sometimes, it seems . . .'

'Like a chore? Do you force yourself? When you fuck me for hours, is that like you're on the scaffolding, constructing a floor of the tower?' Victoria laughs.

'Not at all,' I reply. 'But I'm hungry. If you suggest we make love instead of ordering something to eat, then I probably will treat it like a chore!'

'I hope you would at least think to say "No, Victoria, I'm hungry, I don't want to make love any more!"'

'It's not always easy to resist you. Desire is sometimes stronger than willpower.'

Victoria looks like she's thinking, so I speak next: 'How long was he your lover for, the guy who dumped you just before we met?'

'Two and a half years. I thought you were hungry?'

'Two and a half years!'

'What's so surprising?'

'That you're capable of having a lover for such a long time. Nothing like that has ever happened to me.'

'Yeah, sure. I know you men, and your declarations of innocence . . .'

'I never said I'd never had a mistress. But I've never been with any of those women more than twice.'

Victoria looks at me without replying.

'And before him – before that lover – how many were there?'

'Hardly any. Nothing important. It was pure chance that I met you just as it was ending with my previous lover. Don't start imagining that . . .'

'I'm not imagining anything at all. As you can see, my imagination is fairly limited: I didn't anticipate any of this. Anyway, I'm probably being very naive in believing this version of events. You've probably had a constant stream of lovers since the very beginning of your marriage.'

Victoria picked up the menu from the bedside table.

'I told you I hadn't. What do you want?'

'Same as last time: chateaubriand with Béarnaise sauce.'

'Grilled sea bream for me.'

'So that's why you didn't spend the night with me at the hotel, and you claimed you had to change your clothes? When you told me that a woman in your position couldn't turn up to the office two days running in the same outfit, remember?'

'I'm still surprised you swallowed that!' Victoria said, laughing. 'I had to get home before my daughters woke up, and changing my clothes was the best excuse I could come up with . . . Anyway, I'm going to call room service. I think we should have a *grand cru*. We ought to celebrate all these revelations!'

One lunchtime, while we were talking on the phone, Victoria told me that a meeting scheduled for the next morning had been cancelled, and that she found herself – 'and this is unheard of for someone in my position' – with a completely empty window of time in her diary. Her assistant Johanna had not yet got round to filling this gap with any of the meetings on Victoria's waiting list.

'I have fifteen minutes before she comes back from lunch. So what are you doing tomorrow morning?' Victoria asks me abruptly. I tell her I'll be on the construction site. But I already have a hard-on – I can guess where she's going with this – and I start to stroke myself through the wool of my trousers. I've just eaten lunch: the sandwich packaging, a rolled-up paper napkin and a nearly-empty can of 1664 are arrayed on my desk. My colleagues have gone to have a coffee at the Valmy; I told them I would join them later. 'You think you can?' Victoria asks me in a suave voice.

'Can what? Free myself up to see you?'

'So we can fuck like crazy for an hour tomorrow morning. I'll tell Johanna that I'm replacing this meeting with an important appointment with I don't know who – my notary, for instance – and we can make the decision now, spontaneously, without thinking.'

'What time can you be in Paris?'

'I can take the Eurostar that arrives at 10.17. I'll book a room at the Terminus Nord and I'll be in bed waiting for you at 10.30. I'll take the Eurostar back to London at 12.13, so I can arrive there about 1.30. I've got an important meeting at 2 p.m. I'll be a bit late, but that doesn't matter.'

'You're completely mad.'

'Are you complaining? How many women do you know who'd decide to spend five hours in one morning on the Eurostar to make love for an hour and a half?'

'I don't know any other woman who'd be capable of it. I'll make arrangements to be at Terminus Nord from 10.30 to midday. I'll sort something out with Dominique so my absence isn't a problem.' Victoria is practically purring with pleasure. She tells me this is wonderful, that she's happy, that life is insane. I interrupt her to say: 'Capitalism is pretty cool, in fact. The lives we lead, when you think about it . . .'

'You're telling *me*?'

'To be honest, I'm wondering if your values are not more fun than mine . . .'

'Finally, the penny drops! I did tell you I'd turn you right wing! You can see now how idiotic it is, how backward, to be a socialist in today's world . . . to stay frozen in rigid principles that date back to another century!'

'It's certainly not backward. It depends what we're talking about.'

'What kind of satisfaction does socialism give you? What kind of euphoria does it promise, apart from revolution? Which will never happen anyway. Whereas with me, have you seen what it's like? It's real – and instant!'

'What's certain is that the lives of you rich people are perfect for pleasure-seekers. Today's true libertines are undoubtedly on the right. Eroticism has changed political opinion: I'm beginning to be convinced of that.'

'That's exactly what I think. In the seventies, sex was on the side of the hippies. Nowadays, it's on the side of the CEOs! Believe me, David, that is valuable information – and completely true! You've discovered a very well-kept secret.'

'I wouldn't go that far. But the fact that you're able to travel from London, in the middle of the week, to make love in Paris for the duration of a film . . . I find that fascinating. And extremely arousing.'

'I love that. It's true that our meeting tomorrow will last as long as a film.'

Two days later, I received a long message from Victoria – under its usual title, 'Meeting Minutes' – describing our rendezvous at Terminus Nord, that old and majestic hotel located in front of the Gare du Nord like an ocean liner made of stone.

In this message, she writes that she circled room 548 'like a panther' while she waited for me to arrive. She relates how, for once, we didn't bother with conversation in a bar, nor filter our perceptions with head-spinning pink champagne, but that we leapt passionately upon each other. Or, to be more precise, she says in the next sentence, she leapt passionately on me. She sensed some reserve in me, a reluctance to abandon myself, as if I were turned inward rather than outward to the joy of us seeing each other again. 'Doubts?' she wondered, seeing me 'so pensive, and a bit unwilling'. She wonders if we should have given ourselves more time before starting on the sex as if it was a mountain we had to climb. Or, at least, this is what she thought a bit later when, lying against my body, she listened to me tell the story of how I was mugged at the end of August in front of a cash machine in the 20th arrondissement, at about two in the morning. She notes that we were, at this point, giving ourselves time to get to know each other. 'Time is essential. But where to find it in these multifaceted and increasingly fast lives?' She writes that, while I was telling her about this assault, she watched me, she discovered me, she saw both the little boy I must once have been in the playground and the adult man who experienced this incident. She imagined a slightly awkward, shy child, with a gorgeous face, hair the colour of wood, and very long eyelashes; a slim, pale, gentle boy. She writes that she asked me if I was bullied during breaktimes when I was young: I admitted I was, and she thought that she would have taken me into her gang and nobody would have been allowed to lay a finger on me; she would have defended me tooth and nail. At that moment, while she was thinking this, she told me that I was wrong not to defend myself against the three thugs who'd forced me to withdraw a large sum of money from the cash machine. She told me that, in those circumstances, she would have defended herself and that no one would have been able to steal anything from her unless they tore it violently out of her hands and suffered all the punches she could land. I told her it was completely stupid to risk being maimed for €300. Victoria replied that you had to make people respect you in this life, and never accept another's domination. I said that, faced with three thugs armed with knives in the middle of the night, you have no choice but to obey. She said that wasn't true at all, that you had to resist, and that it was a question of principle, and I cut short this conversation, which was getting tiresome, by saying that we clearly didn't have the same principles. Victoria concludes this part of her message with the words: 'I annoyed him a bit, I'm afraid. It's true I was a bit rough there.'

Next, Victoria notes that what she absolutely wants to record in writing, so she never forgets it, is that dizzying last half-hour, when our bodies seem to find the perfect rhythm.

'He was hard as a rock. I was on top of him. A swell of pleasure went through us, from head to foot . . . How can I describe that unique journey, and at the same time my certainty that it could not have happened without him – without his presence, without his caresses?

'When he felt how hot and wet I was, he suddenly called me a slut. He said I loved that, and I was a real slut.

'I was disturbed, frightened, ashamed, indignant. I did not appreciate being treated so badly when I was at the height of my pleasure, concentrated on our rhythm, on my body's orgasmic shudders. I was so whole and honest at that moment, I would have preferred nonsense words, or words of love, or a groan of pleasure, rather than a word as crude as 'slut'.

'Do I scare him? He told me I was insatiable, that it seemed like I could never get enough . . . but how can I be anything else when the slightest brush of his fingers puts me in a state like that?

It hurt me to hear that word at a moment when I had given myself completely to him, and at the same time, perversely, the word excited me. He realized he'd hurt me, though. He asked me if that word shocked me. I said that it did, and that I thought it was inappropriate in this context, and then – the bastard – he said, in that case, how come I got even wetter when he spoke the word in my ear. My God, the traitor! Saying that to me! And he was right! David looked me in the eyes, smiling, while I continued to ride him methodically (I hadn't stopped sliding up and down his cock). He repeated that as soon as he called me a slut, my pussy had started pouring . . .'

A bit further on, Victoria writes a paragraph that I think is extremely important to an understanding of our story:

'But I'm still searching . . . I still don't understand how to make him come. What triggers his pleasure? What is his key?'

I didn't know the answer to that myself, and that was exactly the problem I was facing in my relationship with Victoria. I couldn't find the trigger – or the key – that would allow me to come.

Victoria turned me on – my constant erection was solid proof of her appeal to me – but I couldn't manage to liberate my imagination in such a way that I could produce an orgasm. The mountain I was trying to climb was smooth, without notches; it was like scaling a metal wall. My pleasure couldn't haul itself up to the light I glimpsed at the summit; it was stuck down below.

I had never imagined that such a problem could occur to a man; I always thought that the two hazards of male sexuality were impotence and premature ejaculation. If someone had told me about the existence of this difficulty, I would have been surprised that it was not specifically a feminine problem, but my relationship with Victoria made me realize that a man, too, can struggle with this. Finding no way to come was a bit like being locked in an empty room that kept growing larger, the more you concentrated on trying to find a door. Or, to use a different metaphor, it was as if I were searching for the rope that could pull me up to the height of pleasure. This rope might be a thought, an image, a fantasy, Victoria's groans, a feeling caused by a vision of part of her body . . . but nothing clicked; every thought my mind came up with proved incapable of getting me going. I made love to Victoria, but never saw the rope anywhere near me – and when I did finally think I'd found it and I started to grip it, I discovered a few seconds later that it wasn't connected to anything, that it was slack. Even when I drank in the spectacle of Victoria coming, when I stared at her magnificent breasts, heard her cries, examined her small feet, her statuesque hips, or her adolescent face transported into the heights of ecstasy, my erect cock and my yearning mind were exactly like a man in the desert walking towards a mirage.

'He joined me when I was in the shower. My train was going to leave in twenty minutes, and I was in a rush. But he had a glorious hard-on and he complained that I was going to leave him in this state. So I told him to masturbate in front of me, and he did.

'I watched the way he did it. It was quite feminine: gentle and slow, just under his glans, a small gesture – firm and gentle – concentrated on one single tiny point . . . and, watching him like that, I understood. He needed time. A wonderful discovery. It was perhaps our secrecy, our urgency – in contrast to marital time, conjugal time – that was preventing him from coming. Perhaps this man could only come in the security of a slower, calmer time.'

Victoria concludes her minutes by writing that the slightest memory of this hour and a half spent with me in that room at the

Terminus Nord causes pains of nostalgia in her stomach. She wishes we could devote more time to each other, that we could find somewhere peaceful and unhurried.

During our meetings and conversations (particularly when I drove home in the evenings, when I put the speakerphone on and we got to talk for quite a long time), Victoria told me about large swathes of her past. She submitted to my interrogations with apparent goodwill, never showing the slightest reluctance to answer any question I asked her, but I sometimes sensed that she was not telling the truth, or was gracefully evading the subject. I had to be extremely insistent, or confront her with her contradictions, to corner her into agreeing to enlighten me. These slow unveilings took place in a light-hearted atmosphere, on both sides. It was part of the game that Victoria did not reveal anything voluntarily, because it ended up being clear that her past was perhaps a little racier than I might have expected when I first met her, and racier than my own past too.

'There's something I'm wondering about. It's a complete mystery to me,' I told her one day. 'You'll probably find it naive, but for me it's a genuine question.' We were in a room at the Louvre Hotel that evening, looking out over the Palais-Royal. 'I'm listening,' Victoria replied, mocking my naivety in advance. 'So what is your question?'

'How a woman like you, having grown up with a bourgeois, conservative, religious background . . .'

'With very strict principles . . . if that's what you mean.'

'Exactly. You husband sounds like he's someone respectable. He trusts you. I imagine him to be sensitive, perhaps a little fragile. You've mentioned your mother-in-law a few times — some kind of dreadful duchess living in a chateau . . .'

'She never accepted me – because I came from a less important family than theirs. But do you know what shocks them most, including my husband?'

'No. Tell me. But don't try to change the subject – I know you.'

'I'm not changing the subject – we'll come back to that. I'm just making a digression that I think will interest you, given that you claim to be a feminist.'

'I really am. If not, I wouldn't be here with you in this room.'

'I know. So, listen: they resent the fact that I don't need them; they resent my independence. If my husband lived alone, his mother would support him financially. His income is much smaller than mine, even when he releases a CD or gives concerts or wins a prize . . . He really dislikes the idea that I am supporting our family. It compromises his conception of the father's and mother's roles. He resents the fact that he is not fulfilling his own ideal of masculinity. He would like to be able to feed us all with his art. I understand that. Money is a taboo subject in our house: my responsibilities, the progress of my career. I can't tell my husband I've had a raise, or that I've received such and such number of stock options, or that my boss has widened the scope of my position: he would think I was trying to rub his nose in my superiority. Perhaps it's simply my success that he dislikes. A lot of men can't bear the idea of a woman being successful. No matter how mature he is, my husband can't escape this mindset: he doesn't know how to deal with the simple fact that I'm powerful, that I earn lots of money, that headhunters from all over the world are constantly seeking me out.'

'I could never understand that kind of attitude.'

'I pay for practically everything, but nobody must ever mention that. The subject is taboo. My husband's in denial about it. As long as this reality remains unspoken, everything is fine between us. In the eyes of my in-laws, however, I am undoubtedly an example of the very worst of the modern world (but not quite for the same reasons as a socialist like you might think this): for them, because I was vulgar enough to want to supplant my husband on a symbolic and material level, they see me as a whore, selling herself to the system to earn money, relieve boredom, overturn conventions, make myself look interesting, make myself the centre of attention. The simple fact that I have a career upsets them – as if I am constantly about to use it against them, and they are defending themselves against this potential threat. As if my mere appearance were in itself a demand that they feel bound to reject out of hand. In reality, as you can imagine, I am not demanding anything from them: whatever I do, I do for myself. I don't know how to explain it to you. They implicitly blame me for having trapped my husband by becoming the powerful woman that they have seen me turn into over the years, when the girl he married was merely a harmless student. By becoming what I've become, I have shown a lack of respect for my husband. I have been tactless towards him. I am guilty of bad taste. I am my husband's embarrassment, but it is not my husband who is guilty of bad taste – it is me, and me alone.'

'You've made my point. What you're saying confirms to me that you're living in an extremely codified world that doesn't allow any deviation from its governing principles – the first and most important of which is that the husband is the head of the family. You've already flouted that first principle: you've done exactly what you wanted. After that, there is another principle . . .'

'I think I can see where you're headed with this.'

'Exactly. At what point does a woman from your background decide to take a lover? At what point does a woman like you, assumed to be faithful to her husband, start lying to him? I've never really seen this happen. I've never led a woman from your background into adultery. For me, this is something beyond representation – this moment when, in a woman's conscience, the decision is made that she's going to offer her sacred body to a man other than her husband. I'd like you to describe that moment for me.'

'You've asked me that several times before, you know?'

'But you've never answered me clearly. You evade it, you smile, you talk about something else, but you don't answer the question.'

'Going to such trouble to obtain a glimmer of truth . . . you deserve a reward.' Victoria takes my cock between her hands and begins to slowly stroke it. I interrupt her: 'Thank you for being so appreciative of my efforts to get to know who you are. But please be so kind as to answer my question without trying to corrupt me.' Victoria laughs, but doesn't remove her hand from my cock. She says: 'Also, the way you've just phrased it, I understand your question better. Before, it seemed like you were merely curious about my marriage.'

'So, are you going to tell me?'

'You'll be disappointed. You'd have to ask another bourgeois woman to get a description of this mechanism: to see it working in reality, to hear it creak like a weather vane in her stunned little imagination.'

'I don't understand. What do you mean?'

'That the opposite actually happened. The decision to marry my husband lit up one day in my liberated woman's mind.'

'You're playing with words, as I should have expected. You do the same thing every time you're embarrassed by a question: you play with ideas and concepts, you give things a reflective sheen until everything ends up being mirrored in everything else.'

'That's not true at all. Listen to me. I understand what you mean: a woman who has never cheated on her husband can't cheat on her husband – or it must be painful, it must tear something very intimate from inside her. If I had been in the situation where I might have said to myself, "Shall I cheat on my husband?", then I might have stayed faithful. To be honest, I doubt that I could have. But that doesn't matter, because the question never arose.'

'I'm afraid I don't follow you.'

'I was already cheating on my husband when we first began to like each other. I continued cheating on him when he asked me to marry him. I cheated on him again when we were married. My husband made his vows, before the mayor and before the priest, with a woman who was cheating on him.'

'What do you mean? Tell me in more detail. You're going too fast.'

'I finished the first year of my PhD. I was doing work experience at the Agence France-Presse; I was interested in journalism. While I was there, I met a thirty-five-year-old man who became my lover. We made love once or twice a week. We weren't in love: it was physical and sexual. It was during this period that I met my husband. We were introduced by friends at a party. I was fascinated that he had won first prize at his Conservatoire and that he had started playing concerts – he was even going to make a CD. He called me a few days later to ask me out, and invited me to dine at La Tour d'Argent. Afterwards he walked me home, and kissed my hand when we said goodbye. We saw each other like this for several weeks. He wrote me very beautiful letters. One evening, in front of the entrance to my building, he kissed me on the lips. I adored him; I wanted to make love with him. I asked him if he would like to come up for a drink. Smiling, he declined, and then walked away. I was really turned on. I remember masturbating when I got back to my room. In fact, I think that very evening . . . Yes, I'm sure of it, but I hardly dare admit it to you . . .'

'Go ahead. We've come this far . . .'

'I was so keen to make love that I called my lover and spent the night with him.'

'No comment for the moment. Continue.'

'You make me laugh. Two days later, my future husband invites me to dinner. He tells me he wants to ask my father's permission for my hand. He wants to know what I think. I immediately accept his proposal. We were married in June, just over six months after our first meeting. We waited for our marriage night to make love. We were united as in the old days, as two virgins.'

'Do you think he'd ever made love with another woman?'

'I don't know, and I never asked him.'

'What's certain is that your husband married a woman whom he knew was capable of marrying him without having slept with him. That's very powerful, symbolically. In his eyes, that instantly and unquestionably made you a serious woman.'

'Exactly. And I was aware of it.'

'So, how did you come to cheat on him?'

'Ask any woman, and they will tell you that, having accepted his conditions, I gave my husband something of great value. So, by a curious paradox, we were quits. He owed me a sacrifice, which meant I was free to behave as I liked until our wedding day. As I had no sexual relations with him, I wasn't cheating on him by sleeping with my lover. My old Maths teacher always used to say that you could add apples to apples, but not apples to pears.'

'And when you were married?'

'I met up with my lover for a drink now and then, but it was so natural for us to make love that we had great trouble resisting.

We couldn't find any valid argument not to give in to our desire to jump in a taxi and go to his apartment . . . and, above all, fidelity was not an argument. On the contrary: we were faithful to something very beautiful that passing time had made ever more sacred, just like marriage. In the end, he met another woman and married her, and after that he didn't want to continue with me.'

'So you were left in the lurch.'

'Exactly. I was left in the lurch.'

'You're being sarcastic, but that's what happened. You found yourself without a lover to satisfy you. So you took another one.'

'I had to wait fifteen years for a new lover – when Laurent entered my life.'

'I don't believe you. And the basketball player you mentioned inadvertently the other day?'

'It wasn't inadvertent. I knew what I was doing when I told you about that man.'

'So he was your lover.'

'I only slept with him once.'

I smile at Victoria. 'Only once? Why only once?' She doesn't reply. 'Come on, tell me. I want to know.' I start to stroke the insides of her thighs, moving upwards little by little. 'Come on, Victoria, you know you want to. Tell me about your basketball lover.'

'What do you want to know?'

'Why did you see him only once?'

'For exactly the same reasons that you only saw your mistresses once.'

'I don't understand why you're refusing to tell me about your lovers. I know – I can sense – that there have been lots. I promise I won't be shocked.'

'Perhaps I'll tell you one day. But not now.'

'So you admit you're hiding things from me.'

'I don't admit anything at all. This is all your fantasy.'

'But you just said . . .'

I didn't learn anything else that evening. My fingers, that had been creeping up her thigh, finally slid inside the slit of her cunt, and we made love until the moment when we had to separate. But we continued this conversation at different times – by telephone and during the meetings that followed.

'You almost admitted it to me, the other evening, when we were coming out of the restaurant.'

I am standing behind Victoria, caressing her shoulders, while watching us in the mirror hung above the dresser, in a suite of the Louvre Hotel.

'What did I almost admit?'

'That you cheated on your husband, before Laurent and before me. You strongly implied it.'

'I had a fling with that basketball player, yes. And no, I didn't sleep with him only once. He was the first of my lovers, and we were together for a reasonably long period – about six months.'

'Finally you admit it. I love hearing you tell me about your life. I can sense it's inexhaustible. It's a bit like taking the first few steps into a forest: I can hear animal noises, strange cries in the treetops. I don't know if the forest is deep or old, but I think it is. I don't know if the forest is dangerous, if the animals who live here are aggressive, but I'm afraid of them. At the same time, I have to keep moving forward – because you keep dangling secrets in front of me, confessions you're going to make, a scrap of truth that will be revealed to me.'

I've been talking to her while watching her face in the mirror. I am still standing behind her, kneading her breasts through her silk blouse. She turns around slowly, her back to the mirror, and kisses me on the lips. We kiss for several minutes, hardly breathing. Then Victoria breaks away, looks at me gently and begins to speak: 'He was the first of my lovers.'

'How did you meet him?'

'Through a girlfriend who works in communications for a major firm that was, at the time, the main sponsor of the French basketball team. She invited me to a match in Bercy. We went in the changing rooms during the third break. I felt an instant attraction for one of the players, and it was mutual.'

'Just like that, in the changing rooms?'

'It was a huge turn-on. The sweat, the muscles, all those impressive bodies. They'd won the match. I'd said to my friend, come on, we're not really going in the changing rooms, are we? It's too private! But in fact, there are lots of people hanging around down there after a match, and we had a badge. I went into the changing rooms and the first thing I saw was a man's face: something passed between us straight away. He was topless, wearing only underwear. We stared at each other for a few seconds, amid the post-match noise and shouting and chaos. My friend saw it all happen.'

'And then . . . ?'

'We made love all night.'

'And you saw each other again.'

'We saw each other again. We became lovers. It lasted six months. We made love regularly – once or twice a week. I was working in Paris at the time. I even arranged some trips so that I could follow him for the French team's away matches. I was travelling less then than I do now, though, so it was complicated to set up fictitious journeys. I took a room in the same hotel as the French team, and he came to see me in the middle of the night.'

'And why did you stop?'

'I got a phone call one morning from his wife. She told me

that she knew he had a mistress. She asked me to disappear, to leave them in peace. I love that phrase: *leave them in peace*. Men are such cowards. It's better if they're not found out. As long as the wife knows nothing about it, there's no problem – they're heroic. But if they get stung, suddenly it's like they're victims; they claim that their mistress is harassing them.'

'When was this?'

'Three years ago,' Victoria says without thinking. 'About three years. Three and a half.'

'Just before Laurent.' I can see she is embarrassed by this observation. Her expression clouds over. She moves away from the dresser and lies on the bed. I join her there and say: 'It doesn't bother me that you've been collecting lovers, one after another, for twenty years. What I don't understand is why you pretended to me that you were a goody-two-shoes.'

'Oh, you think?'

'Remember in London, early in the morning, you told me you'd never felt such urgent desire for a stranger before, and certainly that you'd never given in to it. You said you didn't recognize yourself when this happened, and the next morning you felt outraged.' I pause, then continue. 'You described yourself as feeling mortified. You even called me a womanizer . . .'

'Which you are,' Victoria cuts in. 'You can't deny that you hunted me down – that I was a prey for you.'

'That's not true. I liked you. I wanted to get to know you. It's not the same thing.'

'You saw me, and you approached me. I was hunted. That's something that has always bothered me. That still bothers me.'

'That's what is difficult to understand. Why don't you admit that you're not a goody-two-shoes and that you've had lots of lovers? Perhaps you've even hunted men. Perhaps you've been the hunter, not the prey.'

'Why don't I admit it? Because it's not true. I'm not like that. I had those two lovers, and then you. I'm just lucky, that's all.'

I liked questioning Victoria about her past – I acknowledge that – but Victoria, on the other hand, very rarely asked me anything about my private life. In fact, I admired her ability to make the most of the present moment without ever worrying about the background to our meetings. The idea of something happening off-screen didn't exist for her. The only thing about me that seemed to captivate her was that I was standing there in front of her when we met at the bar of her hotel and she devoured me with her eyes (unless my expression betrayed my worries – in which case she would affectionately question me about why I was upset). Nevertheless, one day, I remember, Victoria told me that she was going to be the one asking the questions. I had to promise her not to evade them. This happened at the Concorde Saint-Lazare. It had been raining hard for hours, and we were at the hotel bar, drinking champagne. I looked Victoria in the eyes: 'You want to ask me questions? What do you want to know?'

'For example, your wife – how did you meet? What does she do? What's her background? I want to know as much about your life as, I've begun to realize, you know about mine – a lot, in other words.'

'It's rather a long story. Difficult to explain. I don't know if we . . .'

'If we'll have the time?' Victoria interrupts, looking at her watch. 'We met up early. It's 7 p.m. – or 7.10 p.m., to be precise. It's raining. We're not going to go out. We have until midnight, I imagine,' she says playfully.

'I imagine,' I reply.

'You're always so discreet. You jealously hide your private

life from me. Tonight, I'm rebelling!' she declares in a loud voice. 'Tonight, I want to know everything!'

'Quietly, Victoria. Stop laughing so loud – everyone's looking at us.'

'So? What does that matter? Are you scared they'll know we're an adulterous couple? Or that a colleague might recognize you?'

'It's not just that. I find the attention embarrassing.'

'My God, you're so serious and puritanical when you put your mind to it! But tonight, I'm in a good mood. That's why I want to crack your shell,' Victoria says, leaning across the table to push her hand under my belt. I don't really like it when she's like this. I hate it when adults act like excited children, supposedly because they've had a tough day and they want to get rid of their stress. Sensing my reluctance to let her fondle me in front of strangers, Victoria straightens up and acts seriously again (though I can tell the seriousness is forced). In the end, her ingenuousness makes me smile. I extend my hand towards her, and she takes it in hers. 'You're so serious that you can't even bear it when I try to make a joke. You make me feel like I'm committing a faux pas, or ruining the poetry of your inner life. Any time I try to be a bit funny, or act a bit silly, you instantly recoil. You look almost disgusted.'

'My wife accused me of the same thing, a long time ago.'

'Not any more?'

I burst out laughing and end up confessing: 'I think that, having reproached her in the past, I killed any desire she might have had to be humorous!'

Victoria laughs in turn. 'Well, I think we've made progress,' she says. 'You see – it's good to talk about you. Now, where were we?'

'I can't remember. I think you wanted to question me about my life.'

'Have you always been attracted to the same kind of woman? Or have your tastes changed?'

'I'll tell you a secret. I think, because of my background, the idea of being picked up by a woman from a privileged background is probably my oldest fantasy. When I was an adolescent, I must have masturbated hundreds of times while imagining making love to a woman like you in a four-star hotel, or in a wood-panelled apartment in a posh part of town. It's funny – I've never made the connection, I'm thinking about it now for the first time – but I remember a young woman, in one of the magazines I had, called Patty.' I stop, and look at Victoria's face. I mutter: 'It's completely crazy.'

Victoria looks at me in surprise, uncomprehending. 'What? What do you find . . .'

'It was you.'

'Who? This young woman?'

'You're Patty. I met Patty! I had to wait till I was in my forties to make love with this woman whose photographs filled my adolescent dreams!'

'You are completely crazy. What was she like, your Patty?'

'Exactly like you. Exactly the same physique. For me, Patty was the ideal woman: not only for making love, but for living together. When I wanked, I used to imagine that all those women in the photographs were my wife: we were married, we had children. Conjugal sexuality is what excites me, not the fantasy of screwing a girl on the beach, having chatted her up in a nightclub. Your body is, in almost every respect, the same as Patty's dazzling, opulent body – one of those conservative bodies that you want to marry. I remember she wore a pearl necklace that hung over her breasts. Her breasts were a bit too big – yours are much better; they're perfect. Patty's breasts were marked by breastfeeding: that turned me on. You are the incarnation of my bourgeois-wife fantasy, as it was at the beginning of my adolescence. You've got the face and the body.'

'Wow, that is crazy,' Victoria says sarcastically. 'And what is it, for you, the bourgeois-wife fantasy? I'd be curious to know your definition.'

'Physically discreet, almost drab, but if you dust the surfaces you can bring back a shine – like with something found in the ground. It's a body designed for procreation, for going to church, for giving pleasure: you have to make love occasionally, if you want to have children.' This makes Victoria smile. I continue mockingly: 'Virtuous and sexy, in equal balance. Those are the two qualities I like to see united in a face and a body – sex and procreation, penetration and labour, pleasure and duty, brazenness and discretion, transgression and obedience, the slut and the mother – and that includes women who don't have and may never have children. That has nothing to do with it. There is a split in the essence of the mother – a split that is also subtly transposed in sexuality. The mother is tender and strict, supple and rigid, conciliatory and severe, sometimes authoritarian. In fact, it's that face – the maternal face, when it exists – that appears first, before the other one. You can think that a woman you meet is perfectly ordinary, and then you glimpse, in the transparency of the maternal face, that of another woman: the sexual face. I can see these two elements in constant opposition in you; it's a major part of who you are. Not all women possess this face – not even all mothers have it. You have to seek it out. You find it occasionally – more frequently among bourgeois women. That's not difficult to understand: it's a social background where people are concerned about balance, much more so than in other social backgrounds. The mother does not win out over the woman, nor the other way round. The two are balanced in a fascinating paradox. The slut and the mother in the same face: it's a cliché, but fantasies are always based on clichés. This one really turns me on. Your face gives me a hard-on.'

'I'm not sure how to take that!'

'Take it as a compliment. Men aren't only attracted to those conventionally sexy girls you see in adverts. The eroticism of the bourgeois mother – particularly when she is a powerful, determined, intelligent woman – is like a neutron bomb for me. I adore your face: it turns me on. Being turned on by someone's face is quite rare. Turned on by a woman's face the way you are by her breasts or her bum.'

'My face turns you on more than my pussy?'

'In a way. Sometimes, when I get to this bar and I see you from afar, reading a document, I can see only the slightly severe face of the woman who runs things, organizes things, raises her children, lays off cartloads of workers. I don't recognize my desire in the thoughts that led me here, and I want to run away.'

'You're getting your own back because I said you had no sense of humour,' Victoria laughs. 'It's pathetic.'

'But almost as soon as I sit down opposite you, the two images – the mother and the woman – readjust to form your face. It's like seeing an image in 3D. And then, when we make love, at some points you look twenty-five years younger. You look like a sixteen-year-old.'

'You've told me that several times.'

'It's as if you were different people, and even you yourself didn't know if you're this woman rather than that woman. I keep seeing strangers – the same strangers, again and again – in the woman that bears your name.'

'And your wife? What background is she from?'

'Military. Middle class. The worst imaginable kind of middle class: people who live like aristocrats because of the codes and customs of military life.'

'I get the feeling you don't like your in-laws very much. That makes two of us!'

'Maybe that's the story of our relationship. We're both loved by our spouses, but hated by our in-laws. So, a part of us feels free to seek elsewhere for this dose of love that's been denied to us.'

Victoria is clearly in a very good mood, and she laughs loudly. 'I've never looked at our affair in that light, but you're right – that's exactly what's happening! As far as I'm concerned, anyway.'

I told Victoria about how I met Sylvie, and the first two years of our relationship. I didn't hide the fact that she was not exactly the woman of my dreams; I acknowledged that, at that time, I thought I would meet the love of my life a bit later. I explained to Victoria that I imagined this ideal woman the way you might think of the heroine of a book you've just read, in a manner that was at once precise and intangible: 'Sufficiently alive and inspired that I could dream about her fervently, but not sufficiently realistic that I would have recognized this woman if I'd met her in the street.' In other words, the idea I had of this woman was so evanescent that it made no difference to my relationship with Sylvie. 'This woman had so many blank spaces, and sometimes those blanks inspired me. But the woman never appeared. And so I stayed with Sylvie.' Victoria looked at me as if the thought that she herself was this long-dreamed-of woman had briefly crossed her mind. She asks me: 'In more than twenty years, you never met the woman of your dreams, so you stayed with your compromise choice?'

'It's a bit more complicated than that. First of all, I'm obviously not making myself clear. Sylvie is not my compromise choice – let's not exaggerate. But, above all, something happened that forced me to stop thinking in these terms. I could no longer wait for my ideal woman.'

I tell her about how Sylvie's symptoms first appeared, her hospitalization at Val-de-Grâce, her allergy to the neuroleptics and the coma it caused. I describe the five days I spent talking to her in her sleep. I tell Victoria about the meeting with Sylvie's father and the accusations he made against me. Victoria is moved: I see her wipe a tear from her cheek. I say there is nothing to cry about, that this is a happy story which ends well – the proof being the two children born from our union. Victoria replies that it must horrific to see the person you love in a possibly irreversible coma: 'Even more so as you were in a violent conflict with her father. I think that's maybe the hardest thing.' I reply that this coma ended one morning when Sylvie woke up, but she had partially lost the ability to speak and write; she could express herself only with the most enormous difficulties. She wrote me postcards that you might imagine the work of a child in primary school. She also had trouble getting around. She had been moved to a room in Val-de-Grâce that looked out over the Boulevard de Port-Royal, and she stayed there for about three weeks. I went to visit her, avoiding the times when I knew her parents would be there. Sylvie barely spoke at all. I made do with smiling at her and holding her hand. Sometimes I read her Edgar Allan Poe's stories or Henri Michaux's poems. I told Victoria that, during the first walk that Sylvie was allowed to take after coming out of her coma, we walked in the French gardens of Val-de-Grâce for about fifteen minutes: she moved slowly, and I held her arm. We were surrounded by many other convalescents who, like us, were enjoying the sunshine: pyjamas and nightgowns outnumbered coats and anoraks; some people were in wheelchairs, while others carted around their mobile drips. I remember finding this walk a bit upsetting. It seemed to me that, given my violent dispute with her father, I couldn't really stay with Sylvie. I'd practically decided to break up with her once she was back on her feet and her parents had picked her up. Basically, I didn't think it was right to break up with a young girl unable to speak or write, and consequently unable to defend herself – to express her anger or disapproval. 'You didn't love her any more?' Victoria asks me. 'You told me earlier that when she was in the coma, you told her you loved her . . .' I replied to Victoria that I'd had no idea how I felt. 'Remember I was only twenty. I was just overtaken by events. I didn't know if I was coming or going . . .' I had the impression that my feelings for Sylvie had been intensified by the danger; the fear that she might die had, for five days, put me through feelings of love comparable in intensity to what you feel when someone leaves you. 'Sylvie was leaving me through death, not because she'd decided to, so my feelings were even worse – more violent and hopeless.' But once Sylvie came out of the coma, I felt curiously liberated from the duty of loving her. I'd given everything I had; I'd sat at her bedside for five days and poured out my most intimate feelings in order to try to save her. She'd survived, and I felt dead. I'd fallen into a vast emptiness where, it seemed, my sensitivity had been destroyed. Sylvie's father would soon pick her up, and everything would get back to normal. The incident with the pink notepaper and the attic room would be erased from all our memories like an unfortunate mistake that the lieutenant-colonel would take pleasure in repairing. It was time for our destinies to go their separate ways.

'It's a very moving story,' Victoria says.

'You're right – it is. But you'll see: this is only the beginning.'

'Would you like another glass of champagne?'

'I'd love one.'

So, I tell Victoria that, when Sylvie came out of hospital, she moved in with her parents. Due to the coma's after-effects, she would need a fairly long rehabilitation process before she could resume her studies. Just before she left Val-de-Grâce, I'd told Sylvie: 'See you soon. I'll come and visit you. Call me . . .' But I knew that her parents would not allow us to see each other again. 'And anyway, as I told you earlier, I wanted to break up with her. But it's difficult to dump someone who's been through something like that, and who seems diminished, unable to express themselves.' In fact, I found out later that, just after arriving at their house, Sylvie had told her parents that she wanted me to spend the weekend with them, and they had violently rejected this request, telling her that they did not want to hear my name mentioned again. She'd been dependent on me for two years, and this dependence had led her to get lost in the darkness of a world that was alien to her. Now that she had, thank God, come back to the light of a normal existence – to the world her parents had raised her in, and which they were happy to welcome her to once again during her convalescence – she needed to take advantage of this to start again at square one. 'You'll see, my love. In a short time, this boy will be nothing to you but a bad memory. Later, you'll meet a normal man and you'll wonder how you could have made such a terrible mistake. You'll find it as difficult to understand how you could have chained yourself to this poisonous boy as we ourselves did while we were trying to accept it for two years. If only we could have told you earlier about how bad he was for you . . . We're not really surprised that your relationship ended so tragically. We'll do all we can to make sure this little shit can no longer put you in danger. We'll protect you from yourself and from the feelings you have for him. Trust us – we know what's good for our daughter. You don't how much damage he can do you.'

Sylvie, powerless, listened to them without being able to respond. She tried to string a few words together, and her mother immediately interrupted her to say that she shouldn't tire herself out talking about this. Sylvie ended up understanding what had occurred between her father and me during her coma. She tried to imagine how we could have become so bitterly opposed. Not that she had ever underestimated the differences of opinion that separated us, but she couldn't understand how such a serious incident could lead to a confrontation; what reasons for an argument her coma could have provided for the two men who were most concerned about her. Sylvie tried to phone me one evening. I answered, and heard a small voice say: 'It's Sylvie.' Even that was difficult for her to articulate. Our conversation lasted a few minutes, but we didn't manage to discuss anything important. Sylvie couldn't ask the one question that she was desperate to ask (although I'd guessed what it was: she wanted to know if I still wanted her, or if I'd decided to obey the orders that she presumed her parents had given me), but I didn't think it was fair to tell her my decision over the phone. I told her we would see each other when she was better and was capable of coming to Paris. I told her I would wait for her, and I hung up as she was stammering in an attempt to wish me goodnight.

A few days after this brief phone call, Sylvie turned up at my apartment. I found her sitting on her suitcase in front of my door one evening, when I came back from my day at the architecture school. 'Sylvie! What are you doing here?' She laughed. She looked extraordinarily happy. I realized that she'd escaped from her parents' house. She was happy at having made this decision (in these extremely trying circumstances, she was more like a hussar than ever). She tried to tell me what had happened. At certain points, she paused, searching for the right word, her eyes raised towards her forehead as if she might look inside her own memory. Then, shrugging, she gave up on the attempt, and continued her story. Each sentence seemed to be an expression of the immense joy she felt at having escaped. We talked through most of the night. The conversation went very slowly. She had trouble moving her lips, moving her limbs, moving about. I wondered how she'd managed to get to the station, how she'd caught the train and then the metro. I found out she'd hitched a lift with a lorry that was delivering food to the barracks. The driver, charmed by this impetuous young woman, had ended up obeying her theatrical demands: in order to hide from him her inability to express herself clearly, she'd pretended it was a game, laughing and shouting 'To the station! Quick! Let's go! To the station!' She'd stolen money from her mother in order to pay for her train and metro tickets. By early morning, it had become clear to me that Sylvie would never give me up: she would prefer never to see her parents again than to be separated from me for the rest of her life. Not only that, but she told me she could never forgive them for having taken advantage of her coma to settle their scores with me. To her, that seemed disgraceful, monstrous. I told Sylvie I didn't think this was the right time to make definitive decisions, that things would calm down. It would be idiotic to estrange herself from her parents. But to make her feel safer, if she wanted, she could stay with my parents – they would be happy to have her. I feared that Sylvie's father would come to drag his daughter violently from my apartment, and that things would end badly. I called him to reassure him. He thought I'd manipulated his daughter into escaping the barracks. I tried to get a few words in over the roar of his voice, a few sentences that might calm him down: I told him that Sylvie would come and see them again when they'd agreed to her conditions about being able to keep seeing me; I told him that she was in a safe place, and that they could sleep soundly ('She's not staying with me,' I told him, 'so there's no point coming here and smashing down my door. She's with mutual friends'). Her father threatened to file charges for abduction, but his daughter was of legal age. The next day, Sylvie wrote her parents a postcard that said, in essence: 'Everything's fine. I want to stay with David. If you don't agree, tough shit. I love you.' I only knew about this once the postcard had already been sent; otherwise I would have dissuaded Sylvie from pushing her parents away so brutally, without leaving the door open for them.

Sylvie remembered a few of the things I'd said to her during her coma. Or, rather, during the night, her memory communicated phrases to her consciousness – phrases she was unaware I'd spoken to her in my pain. Several mornings in a row, Sylvie woke up and told me about her dreams: in these dreams, I'd said things to her; she repeated them to me, and I realized they were the words I'd whispered into her ear during the five days of her coma – in particular, my desire to have children with her and my fear that she would give me only boys. Sylvie asked me if I'd been sincere when I made these promises, or if it had only been to make her wake up. I said that my words had been sincere. 'And they had been – that's not in dispute,' I told Victoria. We seemed to be mirroring each other: the promises I'd made perfectly reflected the desires she felt. And Sylvie was so diminished: her body was so much like a motionless prayer that I got the impression her desires had come to claim what they were owed by those promises I'd made. I was having great difficulty working out how I felt about Sylvie. The state she was in inspired such sadness, compassion, even pity, and these emotions mixed with the tenderness evoked by the memories of our first two years together to form what, from afar, might have resembled love – but which was, I knew, perhaps merely an illusion. And my youthful ideals? The woman of my dreams? Perhaps she was Sylvie. Perhaps she was Sylvie, strengthened by this experience (sometimes I thought that what she had been through had given her a density she'd not had before) . . . or perhaps not. It was at this point that Sylvie's parents – unable to bear the affront of their daughter disobeying their commands about her and me – gave her an ultimatum. These were unbending people – military people. She had decided, against their wishes, to make her life with the man who had insulted her father, so they wrote her a letter in which they ordered her to choose which side she was on. If Sylvie decided to stay with me, she would never see them again. They would renounce their daughter for ever unless she split up with me and came back to them and repented her sins. I didn't know about this letter when Sylvie received it. It was only years later that I found out about this loathsome attempt at blackmail, and the heroic reply Sylvie sent them. (If she had spoken to me about this, I would have advised her not to respond straight away, but to let some time pass.) This was a massive strategic error by Sylvie's father, who thought of life as a never-ending show of strength by those in authority. He had sent her the equivalent of a formal warning with a threat of an exemplary punishment if Sylvie didn't comply with orders. They must have imagined that it would make her tremble with fear, that she would fold under its pressure. This kind of attack is launched only by those who are certain of victory against what they imagine to be their target – otherwise the risk is too great. But Sylvie did not surrender. She stood up to them. Apparently they reiterated their threat soon afterwards. She said no for a second time, and the break was made. Each side said they would never see one another again. And they never did.

'Never again?' Victoria asks. 'That's unbelievable.'

'Sylvie would sometimes tell me that they'd see each other again after we'd had our first child. She wanted that to happen. In her mind, the door was not completely closed.'

'But having children didn't change anything?'

'Her parents died in a car accident.'

'Oh God . . .'

'They died before she was able to place our first child in their arms.'

'I see what you mean. It's horrific.'

'Do you remember *Asterix and Cleopatra*?'

'I read it a long time ago.'

'At one point, the pyramid door closes behind Asterix and his friends. When Sylvie's parents died, a heavy door closed behind me. I was trapped with Sylvie in the story of our relationship like Asterix in the pyramid. And why not, I guess? There's nothing to say this wasn't the right path to take in my life. On the other hand, one thing is certain: I will never get out.'

'That's why, when I told you that I was married and I would never leave my husband, you said you would never leave your wife either.'

'Sylvie sacrificed her relationship with her parents to choose me – and they died before she could be reconciled with them. I bear the immense weight of that responsibility, the weight of her entire life. Sylvie is very fragile. She's forever dancing on the edge of an abyss. I live in constant fear that she will fall.'

'That she'll fall in what?'

Victoria starts laughing.

'It's not funny.'

'Sorry, it was a nervous laugh. I don't know what's got into me.'

And, instead of stopping, Victoria puts her hand in front of her mouth to hide her smile. I can see a flood of hilarity in her eyes, and also a glimmer of entreaty: I should not blame her for these inappropriate hysterics.

'I don't see what there is to make you laugh in this story . . .'

'Neither do I,' she replies. 'It's probably because it's so sad.

It's horrible.' Victoria continues laughing hard. I watch her and wait for the fit to pass. Finally, she calms down. Her mascara has run down her cheeks: she tries to wipe it off with a Concorde Saint-Lazare doily. 'Oh, I'm sorry! But when it gets going, that kind of thing, it's really hard to stop.'

'It doesn't matter.'

'You said that you lived in constant fear that she'd fall, and as you'd just been talking about Asterix, I imagined her falling in the cauldron of magic potion – like Obelix, you see? That's all it was. I'm sorry.'

I stare at Victoria's face for a few seconds.

'I'm hungry. Shall we go and eat?'

'All right,' she replies. 'We could go to Mollard . . .'

'Excellent idea. I want oysters.'

'You can have lobster. On me.'

'Perfect.'

'Give me a minute. I'll be back.' And Victoria walks from the bar to the Ladies, carrying her handbag.

We were walking in the Opéra district. Victoria, who'd had a meeting that morning in Paris, had taken a room in the Grand Hotel for the afternoon. I'd managed to get away from the construction site early enough to meet her at 5 p.m. at the Café de la Paix, where we'd drunk tea before going out for a walk.

As we walked down Avenue de l'Opéra, I confessed to her: 'Sometimes I think I should leave you. But it's impossible. You make me happy. When I open my eyes every morning, I think of you. You are the energy that powers me. You are always the first thing I think about each day. Only after thinking about you do I think about the rest of my life: my wife sleeping next to me, my children, the Jupiter Tower.'

'It's kind of you to say so.'

'It's true. If you weren't in my life, I wouldn't have the strength necessary to make the Jupiter Tower rise from the ground. I want you to know that.'

We walk in silence.

'So, if I understand correctly, you're going to leave me when the tower is finished.'

'Perhaps.'

'I know you will.'

'That is sometimes what I think I should do. But I'm afraid my life will become a bit like a desert again without you. It would be like having a huge crystal chandelier hanging above my existence, and then one day someone replacing it with a bare bulb in a socket.'

'A bare bulb in a socket. I love your metaphors.'

'Life's a bit like a bare bulb in a socket, though, don't you think, once the idea of dreaming is removed from it? I'm not talking about my wife and children. I adore them. But your presence puts them in a different light: in some ways, I love my family life more when it takes place in this wonderful glow that you give out.'

'Let's not question it for now. Let's just enjoy the moment.'

'You're right. We'll see later.'

We go to a shoe shop that I've told her about several times before. I love high heels, and Victoria's feet are beautiful. She wanted me to take her to this shop so she could buy a pair of shoes I liked. I show her some in the shop window: 'I like those a lot, for example.'

'They're wonderful.'

'These would suit you too.'

'I'm not sure. They're a bit . . .'

'A bit what?'

'Extravagant.'

278

'Maybe they are. But the others aren't at all. They're just black patent leather court shoes with high heels.'

'I've never walked in such high heels before. They're so thin! I'm not sure I'll be able to manage it.'

We go in. She tries on several pairs. She walks across the shop, watching her feet in mirrors. I am standing next to the sales assistant, who whispers in my ear: 'This pair really suits her.' Strapped into a fairly severe grey suit that emphasizes her hips, Victoria's body radiates an intimidating authority. I glimpse her toes emerging from the black leather selvage. The instep is rounded. Victoria moves imperially towards us, slow and assured, graceful. She is taller than me now by a few centimetres. My cock is hard. She looks me straight in the eyes, smiling, and says: 'You prefer these ones, then?'

'That pair, yes. The black patent leather heels. It's like they were designed for your legs.' I watch her walk around the shop: her body has become an explosive event. 'And, strangely enough, I don't have a problem walking,' Victoria says as she moves away. 'In fact, I love the feeling of being so tall.' I ask the sales assistant how high the heel is. 'Five inches,' she replies. The Pigalle also comes in four inches, but it's not as good.'

'And the shoes she came in with?'

'They're two and a half inches,' the sales assistant replies. I say to Victoria: 'For a woman who claims she's never walked in really high heels, you're doing pretty well. In fact, you look like a queen.' Victoria goes up to the sales assistant and says: 'I'll take them.'

'Wonderful. Would you like to see anything else?'

'No, thank you. That will be all for today. But I think we'll come back,' Victoria adds, shooting me a mischievous glance. The sales assistant leads us to the checkout, puts the shoes in the box, and the box in a paper bag. She takes the credit card that

Victoria holds out to her. 'Thank you, madame,' she says. Victoria enters her PIN, takes her card and the receipt, and I pick up the paper bag and we leave. 'Goodbye, madame. Goodbye, sir,' the sales assistant says, closing the glass door behind us.

We walk a little way on the street and enter the magnificent covered passage of the Galerie Véro-Dodat that opens up to our right. Victoria takes my arm and then stops me. I look in her eyes. She kisses me on the lips and says: 'Thank you, David. Without you, I would never have dared buy myself shoes like these.'

'They suit you wonderfully.'

'It was a pretty erotic experience. I'm soaking wet, in fact. Walking in those shoes while you and that young woman watched me . . . I would happily have taken her with us, if you want to know the truth!' Victoria bursts out laughing and starts walking again. I say: 'I agree entirely. There was something highly sexual about seeing you like that, perched on those high heels – as if you were naked. You're beautiful, and those shoes magnify your beauty. They turn you into a kind of goddess . . . or a Trojan horse.'

'A Trojan horse? What on earth do you mean?'

'Something impressive that's taken somewhere. It inspires respect. It's revered . . .'

'And what kind of army is hiding inside this Trojan horse?'

'You know perfectly well what it's hiding. Anyway, we'll find out for certain pretty soon,' I say to Victoria, lifting the paper bag containing the precious box to eye level.

'Do you know how to get to the Grand Hotel?'

'Yes, it's easy. The Opéra is just down there.'

'It's funny; with each of my lovers, I discover a new fantasy, a new ritual. With you, it's shoes. With Laurent, it was disguises. But I prefer your heel fetish – it's not as radical.'

'What do you mean by disguises? What did you do?'

'He loved setting up scenes, getting me to act out stories that he prepared in advance.'

'Meaning what? Give me an example.'

'He loved pretending to be a stranger. He arranged for me to be at a certain place, at a certain time – on the street, not in a café. I turned up and I saw him waiting, leaning against a wall: a stranger, a bearded man with long hair. He was in disguise. He'd got hold of clothes that were not at all his usual style. He wore different glasses – enormous, metal frames, etc. He approached me as a stranger would approach me – as you approached me in the shopping centre – and we played. I told him to leave me alone and moved a few metres away. He came up to me again a bit later: I got furious. I left. I could sense him following me. He seemed to give up the hunt, but then strangely I saw him suddenly appear from a hotel entrance ten minutes later. I don't know how he got ahead of me. I told him that if he kept following me, I was going to call the police. I took refuge in a café. He sat at a table next to mine and began trying to chat me up – in the crudest way possible. He told me he'd sensed, from the moment he first saw me, that I wanted him. I played the ingénue. He loved it when I played the ingénue. He started talking dirty. After he'd chatted me up, he suggested that we went to a nearby hammam, and I said yes. So we ended up in a hammam, surrounded by men, and he gently caressed my breasts in front of them. Nobody was allowed to touch me. All the men watched. Afterwards, we would go and make love in a seedy hotel. We loved two-star hotels with big cockroaches crawling all over the place. He fucked me, still in disguise.'

'Did you do that often?'

'Often and regularly.'

'He invented a new story each time?'

'Yes, absolutely. A new scenario each time, new places. The

problem with basing a romantic relationship on those kinds of crazy fantasies is that you run the risk of always having to go further in order for it to keep working. In order not to collapse into ridicule or self-parody, or simply in order to keep satisfying us, these rendezvous had to be constantly reinvented – we had to keep going further, keep crossing boundaries. It's a spiral that makes you want to get rid of the frustrations that result from the repetition of the same scenes – do you understand? It's not like with classic sexuality, where the intensity comes from the sincerity, the commitment. Those scenes were completely artificial. If you're going to play, then play – and see the game through to the end. You understand? It's possible to be drawn, in spite of yourself, into the spiral of the game, and it was that spiral I wanted to escape from when I broke up with Laurent. I broke up with him for exactly that reason.'

The adage of Poe's purloined letter.

Because she said all this so naturally, I didn't understand that what Victoria was confiding in me was so important. I imagined these were nothing more than ordinary phrases, slightly exaggerated in a conventional way (people like to accentuate the significance of their memories, particularly if they wish to excite the attention of the person they're talking to), never guessing that she had composed these phrases for the meaning they revealed if examined in the purity of their instantaneous impact on the listener's imagination. I would have had to grasp their truth the second they were spoken, not listen to them with a slight delay (as is often the case in hazy, distracted conversations), nor see them as subjective visions of what they described, or as figures of speech. These phrases she spoke to me were not figures of speech: they expressed a truth that I was incapable of understanding. I merely said: 'What do you mean by that?'

'Nothing. Just that. I'd had enough of these artificialities. We needed to move on to something else.' Then: 'For example, I can't wait to be naked in these beautiful shoes, standing in front of you, and to see you get hard. I put stockings on today. Flesh-coloured – your favourites.'

We locked ourselves in the room that Victoria had booked at the Grand Hotel. It had a glorious view of the Palais Garnier. We made love. She was naked except for her high-heeled shoes. I almost came. We ate dinner in the room. I admired the architecture of the Opéra through the window, illuminated in the night: it was spellbinding. When Victoria took her shoes off, she didn't toss them on the floor like mere objects; she placed them, as if they were holy relics, on the desk. She remarked on them occasionally: 'I'm going to buy myself more pairs,' she decided. 'Will you come with me?'

'Of course.'

'Maybe we'll even manage to seduce the pretty sales assistant!'

I left for home just after midnight.

Some time later, I am eating lunch with Dominique at the Valmy, a restaurant in La Défense where we often meet. It's close to the construction-site offices, so it's kind of become our cafeteria. When the weather is good, its large terrace on the flagstones of La Défense is a pleasant place to drink a coffee and smoke a cigarette.

The waitress in the Valmy had just placed our starters on the table when my BlackBerry started vibrating: I'd received a text. Since we've been here, Dominique has been telling me about the troubles in his love life. I suspect he's been suggesting this lunch for two days in order to pour out his anxieties to a close friend. Dominique's problem is that he dreams of falling in love. Since he left his wife, his sole obsession has been to find another one.

For months, I have been telling him I find it strange that a man of almost forty, who's been married three times, would not want to take advantage of being single. Why is he so keen to start a fourth family rather than enjoying some adventures, playing the field? He's had five children from these three marriages: the youngest was only four months old when he left the mother last year, to everyone's surprise. His feelings for her had started to fade from the moment when her belly got round (though the timing was a coincidence: he'd enjoyed the four previous pregnancies, and had always liked to make love to his wives when they were pregnant), and before she gave birth, he had long ceased feeling anything for her at all. Still, out of decency, he had waited four months after the birth before telling the mother that he was leaving her. He was the one who thought four months was a reasonable time to wait: at the time, I'd told him that it seemed a bit short to me, and that he ought to make the effort to stay with his wife for at least a year. But Dominique had refused: he absolutely had to leave her. The announcement of this split shocked Alexandre's mother all the more as it had been Dominique who insisted that she have a child (she was forty years old and already a grandmother, so she would willingly have passed on this – particularly if she'd known she was going to be left alone with the baby less than a year later). It left her so devastated that it was worrying: she couldn't seem to recover at all. Since then, Dominique had been avidly searching for the young woman he wanted to share his life with. And one of the women he'd met – and with whom he'd thought it might be possible to have a long-term relationship – had, on several occasions recently, made him seriously question that assumption. That is what he was telling me (we'd just got started) when Sylvie sent me a text. 'Excuse me, it's my wife. I'm going to see what she wants,' I say to Dominique. I read the text she's sent me: 'I'm at

Carrefour. I don't know what kind of meat to get. What do you want?' I reply: 'Whatever you want. It doesn't matter.' Then I send the text before saying to Dominique: 'Excuse the interruption. It was my wife. What were you saying?'

'This is excellent. What's yours like?'

'Not bad. I'm hungry. It's been a tough morning. Still, the lads have worked really hard today. I think we'll finish the floor tomorrow – two days ahead of schedule.'

'You've got so much energy – it's incredible. I don't know what's got into you recently. It's like you can move mountains. You amaze me. Today is 23 November: if we keep going at this pace, we could complete the shell ahead of schedule – around 10 January. I've done a projection – I'll show it to you. It's staggering what's happened to us.'

'I didn't want to get fucked by this building. I decided I would have it, instead of it having me,' I tell Dominique as I lift the fork to my lips. Then I notice that Sylvie has replied to my text. I open her reply: 'But I'm asking you to choose because I can't. Be nice, please!' I write, 'Buy some ribsteak. I love you,' and send the message. I say to Dominique: 'Sorry, but I had to reply. So this woman – your new girlfriend – it's not working as well as you hoped?'

'She's completely mad. One day, everything's fine: she tells me she loves me, she wants to see me, we spend the night together. And the next day, I have no idea why, she sulks: she says she doesn't want to see me any more, and she stays on her own with her daughter.'

'Oh, she's got a daughter? You didn't tell me she had a kid. Oh, hang on, I've got another text from my wife.'

'Yes, I did. Don't you remember? I told you she'd been married and she had an eight-year-old daughter,' Dominique replies while I open the message from Sylvie: 'I don't know what's up with me today, but seriously I can't seem to get out of this shop. I've been here for two hours and my trolley is empty.' Dominique asks me: 'What's the matter? Is something wrong?'

'No, it's OK. It's my wife. Hang on – I really need to reply to this.' I write: 'Don't worry, it's fine. Get a big salad to go with the ribsteak and go back home. We'll do the shopping together on Saturday. I'm in a meeting now, but I'll try to get home early. I love you.' I send the message, then say to Dominique: 'So? Sometimes she wants to stay on her own with her daughter, without seeing you?'

'Yeah, and why not, I suppose? But it always seems to be done aggressively, as a punishment or out of revenge, and I don't understand why. It's like she wants to pay me back for something, but I don't know what that something is.'

'Yeah, that's strange.'

'She's really violent too. I've never seen anything like it. The other night, for her birthday, I decided to take her to a really nice hotel – something classy, you know. So we went to the Palais-Royal – the Louvre Hotel, I don't know if you know it . . .'

'Er, yeah. Well, I know *of* it,' I say, blushing slightly. I am staggered by this coincidence. So I might easily have bumped into Dominique in a lift in the Louvre Hotel – me with my magnificent head of Human Resources (who must be two feet taller than my friend), and him joined at the hip with his slender, volatile young girlfriend – but at the same time, I suppose that the scene he's about to describe to me took place on a Saturday evening. I get a reply from Sylvie, which I read: 'Thank you, that's kind of you. Thank God you're there. I'm going home now. I love you. See you tonight.' I reply to this with a winking smiley. Dominique is waiting for me to look at him again before he continues his story. 'We ate dinner at Café Ruc, a classy restaurant just next door, then we went up to the room. There's a beautiful view of the Comédie-Française. You see, I wasn't taking the piss. I even ordered a bottle of champagne. I'm not a billionaire, just an ordinary man, but I gave her the works! We made love all night. It was great, seriously, like a honeymoon. The next morning, I'm in the shower, and I hear screaming. I come out: she's on the bed, reading texts on my smartphone. She throws it at my face. Look, you can see the mark where it hit me' – and Dominique shows me a fairly deep cut, with dried blood, on his left temple. 'She'd found a text I sent to a girl saying, "I'm sucking your tits".'

' "I'm sucking your tits"? You send texts to girls saying that you're sucking their tits?'

'Well, yeah, I agree, it's not a great text. I must have been drunk. It's this girl who's been after me a bit. Nothing's ever happened with her, but sometimes she sends me dirty messages at night. I replied saying that – nothing more.'

'So what happened?'

'I couldn't make her see reason. She screamed for three hours. Three hours! Can you imagine? Just for a text I'd sent to some girl who means nothing to me. "I'm sucking your tits"!'

'To be honest, Dominique, I do think "I'm sucking your tits" is pretty bad. I would have screamed too.'

'What? Hang on! I pay for a luxury room in the Louvre Hotel and . . . fucking hell, do you know how much that costs?'

'A lot, I'm guessing.'

'Guess.'

'All right, I get it. The room was expensive. So . . . did you manage to calm her down?' And that's when my BlackBerry starts vibrating again: I've got a new text. 'That'll be your wife again. Go ahead, don't worry about me. Reply to her,' Dominique says politely as the waitress arrives. 'Have you finished?

Shall I take the plates away?' she asks us. 'Yes, that's fine. I've finished,' I say, opening the text, which is actually from Victoria.

'You don't have much of an appetite today!' says Dominique.

'I'm saving myself for the *daube Provençale*. And I'm a bit worried about my wife . . . She won't stop sending me messages.'

'Ah, women! When you don't look after them properly, you lose your appetite!' the waitress says, carrying away our plates. I open the text: 'Read your emails! It's urgent!' So I check my inbox while Dominique does the same thing on his BlackBerry. I know that Victoria is in Ho Chi Minh City, where she had to meet her Human Resources teams, and that she has to leave Vietnam today for Bangkok. 'I'm on cloud nine! This country is heavenly. I've just come from a massage with a young female colleague: both of us were massaged by men. It was so wonderful that, when it was over, I wanted him to make me come. The girl I was with said she could see it in the way we looked at each other, the masseur and me, when he stopped massaging me. She told me that, although I hadn't realized it, I'd been groaning all the way through the massage. I wanted him to touch me between my legs. I was so wet! I thought of you. I think that if I'd been alone with him, I would have got him to make me come with his fingers. I'd have torn off his loincloth and taken his cock between my hands. But it was impossible, with this colleague lying next to me. You can see what kind of state you've put me in – all this because of our meeting in the Louvre Hotel three days ago in my Louboutin shoes. I've got them with me here. I love them. Everyone looks at me when I wear them. I miss you. The masseur's expert hands got me so wet that I think I'm going to make myself come in the toilets of this café. More caresses, more! I'm sending you kisses . . .' I put my phone back on the table and look at my friend Dominique. After a few seconds, he says:

'What's up? Is something wrong? You don't look very well. Is it your wife again?'

'No, it's fine. It's nothing.'

'I can see there's something bothering you. What is it?'

'Yes, it's my wife, but it'll be fine.' At that moment, the waitress arrives with our plates. She places them in front of us: the *daube* for me, and a steak and chips for Dominique. Silently, I salt and pepper my food. Dominique reaches out, and I hand him the salt shaker. Steam is rising from my meat. Victoria's long message has made me sad, slightly bitter and pathetically jealous. The fantasy she shared with me is banal, clichéd. But even though I try to reason with myself, even though I tell myself she wants to bring me into a shared erotic fantasy, and this is the proof – the undeniable proof – that I was the one she wanted, I can't get past the idea that, an hour earlier, Victoria felt desire for another man. She wanted him to fuck her. I am desperate to read the email again. It's on my smartphone, which is placed to the right of my steaming plate (I've just tasted the *daube*, and it's delicious: I tell the waitress, who has just come to ask us how our food is, 'It's excellent. My compliments to the chef!'), but I don't dare. Images flash in my head: the look that Victoria shared with the masseur (in which her colleague saw desire); Victoria's desire to touch this man's cock so she could make him touch her and bring her to orgasm. I see the Asian man's fingers slide inside Victoria. I see her hands gripping his shoulders while I look at the bits of carrot and meat on my plate: they resemble brown corduroy. These images, these sensations are hurtful. I can feel them circling my body, my thoughts, my mood, like foreign bodies. They are lumps, unpleasant impurities, annoyances. And yet the erection I got while reading Victoria's words has still not diminished. The *daube* I'm eating and the sight of Dominique's face – which I look at while feigning interest from time to time, in silence – have not been enough to put an end to it. I'm hard as a rock. Blindly, my pain shows me Victoria lying naked, burning with desire, while this young man's hands touch the forbidden parts of her body. And suddenly, I see myself – faced with the devastating competition offered by this masseur – as merely one of many men able to satisfy her. I see myself as just one in a long line of dicks. After a lengthy silence, Dominique asks: 'Do you want to go and call her?'

'No. I'm sorry. It'll be fine.'

'Seriously, if you're worried about her, you should . . .'

I interrupt him: 'Anyway, what are you going to do about this woman – your volatile girlfriend?'

'I don't know. I'm wondering. I do like her.'

'That's not the feeling I get. Seriously, Dominique, I don't get that feeling at all. You should dump her.'

'But . . .'

'If you were just having an adventure, if you were just in it for the sex and having fun, I wouldn't say this. But you're looking for the love of your life. I don't see how this woman can correspond to that desire. Or if she does, it'll be a turbulent relationship, full of conflict. If I were you, I'd dump her. Get out while you can, if you want my opinion.' I see Dominique thinking about what I've said. He nods his head vigorously as I speak while he chews his steak, but he also makes certain movements that seem to qualify his general agreement, as if to suggest that things aren't quite that simple, and that this woman does have certain qualities. He ends up saying this in words: 'You have no idea how much I envy you for having found the love of your life. I envy you the happiness you have together. I envy you the solidity of your relationship. You're a role model for me – I think it's wonderful. My life is a failure. I would have loved to live with the same woman for thirty years, but that wasn't possible. Each time, I realize, after a while, that I've made a mistake,' Dominique says, staring at the sauce of my *daube* as if he even envied me its dark, soft, comfortable colour – as if it were a metaphor for the conjugal smoothness he dreams about. Suddenly he lifts his head: 'Aren't you ever tempted to look elsewhere? Don't you ever have doubts? Don't you have to force yourself, sometimes, not to go off with a woman – I mean, not to sleep with a woman you've met, who you like? It must happen, surely, that you meet women you like, who you find attractive . . .'

'Yes, of course it happens.'

'And . . . ?'

'And what?'

'David! Stop pretending to be innocent. You know perfectly well what I'm talking about.'

'I'm not saying I've never given in to temptation, in twenty-two years, but . . . Dominique, this is just between you and me. I never, ever talk about it . . .'

'Of course,' Dominique replies. 'What do you take me for?'

'But having a mistress? No. Absolutely not. It's a principle I've never wavered from. Yielding to a woman's charms . . . sure, why not, even if it's rare . . . but only once. I'm happy with my wife. I don't want to leave her, and I don't want to take any risks that might put our relationship in danger.'

'I'm going to tell you a secret.' My BlackBerry beeps: I glance at the screen: another message from Victoria. I pick up my phone and say to Dominique: 'Go ahead, I'm listening. I'm just going to see what she wants. She's not very well at the moment.'

'I figured as much,' Dominique replies. Victoria writes: 'So, what effect did that have on you? The Vietnamese head of Human Resources and I are thinking of going back: my masseur was so sexy, and I am desperate to make love – you can't even imagine! If you don't reply to my email, I'm going to have to go back to the masseur so he can take care of me. I'll tell you all about it, in any case . . .' I remove the message from my screen and return my attention to Dominique, who is telling me that he's never made love to the woman of his dreams. 'What do you mean, you've never made love to the woman of your dreams?' I ask him, while sorting through the emotional dregs that Victoria's latest message has left in my mind: irritation, resentment, sadness, humiliation. And, above all, a feeling that at this time was in its early stages but which would become increasingly overpowering: envy that her life was varied, luxurious, limitless and entertaining, while mine was chained to the foot of the Jupiter Tower. Victoria was enjoying the most pleasant aspects of contemporary reality while I was constrained by the limits that it imposes on most of us in order to help a small number of people grow wealthy. Watching Victoria, I understood that globalization had given birth to new ways of life – ways of life we can't see clearly because we are below them, as if an extra floor had been constructed, and a group of hand-picked individuals were running the planetary machine by moving constantly from one country to another. They have now reached a point where the disappearance of the idea of borders leads to a relationship with reality based on mobility and the constant interpenetration of the personal and professional, the private and the social, pleasure and work, gratification and efficiency, due in particular to time-zone differences and the supposed sacrifices they have to make (when in fact they love that). Combined with salaries so high that they might imagine their existence is a burden, this overlapping is naturally accompanied by many benefits (which easily outweigh the inconveniences): I saw Victoria's life as being the most enviable imaginable, in spite of the fact that she indisputably worked extremely hard. (Then again, I too worked extremely hard. Apart from about twenty meal vouchers, however, the system for which I pushed myself to the point of exhaustion gave me no gifts of pleasure; I never received any consolation, whereas my powerful mistress received it on a daily basis.) So, not only was I jealous of the Vietnamese masseur, but of the circumstances that allowed Victoria to quiver beneath his hands. And these two feelings came together to form a particularly exquisite resentment, as sophisticated as was her life. It is never pleasant to admit to such petty feelings, but I have to acknowledge that I was beginning to feel bitter and envious towards Victoria's existence. Sitting in this restaurant in La Défense, surrounded by secretaries and managers, I felt I was the butt of some cosmic joke. Dominique replies: 'I'm not going to go into the details of this thing, but I would imagine that, since you've been young – or, let's say, since your adolescence – you've been massively attracted to one particular type of woman, something very precise. Let's say – just hypothetically – a very small black/ Asian woman, ultra-slim, with narrow hips like a boy's, but with large breasts, enormous breasts, and long curly hair, as thick as a lion's mane. Like Grace Jones. Do you remember Grace Jones?'

'I remember her having a shaved head. Did she have hair like a mane?'

'Maybe I'm getting her mixed up with someone else?'

'But is that your fantasy, what you've just described? Or is that just an example?'

'Promise me something?'

'Sure. What?'

'That you won't talk to anyone about this, ever. I'm a bit prudish when it comes to this.'

'I promise I will never mention it to anyone.'

'All right . . . then I admit it. That's it – that's my absolute fantasy, more or less. You see them like that in the street occasionally, but it's rare. Sometimes you see them on TV, playing nurses, in American series.'

'And . . . ?'

'And . . . ? You think that's normal? That, at over forty, I haven't managed – not even once – to get a girl like that into bed? It's great being alive – I'm not complaining, it's incredibly lucky. But, frankly, what's the point in being born if you can go through life and not be granted a wish as simple as that, when for you it's absolutely essential? Think about this with me for a couple of minutes. Concentrate. You'll see that it's truly traumatic. Something you've dreamed about since you were sixteen! Now you're just over forty and this thing you've been dreaming about since sixteen – a simple thing, I'm not asking for the moon – well, you've never experienced it. I've never been to bed with this long-haired, ultra-slim, big-breasted black/Asian woman that I just described. And, I have to tell you, now I'm middle-aged, that makes me deeply sad and terribly disillusioned . . . I'm at the point where I hardly believe in anything any more. On certain mornings, when I wake up, I almost feel like crying at the idea that I am probably going to die without having been granted this simple wish, which you'd expect everyone to be granted: meeting the woman of your dreams. I was naive enough to believe that – given how hard I work; given, I don't know, how diligently I try to do things well, to play the role I've been allocated – I was naive enough to believe that at least I'd be granted this. And if I'm not, I can tell you that I will die a bitter man. The final light I glimpse, as my life is extinguished, as I close my eyes for ever, will be like a last mouthful of bitterness, the whole world reduced to this single teardrop of bitterness – the black/Asian woman who never came into my life. Fucking hell, David, it's shit . . . I'm sorry, I don't know what's got into me.' Dominique uses a knuckle of his middle finger to wipe a small tear from his right eye. I pat him affectionately on his shoulder and say: 'I love it when you get lyrical, Dominique.'

'I'm tired. Sorry, it's this fucking site. Those bastards will end up killing us, the way they're making us work. Look at the state I'm in, and it's only November. Ah, fuck it. Shit . . .'

'We'll get through it, don't worry. I've got things in hand.'

'No, but seriously, David, apart from that . . . with this thing about the ideal woman, I'm right, aren't I? Don't you think it's sad?'

'Yes, Dominique, you're right to be upset. It is sad. Do you want a coffee?'

'Yeah, a double espresso. And you, the woman of your dreams – have you already met her? Physically, I mean.'

'I don't have an identikit portrait of the woman of my dreams. It's more like an idea, a substance. If I had to sum up my dream woman in words, it would not be an appearance, but a concept.'

'And what is it, this concept?'

'Sorry, I'm going to keep that to myself. It's a secret.'

7

I was woken suddenly last night by the sound of them banging on the door.

I've been having the same nightmare every other night for the last three months. I sat up straight, covered in sweat, in the darkness of my hotel room, just as I had sat up straight in my own bed, next to Sylvie, that morning when this event actually occurred. I went to the bathroom to drink a large glass of water. On the day in question, however, astonished that there could be such an uproar so early in the morning, I headed towards the source of this racket to find out what was causing it. It was about six in the morning. (My alarm clock goes off at quarter past six, but as I'd slept very badly, I was having great difficulty waking up.) I wondered why someone was banging so insistently at my door. I thought perhaps something had happened to one of my neighbours – a heart attack, for instance – or that there'd been a traffic accident in the area. Or perhaps it was a dream? But that idea slowly vanished as I walked towards the tumult, emerging from the haze of sleepiness as I got closer. I approached the door warily, and then I heard, 'Open up, it's the police!' I unbolted the door and a flood of human flesh smashed me against the wall of the entrance hall.

Last night, having been more frightened by this nightmare than usual, I didn't feel like returning to bed after I'd drunk the glass of water in the bathroom. It's 3.20 a.m. I go downstairs, trying to be as quiet as possible. But when I open the door of the living room, I find the hotel owner sitting on an armchair in her dressing gown, barefoot, with one leg dangling and the other tucked underneath her. She is wearing glasses and reading a book. Hearing the door, she lifts her head and smiles at me. I move closer and the two of us laugh silently at this unexpected meeting. She gestures to the sofa that sits across from her armchair, on the other side of the coffee table. She has lit the stove. You can see the flames dancing prettily behind the concave glass. 'What's the matter?' she asks. 'Can't you sleep?'

'Actually, I was sleeping perfectly well, but I was woken up by a nightmare – a really horrible nightmare. Well, it's always the same one: they're banging at my door . . . or, rather, they're trying to knock it down . . . and it takes me a few seconds to realize that it's not the door to my hotel room that's being smashed open. The same thing's been happening to me every other night for the last three months.'

'I know,' the hotel owner replies.

'What do you mean, you know?'

'Our apartment is just underneath. We can hear you screaming. My husband wants to move you to another room, but your room is nice and big, with a good view of the forest. As you're staying here quite a long time,' she says with a knowing smile, 'I think it would be silly to give you a less pleasant room. My husband gets really annoyed when you scream at night,' she says, attempting to reproduce her husband's rage – his guttural pronunciation, his narrowed eyes. Amused, I say: 'Please pass on my apologies.'

'I know who you are.'

I stare at her in silence for a few seconds.

'What do you mean, you know who . . .'

'I saw your picture in the paper when it happened. I was struck by your face. I wondered how a man with a face like yours could have ended up in such a sordid business. I don't know why, but I instinctively took your side when I read about the incident. Poor guy, I thought. Have you been told before how much you look like Joaquin Phoenix? You have the face of someone who does not deserve to get mixed up in a nasty business like that.'

'I don't agree. I'm guilty. I deserve what happened to me. I'm the sordid one, the pathetic one – not the woman who was killed. I realized too late how extraordinary she was. My guilt lies in not having understood that woman until she was dead; in not know-ing until that moment what a treasure I had lost. I failed in my duty to protect her. I was blinded by my prejudices, by my bit-terness and grievances on a whole host of topics. Only when she was dead did I see how great she was, and how small I was.'

'I see you as an idealist.'

'Everyone sees me as an idealist, but the truth is it's very easy to have ready-made convictions, and to express well-meaning opinions, and to make people think your head is in the stars when it's actually in the ground. And what good does it do to posture like that? To say that the world should be a better place, that things should be nicer, that everyone should respect each other? It's ridiculous. Beauty occurs in the moment, or is created by us when we're free. The beauty that Victoria created had to be seized then and there . . . but the idealist is a slow-moving, cum-bersome creature, unchanging, like words carved in stone . . .'

'I'm sorry, but it's still better than being a cynical bastard.'

'Sure, but it's better still to be someone like Victoria – to be so complex that you can't be pigeonholed or understood by those who look at you with an idealist's eye, or a cynic's eye. To under-stand Victoria's complexity, you had to invent a new way of looking or rediscover an unspoiled perspective – almost a child's perspective. She died because of my idealism, which can be, where I'm concerned, a sort of sophisticated stupidity. It's a rejection of space: my idealism encloses a tiny bit of infinity inside a cube and claims that this enclosed space is exemplary, geometric, civilized (pick whatever words you want, it's the middle of the night, and I'm sleepy), but the intended meaning is that the space remaining outside of this cube is immoral, lawless, formless and imperfect. I'm talking about the possibilities that open up to you when you aren't afraid to live. Victoria made this territory hers. She was capable of another kind of idealism – an idealism not frozen in ideas, but based on the principles of the moment, of desire, speed, risk-taking, adventure, movement, energy, transformation.'

'You speak very well for someone who's just woken up from a nightmare.'

'I'm worthless. That's all I've thought about since I got here. I've been repeating these phrases all day long for three months. Victoria transcended all divisions. It's extremely rare to meet someone like that, and to face up to the impossibility of pigeon-holing them. In some ways, she fitted in every box, and in some ways she fitted in none of them. I ran into a conceptual wall. My narrow-mindedness fell apart when confronted with this enigma. In fact, her fluidity seemed like an attack on me. I understand now that I ended up, in my relationship with her, wanting to avenge myself on this freedom that was, for her, a way of life, and that I found too difficult to accept. I was merely a slave: a slave to others, to my bosses, to the system, but above all a slave to myself and to what you call my idealism. I constantly criticized her, suspected her honesty, told her she was hypocritical. I was always reproaching her for something. She went too fast for me. She humiliated me, the way you'd be humiliated if you ran the 100 metres next to an Olympic sprinter. That's probably a more realistic metaphor than the one I used before. She accepted, understood, lived in and used our reality the way Ben Johnson inhabits the space–time continuum of the 100 metres. And I was like a ridiculous tortoise, laboriously carting around its shell of idealism. Do you see what I mean?'

'Not completely, but I can see that you're angry with me!' the hotel owner said, laughing. 'I promise I won't use the word "idealist" in front of you any more, OK?'

'My principles were often a way of rejecting anything that was different, anything that was constantly changing its place and form, anything that moved and lived. My idealism was often a kind of jealousy or resentment, a way of discrediting people who are free. I'm honest, you see: that's the great advantage of going through a tragedy like this. It becomes easy to start again from scratch, beginning with yourself, and you're able to look at yourself more penetratingly. It was about time, at forty-two years old.'

'It will pass. You'll get your self-esteem back,' she says to me affectionately. 'It's fairly normal, considering what's happened to you. Don't you think?'

'I don't think I'll see it any differently, unless I go through a profound change. But anyway, right now I don't have the strength. All I can do is think about what happened three months ago. It's actually worse than if I'd killed this woman with my own hands, driven by some irresistible urge. I'm guilty of having done nothing, of having just been myself – that's why she's dead. I can't accuse myself of a momentary homicidal insanity. Sometimes I think it would be better to be in prison, to be able to blame it on a surge of madness. That way, I could ask society to forgive me by completing my sentence. I would have committed a sin, and I would have atoned for it – everything else would be saved. But that's not possible. It is my self, everything I am, that's to blame for this woman's death. At a particular moment,

I should have reacted in a certain way, and I didn't. From now on, I'm defined by what I didn't do that day. Or maybe it's the other way round: what I didn't do that day is me. The policeman who was with me for the forty-eight hours of custody gave me an unforgettable look when he let me go. I can't escape the accusation in his eyes.'

'I understand what you mean, but you're wrong . . .'

'You can't understand. Nobody can understand a thing like that.'

I get up and stand in front of an old map pinned to the wall. I try to find the village in the south-west where my parents met for the first time one 14 July, and where my grandmother still lives now. Thinking about her brings tears to my eyes. I would rather she'd been dead than alive to witness the fall of her grandson. Most of my days are spent remembering moments from those forty-eight hours in custody; it's like being bombarded by random, dazzling images, like being stuck in a loop bordered on one side by the moment when I saw Victoria leave with two men in a van, and on the other by the look that Christophe Keller gave me when he told me I was free to go. Between these two moments is the death of Victoria, for which I was incarcerated, in handcuffs, when they took me from my house without the slightest explanation; the death of Victoria, for which I was held in solitary confinement – sleepless, destroyed, coveting death – and interrogated for forty-eight hours by a man whose gaze was made so much harder to bear because, in seeking to understand me, he filled me with shame and self-hatred. His intelligence heightened the tragedy I was going through.

That morning, after the policemen surged into my house and three of them shoved me against a wall, I saw a man in plain clothes moving more calmly towards me, set back from the others, hands in the pockets of his anorak and a woollen hat pushed back on his head. His face came close to mine, and he looked deeply into my eyes for a few seconds while an indeterminate number of policemen (I was aware of them from the noise they made) climbed the staircase and spread throughout all the rooms in the house. The plain-clothes man who stood so close to me — black-eyed, melancholic, quite handsome — gave off an imposing aura of interior power. But I immediately sensed in him an undeniable delicacy, something subtle that allowed him to assess situations more discerningly than the kind of policemen who know only how to break down doors and obtain confessions through intimidation. I understood later that this policeman had, from the very first moment, been convinced that I was not guilty of the horribly sordid business for which he'd just broken into my house. And something passed between our eyes at that moment — a glimmer of recognition, as if he'd seen in me a man to whom he might feel close, with whom he might share a friendly conversation at a party. And that is exactly what I myself felt as I was smashed against the wall and I saw coming towards me this wonderful face — unshaven, manly and sensitive — and this penetrating look in which I discerned the spark of complicity. And then his gaze once again grew as hard as that of a policeman who's just smashed down the door of the suspect in a horrifying murder case.

I didn't understand why this improbable episode had just overtaken my life. Then suddenly I had a flash of intuition. I hadn't heard from Victoria since I'd left her, the previous afternoon, near Saint-Lazare train station, with the two men she'd wanted to accompany — except for a single phone call, made three hours later, in which she asked me to join them. I had declined her invitation.

Had something happened to Victoria?

Next, I thought about the briefcase full of cash I'd been given a few days earlier. Had it, for some unknown reason, been traced by the police? It seemed unlikely. In any case, events were occurring so fast and brutally that I found myself unable to think. I was merely a receiver, registering the simple dread of these blazing moments that were consuming me with a pain I'd never known before.

Sylvie had been told to get out of bed and to stand in the doorway to the living room. She'd been given a dressing gown, fetched from the bathroom by a much younger policeman. Vivienne and Salomé, having been led downstairs, had rushed to their mother in tears. She, also crying, had knelt down and taken them in her arms. As if to intimidate me as much as possible, I was flanked by two men who would, I sensed, overpower me at the slightest hint of insubordination. Had Sylvie not been so devastated by what seemed to us an unfathomable disaster, she would probably have questioned me with her eyes to try to understand what it was about, whether I knew anything that might explain it. But the expression she turned on me was merely terrified and beseeching. She looked at me through her tears, already destroyed – all the more so as the two policemen who'd gone to fetch my daughters had formed an implicit border between our two groups, symbolizing the impossibility of moving closer. From this point on, there was a clear and absolute caesura between my life before and my life after: between my wife, holding my two daughters in her arms, and this other man, created by the arrival of the police. This new man is the one I became. And indeed I have not seen Sylvie or my children since that morning, as if those two sentries had drawn a line that would never be erased.

Contemplating the darkness of the forest through my room's black windows, I find myself under Christophe Keller's gaze: I am trying to understand what Victoria's death has done to me. At the very end of the custody period, when the time came for me to leave, I sensed a complex feeling in his expression that seemed to give a name to what I had become – a name I spend all my nights attempting to identify. The only certainty about this name is that it contains a horrific proportion of guilt and shame, and I wish that it didn't. Throughout the night, I examine Christophe Keller's gaze. I feel dirty, and I want it to purify me. I want it to cleanse me, to absolve me and love me.

I went to wait for him twice last week – in the evenings, in front of the Versailles police building – in order to talk to him, and to see his face. But I never saw him come out, and I'm not sure that I would have dared approach him or run the risk that he would turn me away.

Why him? Why this man? Almost certainly because of those forty-eight hours when I opened myself up as I had never opened myself to anyone, in the eye of the nightmarish storm that was Victoria's death. In spite of the fairly precise descriptions I'd given to the police, nobody had yet been arrested (the two men would be found at the very end of my forty-eight hours' custody; they would confess immediately, exonerating me from any involvement in this tragedy). Christophe Keller had the whole of Victoria's electronic diary, which had been found on her Black-Berry, and he read me long passages from it, questioning me, attempting to understand the nature of our relationship, the places we occupied in each other's lives. He was trying to untangle the long, complex threads that had led us to such extremities. I replied to each of his questions as precisely as I could. Not only was this the first time I had confided in someone, but I would never have been able to do it as totally as I did that day, driven by circumstances to pour out personal details under the gaze that this man was levelling at me. I realized that even Sylvie didn't know who I was. For twenty years, she had been living with a stranger who had never confided in her, who had always remained – with others and with her – in a kind of withdrawal, a perfect disguise. Those forty-eight hours had been the first time that my private life was exposed to another's view. I talked about my childhood, my job, my complexes and fears, about Sylvie and her illness. He listened to me, and sometimes he interrupted me to clarify something or to bring the subject back to the concerns of his investigation. He was trying to work out to what extent I had driven Victoria into the arms of the two men who had led her away with her consent. He was undoubtedly trying to ascertain whether I might be charged with manslaughter or failure to assist a person in danger. He knew I hadn't killed Victoria, but he couldn't prove it. The two of us waited, facing each other. Locked in the enclosed space of those forty-eight hours, separated from time and the world, separated from all representable reality (as in the depths of a nightmare where, lost and frightened, my entire consciousness would be trapped, unable to locate an exit, I sought the exit in Christophe Keller's black, probing eyes), we waited for the two men to be arrested.

While his colleagues searched every nook and cranny of my house, Christophe Keller returned to me on various occasions and said things like: 'Come off it – you know very well why we're here. You'd be better off telling us everything now. It'll save time.'

At one point, a policeman came back from the garage and threw the suitcase full of cash on the floor. They opened it in front of me. 'What a find . . . how much is there in this suitcase?' Christophe Keller asked me.

'About €150,000.'

'Where did it come from? Can you explain to me why there's such a huge sum of cash in your garage?'

'It's this . . . it's to do with my job.'

'Do you deal drugs?'

'Of course not. I work in the construction industry.'

'Nobody these days has €150,000 in cash, unless they're dealing drugs. Do you want to explain it later, or now?'

'Is that why you're here? For this money?'

'You want some advice? Given how long we're going to spend together, I would recommend you answer my questions, rather than asking your own.'

'It's a commission. A commission related to my job.'

'You mean a bribe.'

'If you like.'

'Once again, I . . .'

'It's money that was given to me in return for my agreement to do something that was not straightforward, but that is legal.' I was having trouble speaking. The violent presence of those dozen policemen in my home had drained me of all strength. Christophe Keller, who was waiting for me to continue, said: 'Oh yeah? And what was this thing that they were asking you to do?'

'Work more slowly.' And I collapsed on the floor before the two men who were guarding me could break my fall. I started yelling through my tears: '*Are you ever going to tell me why you're here and what's happened? Why don't you tell me? What have I done? What are you accusing me of? I haven't done anything!*'

'You know perfectly well what's happened. I'm just waiting for you to tell me about it yourself. We would appreciate that.'

'Is it because of this money?' I asked him, sobbing. 'If that's what is, you can take it, I don't want it! I couldn't care less about this cash. I have enough to live in this filthy, rotten world! Everything is rotten!'

'What do you mean? What's rotten? You mean yourself — *you're* rotten?'

'No, not me. That! All of that!' I said, pointing at the bundles of cash. 'They forced me to accept the money! They threatened me with reprisals if I didn't take it. And what happens? Instead of arresting the bastards who forced me to accept it, you arrest me – at six in the morning, in front of my daughters! So you can destroy everything!'

And then Christophe Keller began yelling, with a genuinely shocking vehemence. 'For fuck's sake, will you shut your mouth and stop fucking whining? You think that after what you did last night, you piece of shit, that you can cry like a stupid girl about how everything's rotten? Just shut your fucking mouth and tell us what you know! You know perfectly well what I'm talking about!' The shock wave of this crushing exclamation was followed by absolute silence. The policemen had stopped moving about in the house; they all stood still in various strategic places. In that silence, I heard Vivienne and Salomé sobbing through the door of my bedroom, and it broke my heart. And then, as I was too shocked to reply to him, he whispered: 'But who said we came for the money?' I looked at him in silence. Finally, I said: 'You didn't come for that? So why did you come, then?'

'You'll find out later,' replied Christophe Keller in a surprisingly gentle voice, as if he'd just realized that I truly didn't know why they were there. 'First we're going to interrogate you. You're going to tell us where you were yesterday afternoon. Come on, let's take him away.'

'Can I see my wife and children?' I asked Christophe Keller while a policeman handcuffed me. His response was: 'No. You'll see them later, when you've told us what you know.' The clothes I'd worn the previous day were brought by a policeman from my bedroom and thrown on the floor in front of me. I put them on, and we left the house.

There must have been five or six police cars in the street,

parked facing different directions. All my neighbours had come out and were standing in the street outside my house or in their doorways or watching through the windows of their houses. My gaze passed over a few familiar faces, watching me with expressions that made them seem like strangers. Or perhaps it was just being in a situation so foreign to my reality that made the outside world seem momentarily unbelievable. I was bundled inside a car and then we were driving at full speed to the police station in Versailles, the siren screaming every time we got close to a crossroads or a traffic jam.

I turn around. The hotel owner looks at me. With my finger pointing at a spot on her large wall map of France, I say: 'Today, it's a small village that's not featured on any map of this size. But at the time when this was printed, the village must have been relatively big because its name is written there. I found it.'

'What are you talking about?' the owner asks, coming towards me.

'My family village. The village where my father met my mother. I spent all my school holidays there, from my birth until I was eighteen. My grandmother still lives there. She's . . . hang on, she was born in 1919, so . . .'

'She's eighty-seven,' the owner concludes. 'And where is it, this village? Whereabouts?'

'Where I'm pointing – here, in the south-west.'

'I've never been,' she tells me, standing next to me so she can get a better view of the narrow, winding river next to which the village's name is written. 'Is it pretty?'

'It's very pretty,' I tell her, removing my finger. We are facing each other. She moves her face close to mine and kisses me softly on the lips. I let her do it: I accept this kiss without reacting.

She smiles at me.

She tells me her husband is going to leave her.

'What do you mean? What are you talking about?'

'He doesn't love me any more. He's had enough – of me, of his life, of the countryside, of running a hotel.'

'That's a problem, when you own a hotel.'

'He doesn't own the hotel, I do. We've been arguing for months. Not as loudly as you when you have nightmares, but still . . .'

She kisses me on the lips again, and again I don't react. Her arms are around me, and her face is very close to mine.

'I'm a dead man. You shouldn't expect anything from me. I'll never come back to life.'

'I'm not expecting anything from you at the moment. I'm happy to have you in my hotel, in this large room overlooking the forest. You can stay here as long as you want, even when your suitcase full of cash is empty – although that's not going to happen any time soon,' she says with a smile so natural that it immediately defuses the anger that is on the verge of overcoming me. Instead, I just reply coldly: 'I see that you know every detail of the contents of my room.'

'What a way to put it!' she says. 'In fact, I found it by chance, one day when the chambermaid had the flu. When I saw that little suitcase concealed beneath a blanket, I couldn't stop myself looking. I'd be happy if you stayed here even longer.'

'Won't you have to sell the hotel if your husband leaves?'

'It belongs to me. It was founded by my grandmother in the fifties. My husband was a sales rep. He slept here regularly, and ended up staying.'

'I think I'm going to leave.'

'When?'

'I don't know.'

'As you wish. But you could also stay and forget about the two kisses I gave you.' I smile at her. After a brief pause, she adds: 'Go back to bed. It's nearly 5 a.m.'

As we'd been promising ourselves for months, François Gall, José Delacruz, Dominique and I celebrated the completion of the shell by opening a bottle of champagne at the top of the finished tower on the evening of 5 January. This was a private, exclusive party, just for the four of us – separate from the barbecue that would be organized a little later to thank the teams for their exceptional work.

I would have liked to invite Victoria to the construction site so we could celebrate the climax of our romance together by kissing and making love one last time – on the highest floor of the erected tower, exposed to the winds, under the stars, in the middle of the night. But she wasn't in Paris – wasn't even in Europe – the night this farewell ceremony should have taken place. And more to the point, I no longer wanted such a radical end to our affair as I had been contemplating up to then. I called her one day from the bar of the Valmy restaurant: she was trying to fall asleep in the VIP room of some Latin American airport – I forget which country. I told her I believed that we were going too far, that our relationship had become so obsessive that it could put us in danger. I told her we could not keep sending each other, so compulsively, such a staggering number of texts, like drug addicts desperate for a fix. Victoria didn't reply. I could hear her breathing. I told her that the insane intensity with which we'd been conducting our affair for months could not form the basis of a long-term relationship – that we would end up imploding. The fervour we'd brought to our relationship had, during recent weeks, become combined with the no less incredible energy I'd needed to finish the shell of the tower – and this dual combustion had proved extremely advantageous on the twin fronts of our romantic passion and my professional challenge. But, as I explained to Victoria, I did not have what it took to continue such a demanding affair. Interrupting my monologue, she asked me what I suggested, and I replied that we had to calm things down, lower the pressure, give each other some space. I told her that our relationship was speeding out of control, and if we kept going at this rate we would end up going crazy. 'It's too much for me. I can't keep up. I can't give you this much any more. I need a break,' I told her. Victoria started laughing. She said I was talking rubbish. I replied that I no longer had the energy to take on a relationship that was leading us a bit further each day, that demanded more and more commitment from us each day. Victoria told me I was exaggerating, and I told her that she wasn't aware of how essential we'd become to each other. 'Do you realize that the first thing I do every morning is hide in the bathroom to read the messages I hope you've sent me while I've been asleep and to say hello to you, and that the last thing I do, before going to sleep, no matter where in the world you are, is to send you three texts to say goodnight or wish you a good evening? Do you realize that between these two moments, every day, we send each other fifteen or twenty or thirty texts? Do you realize that, unless I know you're in an aeroplane, I start worrying about you if I go a few hours without hearing from you – that I become anguished, that I think you must be dead, that you've had an accident, or that I become jealous and start suspecting that you've given in to the charms of some man who's chatted you up in an airport? Don't try to deny it – you're just the same. You know perfectly well that it's true. We're utterly addicted. Don't you think it's too much? Do you really consider it a reasonable way to live, having to check your phone every ten minutes to see if you've received a message or missed a call? When I'm the construction manager for the highest tower in France and you're the international head of Human Resources for Kiloffer? When we're supposed to have weightier things on our minds than these adolescent hang-ups?' I went on to explain to Victoria that the construction shell had been completed and that the fate of the Jupiter Tower would now rest squarely on my shoulders, that the coming months would demand from me an even more complex and meticulous vigilance than the previous few months – and that was without even mentioning the almighty pressure my bosses would exert on me to make sure I met their theoretically unrealistic deadline. 'They're going to use David Kolski as a chemical agent that will enable the building to absorb more technical operations than ought to be possible in theory,' I told Victoria between two mouthfuls of espresso, as I leaned on the bar in the Valmy. 'Do you remember your chemistry classes, when you learned that nothing is lost, nothing created, everything transformed? That the substance you see vanishing from the cupel heated by a Bunsen burner is actually being transformed into energy? Well, this is the same thing. They're going to sacrifice me in order to meet their deadline; the Jupiter Tower will be the test tube in which I'll be transformed into energy so that it can be fitted out more quickly. When it's over, and the tower is complete, there will be nothing left of me but a sort of deposit, a few ashes – I'll have been burned to a crisp. That's no big deal. It's legitimate to sacrifice a man like me for such massive financial stakes. What am I worth, compared to this bank and its demands?' I concluded, adding that all of this seemed to me incompatible with the mad rush of a full-on romantic passion. I heard a burst of laughter – laughter that seemed to be amplified, bronzed by the sun-filled atmosphere of the Latin American country where Victoria was waiting for her plane and listening to my endless moaning. I laughed too at the somewhat exaggerated lyricism with which I'd described the challenge that awaited me, and I agreed that I was being pathetic. 'But you see what I mean. I need serenity, concentration, confidence and stillness.'

Talking to her that day, I had stomach cramps. It felt as if hands were kneading my belly like dough. I was afraid Victoria would say, OK, I understand, do what you like, but for me it's over, and hang up. I was devastated by the idea of breaking up with her, but the idea of continuing as we had been for the past few months made me feel anguished. The ideal solution would have been for Victoria to sweeten my existence without taking it over, for her to diminish my loneliness without making me regret the insatiable excesses of our relationship; for her to be neither too close nor too far, neither all-consuming nor indifferent; for us to make love from time to time, when she was in Paris. I don't need to emphasize the undeniably pathetic nature of this demand – it speaks for itself. But in this kind of situation, the question of the best possible solution is inevitably unanswerable. You cannot demand an ideal when it comes to assessing the place a mistress takes in a man's life or that of a lover in a woman's – not unless you have already found the person you need for this type of affair. Which was not the case with Victoria. I was asking her to adapt her nature, to adjust to my needs, to domesticate herself in a way that ran against all her most intimate impulses.

Victoria replied that, if this was what I wanted, she would agree that we should give each other more space ('I clearly don't have much choice,' she said), but that she didn't know if she'd be able to bear it. She wasn't sure that the kind of relationship I was asking of her – peaceful and well-balanced – would be likely to satisfy her. 'It's possible that, after a while, my feelings will fade, that I won't feel the same desire for you. If we communicate less, if we take our foot off the pedal, it's possible I'll start to forget you. That's a risk we'll be taking.'

'How can you know what risks we'll be taking? We haven't even tried it yet, and you already know how it's going to end – you're speculating about your feelings starting to fade. As if their intensity was index-linked to the number of texts we send! If I call you less often, you'll stop thinking about me and start looking for another man? How can you say that you might start to forget me if we send each other fewer messages? Is that all our relationship is? Is there nothing deeper to it, no basic need? It's just a kind of addiction to being in permanent contact? Will our relationship die if we don't feed it all day long? Seriously, I sometimes think that the day I'm no longer in a position to satisfy your needs, you'll throw me out like a piece of rubbish and find another man capable of giving you what you need . . .'

'What are you talking about? That never even crossed my mind . . .'

'I'm talking about the truth. In fact, you have no sentimentality at all, never mind any romanticism. You're purely pragmatic, and that goes for your love life too. If you can't consume me any more, or if I'm not available to you, you're no longer interested in me. This is the great evil of our age: having everything we want, all the time, straight away, no matter where or when. And at the slightest disturbance in supply, you change supplier. People are no longer capable of being alone with themselves: they need to be permanently distracted. The thoughtful woman no longer exists . . .'

'Doesn't what I'm saying seem natural to you? Aren't you afraid that if we create a distance between ourselves, we'll become slightly less precious to each other? Out of sight, out of mind. I didn't make that up, you know. People have been saying it for centuries.'

I wrote to Victoria that evening: 'The magic of our first encounter can be prolonged in the long-term only if we bring a bit more introspection and mystery to our relationship, a bit more silence and serenity, if we keep certain fantasies secret and don't share every waking thought. We could communicate more by email, as it doesn't involve the same compulsive, feverish, instantaneous exchanges; it leaves time for reflection, and allows us not to reply straight away. We will continue to see each other in Paris, probably sometimes in London too, and perhaps even in other places far from those two cities if the opportunity arises and we can manage to take it. I haven't forgotten your proposal to let me choose a country from your upcoming schedule where I'd like to meet you for a few days, and your idea of sending me the plane tickets on the day in question; it will be difficult to organize, but all the same I love that idea and think about it a lot. I look at your schedule and I imagine us in your hotel in Rio, or Shanghai, or Chicago . . . The few weeks we've been through together have given me so much. I have the feeling that they've helped me progress in many different ways – yes, I think I can say it like that – so why stop now? That would be absurd, even if I do sometimes have trouble seeing where this relationship is leading us and working out how I can make it fit with my family life in the long term. We need to have the audacity to invent something unique, something different from everything else, that will be our pride as well as our pleasure . . .'

A few days later, I received a Word document containing a letter from Victoria. It was composed using the 'Meeting Minutes' template that she normally used for her private diary. There, I read that my suggestion of rationing our communications had initially struck her as a form of punishment, and that she'd had great difficulty obeying me – her phone had been burning a hole in her pocket. She wrote that she agreed with me on an intellectual level, but in the depths of her soul, her entire being revolted against it. She understood my way of thinking, she understood my reaction to the excesses of the last few weeks, but at the same time she felt hungry for more. She asked me to put myself in her shoes, to try to understand her point of view: it was as if she'd been drinking water from an abundant spring for weeks on end, and suddenly I was drip-feeding her. She went on: 'Have you already forgotten how we were able to inspire desire in each other from a distance? I admit that sometimes our communication was a bit too much. Thinking about it now, I wonder what got into me when I sent you pages from my electronic diary, revealing myself to you so completely and instantaneously. And the things I wrote from Vietnam . . . I must have been mad! As you say, a little introspection and a few unshared thoughts might not be a bad thing. We should ration ourselves, I agree. But, David, I have to confess that the withdrawal symptoms are horrible – this is killing me, and I don't know if I can bear it.'

About ten days later, when our communications had become restricted to long emails, I received one from Victoria that described a party she'd attended in London the previous evening, organized by French expats; it mentioned her overstretched schedule and how she had to 'squeeze thirty-six hours into days that contain only twenty-four'; it explained that she had just spent a weekend in Paris, and that she had enjoyed going to the Opéra Bastille on Saturday evening with her husband; it informed me that she'd planned a brunch at the Marly on Sunday morning with a childhood friend . . . And, at the end of this long email impassively listing all Victoria's activities, I suddenly found myself reading this paragraph, whose apathetic tone seemed to flow straight from the frankly rather boring descriptions that preceded it, but which in reality was nothing less than terrifying: 'Slowly, gradually, time is healing my wounds. What will happen next? Slowly, gradually, I am losing the intensity and madness of our early meetings. This withdrawal from you, that I feared so much, is proving effective. Personally, I think that's a shame. But it's what you wanted, isn't it?'

For forty-eight hours, I was no longer able to stand up because of the cramps in my stomach, which had grown as hard as concrete. The only way I could move was bent over double. I told Caroline I must have eaten something bad at the restaurant, and that I ought to stay at my desk; she went to the chemist's to buy some Spasfon, and Dominique took my place at the construction site for two hours while I remained glued to my chair. There was no question about it: the final paragraph of Victoria's email announced the end of our affair; her feelings for me were fading. As I'd thought, Victoria needed urgency and energy in her love life; she needed excitement and eccentricity in ever-accelerating doses. That was why she no longer cared about our affair. Or perhaps she had never really cared about it – she didn't seem to be suffering unduly at its termination. She was leaving it the way you leave a house, and now I could see her out on the street, striding towards other adventures.

Later that day, I locked myself in the bathroom and let loose the tears that had accumulated inside me over the past few hours. I sobbed like a child, inconsolable, orphaned from every feeling that had absorbed me for several months. Those feelings had become part of my life. Now I found myself alone once again, with only me for company – unsupported, disenchanted, without any of those promises Victoria was so good at breathing into my mind where they floated and popped like champagne bubbles; without the strength and encouragement that her presence had always given me when I was faced with a difficult challenge. Fear had vanished from my life when Victoria entered it; now she was leaving it, fear was returning. I hated the idea that I would no longer tremble with excitement, as if electrocuted, when I heard the beep in my pocket that signalled the arrival of a new text; I was saddened by the idea that I would never again enjoy the divine surprise of discovering, upon waking, that she had sent me twelve while I was asleep; I rebelled against the idea of giving up our wonderful phone conversations during my drive home from work in the evenings. The pain of our break-up illuminated memories of all the spellbinding moments that had studded our times together. There were so many of them, and each time I remembered one I felt like I was being peeled from the inside – I could feel the taste and thickness of blood in my head. I hadn't realized it was possible to taste blood just by thinking about it. But the fact that I could left me in no doubt: my imagination was bleeding.

I had decided not to reply to Victoria's email until I knew exactly what attitude to adopt: whether to accept the break-up or refuse it.

All I felt was pain. It didn't fade. Most of the people I saw told me I seemed unwell. It manifested itself particularly in my voice, which was heavy and lifeless, as if buried. I cried in front of Dominique one morning – suddenly, as if I'd fallen into a hole. He stood up and took me in his arms. 'It'll be all right,' I told him. 'See, it's already over. Please forget what you've just seen.'

On the third day I cracked. I called Victoria to admit that her withdrawal from me was causing me terrible suffering. 'How did we end up here?' I asked. Victoria replied that she didn't like this distance between us any more than I did – 'Perhaps I'm suffering more than you are; how would you know?' she even said – but that the situation made it impossible for her to come and beg me. I said that it seemed odd to have pride in circumstances like these. I told her that this situation had destroyed me, that I could hardly even walk any more because my stomach was so painful, and that, if I had to, I would have no difficulty in kneeling down and begging her, in humiliating myself before her. Victoria replied coldly: 'I'm not like that.'

'But how can you control yourself, suppress your emotions, in a situation like this?'

'My pride never weakens.'

'Even when you're hurt?'

'Even when I'm hurt.'

'So you're cold, in fact. You don't feel anything. I was right the other day – all you need is a man you can consume. Your lovers are interchangeable.'

'And all you need is a presence in your life – why is that any better? You have your reasons, I have mine.'

'You say I need a presence in my life – but in this case it's maybe more than a simple presence, don't you think? Doesn't that seem obvious to you, given what's happened? Even if I refuse to use the exact words.'

'We've always refused to use those words. It's always been an unspoken agreement that we'll protect ourselves from that kind of development. I don't see why that should change today.'

'Because you're in perfect control of yourself and all your feelings? If you decide not to change the way you feel, your feelings don't change?'

'I try, anyway. I build walls. I protect myself. I don't feel like destroying my life just because one morning I gave in to sentimental weaknesses.'

'But haven't you become a bit dependent on our relationship?'

'I'm probably a bit stronger and more determined than you. And a bit better-armed.'

'By experience?'

'Very funny . . .'

'So what are we doing? Are we going to continue?'

'I'm not the one who decided to stop.'

'You've been trying to hurt me all the way through this conversation.'

'I don't see why you say that.'

'You're ice-cold. You don't seem happy that I'm calling you. In barely ten days, you've already had time to distance yourself from me. I find it cruel . . .'

'I had to react! Did you think I would just submit to your decision, and let myself sink? You clearly don't know me!'

'But that doesn't mean you had to protect yourself to the point of forgetting me.'

'Everyone has their own way of dealing with these things,' Victoria replied.

There was a long silence. I didn't reply to what she said, and she didn't add anything. It was like arm-wrestling with silence. She won. I asked, 'So what are we going to do?'

'You're asking me?'

'You don't seem very clear about it either, Victoria! Things seem to have changed since we were last in touch.'

'If you want us to continue, that's fine with me. But I won't accept your demands for limiting our communications or forbidding texts. If we're going to do this, we should do it! We're in our forties – we're not going to hold back now.'

'All right. I see the best way to deal with this thing, to get back to the way it was before.'

'What do you mean, you see the best way to deal with this thing?'

'I see how I can reduce my dependence. You have to know something: if we go back to the way it was before, I will do everything – everything I possibly can – to detach myself from you, so that one day I can tell you it's over. But in the meantime, all right, let's do this, and let's not hold back.'

'Well, at least that's clear. You see, I actually prefer this situation to what you suggested to me last time. So it's a deal: you try to reduce my hold on you – you try as hard as you can to gather the strength to split up with me – and it'll be up to me to prevent you. To make you even more dependent . . .'

That was how we came to restart our relationship at the same crazy pace and in the same crazy ways as we'd pursued it since the beginning.

One evening, while I was driving home and we were speaking on the phone, Victoria told me she had an important announcement to make: 'Do you have fifteen minutes to talk about this, or would you rather we meet up tomorrow to discuss it?' I was surprised by the serious tone in which she made this request. I replied that I was free for about half an hour, so she had time to tell me what it was about if she wanted to. So Victoria explained that she'd just come out of a meeting with the CEO of Kiloffer, who had told her of his intention to hand her responsibility for the group's property portfolio, because the person who normally looked after that department was leaving. As the first and most important of these property developments concerned the renovation of Kiloffer's head office, Peter Dollan saw no reason why he should entrust this operation to anyone other than the head of Human Resources – all the more so as she had the right sensibility for this type of work, particularly in regard to her relationship with architects. 'I swear, that's exactly what he said! I felt like smiling. I don't know how I managed to keep a straight face,' Victoria told me, laughing loudly, while I watched the motorway disappear under my car and wondered where these words might lead us. So, she'd been entrusted with supervising the redevelopment of the firm's head office, and secondarily with starting work on the extension of one factory in France and another in Germany.

It was true that these tasks went beyond the scope of her job description, but at the same time they could legitimately be added to it as they concerned the design of a working environment for Kiloffer's employees. (This was, moreover, the reason why she'd been consulted so closely when the architectural specifications were being drawn up.) Her boss had added that she would be involved in the process no matter what, even if it was only in terms of dealing with the unions on this question of the employees' working environment. 'So, as you'll be dealing with this anyway . . .' Victoria replied that, given the extra work involved in supervising these matters, there would no doubt have to be . . . 'Of course,' Kiloffer's CEO had interrupted her. 'It goes without saying that you'll be suitably remunerated for this additional effort, and we can discuss that whenever you like. You can even recruit one or two people, as well as inheriting your predecessor's assistant.' Victoria said that this was not what she had wanted to tell him, 'But I'm grateful that you've anticipated these concerns.' Kiloffer's CEO had asked her what it was that she'd wanted to say, and Victoria informed him that, if she was going to handle this issue, she wanted to be in complete control of it, from A to Z, and not only in terms of its logistical, functional and administrative aspects. 'I want to be involved in the decision-making. It will be more time-consuming for me, but also more interesting on an intellectual level and more useful on a professional level.' Somewhat taken aback, Peter Dollan asked her what she meant by that. 'He seemed surprised that I should be so demanding,' Victoria said to me while I drove quite slowly in the right-hand lane, listening carefully to her words, unable to imagine where she was going with this. It seemed obvious that she was not merely recounting an anecdote: she wished to inform me about something that directly concerned me. 'To begin with, I think he was just considering giving me responsibility for the boring logistics of this thing, and keeping the cool, enjoyable, artistic aspects for himself! I really trapped the bastard! If you'd seen me negotiating with him, you'd have been proud of me.' Victoria told her boss that she wished to be involved in choosing the architects and to work in close consultation with those who were chosen. 'This is something that fascinates me, not only in terms of my cultural and intellectual interests, but also in terms of Human Resources,' she told Kiloffer's CEO. He had seemed to approve of Victoria's vision and commitment. He told her that he was in agreement with every point she'd raised, and that in any case he was too busy to be able to supervise this topic very closely. He said he would trust her completely with the recruitment of the right teams: 'Strictly speaking, I have no knowledge of architecture,' he added. 'I might commit errors of judgement.' Victoria replied that she'd always been fascinated by architecture and that she could even claim to have some knowledge on the subject. 'Wonderful!' her boss replied. 'In that case, I won't feel so isolated when it comes to examining the projects and taking the necessary decisions.' All he asked of her was that she organize meetings with the agencies she wished to hire so that he could talk to the architects and get to know their signature styles: 'Just a two-hour conversation, you know, so I can find out how they're inspired by our company and its head office, and what their vision is for its redevelopment. So, when it comes to making the decision, I can be fully informed.' Preparations for the three projects had been begun by Victoria's predecessor, so the more technical aspects had already been covered; now, it was a question of selecting the agencies who might perform the best work on Kiloffer's head office – 'bearing in mind not only the types of developments under consideration, but the particular desires that might result from them. So, in terms of style, for instance, that could mean the materials and the colours,' he added. He would leave it up to her whether to organize some kind of competition between several applicants – he had no opinion on this matter; it was for her to decide. One matter to be determined was whether all three projects should be given to the same team, or whether they should go to two or three different teams. 'I haven't decided anything yet,' Peter Dollan told her, 'so you should think about that as well.' He hoped the pleasure she would draw from these new responsibilities would seem like a reward to her: it was the least he could do for her, given the challenges she'd had to face up to in her battle with the unions in Lorraine. He wanted to take advantage of this moment to tell her again how happy he was that he was able to make use of such an exceptional woman on subjects as diverse as the closure of a plant and the decor of the CEO's future office!

Peter Dollan liked to end meetings on a humorous note to show just what a cool, relaxed boss he was.

'So, what do you think?' Victoria asked me.

'What do you mean, what do I think? I think this man is absolutely right to describe you as an exceptional woman.'

'No, I mean . . .'

'I also think that the mission he's given you is fascinating. You're now a construction manager, Victoria!'

'What I mean is, are you interested?'

I was driving. It was night time. I was overtaking a truck, and I had to return to the right-hand lane in order to concentrate.

'I don't understand. What do you mean, am I interested?'

'In being the architect for this thing. In renovating Kiloffer's head office, and then in taking charge of extending the two factories.'

'What are you on about?'

'Listen, I can't stop thinking about this. It could work. It would be brilliant!'

'Victoria, what could work?'

'You becoming an architect again!'

'Stop being silly. Let's talk about something else. I'm not in the mood to joke about this.'

'I'm not joking. Listen, I'll send you the detailed notes; you can come to London for a day; I'll show you the head office; I can even organize a visit to the factory in France. When you get back to Paris, you can take a month to work on it. You develop a project, make a few sketches . . . Then I set up a meeting with Peter; I introduce you to him; you explain your vision to him . . . and I do what it takes to make sure he chooses you. At that point, Kiloffer will give you a contract for the design of its head office and the extension of its two factories; you'll resign from your job and start your own agency.'

I was dumbstruck. I'd just come off the motorway to stop in a service station car park. I switched off the engine.

'But that's impossible. It could never work.'

'Why not?'

'Because!'

'Because what? David, it's wonderful. You'll be able to be an architect again! Isn't that your most cherished dream?'

'Of course it is!'

'So? What's the problem?'

'But it's . . .'

'It's what?'

'Your boss will never agree to give projects on that scale to someone who doesn't even have an agency, someone who was an architect fifteen years ago! Think about it! Come back to reality! He'll instantly guess that I'm your lover and that you're trying to get me in on this. Victoria, he'll want guarantees! He'll ask me what I've achieved as an architect, what I've been doing in recent years. He'll ask for my CV.'

'Not necessarily. With him, I can attack this from a personal angle. He trusts me completely, and he's the sort of person who likes risky initiatives. There's no reason why I can't say to him that I met you through friends, that we are all convinced you have fantastic potential, that you're about to start your own agency, and that I want to give you your big break. I have no doubts about your talent – you have such great depths I've often thought that you're some kind of undiscovered genius . . .'

'Stop it! This is ridiculous. Please, Victoria.'

'But I do think that. That's why I believe I can convince Peter to hire someone like you, even if you're not an obvious match for the kind of candidate we're looking for.'

'You're actually serious about this . . .'

'I'm not saying it's going to be easy. If we leave him the choice, Peter will automatically go for an established architect in a well-known agency, rather than a construction manager who's planning to start his own agency for this purpose, no matter how talented he may be. But Peter is capable of making extremely unorthodox decisions. He's a man who can be persuaded by the magic of words and ideas. It's entirely possible that you could make a powerful impression on him, and he'll tell me he wants to work with you. He's a cultivated man – an opera buff, an aesthete – a bit like you. So, if this works, you'll be his pet project. That's my strategy. Not only that, but you can also project-manage the work. That would allow you to take care of everything: from the architectural conception to the completion of the building. That should be enough to start an agency, shouldn't it?'

'Yes, of course. I could easily form a team and create an organization to take charge of these three projects.'

'And afterwards, with those projects on your CV, you'll find new clients – and your agency will take off! And in the future,

I'll be able to boast that I was the person who gave the famous David Kolski his big break!'

'That's it, Victoria. You think it's already happened . . .'

'What's in your favour is that you can show him a sketch of the project – unlike the other architects we'll meet, who will simply talk about their general architectural vision. You really need to charm Peter with your intelligence and your ideas. That won't necessarily require a huge amount of work upfront: all you need to do is think about it a bit and bring some drawings so that Peter has something to base his questions on. Like that, he'll get to know you and your ideas for the project. I'll coach you on how to act with him.'

I didn't reply. I was walking on the gravel of the car park. I saw an oil stain and a flattened beer can. I kicked at stones while trying not to make any noise as I walked on the tarmac. The lights from the service station illuminated the night. I felt like screaming with joy. My mouth opened wide at regular intervals, as if I were shouting, but only thoughts came out – bubbles of silent euphoria.

'Aren't you going to say anything?'

'I was thinking.'

'Aren't you happy?'

'Yes, I'm very happy. Thank you, Victoria.'

'When are you supposed to finish your tower?'

'In November, theoretically. But I suspect it'll be closer to January, or even February.'

'All right, then, so you quit in September. Who cares if you haven't finished your tower? For once, you won't be the sacrificial victim. They'll finish it without you – it'll serve them right!'

'You want me to start my agency this year?'

'Why not? I'll organize a visit to London for you next week.

You can take a couple of months to work on it. We'll have several meetings in Paris, the two of us, to talk about it, and when we think you're ready – probably around the end of April or the beginning of May – I'll arrange a meeting with Peter for you. You'll hand in your resignation after that, then start your agency, and by September we'll be ready to go. Isn't life sweet?'

A few days later, Victoria's assistant sent me a Eurostar ticket and I went to London to visit Kiloffer's HQ. I met Victoria in her spacious office. I had to hang around for fifteen minutes in her waiting room while she finished what they told me was an important phone call. 'Victoria apologizes for the delay. Would you like a coffee or anything?' a young woman asked me as I was flicking through Kiloffer's annual report. I'd taken it from a coffee table covered with several brochures about the group's various products. A bit later, hurrying out of her office to shake my hand, Victoria said, 'Ah, David, here you are! I'm sorry – come in, come in!' then led me into her vast, well-appointed office, with its glorious view of London. It was strange to see Victoria in her professional environment, and in particular to see her behaving towards me as if I were an ordinary work contact: the idea was that we had met at a dinner party held by mutual friends, and that we hardly knew each other. That morning, Victoria introduced me as the architect who was acting as construction manager for the highest tower in France – 'the Jupiter Tower, in La Défense, designed by a team from London', she took care to point out, before mentioning that I was about to set up my own agency. The young woman who Victoria had asked to be present at our meeting – in order to make it seem more official – was the assistant of the person who had previously been in charge of Kiloffer's property portfolio and who had just left the company. Her name was Irina Rachline: she had Russian origins, and she was good-looking, but what most struck me about her was her scholarly, meticulous, somewhat vexatious personality, manifested in the words she addressed to me and the way she looked at me with her hazel eyes. She clearly took seriously the role Victoria was going to give her in the implementation of these three architectural projects (although I doubted whether the question had ever been addressed directly since she had entered Victoria's service, forcing Irina to cling to vague assumptions). Right from the start, I sensed in her a barely concealed reticence towards me – as if the fact that Victoria's first step in her new role was to have an unscheduled meeting with one of her private contacts did not augur well for the seriousness with which she was going to perform that role; or perhaps, on the contrary, Victoria had presented this meeting as a formality she'd been obliged to accept out of social courtesy. Irina Rachline stared at me in a suspicious and somewhat condescending way, but above all she seemed to be trying to make it clear that she did not like me, or at least did not like the fact that Victoria had agreed to meet me. Or perhaps she wished to let me know that she was not remotely fooled by the masquerade we were putting on for her. At several points, it occurred to me that she was taking out on me her frustrations with regard to Victoria – because, in hierarchic terms, this young woman was not in a position to question the decisions of the head of Human Resources, nor to obstruct them through any kind of uncooperative behaviour. No matter how carefully masked, her sceptical attitude seemed to me to go beyond what was acceptable for someone in her subordinate position – I was mystified that she was able to go as far as she did without meeting any resistance – unless Irina Rachline believed that Victoria had authorized her, in a private meeting held just before this one, not to take me seriously. You can see the kind of thoughts this young woman's

behaviour had led my mind towards, even while I was pretending to answer Victoria's faux-serious questions and the assistant
was recording my answers on paper. Because of this young
woman and her querulous attitude, I left this meeting with the
feeling that the whole thing had been a charade; that I had just
taken part in a scene from a play directed by Kiloffer's global
head of Human Resources, a farce that had fooled no one. The
assistant even handed me her card, at the end of the meeting,
with unconcealed distaste (because Victoria had declared that,
from now on, all communication between Kiloffer and me would
have to pass through Irina Rachline). If all of this had not been
merely for show, then why didn't Victoria correct her assistant's
bad attitude? Not only had she not batted an eyelid at this behaviour, she had seemed utterly indifferent to the insensitive way I
was being treated by this person, whom, it had already been
established, would have no role to play with regard to me. In the
hours that followed, feeling anxious and uneasy, I thought to
myself that something was not right here – but I didn't know if
this impression was based on the simple fact that, having had to
conceal the true nature of our relationship from other people,
this meeting had inevitably been a masquerade. Not only had we
been putting on a performance around the table in Victoria's
office, but we'd had fun doing so. Each time the assistant's eyes
had been focused on the biro she was using to record the words
I spoke on her graph-paper notepad, Victoria flashed me fiendish
smiles and impatient winks, or pinned me with hot stares that
communicated to me just how urgent her desire for me was.
With this young woman as our audience, we were performing a
play that was joyful and boisterous, witty and efficient, as if
the knowledge that we were working cheerfully and enthusiastically had enlivened us throughout the meeting. But I worried
that Irina Rachline had perhaps not failed to notice the overly

sophisticated turns of phrase that excluded her from our complicity in a rather unpleasant way, and that gave the meeting a casual atmosphere that, afterwards, I would bitterly regret. Because it was not in my interests to go all the way to London for reasons that I considered serious, only to let my mistress believe that I was merely messing around. It even occurred to me, as I was rocked by the speeding Eurostar on my way back to Paris, that her reputation as a man-eater was perhaps no longer a secret among Kiloffer's employees. I imagined that most of her colleagues had realized that our meeting was nothing more than the preamble to a ceremony that would take place a few hours later in a hotel room, all the more so because my physical attractiveness had struck them as suspicious; I'd definitely sensed that. And yet at the same time, these strange suspicions were mixed with the reality of an official meeting, on a fascinating subject, paid for by Kiloffer, which had ended with Irina Rachline handing me all the information intended for the chosen architectural agencies. In the days that followed, I managed to reason with myself: I told myself that this feeling of falseness that had caused me such anguish had perhaps been due only to the assistant's hostile attitude, to Victoria's jokey mood, and to the lie that our relationship constituted for everyone we met that morning.

After my visit to the head office, Victoria told me she had some shopping to do, close to her office, and she suggested that – if I had nothing better to do – I should accompany her, then go for a quick lunch together. I agreed, and we went down into the underground car park together. There, we got into Victoria's huge, black, 16-valve, leather-lined 4WD, and she drove it at top speed through the London streets. 'Nothing's too good for Kiloffer's head of Human Resources, eh?' I said sarcastically to Victoria. 'Do you have to close factories in order to afford this kind of vehicle for yourself?'

'Shut up! Don't say that – this is my guilty pleasure. It's not my fault if I love big cars! And it's beautiful, don't you think? I've only had it four days – it's brand new.'

It was exhilarating, being driven so fast and skilfully by Victoria in an outrageously flashy car, but I kept these feelings secret because they made me feel a bit ashamed. I watched her in profile, and she glanced from time to time at each of the three rear-view mirrors – and sometimes, with a smile, at me. Whenever a space opened up in front of her, she accelerated into it, and sped off as soon as the lights went green if she was first in line.

'You're beautiful when you drive.'

'Thank you. I do sometimes get chatted up in traffic jams. So, what did you think of our meeting?'

'I think it's a fascinating project, and that we can achieve something brilliant. But I was a bit bothered by your assistant's attitude.'

'Oh, really? Why?'

'She's strange. How well do you know her?'

'Hardly at all. I started working with her last week. Would you rather we didn't go through her?'

'I don't know. What do you think?'

'The reason I asked Irina to attend the meeting was to put you in the loop officially. But if you have a bad feeling about her, we can continue to work directly with just the two of us.'

'I think I'd prefer that. That girl doesn't like me. I sensed a definite hostility towards me. It's obvious that she'll throw a spanner in the works if she can. I get the feeling she really doesn't want me to be chosen.'

'I don't see why, and anyway she has absolutely no power at all. But if you prefer not to be in contact with her, that's fine – we'll work directly between the two of us. Do you want to see my house?'

'But maybe I'm making a mistake? Maybe you're right, and this should be done officially, so that I'm in the loop. Please, Victoria, don't you want to help me resolve this issue?'

'Do as you like. It doesn't matter – it's not important at all. So . . . do you want to see my house?'

'Your house?'

'Yes. Do you want to visit it?'

'I don't know – that depends. Is it far?'

'No, it's very close.'

'Victoria, what are we going to do about Irina? Tell me what you . . .'

'Listen, just forget about it. I'm going to talk to Peter directly about you. Your candidacy is unusual anyway – it may as well stay that way. You're right: let's forget this girl. I'll ask her to look after the official agencies. I shouldn't have asked her to come to this top-secret meeting . . .'

'Why do you call it top secret?'

'No, it's nothing!'

'Are there going to be official candidacies – the official agencies, in other words – and then me? But that's a risk, then, if Irina . . . Victoria, are there going to be official applications, and then me on my own?'

'But you're going to get favourable treatment. You'll be secretly championed by the boss's *éminence grise*. What more do you want?'

'I want it to work. I want to be chosen. There's no point in me dreaming about this if it's lost before I've even applied.'

'All right, so are you interested in seeing my house or not?'

'Yes, OK. Why not? But where is it?'

'Finally! It's about time – I was getting sick of driving round the block. We're here!' Victoria announced, parking her 4WD in front of an elegant white building in a long and obviously wealthy residential street. 'There it is – everybody out!' she added, laughing. And then, while she was sliding the key into the lock of the front door: 'Don't worry, this is my project. Peter trusts me. I'll take care of everything. All right?'

'Yes, all right.'

'Then please step inside, my friend . . .'

I would never have imagined that Victoria's house would be furnished and decorated the way it was: club chairs, ceiling fans, panther skins and buffalo heads hung on the walls, a stuffed crocodile, wicker furniture, a wooden globe, beige-painted walls and – everywhere you looked – souvenirs from her trips and postings abroad. It gave me a strange sensation, only now dis-covering the place where Victoria lived, after five months together. This visit to her home seemed to give me a more mean-ingful idea of who she was than making love with her had ever done – a false impression, of course, but nevertheless that was what the decor of her house (as she showed me into room after room) suggested to me, as if an immense chasm were slowly opening up between us. It was all the more awkward as this was not something immaterial (like our political and ideological dif-ferences, for example) but something tangible, objective, present. I didn't like this uniformly neo-colonialist decor: I felt like I was visiting a slave trader's mansion in Africa in the nineteenth century (not inappropriately, perhaps, for the residence of a global head of Human Resources). 'It's impressive,' I said. 'You'd think we were in India or Africa. I had no idea you were so into safaris. All these rifles, animal skins and antlers . . .'

'I know! I love this style. I created all this myself as I trav-elled round the world. To begin with, we had my husband's furniture – it was like living with Madame de Pompadour! It was awful. I hated it!'

'I keep expecting a pet chimp to suddenly appear, or a black panther on a leash . . . You don't have a boy to serve me a lemonade?'

'You're making fun of me! Bastard! I hate you!'

'Not at all. I find it charming. You should see my place – there's absolutely no style at all, no single direction.'

'Well, you ain't seen nothing yet. Get ready for a shock – this is the ultimate,' Victoria told me, opening the door to a vast corner room on the first floor, illuminated by four windows: the parents' bedroom. 'So, what do you think? Classy, isn't it?' I moved into the room, where I saw an Eastern-style four-poster bed in sculpted dark wood, with a cone of white tulle descending from the ceiling over either side of the bed's frame. Victoria opened the door to the bathroom, furnished entirely in wicker, with Liberty curtains over the windows. Under two dressing gowns hung on the wall, I noticed two pairs of plastic sandals – his and hers – posed neatly on the tile floor. For a moment, I stared in shock at the sandals belonging to Victoria's husband: I could see the imprint of his toes in the plastic. Then I heard behind me, from the doorway: 'Are you coming?' Victoria took me by the hand and led me towards the bed, where she pushed me on to the mattress before leaping on top of me. As she began to undress me while kissing me on the mouth, I said: 'Victoria, surely you don't think we're going to make love in your bedroom – in your conjugal bed? You're crazy!'

'In my conjugal bed? You have the funniest expressions! Anyway, why exactly did you think we'd come here? To drink a cup of tea?'

'I'd like Darjeeling, please.'

'Make love to me, you bastard! You pig, I hate you!' Victoria replied, covering my lips with hers to stop me talking.

'Do you want me to take you like a lion? Or perhaps a panther?' Victoria started hitting me. I knocked her sideways and pushed my fingers inside her: she was soaking wet. 'Actually it's a huge turn-on to fuck you in your marriage bed. I'm going to take you like a dog in your bedroom.'

'Yes, fuck me! Hurry up! I can't wait!'

I made love to Victoria, without coming, until I had to leave for St Pancras to catch my Eurostar. Victoria drove me at top speed towards the centre of London, not far from her office, where I hailed a taxi. I masturbated in the Eurostar toilets, thinking about Sylvie's body (and coming, standing up, into the metal bowl), and it was only when I returned to my seat, exhausted, that I gave any thought to what had happened to me that day: the strange morning meeting and the ambush Victoria had perpetrated on me in order to get me to make love to her in her marriage bed. I ended up nodding off with some unresolved idea in the back of my mind, exactly as if I'd encountered a problem and I didn't know how to deal with it. This was odd, because not only had I not encountered a problem, but I had actually accomplished something constructive (I'm talking about my visit to Kiloffer's head office). This was late February, and everything seemed to be going well for David Kolski.

We met early – about 6 p.m. – at the bar of the Grand Hotel, close to the Palais Garnier: Victoria had chosen this spot because she was going to the opera that evening at 7.30 p.m. It was a production of *The Marriage of Figaro* directed by a famously radical playwright. Several of her friends had seen it and hated it: 'It sounds awful,' Victoria told me. 'Apparently the recitatives are stammered out by a drunken tramp who crawls across the stage. But we got our tickets as part of our subscription, so we're going to see it anyway. Frankly, though, I fear the worst – there's nothing I hate more than people who think they have the right to ruin music by flaunting their mediocrity.' (Her comments went over my head – I listened without replying or agreeing or showing any interest in the subject – but I suspected her of having conservative, even reactionary, tastes when it came to opera.) Victoria had arrived in Paris that morning for a work meeting with Kiloffer's French legal representatives, in preparation for what I knew to be a crucial showdown with the unions the next day. As she had long been planning to go to the opera that evening with a group of other subscribers including her husband, she would not sleep at the hotel but in their Paris apartment – something she had hardly done at all (except at weekends) since I had known her. (I found it strange that her husband never asked why Victoria no longer came to Paris for work during the week, except for the brief visits she made during the day or the lightning visits she led her family to believe she made between two foreign destinations – when in reality she was in the Louvre Hotel or the Concorde Saint-Lazare, making love with me all night.)

I had opened the thick, strapped folder that I'd brought with me, and placed it on the floor. And, having moved our teacups to the edge of the coffee table, I had laid out the rough sketches I wanted to show her, along with a number of finished drawings. Some of these, in colour, were nicely done and had a genuine aesthetic impact, particularly the larger ones. Victoria seemed surprised by the number of documents I'd spread out on the table, a testimony to the amount of work I'd put in. 'Let's start with the lower floors. I've given a lot of thought to the lobby, the entrance and the panoramic restaurant on the second floor. That was the starting point for everything else, in fact. I don't want Kiloffer's head office to give the impression of a closed world, as is often the case these days with mirrored glass walls; I wanted the building to be open to the city and to absorb its energy, so that there's a permanent to-and-fro. You'll see later that my project consists in replacing all the windows with a more efficient type of glass, but also in glazing the eastern, western and southern facades with a second skin that offers protection from sunlight. In fact, I ought to begin with this drawing, which shows the ultra-sophisticated glass coating I'm going to install on the building, allowing you to make serious savings in energy costs.'

'But is it possible? Can you realistically stay within an acceptable budget if you install a second skin?'

'I'm not going to pretend it's not a major investment. But even in the medium term, it has strong economic benefits. I'll have to do the exact calculations, but in my opinion, the energy savings mean it will pay for itself within only a few years – maybe fifteen years. To give you some idea, energy costs associated with traditional office buildings are generally around 400 kWh per square metre per year. The Jupiter Tower, which is a High Quality Environmental building, will be around 100. With the system I'm proposing, I could promise you energy costs of about seventy.'

'I see what you mean. That's a huge difference.'

'That's the kind of thing that can easily be verified by a feasibility study. After a certain number of years, once you've paid for the installation, you'll have a building whose operating costs are one-fifth of most other buildings. Which, in an era when future energy costs are so uncertain, is a considerable saving. It would also allow you to boast that Kiloffer's head office – due to an intelligent and environment-friendly renovation – meets the standards set by the HQE label; you can legitimately claim that you've spent a lot of money on implementing an innovative technology in order to have a head office that is ecological and respectful of the planet's needs. If you choose this model, you'll be demonstrating your commitment to sustainable development.'

'That's an issue I'm very interested in. You have to understand that our industry is essentially polluting; we emit an enormous amount of carbon dioxide. It's important to us to be able to say that we respect the environment, that we care about ecological issues. Well done – that's great. It's a very important point.'

'I'm glad you like my work, Victoria,' I said to her with a smile. 'So . . . each office has its own air-conditioning system; these flaps, installed on the building's facade, allow inside and outside temperatures to be synched, meaning that air handling is not global, as is usually the case, but local and individual. The air is filtered by the first skin and then circulated between that skin and the facade – I've done a little sketch here to explain the principle, look – and the individual flaps, as you'll see on the drawing, enable the recycled air to be circulated within the offices. So you could describe it as a building that breathes.'

'But what's the point of that?'

'By combining this system with traditional air-conditioning, we can achieve perfect results – an air temperature that is mild and comfortable, and adapted to each person's needs, to varying circumstances, to the temperature differences between night and day, that kind of thing. And in fact, it's these individually adapted controls that enable the biggest energy savings.'

'I didn't know that. You're teaching me something new. Oh . . . Laurent is there.'

'Laurent . . . your former lover?'

'Of course. Who else?'

'What's he doing here? Has he seen you?'

'Yes, he saw us. I'm sure he knows it's you.'

'What do you mean, he knows it's me?'

'I told him about you and me.'

'You still see him?'

'He calls me occasionally to find out how I'm doing. He's

been jealous ever since he found out about you. He wants us to see each other again . . .'

'And . . . ?'

'And nothing. I tell him it's too late, and he should have thought about that while there was still time. I remind him that the last time we were supposed to meet, he stood me up.'

'Which one is he?'

'Try to be discreet.'

'Come on – you can point him out, at least!'

'All right, but be discreet.'

'As if I'm ever anything but.'

'Near the entrance. On the table to the right. He's in profile, wearing a brown jacket.'

'The velvet one?'

'Exactly.'

'Is he in disguise, or is that how he normally dresses?'

'Don't be silly, David. We're not lovers any more, so why would he wear a disguise? He's wearing his mathematician's jacket – the same one he's worn for years – with chalk on the sleeves and fourteen identical pencils sticking out of the pocket. I've never understood why he always walks around with all those pencils. Anyway . . . where were we?'

'We were talking about energy savings.'

'It's funny, him seeing us together. I like taunting him by letting him see me with you,' Victoria says, shaking with laughter.

'He can't stop looking at me.'

'He's going to be so mad about this. I bet I haven't had my last message from him.'

'But anyway, going back to the lobby I mentioned at the beginning . . . I'm looking for . . . here it is . . . this drawing . . .'

'That is a truly beautiful drawing. The building from the

street, at night – it's incredible. This is exactly the kind of thing that Peter will love. It's so poetic and you can see how much thought has gone into it . . . But how did you manage to produce all this in such a short time?'

'I'm glad you noticed. Not bad, is it?'

'I'm impressed.' I placed my hand on hers and squeezed. We smiled at each other. When I looked up, I saw Laurent watching us. I started talking about my designs again: 'I don't want the building to give the impression that it belongs to a secret world, protected from the outside, so for the first three floors – for this entire area – I'm using an extremely transparent glass. So, from the street, you'll be able to see that the second floor is devoted to the company restaurant. I think this will give a human character, almost an intimacy, to the building, which is an essential part of my project. And then this is an idea I'm really proud of – I had it one evening, driving back home . . .'

'You're right, it's incredible. I had no idea you'd put so much thought into this.'

'I haven't slept much in the last couple of weeks. I've been working like crazy on the construction site, and things are fairly difficult at the moment. Maybe it's because life is so tough with the tower that I've been taking refuge in this more inspiring work every evening. I've been spending hours drawing at home recently – at night, while my wife is asleep. To be honest, I'm hugely excited by this project. I feel inspired by it. I can't stop thinking about it, perfecting the finished drawings. I really hope Peter will like it, Victoria. I believe I'm capable of doing an excellent job on this – every bit as good as an established agency.'

'I'm pleased you've put so much into it . . .' Victoria begins, then pauses. She looks like she's suspended in the middle of a thought. I raise my eyebrows. She looks down. I move closer to her, lift her chin, and kiss her on the lips. I look at the table near the entrance: Laurent looks away. I ask Victoria: 'Yes? But? I don't know . . . you look like you want to tell me something . . .'

'No, nothing,' Victoria whispers. Then, almost immediately: 'But we don't know if this is going to work, David – so much is up to chance. I'm worried that you're putting so much into it when the result is so uncertain.'

'But it's worth trying, isn't it? You have to know what you want in life. I'm enthralled by this project. I'm desperate to win this contract and start my own agency. And my only weapon is my brain, my imagination, the ideas I can come up with. Nothing can beat a good idea – an idea that the others haven't had, that they'd like to have . . .'

'Good. I'm glad you're putting your heart into this project. I'll let Peter know how motivated you are.'

'All right . . . so anyway, one evening, I had this idea that I really love. Look – you'll get a better idea of it from this drawing . . . Can you see the part in the centre, where my finger is? Where the lifts will be, going all the way up to the top of the building? Well, as it will be visible from the outside, because of the transparent windows, particularly on the first three floors, I'm going to cover it in a golden, silky, slightly mirrored finish so that it can reflect the lights from the city, street scenes, pedestrians, a passing bus . . . People in neighbouring buildings will be able to see the city reflected in the walls of the central lift shaft of Kiloffer's head office. I've already written all this in a notebook. I'll be able to tell your boss that there'll be a permanent interaction between the building and its urban context – the city of London – as if Kiloffer's head office, rather than being folded in on itself, looked out at the city, thought of the city, dreamed the city and all those who live there. It's a listed company, with shareholders; it's transparent in its dealings, it's turned towards the outside, and it must reflect the concerns of those who have placed their trust in it and who have decided to follow it in its development. Through its golden hue and its reflective quality, the building's spine signifies that Kiloffer's activities are associated with the creation of wealth. There's no better symbol of what a modern, responsible, transparent, listed company should be – reactive to the concerns of its shareholders.'

Victoria bursts out laughing. I begin to laugh with her. Then she says: 'I can't believe what I'm hearing! You, a staunch socialist, are working for the good of capitalist doctrine? You're making speeches on our behalf? David, you should be horrified with yourself – you're turning into a collaborator!'

'It's pretty good, isn't it? Did you notice how slick it is, conceptually? Come on, Victoria, admit it! You pay PR agencies hundreds of thousands of euros to give you idiotic recommendations! Have any of them ever provided you with something so thought-out and developed? And it's based on an architectural project! I'm creating architecture that thinks, that communicates, that makes speeches!'

'I agree completely. It's brilliant.' Victoria starts laughing again, looking at me affectionately. 'I never imagined you'd be able to get inside our mindset like that, to articulate it from within . . .'

'I got really into it. If this can enable me to start my own agency, I'm ready to make any kind of compromise.'

'Sell-out! Opportunist!' Victoria taunts me, laughing. 'You criticize us, but you're worse. In fact, I'm beginning to wonder why you're a socialist at all . . .'

It was at that moment, as she looked over to Laurent's table, that I saw Victoria's face fall. She looked back at me. She smiled. But I could sense that this smile was like a bird perched on a randomly chosen branch, ready to take off again at any second.

The smile had nothing in common with the lips on which it briefly played.

'What's the matter? What were you looking at?'

'Nothing. It's all right.'

'Who's that man? The one who just arrived?'

'Nobody, it's fine. Nothing's the matter.'

'If you say so. You look pretty strange, though.' After a few seconds, I said: 'So, when are we going to see Peter?'

'It's a bit complicated at the moment. He's busy with a massively important project, top secret, crucial for the group's future. Even I'm having trouble getting to see him. In any case, don't forget that we'd said late April, early May – and it's only 30 March today.'

'But as I'm ready, can't we bring the meeting forward?'

'What time is it?' I look at my watch, then look back at Victoria's face: it has gone pale and is trembling slightly. 'Quarter to seven.' I move my hand to take hers, but she moves it suddenly out of the way and sits back in her chair as far away from me as she can. I say: 'All right, have it your own way.'

'I'm going to have to leave you, David.'

'Why? What do you have to do?'

'I need to join Laurent's table.'

'You told me you were meeting your friends at quarter past seven on the steps of the Opéra Garnier. That's only two minutes from here . . .'

'That's true. But by some amazing coincidence, three of my four friends are sitting at that table near the entrance, so I need to join them. I can't possibly leave this bar with you. You need to let me sit down with them.'

'Laurent is one of the people you're going to the opera with tonight?'

Victoria stares at me.

'You told me your husband was going to be there. I don't understand . . .'

Sitting back in her chair, watching me from afar, Victoria watches as understanding of the situation slowly dawns on me.

'The man who just arrived, who sat down after kissing Laurent, that's . . . he's your husband?'

Victoria still doesn't reply.

'They know each other? Fuck me, I'm totally lost here . . . Your husband and Laurent go to the opera together? It seems to me I asked you a question; I'd appreciate a reply. Do they know each other? Are they friends?'

My eyes question Victoria with a silent, powerful urgency. In a faint, annoyed-sounding voice, she replies: 'Let's change the subject.'

'We're not going to change the subject. As far as I can see, you're not really in a position to start choosing our topics of conversation. If you don't answer my question, I'm going over to ask them.'

'Laurent is my husband's best friend.'

'How long have they known each other?'

'They were childhood friends.'

I stare dumbfounded at Victoria.

'The man who disguised himself, who put on false beards and took you to hammams so he could fondle your breasts in front of guys wanking themselves off before fucking you in seedy, cockroach-infested hotels, is your husband's best friend? This man, who you told me you'd left because he wanted to go too far in these crazy fantasies . . . you and your husband go out for dinner with him and his wife, the four of you together? You share an opera subscription and sometimes go on holiday together with your kids in summer? You manage to live this double life?'

'Without any problem at all, if that's what you want to know.'

345

What I have just discovered is huge. It is fascinating. This is no longer just a difference in taste or opinion; it is not merely that I find myself in disagreement with Victoria's mindset or lifestyle; I am confronted with some kind of mutant whose adaptive capacities to the most extreme situations are astounding, almost inhuman.

'This is unbelievable. So, to sum up, there are, in this bar: Victoria; her husband; her current lover; her previous lover, who turns out to be her husband's best friend; and I imagine that the peroxide blonde is Laurent's wife . . . all of this in the same little fishbowl, at the same moment, on your way to the Palais Garnier! Lucky you can count on the support of your ex-lover to get you out of this fix. So, basically, nothing can disturb your little arrangement – unless I seriously mess things up. In other words, unless I get up and walk over to that table to explain to them who I am, and to tell Laurent that I know who he is.'

Victoria stares at me without replying. For a brief instant, however, I sense a hint of hatred in her look. 'What effect does that have on you, seeing your system from the outside?'

'What do you mean, my system?'

'I call it a system because there's nothing else it can be called: not to be able to imagine your existence without always having at least one lover. I'm certain about this now. It's there before my eyes, a tangible reality: you cannot conceive of living in any way other than having multiple lives that never overlap.'

Victoria's face lights up briefly, as if illuminated for a few seconds by my words, like a ray of light that shines out between two clouds. She says: 'I've never looked at things in that way, but you're right: yes, in some ways, this is a system. I always thought it was chance that I never ended up without a lover; I always thought it was just how circumstances had arranged things, that I had nothing to do with it. But no: you're right, in fact. Without a lover, I would pine away. I've always managed things so that I have a lover, but I'd never been aware of it before. What you're saying is funny but true. Yes, it's a system.'

'Shall I tell you what fascinates me most about this situation?' Since her husband's arrival, Victoria has been unrecognizable: I have never seen her so fearful, almost submissive, hiding in the depths of her armchair like a little girl. Each of her replies to my questions is preceded by a few seconds of silence, and the replies are not so much responses as a way of pushing me far away from her body, keeping me at a distance. That evening, I saw just how much Victoria respected her husband. I hear her whisper: 'Yes, tell me. What fascinates you?'

'It's that Laurent still hasn't told your husband that you're here. Everything's happening as if you haven't been seen. He's protecting you. He's protecting himself. The three of us are linked by a form of solidarity that, personally, I find quite sordid. This situation is nothing like me; I don't recognize myself in it at all. It's as if I'd been artificially transported into a reality that has nothing to do with me, but where you and Laurent are demiurges. This is your world, your universe, your mindset . . . I have nothing to do with any of it. I find it sordid and unhealthy.'

'You can't understand it, David. You could never understand us.'

Victoria has not raised her voice, but these two sentences are delivered in a fast, hard tone. I feel wounded by their impact. The word 'us' sticks in my thoughts like a bullet in muscle.

'What do you mean, "*us*"? Why say it like that – "you could never understand *us*"?'

'Because you see things from a basic viewpoint. You have no elevation of mind. We have never believed that moral prohibitions have anything to do with us, we have never let them limit what we can do. *We're happy to leave them to you – those of you*

347

who need guidelines. In fact, I'll go further: we're aware of belonging to a kind of aristocracy – a class of people who know how to wring pleasure from powerful, abnormal, extraordinary situations. There are men – and they are very rare – with whom it is possible to free yourself from conventional forms of behaviour. Laurent is one of those men. Most people are afraid: they put up barriers. You, clearly, prefer to do things by the book. You lack courage.'

Victoria is talking to me coldly, in a low, calm voice. I get the feeling she wants to devastate me. (Someone sitting further away and vaguely watching her face would not suspect for a second that Victoria was verbally executing me: her face is marked by a faint smile that might be mistaken for a sort of romantic languor – whereas in reality, activated by the words she's speaking, it is a contemptuous smile. Even her calmness, in combination with what she's saying, is offensive.) It's fascinating how Victoria has managed to invert the power relations, smashing me against the wall of my own moralizing. Caught in the trap of an accusation I've begun to level at her, she defends herself by attacking: she excludes me from the complicity that linked her to Laurent in order to make me look smaller, expose my pettiness. I don't say anything in reply. I understand what she means. She crushes me with all her power. I sit silently in my chair and let my gaze wander over the drawings that cover the table: I see them upside down, as they are all turned towards Victoria.

'Ordinary mortals have neither the capacity to do these kinds of things, nor the capacity to understand them. And some of them do not have the capacity to tolerate these things either. I'm sorry for you if all this is beyond you – but, please, don't come moralizing to me. I don't have to justify what I've done to anybody. You will never make me say I feel guilty: what I went through with Laurent was glorious. I hope, one day, you can have experiences as incredibly beautiful with a woman as those I lived through with Laurent when we were supposedly transgressing your morality,' Victoria says in a sardonic and cruelly irreverent tone, attempting to imitate the intonation and facial expressions of a naive, offended and somewhat stupid person.

'Why are you talking to me like that? It hurts me to hear you speak to me in this way. There's no need for you to be hurtful.'

'I'm not being hurtful. You're the one saying I'm sordid. You can't understand: I'm not sordid.'

'All right, I'm sorry. I take back the word "sordid". I just wanted to express how uneasy it made me feel to find myself part of this situation . . . but never mind. I understand what you're saying. I wouldn't be capable of living like that, but I do understand – and I don't condemn you for it. In fact, I envy your ability to be so free.'

'Good. Thank you. And I apologize, in that case.'

'On the other hand, I feel like I'm at the edge of an abyss. It seems to me you're capable of anything. I don't know who you are any more, or what you're doing. I don't know if you're telling the truth. How do I know you don't have two lovers? How can I be sure you haven't actually got back together with Laurent? I've just witnessed your extraordinary capacity for segmentation and concealment: it doesn't shock me, but it does scare me. I fear I'll end up a victim to it. You boast about your ability to live outside all conventional morality, and at the same time you reassure me that you always tell me the truth. How can you expect me to believe you? With you, it's impossible to know – at any given moment, irrespective of the subject in question – whether you're telling the truth or not. Tonight has made me certain of that.'

Victoria does not reply.

'You know, when we met, we were each part of a system.

My system was to have a mistress now and again, fairly infrequently, and to see each of them only once. Your system was to always have a lover, without any kind of discontinuity at all. I could have made you part of my system – I could have disappeared the day after our night in London. But what happened was that you lured me into yours. I am currently, for the first time in my life, part of someone else's system. Sometimes I resent it, as you know; at various times, I've tried to escape it. But through different means, you've always managed to keep me part of it. And now I find myself trapped in this system . . .'

'Nobody's forcing you to stay in it. I don't understand why you use the word "trapped".'

'I've trapped myself. Through my dependence on you, by my need for you. And now I've discovered that I am, in this system, just one among many . . .'

'What are you talking about?'

'I don't see what there is to stop you widening the field of your experiences without my knowledge. I'd naively imagined that what I could see of your life was the reality, but maybe it's only part of a much bigger reality, most of which is hidden from me. Maybe your life is very different from the way I imagine it? Maybe I'm in exactly the same position as your husband, except that I'm on the first floor while he's down at ground level? Maybe there's another man, above me, who I don't know about, and who knows a bit more than your husband and I do, because he's aware of our existence? Maybe there's another man up on the third floor? Or even a woman? Or maybe you segment your life into utterly separate compartments, and none of us are aware of each other's existence when in fact we're all living on the same floor?'

'You're out of your mind, David – all of this is in your imagination. I swear to you you're the only one. I have no one else in my life . . .'

'No, I'm not out of my mind. All I'm doing is following your system to its most logical conclusion. As I said before, it doesn't shock me: contrary to what you thought earlier, I'm not making any moral judgement on you. I'm just scared, that's all. Your system makes me fear for myself.'

'You have no reason to be scared. I promise I'm faithful to you.'

'It's not a question of fidelity. You can sleep with whoever you like, wherever you like – I don't care. It's a question of hidden reality. Your reality is a construction, and I can perhaps see only the part of it that directly involves me. I don't accept the idea of this partial vision. I want to be panoptic; I want to be able to see every little corner of your reality.'

'I'm not hiding anything at all from you.'

'You could have told me that yesterday. And this evening I would have found out that it was untrue.' Victoria doesn't reply: my words have struck her dumb. I continue: 'Promise me one thing, Victoria. In return for me allowing myself to be drawn into your system . . .'

'Go on.'

'I just want you to tell me the truth. To tell me if I'm number one . . . or number three. To tell me if you spend the night with another man during your travels. I want to be certain that you're not lying to me. Given what I know about you now, even the smallest lie would be unbearable. Everything has to be transparent between us now – that's essential. If not, it will become impossible to trust you at all.'

'I promise. But I really have to leave you now. I'm sorry.'

Victoria called the waiter and paid for our cups of tea. I picked up all my drawings and put them back in the thick folder. We stood up, and I helped Victoria into her coat. As she turned towards me to button up her coat, our eyes met. That mingled gaze was at once tender, frustrated, worried and uncertain. She told me: 'We should pass alongside the bar. That way, when we leave, we'll be a bit further away from their table.'

'You look terrified. Are you afraid?'

'A bit. I have to confess that this situation scares me.'

We walked towards the bar, and then alongside it. As we passed the table, under the gaze of its four occupants, I suddenly stopped and turned round to look Victoria in the eyes. Her face was frozen in panic. Slowly and calmly, enjoying every moment, I smiled, savouring it like a spoonful of melted chocolate, 'Are you frightened, Victoria? Is something wrong? Surely you're not going to collapse, here, in front of everyone? That would be very bad timing . . .'

'What are you doing, David?' Victoria asked me between clenched teeth, while attempting to appear as natural as possible. (The disparity between the extreme pitch of her emotions and the need for her to maintain a friendly expression was awe-inspiring.)

'What am I doing, my dear Victoria? You want to know what I'm doing?'

'Well, mostly I just want you to stop this stupid little game. Come on, hurry up – we need to get out of here. We can talk in the lobby.'

'I'll tell you what I'm doing, my love: I'm saving the day. I'm going to take your hand,' I said, taking her hand, 'and I'm going to squeeze it for a few seconds, quite openly, in a fawning, slimy and vaguely contemptible way, like a man who's trying to seal a lucrative contract.' And I squeezed Victoria's hand the way I'd seen certain businessmen do on the Jupiter Tower when they were trying to sell us some equipment. 'And then, Victoria, I'm going to say something along the lines of: I'm delighted to have made your acquaintance; it was a genuine pleasure to have had such a frank and profitable meeting. (Have you noticed, by the way, that all of them, including your husband, are carefully watching us?) And above all, I am going to tell you how happy I am that you liked my renovation project. Do you think you'll be able to get back to me quickly with a date when I might meet with you in London?'

'Uh, fairly quickly, yes, I think so,' Victoria replied.

'Wonderful. That's great. I'll be delighted to meet Peter Dollan so I can show him what I have in mind. And, once again, if you need any extra drawings, or if I have any thoughts about your factory in Lorraine, I'm perfectly ready to put aside some time to go and visit it, so that I can provide you with a costing and analysis for the project as soon as possible,' I told Victoria, with the kind of facial expression that people use when saying this kind of thing. 'And, you see, when this little scene is over, you'll be able to go and sit down with them without any problem at all. You won't have to justify anything. I'll have neutralized the situation. All you'll have to say to them is, "God, what a bore that man is! I couldn't manage to get rid of him. He's a failed architect who's trying to flog me his services." And now, Victoria, I will say goodnight. I hope you have a wonderful evening at the opera.'

'David, I don't know how to thank you. I'll send you a text when it's over.'

'Goodbye.'

I released Victoria's hand and left the bar of the Grand Hotel. Then I went home.

A few days later I got an email from Victoria, who was in South Africa for a week-long 'road show'. She'd worked in Johannesburg with her Human Resources team, and then visited factories in various parts of the country. At that moment she was in Port Elizabeth, and when the afternoon was over she would leave it to spend the weekend in Gorah Elephant Camp with a few colleagues. They were going to explore a nature reserve and go on safari.

The hotel where she was staying was in an extremely beautiful renovated colonial house, made entirely of wood and furnished with wonderful taste (reading this, I immediately imagined a decor similar to her house in London): 'I feel like I'm staying with a typical but surprisingly adventurous old aunt, who has many tales to tell. It smells of wax. Everything is decorated in dark, varnished wood and ethnic fabrics in shades of beige and brown,' she wrote. Because she had arrived quite late the previous evening, the restaurant was already closed. She was welcomed by a 'young man with an astonishing presence' who offered to find her something to eat from the fridge in the kitchen. He took her bags up to her room, then told her he could serve her a snack in one of the ground-floor rooms in about thirty minutes' time.

Victoria's room was magnificent: a four-poster bed; a large balcony overlooking a beautiful tropical garden; a spacious bathroom with an authentic old tub standing on lions' paws, in which she lazed for a long time before going downstairs to one of the ground-floor living rooms where she devoured the meal the young man had kindly prepared for her from a silver plate (cold meats, cheese, fruit and cakes). She'd drunk mineral water and red wine, and the young man checked in on her frequently to make sure that everything was to her satisfaction. Victoria wrote: 'He was tall, athletic and astoundingly handsome. He had a sweet gaze, and he flirted with me gently. The worst thing was that I was really charmed by him. He must have been about twenty-six.' There was something strange about this luxurious house that made her uneasy, but it took her a while to work out what it was, particularly as she didn't know what part the young man's charm was playing in her feelings. I myself was beginning to find this email strange. I kept rereading these words – 'The worst thing was that I was really charmed by him' – and they made me reel with pain and, at the same time, with pleasure – just as I had done the day I read her message about the masseur. She had not understood the cause of her unease until the young man revealed it to her: they were the only two people in the building. When he told her that, she saw a message in his eyes that could not have been more eloquent: they were free to enjoy themselves as they wished . . . 'This realization felled me,' Victoria wrote. The situation was all the more unsettling as the looks this young man gave her grew ever less disguised. 'I was sweating, and I could feel that my face had gone red. I was afraid he would guess that I was turned on, and that he'd become more forward.' Feelings of intense vexation and painful jealousy had begun to darken my mood, but I read Victoria's email avidly – taking it slowly so I wouldn't arrive prematurely at the climax that I both dreaded and hoped for. Because the truth, however intolerable, was that I was growing ever more aroused by the thought that Victoria would surrender to her desire, and that her email would end with a description of the pleasure she received from this young man. Yet I also knew that this climax would cause me great suffering.

Victoria had tried to divert the young man's attention by talking to him about the beauty of that vast house. She questioned him about its history; she asked him what date it was built, to whom it had belonged, how long it had been a hotel, etc. He offered to give her a tour of the property, so they walked from bedroom to bedroom, with him showing her the most beautiful ones, as well as the living rooms that were located on various floors. The email I was reading seemed interminable. Victoria wondered over and over how she would behave when the inevitable moment came, and the young man made his move. The two of them ended up standing on the balcony of a bedroom, in the moonlight, in the mild night air, overlooking the tropical garden. The young man put his hand on the guardrail, next to Victoria's elbow. His skin grazed hers, and she felt her breathing accelerate. She looked at him with a faint smile. She didn't move. They stayed in that pose, joined by the electrifying touch of skin on skin. 'For a minute, everything was in suspension,' Victoria wrote. All it would have taken was for her to press her skin against his, or for her simply not to move away, and their night would have tipped over irreversibly into something else, she explained to me in her message. They had begun to lean closer together . . . 'Oh, the terrible temptation! The deliciousness of that moment when all was in my power,' I read, enthralled, on the screen of my BlackBerry. I was unbelievably turned on. My cock was hard. I was close to coming.

'I resisted,' Victoria wrote, in a new paragraph.

She removed the edge of her left elbow from the portion of his skin it had been touching. The young man politely excused himself, as if he'd been bothering her. She wished him goodnight, then locked herself in her bedroom, 'feverish and impatient' (two words I bled dry with my imagination over the next few days). She lay, tossing and turning, in her bed for a while, naked, unable to fall asleep, 'repenting my stupid bloody virtuousness' (an expression that became stuck painfully in my mind, close to the two wounds she'd already inflicted on me). Finally, she got up and opened the French windows that opened on to the garden, hoping the fresh air might calm her down. She put her hand into a fruit bowl, intending to take an apple, but by chance her fingers found a banana – 'a lovely, long, firm banana, slightly curved,' Victoria wrote. She inserted the banana into her vagina. The fruit's coolness contrasted with the heat inside her. Victoria wrote that she thought about my cock, because I was so good at taking her and making her come. She went on: 'In an incredibly real-seeming fantasy, David was suddenly with me in my African night, against a backdrop of unidentified sounds. He was behind me, holding me close to him. He grabbed the banana and began sliding it in and out of my vagina. His cock grew hard and I felt him trying to penetrate my other hole. I was terrified by this idea, and also turned on. The anticipation of that agony and delight intensified the pleasure I was taking from the banana . . . Then I lost my balance and fell on the bed, groaning with physical pleasure and relief, biting the sheets so that the young man wouldn't hear me. God, how I came! David, I wish you'd been here . . .'

This account, under the usual title 'Meeting Minutes', was supposed to be an extract from her private diary, and therefore a truthful retelling of an actual experience. But, although there was no reason why Victoria should alter the truth in writings intended for her own archives (unless she was perverse enough to write them specifically for me, counting on their aura of authenticity as a way of falsifying events in her life that she didn't want to admit to), I found it difficult to believe that she had resisted the temptation. 'What stopped you? I don't understand what held you back,' I said to her on the phone a few hours after opening her email. 'Why didn't you make love with that young man if you were attracted to him? Nobody would have known.' Victoria replied that it was weird of me to suspect her of having surrendered to this young man's advances when she'd gone to such lengths to tell me how she'd struggled against the ferocity of her desire. 'Did you want him?' I asked. 'Did you want him to make love to you?'

'Of course I did, but I was a good girl. It was you I wanted.

I missed you. I wanted you to make love to me. I was desperate for your cock. That's why – alone in that house, with such a handsome man – I almost gave in. Everywhere I go, the thought of you is with me, giving me a constant desire to make love. That man would have been nothing more than a sex aid.'

'You should have done it, then. You should have fucked all night with that athletic young man . . . and afterwards you should have told me about it.'

'Is that what you would have wanted me to do? Surrender to temptation, and tell you about it?'

'I'd have preferred that to a lie. If you'd told me in detail about your night, I'd have known it was true: that things had really happened like that. Whereas now, I'm not sure I believe you. I'm jealous because I think you may have succumbed to temptation and that you're hiding it from me in order to spare me pain.'

'Would it have turned you on if I'd made love with that boy and told you about it?'

'Would it have turned me on?' I repeated, taken aback by the suddenness of this intimate question.

'Yes. Would it get you hard if I was fucked by another man and told you about it?'

'I don't know. It's painful to think about it, but I think it would turn me on a bit, yeah.'

'Did you have a hard-on when you were reading my email?'
'Yeah.'

'Would you like me to fuck someone else and tell you about it?'

'I think so. Maybe. But mainly because it would prove to me that you'd decided not to hide anything from me – that you're being entirely honest with me. I was really traumatized by what I discovered at the bar of the Grand Hotel the other evening. I can't stop thinking about it. I can't stop thinking that you're manipulating me. I'm almost certain you made love with that guy; at least if you told me about it, I'd be getting something out of your system. I often think that I'm merely a cog in your machine. I don't want to be the victim of your way of life.'

In an extract from her private diary that I received a few days later (and which made me wonder, as I read it, why she'd sent it; it consisted of three pages recounting, rather boringly, the end of her South African trip), I came across a series of paragraphs in which she mentioned that telephone call. The deeper meaning of these lines would only be revealed to me a few months later; for the moment, all I took from them was that she had not really understood what I'd meant when I'd asked her to describe her sexual escapades. For me, it was a question of protecting myself from Victoria's limitless freedom; a way of ensuring that she wouldn't enjoy it at my expense. This was not the first time she'd made discreet allusions to the perversity of her lovers (I'm thinking of what she told me, as we were leaving the shoe shop, about the downward spiral she'd been drawn into by Laurent, which – she'd tried to explain to me – she needed to distance herself from in order to protect herself; she mentioned that again in this email), but I didn't feel concerned by this 'perversity', whether with regard to me or to her lovers in general. Just as my ears had not really registered the seriousness of her meaning when she'd talked to me about it in the Galerie Véro-Dodat, now my eyes slid smoothly over the spiky angularity of her words, strangely unscratched by their sharp edges – because, for the moment, my perception and her syntax were strangers to each other. Only when my hand, rather than my eyes, touched on this thorny issue a few months later would I feel its wonderful, dangerous harshness. In that instant, I would become as 'perverse' as her other lovers had been – and I would discover that this 'perversity' was something that had always been part of me.

These were the crucial few paragraphs:

'I was thrilled that he called me, and that he seemed to be missing me so much, but at the same time he said some monstrous things that I probably ought to consider in more detail. He said he was afraid of me, for example, and that he wanted me to be seduced by another man; he said he wanted me to make love with that man all night and then give him a blow-by-blow description – in order not to be possessed or manipulated by me. A bizarre idea . . .

'This perversity reminded me of what I'd fled from, exhausted, with Laurent.

'How do I escape the vicious circle that seems to be repeating itself? Is perversity the only end, the sole prerogative of such passions?

'Are women of my age condemned to meet men, bored by years of ordinary relationships, who want to pursue their fantasies to extremes? That's what I fear . . .

'I didn't want to hear this. I didn't want to react.

'How can he say that to me? How can he kiss me like he does, how can he be so hard with desire for me, and at the same time threaten me with all this destructive madness? It disturbs me so much.

'I'll give it more thought. It's something that needs to be thought about carefully. Is he being serious? Or is this just the after-effect of last week's incident in the Grand Hotel, a sort of revenge for what I put him through?

'I constantly tell him how wonderful, how extraordinarily cool-headed and generous he was that night, like a knight in shining armour. Lying in this large white bed, unable to sleep, I think how protected I felt that evening, when so many people were in the same room, unknowing. That's it – I've finally found a name for the strange sensation I felt when he took my hand and looked in my eyes: his expression told me 'I'm staying calm',

'I'm not running away', 'I'm going to take my time' . . . and I felt protected by this man, who suddenly picked up his lines and began playing his part in the situation, rather than abandoning me (as he had every right to do) with a "goodbye and good luck". He showed his class that night.'

Then this extract from her diary concluded with a long disquisition on South African society.

What was beyond doubt was that since receiving that email from Victoria detailing the night she spent in the colonial house, I masturbated every day imagining her in bed with the young man she'd fancied.

Was this perversity on my part? But, if it was, why did she send me an account of her experience?

There were now two glorious scenes in my mind, put there by their passionate heroine, Victoria. And these two scenes had become the matrix for a variety of inexhaustible fantasies. Everything came from those seconds of hesitation: when the masseur saw the imploring look in her eyes, and when the young South African felt Victoria's elbow touch his hand. A mass of fictions were set in motion by these two moments. She took the masseur's hand and pushed it between her legs. She rubbed her elbow against the young man's hand. The masseur slid his fingers into Victoria's wet pussy, and the young man kissed her on the mouth. A bit later, the masseur made her come with his fingers while the young man moved over her body and penetrated her with his cock.

Two weeks after I received that email, I left for a week in Florence and Siena with Sylvie. It was the Easter holidays, and we'd left our children with my sister and her family. Apart from my stays in London, I had not left Paris since the previous summer or given myself a single day off (including Christmas and the New Year) because of the huge amount of work I had to complete. I was starting to feel exhausted; my paid leave was accumulating; and I decided that now was the time – just before the final straight – if I wanted to get away for a few days. I asked Sylvie where she'd like to go for a romantic break, and she replied that she'd always dreamed of Tuscany. So I organized a trip to Italy for just the two of us.

In spite of the difficulties I was beginning to encounter on the construction site, I remember feeling happy during this period. I was fully immersed in the project Victoria had entrusted me with, returning to it over and over again to improve old drawings and make new ones. Each evening, when I got home, I locked myself in my office to work, writing down my ideas and backing up my proposals; the more I developed my project, the more certain I felt that Peter Dollan would not be able to dismiss it. In odd moments of euphoria (stoked by my conversations with Victoria, which were increasingly frequent and optimistic on this issue of my application and its chances of success), I told myself that none of the agencies I was competing with would have analysed the question so deeply or come up with such persuasive solutions as I had. Finally, at forty-two years old, my talent would receive its due. So I started dreaming again: I rediscovered the state of mind I'd had when I first arrived in Paris and naively imagined a great destiny for myself.

I loved Florence and Siena. I'd never been to either place before. I was happy to stand beside Sylvie in museums and churches, the two of us holding hands, and share the emotions we felt when we looked at the masterpieces on the walls. I was happy to drive with her in the countryside and look out at the same glorious, rolling landscape. The weather was wonderful, and we ate lunch outside at trattorias almost every day. I'd decided to leave my BlackBerry in Paris, and to call Caroline every other day to reassure myself that no disaster had befallen the site. Consequently, I'd warned Victoria that we wouldn't be able to send each other texts or emails, which seemed better to me in this kind of situation. The day before my departure, she'd told me she was going to talk to Peter Dollan about me on Wednesday – in the middle of my Italian trip, in other words – and I'd made her promise to send me an email telling me how he'd reacted, so I could find this out as soon as I got home on Sunday evening. As I didn't doubt for an instant that Peter Dollan's reaction would be positive, I was able to imagine the end of my holiday with the same excitement I'd felt at its beginning. And between these two events were all the splendours of Tuscany: the blue of the sky; the churches and their altars; the winding, cypress-lined paths; Masaccio's frescoes on the walls of the Brancacci Chapel.

I hadn't seen Sylvie look so happy in years. I felt in love with her. She was right for me. I bought her a pair of shoes that she'd spotted in Sergio Rossi.

We made love every night. This was the first time we'd made love that often over a period of several days. I wanted her, and she wanted me. We felt good together. The hotels I'd booked for us were luxurious and comfortable. And every morning, in the toilet, I would make myself come while thinking of Victoria: making love with Victoria; visualizing Victoria in bed with the athletic young South African; imagining her making love before my eyes in a room at the Concorde Saint-Lazare with a stranger picked up on the internet. So it was that a relatively elaborate fantasy began to establish itself as the basis for my morning masturbation sessions in the toilets or under the shower of our hotels in Florence and Siena.

I found a man on the internet who seemed to have the same physique as Victoria's young South African athlete. I arranged for him to turn up at the Concorde Saint-Lazare at a particular time: he had to pick up an envelope from reception in which he would find the key to our room. I asked him to make his appearance at a certain, precise time, not to make any noise, to undress discreetly in the doorway. I told him that my wife didn't know about him, and I wanted it to be a surprise. About twenty minutes before he was due to appear, I began making love with Victoria, having first blindfolded her: everything was precisely timed. I took her in the usual way, but – in the middle of our lovemaking – I asked her if she'd like to have the young South African in bed with her, if she'd like to be able to touch him. Victoria said yes, she'd like that a lot – to stroke his muscles and see his cock. And so, having undressed in the doorway, the young man quietly moved towards us. I gestured to him with my eyes that he should join us, and he knelt near Victoria's head, admiring her, his cock erect. 'Would you like a man to touch your breasts while I fuck you?' She sighed yes, and the young man began caressing her breasts. She started at the first touch of his fingers on her skin. I whispered in her ear that there was no danger, that she should relax, that she would enjoy it. The man touched her stomach and her breasts; he stroked her thighs. Victoria became even wetter. I saw her hands seek out the stranger's cock.

Often I ejaculated before the young man even had time to penetrate her. Sometimes, however, I took long enough that he gave in to her begging and fucked her while I watched. Victoria's orgasms seemed twice as intense as usual.

During the weeks that followed, I masturbated numerous times while thinking about our two faces kissing, then being pushed apart by a man's cock that Victoria ended up taking in her mouth, a few centimetres from my lips. One image repeated itself regularly: I took Victoria doggy-style, holding her upright by pulling firmly on her chest, while a man stood, naked and erect, before us, his cock rubbing against our two faces. It touched Victoria's face, and sometimes bumped into my cheek. She teased the head with her teeth.

When I got back to Paris, I leapt on my BlackBerry. But it was in vain that I searched for a message from Victoria – among the many she'd sent me – telling me what had happened at the meeting with Peter Dollan. On Wednesday 19 April, there'd been a message in which she told me about a party in Covent Garden – but without the slightest mention of the meeting nor any indication that it had been cancelled.

I called Victoria the next morning, and she told me that the meeting had been postponed. A new date had to be fixed with Peter Dollan's assistant. She was going to take care of it in the next few days.

8

The boss of the property development company received us in his office on Avenue Montaigne on the day after Labour Day. I remember the irony of this concurrence of dates.

We were seven weeks behind the original schedule. Not only had we squandered the breathing space that the accelerated work on the shell had given us (I remember, back in early January, the delay had been only three weeks – hence the euphoria and the champagne corks flying towards the stars that night, at the top of the erected tower), but recently we had also been slowed down by a number of new difficulties: the painting company had gone into administration, and the installation of the power supply for heating and lighting had been delayed by two months. As we had, for several weeks, not been in a position to show the bank the most recently completed floors (called for in the schedule in order that its experts could make inspection visits and provide us with a snag list), it had begun what looked like preparations for legal action. 'We've been receiving registered letters detailing the delays and the high number of snags relating to the already completed floors,' the boss began. 'These letters are, of course, very polite. For the moment, they contain only observations, but let's not kid ourselves: the bank's legal department is already in the starting blocks; they're compiling a file, and they will undoubtedly take us to court if we fail to finish the building on time. To put it another way, we are already in pre-litigation.

It's extremely worrying, particularly with the rumoured delays. I've heard it said that we might end up three or even four months behind. That is absolutely unthinkable,' the boss concluded.

The meeting on 2 May was very similar to the one that had taken place on 6 September in the same location, but it was distinguished by an element that had been absent the first time round, probably in order to make the second even more ominous: the staggering scale of the financial stakes. It was true that, even in September, the boss had already mentioned the threat of penalties, but the shell was merely the first stage in a process that would continue for several months. (Because the deadline seemed so distant, the fear of not meeting it was diluted by the esoteric hope that things might get better.) But now we were on the final straight – the countdown had begun; the finishing line was visible – and we were in a phase of completion, with the deadline fast approaching like an unfalsifiable verdict. Either we finished on time or we didn't. Either the delay was acceptable or it wasn't. Either the property developer would manage to negotiate a new level of affordable penalties with the bank or the scale of the delay would make that impossible.

The contract stipulated that the property firm would have to pay the investors the sum of €150,000 for each day's delay, and €230,000 per day after a period of six weeks. It was an easy calculation, but the boss of the property firm used a calculator to make it. 'Which gives us,' he said, tapping the keys with his fingers, 'if I'm optimistic and I assume a delay of three months . . . You see, I've decided to be nice to you . . . So that makes . . . we'd have to pay €18 million in penalties.'

Eighteen million euros.

That was the figure that the boss pronounced, sombrely, amid funereal silence, in a meeting room filled with contract managers.

Nobody dared to comment on the result of this calculation. There was no need for the boss to look at me in order to place this load on my shoulders; I had been carrying it for several weeks. I had become the incandescent embodiment of the completion process, as if the construction of the building were my trial, and the delivery date my own personal verdict: acquitted, or condemned.

When I think about this now, it seems to me that, because of this sense of responsibility that characterized my relationship with reality, I allowed my personal life to be contaminated by problems that ought to have remained strictly professional. I let the Jupiter Tower become part of me; I let it take over my life. Why did I internalize the property developer's horror at this hypothetical delay to such an extent? What harm could it do, ultimately, to fail with a project once every twenty years? It was as if those €18 million haunted my imagination like some gargantuan nightmare, and that I had to rid myself of them using only the means at my disposal – all so that the president of the bank could cut the red ribbon, while no one had any idea of the agonies that had gone into constructing the skyscraper. The property developer could shake the CEO's hand amid the applause of the inauguration ceremony; with the deadline having been met, the two men could publicly congratulate each other on their success, while, lost in the crowd, anonymous, I would stand in silence, my vital forces having been drained in order for this operation to be completed on time. The only way I could have rid myself of the absolute obsession that meeting this deadline had become for me was if I'd met Peter Dollan and he'd told me he was giving me the three architectural projects. In that event, I would have quit the Jupiter Tower and started my own agency. I would have flown towards my destiny. I would have become another man. But Victoria's reply never came, and the meeting with Peter Dollan kept being delayed. This endless procrastination intensified my anxiety, and made the Jupiter Tower seem like a cell in which I was held prisoner and tortured.

Having told us several times that the delay was going to cost him €18 million, the boss turned to Jean-François, my direct superior, who said: 'We'll do what it takes to ensure this delay is reduced. David has everything ready on the ground to make the builders work flat out.' Every face in the room turned towards me. Looking the boss in the eyes, I promised: 'Absolutely. I've taken various measures to increase the efficiency of the site, to clear up problems more quickly, and to increase productivity by better synchronizing our service providers.'

'Give me an example.'

'For instance, I've established a Wednesday-morning meeting, in addition to the usual Thursday-morning site meeting, which is both a kind of rallying call to motivate the troops and a chance to bring up difficulties and find solutions. The weekly meetings are no longer enough: we have to break the routine and institute a kind of state of emergency. These Wednesday-morning meetings are a chance to press on everyone the fact that we're in a crisis situation, and to tell all our employees and colleagues that they have to push beyond their physical, mental and financial limits. That's what the atmosphere is like now. Otherwise we won't succeed: the delay is so huge that it can only be significantly reduced through the most exceptional efforts – I might almost say inhuman efforts – from everyone concerned, no matter what their position in the hierarchy. This is just like the shell, only worse. The situation is more serious now than it was when we were struggling to complete the shell. The building companies need to put more people on site and they need to lead them better . . .'

'Don't make me laugh,' the boss interrupted. 'We've already

told them a thousand times that they need to increase their workforce!'

'That's no reason not to repeat the demand. I'll repeat it to them as many times as it takes, every Wednesday morning, until the Jupiter Tower is finished.'

'Are you sure these Wednesday meetings aren't just a waste of time? Is meetingitis really the best solution?'

'It's not meetingitis. Those sessions allow us to consult, to coordinate, to prioritize. They allow me to get my message across. I talk to them, I galvanize them, I scare them. I encourage them to be honest about their problems. Even though we're only a few months from the deadline date, some people are still working away quite calmly, taking their time, hiding problems from me, as if nothing important were at stake. I have to pin those people down; I have to be firm with them.

'He's right,' Jean-François broke in. 'I stayed at one of those meetings for half an hour the other day. It was really useful. Quite a few problems got cleared up . . .'

'I'm not convinced,' the boss interrupted. 'We need to take radical measures. We can't continue like this without anything changing. I don't know if you understand this, but . . . fucking hell! *Eighteen million euros!* Wake up! It's imperative – I say *imperative* – that this delay is massively reduced, if not eliminated altogether. I'm warning you: if nothing happens in the next few weeks, some of you will pay for it! Heads will roll! There, you've been warned. The situation cannot remain like this. Gentlemen, to work! We'll talk again soon.'

I called Victoria as soon as I came out of the meeting.

'You don't sound well. What's the matter?' she asked me.

'I've just come out of a meeting with the developer of Jupiter. It was really tense. Threats were made. They think we're a bunch of wankers. I'm exhausted: I work eleven hours a day, and

I'm carrying this site on my own. And yet when I sit across from this man and he looks at me, I feel like I weigh no more than a feather – like I have no value in his eyes.'

'Don't let him do that to you! You need to respond! I know his type – those technocrats. If you want them to respect you, you have to show them how strong you are.'

'I'm not letting him do it to me! I made my arguments.'

'Ooh, he's getting annoyed now!' Victoria said, laughing. I could tell from her cheerfulness that she had no idea what was at stake or how upset I was. I continued: 'If the delay isn't reduced, which seems the most realistic scenario at the moment, but . . . well, we can still hope to rectify the situation and finish on time . . .'

'Of course you can! Obviously you'll finish on time!'

'They're not going to let me breathe. They're going to put me under huge pressure. It's too much for one man alone. I don't know how I'm going to cope. We risk paying €18 million in penalties . . .'

'Oh, wow,' Victoria interjects. 'I'm beginning to understand why they're unhappy. I wouldn't like to be in their shoes.'

'But I'll make it. I swear, I'll do it. It's a question of honour. I can't stand the idea of failing at something, even if the price of success is falling ill or dying of exhaustion. I'm not going to give up on this.'

'I'm certain you'll pull through.'

'If I have to create my agency this autumn, I at least want the situation I leave behind to be improved, to be relatively healthy.'

'I prefer hearing that and seeing you in this state of mind. I don't like it when you talk like you did earlier – you sounded like a loser, a defeatist.'

'A loser? A defeatist? How can you say that to me? You're incredibly annoying with stuff like this, Victoria. I can never complain, not even for a few minutes, despite the fact that my situation is a nightmare. I have to grin and bear it, pretend everything's fine. It's inhuman. I'm not a loser. I'm going to prove that to everyone. I'm not a depressive either . . .'

'I know,' Victoria interrupts me. 'All I was saying is that I prefer it when you're determined rather than giving up without a fight. What are you doing now?'

'I'm going back to La Défense. I've got a meeting about clearing the snags.'

'Clearing the snags? What does that mean?'

'And you're a construction manager? You ought to know what clearing the snags means!'

'Explain it to me, instead of taunting me. You can be pretty annoying too.'

'When a client visits a building, he has to note down all the faults he finds, the things that don't work or that don't comply with his specifications. That's what we call the snags. The building companies have to correct them in order for the client to be able to clear the snags. One of Jupiter's problems is the snags on the finished floors: there are thousands of them, and the numbers are increasing exponentially as we go along. There are so many of them that if the builders decided to spend all their time eliminating them, they wouldn't be able to move on to the next floor. It's crazy – not only are we working on a 230-metre tower with fifty floors that we're struggling to finish on time, but we're also drowning in thousands of tiny details. There are just so many problems – small ones as well as big ones. On the one hand, we still have 90,000 square metres to fit out, and on the other we have tens of thousands of snags. It's a bit like those swarms of grasshoppers that attack harvests: thousands and thousands of problems are invading our reality, devouring our energy, our days, our nerves and our teams. It's driving us all mad.'

'Give me an example of a snag.'

'A chipped ceramic tile in the Ladies toilets on the 32nd floor, south side. A black stain in a corner of the skirting on a white, just-painted wall on the 18th floor. There are thousands of those kinds of details.'

'The bank has people who check all this stuff?'

'People who check all this stuff? Are you kidding? They've got a team of a dozen people who do nothing but that, who examine the building in the smallest detail and note down the tiniest defect! I was walking round the tower with the head of the bank's property division the other day. I get on well with her. She's someone who's aware of the quality of the work we do; she respects us; she realizes how much energy we're putting in to try and reduce this delay. But, all the same, she does her job, because her bosses are exhorting her not to let us get away with anything. All of a sudden, while we're in the middle of a conversation, she stops walking. I turn round and ask her what she's doing. She replies that it sounds hollow – one of the carpet tiles sounds hollow. I move closer. She uses her foot to tap at different places in the carpet, over an area of a few square metres – tap-tap, tap-tap, tip-tip, tap-tap. Listen, she says: it sounds hollow. It makes a different sound. What is it? I tell her it's nothing, but she won't let it go. She says it's not right, that the problem must be rectified. I tell her that, given the position we're in now, we're not going to stop for this kind of unimportant detail. She replies that no detail is unimportant, that the tower must be perfect. I say that, at this rate, we won't be able to finish it in five years. She says, that's your problem – you'll pay the penalties for five years. She calls one of the young men who's accompanying her and, in front of me – as if to show me that she will not make any compromises and that the balance of power is clearly in her favour – she asks him to note down that this carpet tile sounds hollow. She even tells her subordinate off for not having noticed it during his inspection visit. The young man replies that he's going to check the entire floor to see if any other tiles make a tip-tip sound when they should make a tap-tap sound. She replies that that is an excellent idea, and he says they could even do it on every floor. She says that's exactly what they should do. It's hard to believe, but I swear to you it's true. In the days that followed this, I came across this young man on several occasions, in various parts of the building, tapping the floor with his foot.'

'The people in the bank must be mad . . .'

'You see what I mean when I talk about swarms of grasshoppers devouring me. When I try to go to sleep at night (I usually can't until I've walked around for several hours), I feel like thousands of facts and problems are nibbling at my brain, and there's nothing I can do to stop them. The troubles of my day keep turning up in my thoughts, no matter how hard I try to interrupt them with sleep, to replace them with the calmness and silence of the night. The young guy keeps pacing all the floors of my brain, going tap-tap with his foot on every single carpet tile. There are hundreds of them doing things like that, asking me questions, sending me emails, telling me stuff, inside my head, all night, while I'm trying to fall asleep.'

'I'm going to have to leave you. They're waiting for me. Sorry.'

'Have you had a chance to see Peter yet, and talk to him?'

'No, not yet.'

'But you were supposed to see him last night.'

'I saw him, but it was about something else altogether. He wasn't in the best mood to talk about this. I sensed it wasn't the right moment to bring it up.'

'You tell me that every time.'

'No, this is the first time I've used that reason.'

'Today is 2 May. I showed you the first drawings on 30 March, and gave you the complete folder on 15 April. I've worked like crazy on this project, and you still haven't talked to Peter about it. I don't understand.'

'I'm going to do it. I promise you I will. I believe in this. You need to stop worrying, and trust me. I know Peter inside out; I'll know when the ideal moment comes for me to talk to him about it and arrange a meeting for you.'

'And Irina?'

'What about Irina?'

'Is she making progress?'

'She helped me make an initial list of possible agencies whose work we like. I should see her next week to whittle that list down to two names, plus yours. I also have to talk to Peter about that list. I'll tell him about your application at the same time.'

'When, though?'

'I don't know. I'm going to China the day after tomorrow, and I'm staying there for ten days. I hope to be able to do it on my return, around 15 May. Are we still seeing each other tomorrow night?'

At this point in the conversation, I turned around to look at a young woman I'd just passed – a tall, spectacular girl, a bit like Victoria but younger. That was how I came to notice two men who had also stopped. They were staring at me. I looked at them: first one, then the other. Their faces were familiar. I was sure I'd passed them before. (And suddenly I remembered that they'd occupied the table next to mine the day before yesterday at the Valmy, when I ate lunch with Caroline, who had made it her mission to make me sit down and eat more than my usual sandwich.) The two men smiled calmly at me, and stood there immobile, waiting for me to start walking again so they could start walking too. Clearly, they were not in the least bit bothered about having been spotted. In fact, to judge from the smiles on their faces, this development amused them. Perhaps they had decided, or been told, to reveal themselves to me today? The revelation of their presence was a message in itself, but what did it mean? With their almost platinum-blond hair, pink skin and huge builds, the two men looked noticeably foreign.

What do you call it when you tail somebody openly, without any attempt at concealment? An intimidatory measure? A surveillance operation?

My heart was beating wildly. Victoria grew impatient with my silence. 'David, are you there? Why aren't you saying anything?' I started walking again and replied: 'Yes, sorry, I . . . what were you saying?'

'Are we still seeing each other tomorrow night?'

'Of course, yes. I kept my evening free for you.'

'I've booked a room in a new hotel. I had an idea the other day – it's a surprise. I suggest we meet in the bar of the Meurice Hotel on Rue de Rivoli, opposite the Tuileries.'

'All right. What time?'

'What's the matter, David? Your voice is strange. You sound like you've just done a sprint – you're all out of breath.'

'I'm being followed by two men.'

'What do you mean, you're being followed by two men? What are you on about?'

'I swear – they're walking behind me now. I've noticed them, unconsciously, in the last few days, but it's only now that I've put everything together. Several times I saw the same car behind me – an Audi Break. I even saw it parked at the end of my street the other morning, when I left for work. I thought it must be a coincidence. But they're here now, on Avenue Montaigne, and they're following me. It's obvious.'

'David, this is nonsense. You're tired. The site is getting to you.'

'All right, so you think I'm going mad. What time are we meeting?'

'I'll be free at 6 p.m.'

'No, a bit later. I've got a meeting at 5 p.m. I'm up to my neck in it.'

'Let's meet for dinner, then – at 8 p.m.?'

'OK, 8 p.m. I'll call you this evening on my way home.'

'All right, talk to you later. Good luck. And, above all, don't let those men catch you!'

I hung up, and went down to the underground car park to pick up my car.

Ten minutes later, while I was driving along Avenue de la Grande-Armée towards La Défense, I glimpsed an Audi Break in my rear-view mirror, following me three cars behind.

Prior to our infamous meeting at the Buddha Bar on 19 June, I saw Victoria in Paris on 3 May, 10 May, 21 May, 1 June and 12 June.

I was unable to arrange a meeting with Peter Dollan. Each time I asked Victoria what was happening, she told me not to worry, to be patient.

I suspected Victoria of manipulating me, of stringing out this fiction with the sole aim of satisfying her needs – or of obtaining the measure of fantasy required by her pragmatic existence as head of Human Resources. Bearing in mind what I'd learned of her past, it was hardly inconceivable that she would lie to get what she wanted, whether romantically or professionally. From everything she'd told me about her job-cutting mission, it was clear that she was telling the unions the exact opposite of what she had in mind; why wouldn't she do the same thing with me?

My hopes for this meeting, my dreams of success, were so precious to me that I really didn't want these suspicions

confirmed. So I chose to believe all her explanations, never setting an ultimatum or demanding a more formal commitment.
Each time I said to her, 'I don't understand – what's happening?
If it's not working, if Peter said no . . . that's not a problem. I
expected his response to be negative. But tell me, so I can move
on to something else,' Victoria replied: 'What are you talking
about? Of course he hasn't said no! He's going to say yes – I
believe that absolutely. You're going to start your own agency.
It's just a question of time.' For me, this constituted a momentary proof of her sincerity. The day the meeting was finally
supposed to take place, Victoria didn't mention it. I had to ask
her about it, twenty minutes into a phone call: 'So, that meeting
about the architectural projects – how did it go?' And Victoria
replied that Peter Dollan's assistant was going to call me to
arrange a meeting. 'That's how you give me the news? Is that all
you're going to say?' I asked, astonished.

'What else do you want me to say? He told me to ask his
assistant to set up a meeting for you.'

'But that's brilliant news! You don't seem very excited,
though. You didn't even bring it up yourself – I had to ask you
about it.'

'I wanted it to be a surprise.'

I had noticed that, when Victoria lied, she attempted to evade
difficult questions by saying something so absurd that it derailed
the entire conversation. By stopping it in its tracks, the original
problem was forgotten as attention focused on the new
absurdity.

Something else I'd noticed, particularly in her texts, was that
when she wrote in English, it meant she was lying. If I asked her
a question that she didn't want to reply to with a negative, she
wrote: '*Why not?*' or '*I don't know*' or '*We'll see*' or even '*Yes*',
when what she actually meant was 'No' or 'I don't think so'. If I

asked her when she was coming back and she replied '*Tuesday*' rather than 'Mardi', I knew she wasn't coming back but she didn't dare tell me. Me: 'Did you talk to Peter, like we agreed?' Her: 'No. He's gone on a trip.' Me: 'Damn!' Her: '*Sorry*.' Me: 'When's he coming back?' Her: 'Next week.' Me: 'Are you going to see him?' Her: 'Lots of meetings planned.' Me: 'Ah, great! So we'll finally have some news!' Her: '*I hope*.' Me: 'But you're going to arrange a meeting about this with Irina, aren't you?' Her: '*Of course*.' Me: 'So everything's fine.' Her: '*Yes*.' Me: 'What are you doing now?' Her: 'Meeting with lawyers.' Me: 'How's it going? Are you happy?' Her: 'Yes. I've got to go. Talk to you later.' Victoria had no idea that this kind of conversation was utterly transparent to me, because she was unaware of the tic she had that betrayed her dishonesty.

'You wanted to surprise me? That's why you didn't call me when you came out of your meeting with Peter?'

'His assistant will call you tomorrow to arrange an interview. I didn't want to spoil the surprise.'

'All right, I understand. But tell me, how did he react to my designs?'

'He thought they were wonderful.'

'Really? He liked them?'

'*Well* . . . he didn't really have time to study them properly. I mainly talked about you, about your profile. I showed him your folder, so he's aware of how much work you've done on this. He agreed to meet you.'

'When?'

'*At the end of July, I think. About.*'

'The end of July? But that's so far away!'

'He's not free until then.'

'Don't you want me to call his assistant myself? So we can work out the best date possible?'

'No, leave it to her. She'll call you. She's very busy.'

Another absurd phrase.

'So I can't call your boss's secretary because she's very busy?'

'I've told you she's going to call you. Let her do it her own way. Procedures must be followed. *It's much better like that.*'

Do it her own way?

Procedures must be followed?

It's much better like that?

Listening to Victoria, I couldn't rid myself of the feeling that she was lying to me. There was something false in her voice, in the words she used, in all these bits of English. I tried to offset my suspicions by asking as many questions as possible, giving her the chance to form a reply coherent enough to clear up my concerns. But the longer this conversation went on, the more certain I became: Victoria was getting bogged down in her own lies.

The Kiloffer CEO's assistant did not call me the next day, nor the day after that, nor any of the days after that.

In a logical extension of my resentment towards Victoria, I began to feel increasingly repulsed by her. As the time drew close to meetings in her hotel, I felt ever less keen to go.

I had always experienced a vague reluctance in the hours just before our meetings, but this feeling had generally meta-morphosed quite quickly into desire. For several weeks now, though, the sight of Victoria sitting in a chair in the bar of her hotel had been like an offence against the world's tranquillity, and I had felt my reluctance solidify into resentment and depression. I became the most unpleasant company imaginable: monotonous and offensive, frontal in my attacks, slimy in my insinuations, dogmatic in my diatribes.

I spoke in endless monologues in order to put off for as long as possible the moment when Victoria would lead me to her room. Once we were there, I sat despondently in a chair – my knees pressed together, my hands wedged between my thighs – and kept on talking until Victoria dragged me into bed and raped me.

I felt like a whore. I was aware of prostituting myself in order to win the project I so desired. All day, I was a slave, and several times a month I was a prostitute as well. It was undoubtedly this feeling that was at the root of my behaviour: I tried to diminish my unease by attacking Victoria. Beyond the fact that these monologues allowed me to delay the moment when I had to give my body to Victoria, their purulence betrayed my internal decay and the disgust I felt for myself.

I ended up naked, held down against the sheets by Victoria's body, which rocked selfishly on my erect cock. Once we'd started having sex and she told me to go faster, to take her, I fucked her the way I worked on the construction site: exhausting myself with the feverish, frantic, despairing extremity of my effort, squandering my vital life forces on her. I no longer belonged to myself. I was in a state beyond tiredness. I gave myself to Victoria in bed as I gave myself to others at the site.

If I had known for certain that this architectural project would never happen, I would have broken up with her then and there. But I was afraid that, by doing so, I might be making a huge mistake.

In a fragment of her private diary that Victoria sent to me during this period under its usual title of 'Meeting Minutes', I read the following: 'I am pensive and unsettled. Our last few physical encounters in Paris have been strange. There were those interminable conversations when he wouldn't stop talking – when *we* wouldn't stop – because he kept goading me, picking fights, forcing us to confront each other, to hate each other, emphasizing our differences . . . Since the day we met, we have argued about ideology – it's the salt in the delicious sand-wich of our two worlds, our two personalities – but recently it seems to me that this little game has got out of hand. I think he's suffering. I can see him buckling under his fatigue, gradually shrinking, and I want to put some happiness back in his life . . . but how? It's all the more difficult because, for a while now, he's been getting less and less tame, like a pet that won't let you stroke it. I sometimes think he must be angry with me about something, but what? What could I have done to annoy him so much? When I see him sitting like a statue in his chair, talking and talking when I wish he would just kiss me, it makes me want to go to the opposite extreme: to go all the way in those fantasies that his body and his way of making love inspire in me, even if it means taking dangerous risks . . .'

I had begun to suffer from Victoria's way of life, her freedom, her privileges. Her lifestyle was torture for me: locked in a tower with an ever-growing delay, I felt dead to the pleasures of life. I couldn't stand watching her jet all over the world any more.

I couldn't help feeling bitter, knowing that Victoria was rub-bing shoulders with the people who cause all our problems. When you're at the top of the pyramid, in the company of others at the same level – and this was the case for Victoria – there is no one who can make trouble for you. You are paid, in fact, to create it for others through the constraints you impose and the strat-egies you implement. I could experience this every day at the construction site where, because of a series of decisions taken by certain executives a few years earlier, it was clear that everything had been calculated to make it impossible for us to work in good conditions. Their attitude was: 'They'll just have to manage. Cross that out – don't write three years, write two and a half years. I'm telling you, if they have to build this tower in two and a half years, they will. That way, we can start making money from it six months earlier. And, best of all, we save ourselves six months of labour costs . . .' Could I ever call into question the decisions of these people? Could I make them accountable for their recklessness? Sheltered by the certainties of the world they live in, they simply wait for the building to be completed. Everyone blames me, when they should be blaming the real culprits.

In my most poisonous ruminations, I told myself that Victoria belonged to that privileged aristocracy who were never called into question, whose lives were beyond all judgement, who acted in concert to ensure that their salaries and standards of life remained as high as possible. When I read that such and such a boss's profit shares can end up in an ordinary year at about €3 million, I wonder how such largesse is even possible – and the answer is clear: this is an international norm, a custom established within a certain class by that class's own united, globalized members. On the other hand, they are also committed to cutting costs, as much as possible, in these companies that are so generous to them – in order to increase productivity and pay larger dividends to the shareholders. Even when these executives show themselves to be incompetent and have to be fired, they are rewarded: instead of smashing like a vase on the hard tiled floor of their failure, they fall on to a soft mattress stuffed with several million euros.

I am not suggesting that Victoria didn't work hard. But the system to which she belonged allowed her some very pleasant consolations in return for the stress she was subjected to. When, half-drunk, she described to me the evenings she spent in large Asian or Latin American cities, I had to fight off fits of bitterness. Reading an email like this one – 'It's a hot, beautiful night, filled with the sound of crickets. The hotel, in a renovated palace, is magnificent. We had dinner in an incredible place, just outside the city. I ate grilled grasshoppers! We came back on these motorbike-taxi things – it was funny, we laughed a lot. Now I'm sitting at the edge of a pool covered with water lilies in the tropical garden. I will fall asleep on silk sheets. They gave me the biggest room – apparently Mitterand adored it. I want to make love. I'm thinking of you. Goodnight . . .' – I often felt like flinging my BlackBerry across the living room of my house, where – drained by the horrors of my day, incapable of doing anything but vegging out – I was watching some stupid TV programme.

One night, when I insisted, Victoria had admitted to me how much she earned: €350,000 per year, plus stock options worth, on paper, about €3 million. She owned her house in London (worth €2 million) – bought with her own personal funds, not with her husband's family fortune – having sold an apartment in Versailles that she'd bought a few years earlier. As she'd always lived abroad, she had always been able to earn very good money.

Finally she asked me: 'And you? How much do you earn?'

'I hardly dare tell you. In one way, it's a lot, if I compare it to the salaries of some of my colleagues, or to what the vast majority of French people earn. But, considering my responsibilities and the pressures I'm under, and compared to the profits certain people will make from this tower if I bring it in on time, it's also scandalously small. I don't even have a profit share, or any success-related bonuses. Whether I succeed or fail – financially, it makes no difference. They know I'm a good, obedient soldier, so there's no point in them dangling the prospect of an additional reward if I achieve their impossible target . . . so they don't bother dangling any additional reward at all. I don't need to go into detail – you know how it works . . .'

'All right, but how much?'

'Before tax, I earn €5,500 per month for fourteen months.'

'Huh? Are you serious? Five thousand five hundred euros per month?'

'Which makes about . . .'

'You only earn €5,500 per month?!'

'I know. The funny thing is that, quite often, when I tell people how much I earn, I feel ashamed – either because it's too high or because it's too low. Five thousand five hundred euros per month is simultaneously a lot . . . and not very much at all. It all depends who you're talking to.'

'It's incredibly low.'

'Each time I ask for a raise, they refuse. If I asked for a bonus tomorrow – even of just €4,000, so I could go on holiday with my family, who I've barely seen in the last six months – they would refuse. That's what makes me sick, particularly when I see your lifestyle, with all those business trips that you extend with safaris or stays in colonial mansions . . . all those wonderful restaurants, those massage salons, those luxury hotels . . . All those air miles you accumulate from your business trips and that you use for family holidays, taking your children abroad: that air-miles system is one of many examples of your class's privileges. Why aren't executives' air miles paid into a mutual fund for the benefit of ordinary employees who can't afford real holidays? Do you need this system of air miles to buy your plane tickets when you earn €350,000 per year? That's what I find disgusting: you've got it all worked out between you, so that you have the best of everything, and nobody can contradict you. Why should air miles earned through business trips be poured back into your private life? Why don't you give those miles to your assistants? For me, this is clearly an abuse of the system . . . but it's become a sort of institution.'

'Oh, stop making speeches! I feel like I'm listening to José Bové or some other simplistic socialist. I'm used to a rather higher level of thought from you. What you're spouting now is the most repugnant kind of self-righteousness.'

'We're drinking pink champagne in a hotel room in the Louvre with a view over the Palais-Royal, and all of this is paid for by Kiloffer. That's great, I really enjoy it. But at the same time, tomorrow, one of your subordinates will refuse a raise of €150 per month to a secretary . . . and meanwhile you're closing a factory in Lorraine, putting 400 people out of a job.'

'Don't make false comparisons like that, David. It's just facile.'

'It's not a false comparison. Kiloffer is paying for us to drink champagne in a room in a palace on the basis that you deserve it. You've spent eight hours battling heroically – and, I'm sure, with great talent – against unionists determined not to let you spin off Kiloffer's heavy industry division. With the help of your army of lawyers, you've managed to circumvent the Works Council. You were whooping for joy on the phone earlier, as you told me you'd won a crucial battle, that your strategy had been perfect, that you'd pulled the wool over their eyes. You were yelling that you would soon win the war, that we were going to have a great time . . .'

'Surely you're not going to reproach me for wanting to give you pleasure,' Victoria replied teasingly, lifting the glass of champagne to her lips.

'That's what I'm discovering through you. Under the pretext that companies have to be run by someone, and that running a company is something relatively complex and exhausting, you've established the principle that in order to run a company well you must have comfort, tranquillity and bonuses as regularly as a child needs hugs. You have to travel in first class because you need to be well-rested when you get off the plane. You have to drink the best wines, sleep on the best mattresses, stay in the best hotels, luxuriate in the most spacious bathrooms . . . because, if you don't, you'll be less efficient; your concentration won't be quite so perfect during those bloodstained meetings with the unions; the companies you run will be less profitable; people will end up on the dole. Your responsibilities are so massive that you have to be pampered like film stars or greyhounds or those fragile old Bentleys with engines that require the most careful maintenance. You can't take the metro to the airport because you might catch a cold, and of course you can't wait for your plane with all the plebs so you shut yourselves away in VIP lounges where everything is free: drinks, food, newspapers from all over the world, etc. That's how it is: you've got it all sewn up between yourselves to ensure the best lifestyle possible.'

'You're just mean-minded and envious, that's all.'

'You know as well as I do that your professional efficiency would not be in the least bit affected if Kiloffer cut your personal expenses by 50 per cent. Or if you – out of decency and respect for the people you're putting out of work – decided to cut your own personal expenses by 50 per cent.'

'You're jealous, so there!'

'Exactly. I'm jealous. I suffer because I'm exhausted and I'm not sufficiently rewarded for the sacrifices I make. I feel like I'm on the wrong side of the fence: I'm very close to the fence, but on the wrong side. The proof being that you and I are here together. I'm not a labourer . . .'

'That's not a proof of anything. I'd be perfectly capable of bringing a labourer to the Louvre Hotel to make love with him. In fact, one of the unionists I've been negotiating with . . .'

What I found particularly ironic was that Victoria's job consisted of assessing the potential of Kiloffer's employees, but nobody – with the sole exception of the CEO – was assessing her. Nobody was pronouncing the slightest judgement on her abilities, or her performance, or her way of working. Because of the position she occupied, I had the feeling that she was the only person in the company not to be examined by anyone. She was the blind spot in the system of surveillance that she herself ran.

One day, when I asked her why she travelled so much, she replied that she had to meet her Human Resources teams in the group's foreign subsidiaries on a regular basis: she had to oversee the strict application of Kiloffer doctrine on a number of subjects including recruitment, remuneration, profit-sharing, internal promotions, skills development, company culture, respect for the environment, etc. She took advantage of these trips to make sure that everything was working properly: she would go to see the labourers, who had no idea who she was, and ask them about their working conditions; she would mix with ordinary employees in the staff canteens to hear what they said about the company and its leaders, with the aim, or so she claimed, of understanding their needs more closely and giving them satisfaction. But, as she herself admitted, it was also a way of discovering what the subsidiary's leaders were hiding, identifying personnel problems that the local head of Human Resources had not thought it worth bringing to her attention. Sometimes she managed to put the cat among the pigeons by escaping the bubble in which they tried to keep her enclosed (they wanted to make her eat lunch in the management dining room, or take her to a restaurant, and they never wanted to leave her alone in the factories): she loved seeing the panic her little escapes could provoke in the subsidiary directors when they were informed that Victoria de Winter had slipped away from the assistant who was accompanying her and was now walking around the site on her own, talking to everyone, entering people's offices.

When she went to visit the group's foreign subsidiaries, Victoria had to meet young executives with the potential to become future directors of Kiloffer. Part of her job, now, was to anticipate the progressive renewal of the group's leadership, and to ensure that the brightest talents were not allowed to leave the company. So, the directors and Human Resources heads of Kiloffer's subsidiaries were responsible for making Victoria aware of the company's most talented young staff (or those who had become known, at one time or another, for some glorious or surprising act, of whatever kind, even if it belonged to their private life: if a young woman had saved a child from drowning by diving into an icy river, for example, or – more modestly – if she had won a tennis tournament) so that she could audition them and form her own opinion. Hence the safari she'd organized in South Africa, which had allowed her to spend a little longer with a few of these rising young stars, in order to get to know them better. After that, she could enter these people in the category of 'Young Talents', then in the 'Top 40', and then in the 'Top 10' – in other words, the forty and then the ten people considered to be the group's most precious treasures. It goes without saying that everyone in the company, all over the world, was competing to be admitted into one of these three categories, and that those who belonged to them were possessed of a particularly prestigious aura. It was also possible – if you underperformed, or caused Victoria or Peter Dollan to be disappointed in you – to be removed from the 'Top 40' or the 'Top 10', even if you'd been on those charts for a decade. Victoria revealed to me one day that certain people didn't age well, with some of the young stars she'd helped create fading like flowers. Within the 'Top 40' were various strata where people were moving up – or not. These adjustments were decided once a year by the Executive Committee, led by Victoria and Peter Dollan: the two of them could direct the destinies of hundreds of individuals by moving their names up and down these Excel tables, by adding + or – in the boxes alongside each name. Everyone accepted the principle of these manipulations, which made them, in my eyes, like children – over-qualified, extremely well-paid children, admittedly, but children all the same.

Each year, Victoria's central office organized a seminar in a chateau near Paris, bringing together a few of these 'Young Talents' from all over the world, as well as some employees who had recently come to notice. The official objective of this seminar was to cultivate the company culture; to reinforce the values on which it was founded; to permit encounters between people from different countries, jobs and perspectives; to pass on new knowledge, etc. In reality, however, the aim of these ten-day seminars was to verify – as in a laboratory, through a series of experiments, psychological tests, hypothetical situations and role-playing games – whether these people were as genuinely talented as Victoria's foreign teams had claimed. The simple fact of being able to impress one's bosses and colleagues (whether on a personal level, or by doing your job efficiently) was not enough in itself to signify the kind of long-term potential that the company was seeking. This had to be proved in a rather more in-depth way than by a simple intuitive approach. More specifically, there were tests arranged each day in the chateau grounds designed to enable each candidate to be assessed according to a number of parameters: team spirit, ability to analyse or summarize, intellectual capacity, propensity to inspire respect and attention, physical endurance, lucidity, quickness of thought, sense of humour, ability to listen, powers of deduction, etc. The participants were divided into five teams, and each team was given a road map on which the five challenges were listed – the same for each team, but in a different order. Ostensibly, the idea behind this was to make a group of strangers from different parts of the world work together. But in reality, Victoria had five employees who went from one group to another, taking notes, making audio and video recordings, and observing how each individual reacted to the various situations they encountered. It was noticeable that, in each group, a leader emerged spontaneously – though, ultimately, this leader was not necessarily the person who would come up with the best solutions or provide the best stimulus for their discovery. The leader was the person who held the road map and read it out to the others, and who tried to hold on to it throughout the test, even if certain others – through means of varying astuteness – attempted to wrestle it from them. Victoria's henchmen took great delight in recording all of this in their notebooks. Victoria used some rather silly beach games to reproduce situations that closely (if simplistically) resembled the kinds of situations encountered in the employee's professional life, and in this way was able to divide people into categories. It was an instantaneous way of revealing their qualities and their defects, their potential and their limitations, without them knowing what was happening, and without them even imagining what was at stake during these games.

I was horrified. It seemed to me that the very worst of the world was concentrated in the idea behind this seminar for young, globalized executives.

'I wouldn't miss this event for anything in the world. I go every year. It's great fun.'

'What kind of tests are they?'

'For instance, we put a rope on the ground in a circle with a five-metre diameter, and in the centre of the circle we stand an empty bottle with a raw egg placed on top of its neck. We ask the ten people to stand outside the circle, and they are given various objects – a clothes hanger, a corkscrew, a golf ball, a long piece of string, a box of paper clips, a roll of Sellotape, a tennis racket, etc. The point of the game is to bring the egg outside the circle without breaking it. They have to work together to find a solution. The funniest thing is that, among the five groups, those who succeed in bringing the egg out of the circle tend not to do so in the same way: some of them come up with simple solutions, others with more complex, even quite convoluted solutions, and some of them don't manage it at all. We try to analyse why. We've come to realize that, most of the time, the success or failure is due in large part to a very small number of people, sometimes to a single person, who drives the team forward – or weighs it down. We draw some fascinating conclusions from this which, as you can imagine, have repercussions on the careers of our young candidates. It's much better to find out about them now, in the grounds of a chateau, than in the real world, having put too much hope in an impetuous young Texan who made a big impression on us early in his career but who turns out in the long term, or when given an overly elevated position, to be too fearless, too authoritarian, too irresponsible. This kind of experiment allows us to save time, to verify our initial impressions of the people we've identified.'

'I find it amazing that they agree to take part in this kind of thing,' I said to Victoria. 'It's degrading.'

'They don't know about it. It's never made clear.'

'They must suspect, surely?'

'Not necessarily. We present it to them as a way of getting to know each other better and improving their behaviour in group situations. Afterwards, there are meetings, each of them is given a brief report, and there are interviews during which they have the opportunity to justify their actions, etc. Our tests are cleverly concealed behind a convincing facade of personal development. In reality, we discover much more about them than they are led to believe; the projections we make are much more in-depth. In any case, they don't have a choice if they want to climb the company ladder.

'I think these methods are outrageous. It's an affront to human dignity . . .'

'Listen to you! An affront to human dignity! The way you talk . . .'

'I'm serious. It's an attack on privacy. There should be a law limiting the means available to you in your quest for knowledge about the people you employ. It should be enough for you to watch them work, to judge them on their results. You shouldn't be able to observe them outside a work environment. I find it outrageous that you're allowed to watch them play games in the grounds of a chateau. Particularly as they're not given a choice . . . I imagine they're not allowed to refuse?'

'They would lose credibility if they did.'

'If I were in that position, I'd say no. I'd want to be judged on my work, on the way I'm perceived in a professional context. Either you want to work with me or you don't. All you have to do is show some trust, follow your instincts. You don't even have the balls to take risks any more. Hiring people is a human, subjective thing: you're choosing the people you wish to work with, and not necessarily because they're the most efficient at their job. These kinds of practices bleed all the poetry from the world. I wouldn't want to work for a company like Kiloffer if it meant that, to progress, I had to submit to dehumanized processes, at the end of which the head of Human Resources might simply get rid of me. Your methods are as cold as a balance sheet – which is not surprising, as the sole important criterion for evaluating your executives is that they make you as much money as possible. Corporations are increasingly ugly things, and your seminar is the perfect example of why that is.'

'Why don't you come to bed with me instead of spouting all this rubbish?'

'Hang on a minute – we haven't finished yet,' I told Victoria, sitting in my chair while she wriggled lasciviously on the bed, her dressing gown half-open.

When I'd finished reading the pages of her private diary in which she complained about how my monologues and attacks left too little time for making love, I replied to her with a message that ended with the words: 'I agree completely. We've spent too much time talking when we've seen each other recently. I've been criticizing you too much for things that don't really have anything to do with you. You have qualities that my torturers don't have – particularly your body. And I'm intrigued by those fantasies you mention . . . If you put those into reality, I'm sure I will start to regain my energy. And I promise you I'll make an effort to rein in these bitter outbursts: if anything, I'd rather go to an extreme in the other direction, even if – as you say – it means taking dangerous risks . . .'

I wanked regularly, imagining us making love with a stranger modelled on the young South African athlete. But whenever I saw Victoria in the flesh, I couldn't get past the repellence I felt for her body. It was as if I were petrified in my rancour. Reality seemed to be riding roughshod over me – and the way Victoria was taking me for a ride in the most brazen way imaginable played a significant role in keeping me in this state of mind. It came as no consolation that she was ready to pay for my meals, flight tickets and nights in beautiful palaces in far-flung corners of the world in order to have access to my body.

I was sitting on a chair, a glass of fine wine in my hand, my legs crossed, watching Victoria who was lying on the bed waiting for me to stop ranting. She was examining the colour of the Château Margaux 1995 she'd ordered to celebrate the spin-off of heavy industry she'd won from the unions that very day at a stormy Works Council meeting.

'To Kiloffer's share prices going up!' she'd said provocatively, a few minutes earlier, when she touched her glass to mine. 'To my stock options!'

'Don't expect me to help you celebrate the success of your scheming,' I replied. 'You know perfectly well how I feel about this. I lift my glass to the courage of those who fought against you – in vain, sadly . . .'

'You're such a killjoy, it's not even funny! You could at least take pleasure in your mistress's professional success. To us making love, then,' she'd replied mockingly, 'even if I've been waiting almost two hours for you to notice my body here on this bed.' And she examined her toes.

For several weeks now, I'd been criticizing Victoria for duping the unions with her concealed attack – it was perhaps the most divisive subject between us. On the other hand, you didn't have to be a genius to see that she had very little option: if she wanted to achieve the goal set for her by Kiloffer's board, she had no choice but to proceed in stages and to conceal from the unions for as long as possible – by lying shamelessly to them – the true outcome of their negotiations, which was to sell off the company's heavy industry division in order to refocus on new technologies. At the same time, Victoria assured me that she was deeply concerned with the fate of the workers; she said that she was proceeding in this way – with a series of revelations – in order to protect them from their own blindness and knee-jerk reaction, which was to always rebel against any proposals made by management. Since the irrevocable decision to sell off heavy industry had already been made by Kiloffer's administration council, it befell the head of Human Resources to make sure that this transition went through in the best way possible. It was in her interests, of course, but also in the workers' interests: she was carrying through the shareholders' scheme, but in a way that she claimed was as advantageous as possible to its victims.

When I questioned her sincerity, Victoria retorted: 'I didn't make this decision. Peter suggested to the administration council that we give up the heavy industry division, which was dragging Kiloffer down in the financial markets and limiting the value of its securities. Heavy industry is not well thought of by financial analysts, who advise investors not to put their money in this type of sector. Kiloffer's shareholders realized that if the company repositioned itself in the new technology sector, the values of the securities would rise again. So, from the moment when this decision was taken, the workers have been better off dealing with someone like me – someone human, who respects them.'

As I really didn't believe her, and as I felt sure she was entirely on the side of the powerful, I found this soapbox speech of hers rather revolting, as it allowed her to have her cake and eat it. Not only was she screwing the workers over, but she was claiming that they ought to be grateful for the lesser evil she had negotiated for them. I accused her of duplicity. This is undoubtedly the right word to describe a head of Human Resources, who must constantly mix all the ingredients of the problem, the way a winemaker blends grape varieties, so that it's no longer possible to identify her as belonging to one camp or the other, or to easily identify her strategies. It was essential that she should be a credible, respected partner for the two opposing parties, in order to manipulate them both. And at the end of it all, she would receive a huge bonus in the form of stock options in return for the services she performed on behalf of the shareholders, and would go off on a family holiday to a sunny island somewhere.

When I accused Victoria of cynically dismantling factories that were not losing money, she replied that, on the contrary, she spent her time attempting to dampen the ire of Peter Dollan, who constantly criticized her for not going fast enough: 'So, de Winter, where are you with these negotiations? What the hell are you doing? We're not going to waste a whole year on this! Watch out for French unionists – they're the worst on the planet.

They'll bog you down if you don't give them a show of strength. Either you close this factory or you don't. I'm going to give you ten days to sort this problem out – and if you don't, I'll get the lawyers in and do it myself!' All this because she was trying to do things correctly, without yielding to her boss's destructive urges. (He wanted to close the factory while spending as little money as possible, and he'd been driven in that direction by the manager of the threatened factory, who – by demonstrating his zeal to the CEO – hoped to get himself noticed for his managerial authority and to win a promotion within the parent company. This man had suggested several times to Peter Dollan that he ought to take over Victoria's negotiations, on the basis that his methods would not only be more efficient, but also cheaper.) 'To respond to your accusation,' Victoria said, 'I explained to the unions that it was precisely because Kiloffer was generating a profit, because this factory was not losing money, that we were offering them a fair severance package. We are not in a catastrophic situation, on the verge of bankruptcy, with a court administrator. But I have to make them understand that they also have to be reasonable, that they can't push it too far, that the capitalists who run the group are not bleeding-heart poets. I want to help them negotiate the best severance package possible, but only if they're prepared to be realistic: if not, I can't take their demands to Peter . . . and if I can't do that, we can't make progress . . . and if we can't make progress, his stance will harden.'

'Fuck me, you're clever!' I told Victoria. 'You soften them up, you get them under your spell . . . You pretend you're defending them against the shareholders, you manage to make the unions trust you when you belong 100 per cent to the enemy camp . . . It's a truly diabolical strategy.'

'I'm not pretending. I act in accordance with my beliefs. The way I tackle problems is clear and simple – not too nice, or too nasty. I show them that sometimes there's room for negotiation, and sometimes there isn't. I show them I have a direct line to the boss, and that when decisions are taken, they're taken. And when they're taken, they're correct. I can talk tirelessly, for hours, about why a decision is correct. I can prove it.'

'You can't prove that kind of thing. I seriously doubt that you and the unions could agree on what's right, on a severance package that's fair. I seriously doubt you share the same ideas about the subject.'

'You're wrong. I have a strong social streak – seriously. You know what he calls me, Peter, when we're in an administration council meeting, discussing these kinds of disputes, and I ask leave to speak?'

'No. Go on, what does he call you?'

'Mother Teresa. "Oh, hang on a minute, Mother Teresa wants to speak! She's probably going to make us all aware of the plight of the poor widows and orphans!" That's how I'm caricatured at Kiloffer.'

'Everything is relative. It's easy to be Mother Teresa when you're dealing with someone even more inhuman. There are also plenty of people who are more revolutionary than me.'

'Sometimes companies set up severance packages which make them even better off than they were before, to earn more money, or to guard against a possible contraction of their market . . . but this contraction is only hypothetical. It is perhaps nothing more than a pretext. In this case, I believe – and this is what I call my personal ethic – they ought to pay for what they force their employees to go through. There is a price for that – a fair price. Dumping people on the cheap – I'm not like that. That's not the reputation I have. The headhunters targeted me for Kiloffer because of my reputation. That's why they hired me – because I explained who I was, how I worked, what my style was.'

'I never know which side you're on. It's impossible to pin you down. One moment, you're with the workers; the next, you're with the bosses . . . And all this cash they give you to execute orders that come from above . . .'

(As I said that, I remembered that a few weeks earlier – the evening of the day she'd obtained the go-ahead by the Works Council for the closure of the factory – she had wept into her glass of champagne. 'Are you crying?' I'd asked.

'No, it's nothing . . .'

'Yes, you are. You're crying. Your eyes are wet. What's the matter?'

'It's horrible closing a factory, you have no idea . . . The machines stop working, the factory goes silent. There are no more trucks, no more freight trains filled with raw materials. All this activity ends, and there are people weeping. I've seen workers in tears this afternoon, workers who have been in that factory since they were sixteen years old . . .'

'So you're not completely insensitive.'

'What do you take me for?'

'At the same time, though, I suspect this is a way of letting yourself off the hook. They're crocodile tears – an instant, natural emotion that everyone feels. After you've had a good cry about the fate of the poor workers, you feel better . . . and get back to the task of destroying them.'

'It's horrible of you to say that. Do you think I'm some sort of monster?'

'No, I don't think you're a monster. But I do think it's even worse for you to cry about what you've done. It would have been more decent if you'd abstained from that kind of facile emotion.')

In fact, having managed to negotiate a severance package (in other words, to close this factory and halve the productivity of another factory, close by), Victoria had had to go back to the unions (having at least convinced Peter Dollan to give her a respite of four weeks: 'Please, Peter, I can't go back to them now – they'll murder me! They'll slit my throat! We have to wait a bit. Please, let me have a little time!'). She had gone back to the unions to announce that Kiloffer wanted to spin off its heavy industry division, which had never been mentioned before. This essentially meant it no longer being part of Kiloffer – creating an autonomous entity and putting it on the market under a different name. 'But without selling it,' Victoria took care to point out to the thirty-five dumbstruck unionists. They'd demanded: 'Why didn't you tell us this before? What the hell is going on?'

'Because it's only just been decided,' she replied without faltering.

'You're going to sell us off, aren't you? You want to get rid of us! Admit it – that's the truth! That was your plan all along, in fact!' the unionists had yelled, and Victoria had replied, with perfect aplomb: 'Not at all. We will never abandon you – I swear it. You are part of Kiloffer – part of its history. You belong to the 200-year-old, historic sector of Kiloffer. You're staying with us.'

'Yeah, right! You really think we're going to swallow that? You really believe we're going to trust you? It's always the same – we're always the ones who have to pay! You told us for weeks that our sector was at risk, that there were difficult years ahead, that in order to save Kiloffer's heavy industry division, you would have to prune the sick tree – close one factory and cut production capacity in another – so that it could grow new branches the following year. Remember that?'

'I remember. That's exactly what I said.'

'We trusted you. We ended up agreeing that a few branches would be pruned so that the tree could reflower. And now, three weeks later, you tell us that you're giving our tree to a tree nursery.'

'I never said we were going to give up heavy industry – we're just spinning it off.'

'But where has this come from? What is this bollocks? We thought it was over – we trusted you. And now, less than a month later, you come back with a new crazy idea. You're hiding something from us! You're not on the level with us – we can sense it. There's no point trying to con us, Mrs de Winter. We're warning you: this time, you won't get away with it!'

'You work in your nice big offices, you wear your pretty shoes! You want to earn even more money – that's the truth! And we have to pay for it, as usual. It's always the same story. We're the ones who get it in the neck!'

'You manipulated us! You're hiding something! You've got something else in mind!'

'Not at all – we have nothing else in mind. Spinning you off is a way of protecting you.'

'But this time, let us warn you, we're not going to let it happen. We'll fight to the bitter end!'

'You can forget about Kiloffer getting rid of heavy industry, and you can forget about us taking another name! We'll be called Kiloffer till the end, even if it kills us!'

So, for the last two months, Victoria had been negotiating the spin-off of the heavy industry division. After a fierce tug of war that had lasted for several weeks, she had finally managed – on Tuesday 12 June – to get the go-ahead from the Works Council, allowing her to set in motion the spin-off process. Hence the fine wine we were drinking. She knew that the next step was to inform the unions that this spun-off subsidiary had already found a buyer: one month before this, Kiloffer's finance department had made contact with a Brazilian corporation who had made a firm offer. As soon as Victoria had completed her business with the unions, the deal would go through. In a few days' time, she would have to explain to them that they were about to be sold off to the Brazilians, and that this was the best they could hope for in their future.

'But how can you justify changing your mind so quickly? How the hell can you tell them the exact opposite of what you swore to them only two weeks ago?'

'I'll tell them that Kiloffer is a company that makes decisions and acts on them quickly . . .'

'You wouldn't dare tell them that . . .'

'I'll tell them: heavy industry is no longer Kiloffer's core business. But if we sell you to a company where you will be the core business, you'll find yourselves with people who speak your language, who share the same culture, whose main priority is heavy industry, and you won't have to constantly compete with precious materials and new technologies. Because the truth is that those sectors are way more lucrative than heavy industry, and we at Kiloffer want to massively increase our investment in them because their yields are so much higher than in your sector. You'll be loved by these Brazilians for what you are: heavy industry people.'

Who was this woman? What did she believe in? How could she say one thing one day and the complete opposite two weeks later? Where did she get this ability to be all things to all men, never to allow herself to be pinned down, never to feel encumbered by any of the commitments she'd made, of whatever kind?

It was because she was always in movement. Victoria brushed past reality without ever getting caught up in it.

In some ways, it is impossible to lie if you never remain in the same place. You say one thing to one person, and a second later you're on the other side of the planet and your views have changed. You aren't there, in the days that follow, to see the face of the person you've lied to, to see the disappointment in their eyes.

It's only when you stay in the same place, unmoving – like me in the Jupiter Tower or like monks in a monastery – that you see the truth clearly, that the truth gets its hooks in you, that you feel like you owe it something, that you have to face up to it without cheating. By moving around, you're able to hedge your bets. You can forget things more easily, erasing from your mind any evil you've committed or any promises you've made. If the people who ran the world were not always moving so fast (whether geographically or just mentally), they would see the stark truth of what they were doing, and they wouldn't be able to bear it.

This was the system on which Victoria based her existence: never staying in the same place, dividing herself between many different activities and projects, in order never to let herself be trapped by any truth – but, instead, by constantly moving, to be her own truth. Victoria felt no pity, remorse, sadness or anxiety because she was able to dissolve them through movement and fragmentation. Speed is the truth of this world, not the local realities that it allows the powerful to fly over, drive through, or glimpse in passing. Victoria was always at home, always unconstrained. She always had an escape route. The only thing that ever interrupted her headlong rush forward was sex.

With an English mother and a father from Berlin, mainly raised in a country (France) which was not her own, Victoria boasted of being an international woman without any particular roots. She took disproportionate pride in having lived in many different countries, and from being able to move anywhere, from one day to the next, to take a new job, bringing her daughters with her. All those who had never lived outside their home country, she considered backward and old-fashioned, a bunch of anachronisms unable to take advantage of our era. She regularly criticized me for being 'Franco-French', living in a small, inward-looking world with narrowly parochial values. For

Victoria, being modern meant never having a country you could call your own.

When I talked endlessly, watching her lying on her bed, the thoughts she inspired in me seemed to give me a better understanding of the world I lived in. But this gave me no comfort whatsoever, nor did it provide me with a better way of coping with the world's harshness. Quite the opposite, in fact: the world seemed to oppress me even more intimately than before.

It was 19 June, and it must have been about 7 a.m. I was driving to the construction site, listening to Radio France Inter, when I received a text from Victoria. The cars in front of me slowed down, and I was able to read it: 'I'm on the Eurostar, heading full speed towards you. I open *Libération* and wonder if I'm dreaming . . . on page twenty-three there's a boxed article about you. It's wonderful. I admire you so much – you've become a hero. We have to believe. I believe in you. Things always happen if you really want them . . . I wish it was evening already. Today is going to be a tough day, but I'm happy I have the consolation of knowing I'll see you tonight . . .'

I couldn't believe it. An article in *Libération* about me and my work as project manager on the Jupiter Tower! It was true that a journalist had come to the site a few days earlier, accompanying the architects. They had told him about my role in the building's development, and he'd wanted to interview me. He'd told me he would undoubtedly quote me in his article, though its publication date had not yet been confirmed. I hadn't mentioned it to Victoria. I was hoping to surprise her if, perchance, the journalist had featured me in his article.

I tried to call Victoria, but she didn't answer. When the traffic slowed down again, I took a moment to write to her: 'Thank you! That's brilliant! I'm so happy. Can't wait to read it.'

I called Dominique to see if he happened to be near a newspaper vendor, but he didn't answer. I called Caroline to ask her to buy a copy of *Libération* when she got to the train station in La Défense; she didn't answer either, but I left her a message saying that there was an article about the Jupiter Tower in *Libération*, with a small boxed feature about me, on page twenty-three.

Taking a different route from my usual one, I stopped my car on the bypass, under some steps, and climbed them four at a time, then ran along the main avenue of La Défense, below the Société Générale skyscrapers, until I reached a newspaper vendor. I bought four copies of *Libération* from the display stand, nipped into the baker's to buy croissants and pains au chocolat, and, leaping like a dancer, I sped back down the steps towards the bypass, where a policeman was putting a ticket under my windscreen wipers. Having tried and failed to persuade him to let me off, I shoved the ticket in my pocket with a big grin and cheerfully told him, 'Ah, never mind – it can be my little tribute to the beauty of the day!' before driving to the office.

Reaching the prefab buildings that house the contract management's offices, I bumped into Dominique, who was going out to the site, helmet in hand. He said: 'What's the deal with this story of yours? You told Caro there was a piece about Jupiter in *Libé*, but we went through it a dozen times and couldn't find anything. Who told you that?' I stared at him in disbelief. 'Dominique, what are you on about? Are you taking the piss? It's on page twenty-three!'

'Have you looked?' he asked, motioning with his chin to the four copies of *Libération* folded under my arm.

'Not yet. I've just bought them. I picked up a ticket, stopping to get them.'

'Well, take a look. You've been misinformed. Anyway, I'd better hurry up – I'll see you at eleven for the car-park doors meeting.'

As soon as I reached my office, Caroline pounced to demand who'd told me there was an article in *Libération* about the Jupiter Tower. I told her it must have been someone unreliable or with a peculiar sense of humour. 'You're not kidding,' said Caroline. 'There's nothing in there. Not on page twenty-three, and not anywhere else either.' I sat down. 'Hey, I bought some croissants and pains au chocolat – go ahead, help yourself,' I said, opening the newspaper at my desk. On page twenty-three, I found some articles about a rock concert, a dance show and a contemporary art exhibition, plus a few brief round-ups on various topics. But nothing at all on architecture, nothing on the Jupiter Tower and nothing about me. My face must have fallen: Caroline gave me a pitying look as she ate her pain au chocolat. 'Don't worry, it's not a big deal. It'll come out another day. You look so sad, David! What's the matter? Someone told you you'd been mentioned in this article? Maybe it was just held back? It'll be published tomorrow! If they said you were mentioned, you'll be mentioned – don't fret!'

'No, it's not that. It's just a misunderstanding. Thank you – you're lovely – but I don't think I'm going to be mentioned in this article. It was just wishful thinking – I got the wrong end of the stick. I was too keen to hear what I wanted to hear . . .'

'I don't have any idea what you're talking about, David . . .'

'It doesn't matter. Anyway, let's get to work. We've got a hard day ahead of us. Another one. Here, take the rest of the croissants – hand them out to whoever wants one. I'm not hungry.'

Caroline smiled at me, then left the office.

I sent Victoria the following text: 'Your message was in dubious taste. Thanks a lot. It'll be hard to enjoy my evening with you after that.' Victoria replied a few minutes later: 'I'm in a meeting with the lawyers. I have no idea what you're talking about!!!' Me: 'About the article in *Libération*.' Her: '????' Me: 'There was nothing on page twenty-three. You convinced me there was an article about me in the newspaper. For half an hour, I believed it – and it was wonderful. I went to a newspaper vendor, but it was all a lie. There was nothing in there. There will never be anything about me in any newspaper. Goodbye.' About twenty minutes later, she replied: 'But I was dreaming! I dreamed that I opened the newspaper and there was an article about you. It was a dream! It was what I was wishing would happen! Reread the message I sent you – it was clear!' Me: 'It wasn't clear at all. You shouldn't mess with people like that. You shouldn't make fun of their dreams and frustrations and failed ambitions. It was cruel of you to do that. It was thoughtless and nasty.' Victoria replied: 'God, you're difficult! I'm too busy to deal with your moods this morning. We'll talk about it this evening.' I found it incredible that Victoria didn't apologize, that she was not sorry at all for the misunderstanding she'd caused. I'd been hurt by the message she sent me from the Eurostar, which highlighted the failure I'd made of my life. I'd been hurt by the fuss it had caused at the office. I'd been hurt by the cold way she'd reacted to my disappointment. Me: 'I don't know if I'm going tonight.'

Victoria did not reply.

I reread the original message. Victoria was right. It was written lovingly. There was nothing confusing about it. But at the same time, I wanted so much for her to have written that about me, and I couldn't swallow the disappointment she'd caused me, nor the bitter aftertaste this misunderstanding had left in my mouth. This incident had made me realize something: that it had not seemed inconceivable to me that there should be a boxed article about me in a newspaper (even though you never see construction managers, however talented, written about in mainstream papers like *Libération*), which showed how highly

I thought of myself and how badly I craved recognition. My youthful ambitions remained intact. All I had to do was scratch at the thin layer of servility under which I'd hidden them twenty years before, and my adolescent dreams began shining again just as brightly as they had before.

I called her at lunchtime. I told her I'd believed her message, that I'd called my office to tell them about this article, that I'd been made to look ridiculous in front of my closest colleagues. How could she write something like that to me without guessing how it might affect my imagination? 'Do you understand what I mean, or not?'

'Do you really have to make such a meal of it?'

'You could at least say sorry!'

'Why should I be sorry? You never even told me you'd talked to a journalist from *Libération*! How was I supposed to guess that?'

'That's not the point!'

'David! I just wanted to make you happy. I was so pleased about seeing you this evening. I was thinking of you, and suddenly I was immersed in happiness at having met you, and I thought how exceptionally talented you were and how one day I would open the paper and there'd be an article about you! I just wanted you to know that. I can't believe you're criticizing me for this!'

'But that's never going to happen! You're dangling something impossible in front of me. How could you be so thoughtless? How could you be so incapable of putting yourself in someone else's head, understanding their point of view?'

We had arranged to meet at the Buddha Bar, on Rue Boissy-d'Anglas, at about 8.30 p.m. to eat dinner. I spent several minutes searching for Victoria when I arrived, before finally finding her on a banquette in the dark corner of the bar, like a secret I'd had to discover.

As I moved towards her, I was struck by the power of her beauty.

She got up to kiss me, raised up on the high-heeled shoes she'd bought a few weeks earlier. She staggered as she walked, hardly able to believe how tall and desirable she was. Her shoes accomplished for her calves what the skimpy outfit that clung to her hips did for her thighs: lengthening and magnifying them.

I sat on a stool across from her. Her blouse was slightly more unbuttoned than usual, showing a deep and enticing groove between her breasts that greedily swallowed up the gazes of the men who passed close by. Her hair fell sensually to either side of her face like a pair of curtains on a theatre stage. Her clear, luminous face, framed in the centre, seemed undressed: it expressed Victoria's erotic thoughts in a particularly eloquent, sensual, spectacular way.

She was madly desirable, but my bad mood had not left me. I thought her beauty indecent, disrespectful to the misery that had overcome me.

I told Victoria she was radiant. She said she knew. She said she was in a state of barely imaginable arousal. 'All day, men have been looking at me with lust in their eyes. They could sense my desire to make love.'

'You're right. There's something special about your aura today.'

'Shall I tell you?'

'Yes, tell me.'

'It's mainly because I'm seeing you tonight. But it's also because of these shoes. You can't imagine how they make me feel when I wear them and walk among men. I feel like I'm becoming explicit, like my body is an outrage to decency. I feel like a fierce, voracious female who needs to be taken. At the same time, though, I dominate men – I crush them with the desire they feel, which will remain unsatisfied. They'll have to go home and wank in the bathroom of their apartment, thinking of my body while their wives make them dinner. I turn them on – they devour me with their eyes – but that's all. These high heels protect me even as they exhibit me, just like a theatre stage.'

I look at Victoria without saying anything, fascinated by the resplendence of her face, enthralled by her legs which she crosses under my gaze – and, at their ends, this sharpened heel, like a gun at the end of an outstretched arm. And yet I still resent her, am angry with her, want her to pay for what she did to me. She attracts me, but I want to hurt her.

We went into the dining room. They gave us a table sandwiched between two others. We ordered an assortment of sushi and a bottle of white wine. Victoria looked slightly less mysterious in the well-lit restaurant, but just as beautiful. Her radiance annoyed me. I wanted her to care about me, to be sad for me, to appease me, to apologize.

I ate sushi, looking occasionally at Victoria. I had gone back to questioning her over how she could have written me such a cruel message. She responded with a pirouette that meant 'let's not dwell on this unfortunate episode, but have fun and enjoy being together'; she was so happy to spend the evening with me. I persisted; I pushed on into the middle of the territory that Victoria's smile had enclosed. I was clumsy. I told her she didn't seem to realize how thoughtless her message had been. I said I couldn't manage to forgive her, that something between us had been broken, that it would take time for her to regain my esteem. I told her that she probably wasn't aware of this, but sometimes she seemed to be lacking in psychological subtlety, which was somewhat surprising for a head of Human Resources.

Victoria drew back suddenly, and I saw a grey, stormlike light in her eyes. She spoke to me in a biting voice that felt like a slap in the face: 'If you don't stop this immediately – if you say even one more word about this – I will get up and leave.' She stared at me, and her eyes were a stranger's. Her expression was icy. There was nothing intimate between us any more. I could tell that she was ready to destroy me.

My whole body trembled. I kept eating, in silence. When she spoke that sentence, I felt such a sense of injustice surge up inside me that I almost left the table myself.

I told Victoria that it would be better if we split up, that I couldn't see where I fitted in this relationship. 'Our affair doesn't satisfy me any more. This isn't what I want. I don't know what I'm doing any more. It's a shame for our architecture projects.'

She paid, and we left. We walked in the street – a slow, silent, somewhat funereal walk, because of her heels and our sadness. It was the last time we would walk together in Paris. We moved along the pavement without touching, mistrustful, as if separated by something bigger than an argument, as if years of estrangement had suddenly come between our bodies.

Victoria said: 'I'm going to take a taxi. It's difficult to walk like this.'

She lifted her hand, and a taxi halted before her. She opened the door. 'Are we going to say goodbye like this, outside a taxi, or are you getting in with me?' She looked me in the eyes. A few seconds passed.

'Where are you going?'

'The Louvre Hotel.'

'I'll come with you.'

I lay on the bed with my coat on, as if I were travelling. Although I had agreed to go with her, the atmosphere remained tense, filled with unresolved grievances. Each of us believed we had good reason to blame the other.

Victoria sat at the end of the bed for a long time without

saying a word or even looking at me. I watched her in profile. She was still just as desirable. I was hard.

I told her that we'd fallen into an adulterous routine: there was something almost marital in our relationship. 'It always happens the same way: we meet in the bar of your hotel, sometimes we go to a restaurant, we go up to your room and make love for two hours, we talk, we drink champagne or wine, we make love again, and then we say goodbye. We send each other emails and texts several times a day, we talk on the phone, we tell each other how much we miss each other – just like a husband and wife might do three times a day before seeing each other again at home. This isn't exactly what I was looking for when we started seeing each other. I don't need another marriage; I don't need another layer of conjugal stability; one is enough for me. Until now, whenever I've sought out physical relations beyond my marriage, however briefly, it's been because of the appeal of the unknown – to discover new bodies, to seduce women, to experience something new. I feel like we're just repeating ourselves: there's no variety any more.'

Victoria watches her heel as it moves rhythmically through the air at the end of her crossed leg.

I said it seemed to me that Laurent got a better deal with her: they'd had a relationship that was not merely routine; she'd given him the chance to fulfil his fantasies. They'd crossed borders, explored new lands, rather than stagnating in the same place for months. I didn't see the point in having a mistress if the transgressive element that was generally part of an adulterous relationship didn't lead it anywhere new or forbidden. I added: 'I don't understand why you agreed to go to such extravagant extremes with Laurent while, with me, you limit yourself to making love normally, without the need for anything else, as if I were your second husband.'

'Because I trusted Laurent. I felt safe with him. He protected me from my own urges. He brought me back to shore. He didn't let me get lost out to sea. You don't do that kind of thing with just anyone – it's too dangerous,' Victoria said, turning to face me.

I felt like I'd been stabbed in the chest. Victoria's words were insulting enough to be lethal, and she knew it. I felt a surge of revolt within me, and for the second time that evening I came close to leaving. But the words I'd heard had allowed me a glimpse of a landscape so new that I controlled myself. Something arose in my mind to put out the fire of humiliation that was spreading through it. I halted the mechanism that Victoria had started, leading us towards conflict, and focused in a calm, concentrated way on my intuition that something crucial was at stake in that moment.

I took a deep breath, and – in a composed, respectful voice – told Victoria: 'I don't see any reason why you can't trust me the way you trusted him. But trust isn't something you decide upon: either you feel it, or you don't. So it's up to me to make you trust me. I'll try. I'll succeed.'

I noticed that Victoria's foot had ceased its staccato movements. My words had opened up another way out of this night; it no longer had to end with us splitting up. But she heard the implication that this would occur only if she allowed me into the place where Laurent had been before me.

My cock was hard. I knew we would soon make love, and that it would be the most extraordinary thing – physically, sexually, mentally – I'd ever experienced with a woman, something that would instantly alter our relationship with each other, and above all our relationship with reality.

After a long silence, I asked her if she remembered that, during my Easter holiday in Italy, I'd divided my orgasms equally between my wife and my mistress: 'I made love each day with my wife, and I masturbated each day in the bathroom, thinking about you.'

'I remember,' Victoria replied. 'I liked that idea.'

'When I touched myself, thinking about you, I made up stories in my mind. It all started with what you wrote about the desire you'd felt for that Vietnamese masseur . . . and then your attraction to the young South African guy. I started imagining situations in which I'd make love with you in front of another man who, little by little, would begin to join in, to put his hands on your body. As the days passed, these scenarios became increasingly elaborate: I found men on the internet who came to our hotel room; you were blindfolded; I asked you how you would feel if there was a stranger on our bed, watching us; I asked you if you'd like to touch his cock and put it in your mouth; you said you would, and at that moment the stranger began caressing your breasts; you groped for his cock in the darkness; I made love to you while you stroked him. So, that was the kind of story I came up with when I was masturbating: we didn't make love normally like a married couple; that kind of conventional lovemaking was just for my wife.'

Victoria turned towards me and said: 'If that's the only thing that will turn you on, then OK, let's do it.' She stood up. I watched as she put her coat on, took her handbag from the armchair and the room key from the desk. While she was doing this, I'd taken my cock out. I said to her: 'But where do you want us to go?'

'I don't know. Anywhere. A sex shop, a porn cinema, a car park . . . wherever you like. If that's what you need, I agree to let other men fuck me while you watch. Come on, let's go.'

'Not tonight. It's late – there's no time. Come and sit down again.'

Victoria glanced at the erection that reared up from under my coat; she dropped her coat on the carpet and then took off her skirt, her blouse, and her bra. We stared at each other: I stroked my cock as she stood before me in her five-inch heels, naked but for her black stockings.

'You look incredible. I've never seen you look as beautiful as you do tonight. Come here. I want to make love to you.'

She came over to the bed and undressed me. I let her do it. She straddled me and enveloped my cock.

'This is so good – can you feel how wet I am? I've been thinking about this all day. My God, why should we split up . . .' she whispered into my ear before biting it deeply until I began to scream. I thought my ear lobe must be bleeding. I roughly grabbed hold of Victoria's buttocks and shoved my cock hard inside her, as if to hurt her.

'So you want to fight tonight, Victoria? You want war? You want me to fuck you . . .'

'Yes, don't stop! It feels so good! I love it when you fuck me hard like this . . .'

After a few minutes, I stopped. Victoria lifted herself up a little bit so she could look me in the eyes. Our faces were close. She touched her lips to mine. She began sliding herself gently along the length of my cock, from the head down to the base.

'Victoria, I want you to tell me . . .'

'What do you want me to tell you, my love?'

She kept moving up and down me. It was good. It was slow, soft, deep.

'With Laurent . . . what you did. You never really told me. Why was it dangerous?'

'Would it turn you on for me to tell you where and how we fucked?'

'Yes. Go on. Tell me.'

Victoria made love to me for a few seconds longer, intense and silent, breathless and eyes closed. Then she smiled, and opened her eyes: they sparkled; her face was radiant. She started talking again, her movements slow, full, concentrated, her pelvis lifting and lowering, lifting and lowering.

'It all began one night, after a date in a hotel, when we went to an underground car park to pick up his car. I'd noticed that the security guard in the glass office at the entrance was extremely cute. I mentioned that to Laurent, and he asked me if I wanted to fuck him; I said of course not, don't be stupid, I just thought he was handsome and charming. When we got in the car, Laurent asked me to give him a blow-job; it had turned him on to know that I fancied the security guard. You see? I'm cursed. Fate is conspiring against me. My last three lovers have all wanted me to be fucked by other men . . . Laurent started undressing me: I was down to my bra, stroking his erect cock . . . he put his fingers inside my pussy, which was already soaking wet.'

'Like tonight? Or even wetter?'

'Not as wet as tonight, David . . . It would be impossible to be more turned on than I am right now . . .'

'Have you noticed how hard I am? I feel like my cock has grown bigger . . . So what happened after that?'

'I slid on top of him and we made love with my back to the steering wheel. I was scared that someone would find us. There were security cameras everywhere; people could come down to get their cars . . . But most of all, I thought that the security guard would end up finding it strange that we hadn't driven past his glass office to get out of the car park: we'd paid, he'd seen us go downstairs . . .'

'So what happened?'

'I saw his face appear in the passenger-side window. He shone a torch at our bodies in the darkness. The beam of light picked out elements of the scene, one by one, in jerky movements: my face; Laurent's cock, which he tried to see penetrating my vagina; I wasn't wearing a skirt any more. I watched the young man's face greedily, as he in turn watched me in disbelief. But all he did was light up our bodies with his torch through the car window. As I started to come, I smiled at him. The light beam lingered on my bra; I took it off so he could see my breasts. I turned slightly towards him, allowing him a good view of my breasts bouncing as I screwed Laurent. I had an incredible orgasm. It was such a turn-on, being watched by this handsome young man, our bodies illuminated by torchlight as he searched for the most searing detail. Laurent came inside me. I howled and bit the headrest. It was amazing! Then the torchlight went off, and the security guard disappeared.'

'God, I love that! It turns me on. Keep telling me stories. This is the first time I've made love while having a conversation . . .'

'We were in a hotel room. Laurent had bought a dildo. I saw him smearing it with oil. He put it in my anus. It hurt, but it turned me on. He fucked me while I had the dildo in my arse. A bit later, he told me to go down on all fours and he penetrated me anally. He didn't ask what I thought. It was good. I'd never done that before. I'd always refused because I thought it was degrading. It hurt, but it felt good. He went in deeper and deeper, ignoring my cries of pain. I found out I could come from anal sex.'

We made love for a few minutes without speaking.

'So that's why you made yourself come in South Africa by imagining that I was shoving a banana in your pussy while I had anal sex with you?'

'Exactly. Although that's not exactly what I was thinking about that night. Do you want to know the truth?'

'Yes, please. We should tell each other everything, learn to know each other completely . . .'

'I fantasized that the young man came back to the bedroom. You were there too, and we were making love on the bed. I was on top of you, like I am now. You agreed that he could join us. I was dying to make love to both of you, but I didn't dare ask you – I was afraid you'd say no. You said yes.'

'Just like in Tuscany, when I came in the hotel bathrooms . . .'

'He undressed. He knelt behind me and fucked me anally while you and I made love. That's how I came, that night – by imagining the three of us together.'

Victoria stopped talking. I heard her groan. She was getting wetter and wetter. She whispered in my ear: 'I'm going to tell you a secret. Even Laurent never knew this. It's my absolute fantasy – I've never done it. I would like one man to fuck me in the vagina and another up the arse. At the same time.'

'We'll do it, if you like. I want that too. You've no idea how much that turns me on.'

'I can feel it. You're so hard.'

'Another story,' I say to Victoria. 'It turns me on when you tell me these stories.'

'We went to a porn cinema near Saint-Lazare train station. It was full of men. I love porn films – it turns me on to watch people having sex. I got on top of Laurent and we started fucking in the middle of the cinema, in an almost empty row. Men came close to us with their cocks out. There were erect cocks all around us. They wanked themselves off while they watched us. It drove me wild, seeing all those dicks. One of those guys started caressing my anus. It was an incredible feeling. It was the first time Laurent and I had gone that far, that we'd let a stranger touch me. This man's fingers brushed against Laurent's testicles every time I eased down Laurent's cock. I was so turned on by this hand I could feel between our two bodies. I wanted him to take Laurent's cock in his mouth. I had an orgasm. It was volcanic. My howls merged with those of the woman who was having sex on the screen behind me, although I couldn't see what was happening up there. Everywhere I looked, I saw erect cocks, men wanking. I met their eyes. I loved them watching me come. Laurent came inside me. We got dressed and we left.'

We kept making love and talking. Victoria went faster and faster. She moaned ever louder. She was panting so hard, it was difficult to tell what she was saying. Her words came in small bursts, interspersed with yells and sighs, her mouth close to my ear. Sometimes her story was interrupted for a few seconds, then she began speaking again.

'You didn't do anything else? Didn't you try anything with this man who was touching you and Laurent?'

'That was all we did. Laurent took me out of the cinema.'

'Did you want to stay?'

'I was like a madwoman. I'd completely lost my head. I wanted all those guys to fuck me. Laurent took me out of the cinema against my will, practically dragging me by the hair.'

'That's why you said earlier that you trusted him? Because he didn't give in to your pleas when your urges overcame you?'

'Exactly. I lose control of myself in that kind of situation. I'd be capable of anything, of going off with anyone . . . If my defence mechanism stops working – you know, that defence mechanism I've told you about several times, particularly in London . . . it was that defence mechanism that held me back from accepting your invitation to go for a drink . . . I wanted you – we could have been fucking from the first minute. When I'm in that kind of state, when I set my desires loose, I absolutely have to satisfy them. Afterwards, when I think about it, I feel scared. That's why it was essential that I could trust Laurent: I made him solemnly promise me not to let me go too far. I only went into those places – cold, clear-headed – after he swore to me that he wouldn't let me touch another body. When we went to the hammams and he stroked my pussy and my breasts in front of wanking men . . . you can't imagine how desperate I was for him to fuck me in front of them, for us all to end up fucking together.'

'I understand what you mean. I promise you can trust me.'

'I know, David. I'm dying to do it, even more than I was with Laurent . . . and above all to go further. I want us to really do it, you and me . . .'

'Really? But why?'

'Because I like you. Making love with you is more powerful than it was with him. You make me want to go all the way with my fantasies, to try everything. With Laurent, it was mostly a game, an intellectual experience. He was a manipulator, a mathematician.'

'What was it he wanted you to do, that you wouldn't? What did he ask you to do, that in order to get him back you'd finally decided to say yes to, the day you were supposed to meet him in the shopping gallery?'

'That was it. Each time we were supposed to go into a place like that, he tried to persuade me to go a step further. He even wanted me to take lovers, so I could tell him when we made love. It had got out of hand. He wanted us to go to swingers' clubs so I could help him pull girls – he wasn't very good-looking. The problem with that kind of sexuality is that you always want more: after a while, you get bored, and you feel the need to raise the stakes, to go one step further. I was starting to get a bit scared. I suspected him of loving me less than he had before, of wanting me less, and of compensating for the lowering of his desire with sexual distractions and amusements.'

'And what happens? You end up with a lover who's leading you into the same spiral.'

'It's not exactly the same spiral. It wasn't as essential as it is with you. For me, this isn't a sexual distraction or amusement.

I want to do this with you. I've always been fascinated by this fantasy. It's something I want to do with the right person.'

'So you and Laurent never made love with anyone else? All you ever did was display yourselves to other people? You never went any further?'

'We never went any further.'

I pushed Victoria down on the bed and lay on top of her. Then I penetrated her. In the wall mirror, I saw her legs in the air above me, arousing in black stockings and lengthened by her high-heeled shoes, which struck me as being both truthful and concise, like a haiku.

We made love slowly, for a long time, continuing to talk intimately, opening up our theatre of fantasies for one another, inventing stories in which we both played roles in turn. We described scenes; we imagined ourselves in different places. We found ourselves somewhere with naked men sitting on marble steps, the steam from a sauna all around them. 'You'd have picked out a man when we got here,' I said to Victoria. 'A man I'd have wanted straight away,' she replied. 'What's he like? Describe him to me. I want to be able to visualize him.' We were making love. I was watching Victoria's legs in the mirror. 'Dark, maybe Arab, quite hairy, muscular. I look at him; he smiles at me; I lower my gaze to his cock and see that it's growing,' Victoria replies, groaning. 'Really? All you have to do is look at it, and he gets a hard-on?' 'Exactly. His cock is huge . . . I'm a bit scared. I wonder how he'll manage to fit it inside me . . .' 'And what am I doing, while all this is going on?' 'You're touching my breasts. I've put my hand on your cock and I'm wanking you off. Your fingers are in my pussy . . .' Victoria couldn't stop coming. We had never known such intense, continual pleasure between us. We heard people talking in the room next door, separated from ours by a communicating door that presumably opened when a client needed an interconnecting room. The room wasn't well insulated. I said to Victoria that our neighbours must think we were mad. I couldn't understand how they had not started making love in turn. It seemed surprising to me that, having listened to us having sex for two hours, they hadn't been driven into a sexual frenzy of their own. 'Yeah, you're right. I don't know how they're managing to resist. I'd love to hear another woman come,' Victoria replied while I moved inside her. 'Hey, why don't you take me against the communicating door? That way, they'll be able to hear us better,' she added. 'It would be great if all four of us were making love together through the door, just with the noises we make, our cries and sighs,' I said to Victoria. I got up, and that was when I noticed a fairly spread-out halo of dampness on the sheets, where Victoria had been. I asked: 'What's that? Did something just pour out of you?'

'I came so much that I ejaculated . . . It's called gushing.'

'Are you a gusher?'

'Not really. It's only happened to me four or five times, when I've been coming like crazy. At one point, earlier, when we were talking about making love, it was so strong that when I came I felt some liquid spurting out of me.'

'Do it again whenever you like!'

'It's very rare. I'm telling you: four or five times in more than twenty years. I'm thirsty. What time is it? Should we order a bottle of champagne?'

'Twenty past midnight.'

'How much time do you have?'

'I have to leave about one. And I also have to get my car from Madeleine, near the Buddha Bar.'

'I'm going to call room service. We need to celebrate our break-up,' Victoria exclaimed, crawling over the bed to grab the telephone on the bedside table. 'This is the most wonderful break-up I've ever had!'

'I agree. It's amazing, what's happened between us tonight! You have no idea how happy I am. It's like we've spent months walking through a corridor and only now have we found the door to the room of our true relationship . . .'

When I went to pick up my car from the underground car park where I'd left it (going down the concrete stairs, my mind replayed the scene Victoria had described to me, with the security guard's torch beam licking her naked breasts), I found the two men who'd been following me since April (although it had seemed to me that they'd been following me less frequently in recent weeks). They were standing near my car. I started walking more slowly when I saw them. This was the first time they had been in front of me rather than behind me, and that fact frightened me. Clearly, they were waiting for me, but why? I stopped about 10 metres from where they stood, and one of them walked towards me in a way that I found reassuring. In a strong accent, he said: 'We're sorry to disturb you at such a late hour, but we'd like to have a few words with you. It won't take long, and you can go home afterwards. If you'd like to follow me . . .' The other man opened the back door of the Audi Break that was parked next to my car. Accepting the first man's courteous invitation, I walked to their car and got inside. A man in his forties, sitting in the passenger seat, who struck me as being particularly refined, welcomed me considerately: 'Thank you for having agreed to meet me. It's late, so I'll be brief. We can continue our conversation another day if you'd like more time for us to get to know one another, although I think the best thing, for both of us, would be for our relations to remain as limited as possible.'

'Who are you?'

'If, in the next few days, you wish certain things to be clarified, if you have any doubts over how to interpret what I'm about to tell you, please feel free to ask me. All you need do is make a request to one of our two friends. You're able to see them on a regular basis.'

'You haven't replied to my question.'

'I'm a lawyer. I represent the interests of a client who has a proposal to make to you. You're not obliged to accept it, of course. I'll give you some time to think about it. Above all, please don't feel threatened by the circumstances of our conversation: at night, in an underground car park, just after you've been to see your mistress . . . and as you're about to pick up your car to go home to your wife . . . This is another reason why I wish to be brief: I don't want to delay you . . .' the man concluded, with an expression that was in stark contrast to his words. He was clearly threatening me. I looked at his face in silence for a few seconds, before saying: 'It's rather a strange way to go about things, don't you think? You tell me I should not feel threatened, and yet you're obviously blackmailing me.'

'Absolutely not. None of us will say a word to your wife. I was simply summing up the situation. Unless, of course, you are imprudent enough to tell anyone else about this conversation . . .'

'What's this about?'

'I've heard that you're making a huge effort on the construction site, at the moment, in order to reduce the delay on the Jupiter Tower.'

'That's one way of looking at it. It's my job.'

'Good. Apparently you're working extremely hard. You've made it a point of honour to complete this building on time, or at least with the minimum delay possible. Your bosses know how to manipulate you into sacrificing yourself. You are working flat out to meet the deadlines you've been set. Some people admire you for this, but you need to know that certain other people are irritated by it. You'll never be able to hold it together. You ought to take a holiday. Why fight against the natural course of things like this? You know perfectly well that the delay on this building is inevitable. Let go of it. Let things happen as they should . . .'

'I don't understand what you're getting at.'

'Take your mind off work a little bit. Enjoy your days off. Take the family on holiday somewhere nice. We're willing to pay for it. We can help you take your mind off work.'

'What do you mean by that?'

'One hundred and fifty thousand euros.'

'Sorry?'

'One hundred and fifty thousand euros to help you relax, to help you see things differently, to let you work without so much stress and worry. Be cool. What's it to you, after all, if this building is delayed? It won't kill you. Take it easy. Will they give you a bonus if you succeed? I'll give you one if you don't succeed. I'm not asking you to fail, or to hand in your resignation. Quite the contrary, in fact. I require the Jupiter Tower to be as well built as possible. Just don't over-exert yourself: a small delay never hurt anyone . . . She's an impressive woman, your mistress. She looked beautiful tonight, in those high heels. Make the most of it. Spend some time with her. Stop obsessing over this delay. What will be will be. There's no point trying to change things. The construction of the Jupiter Tower is delayed? So what? That's just the way it is. All I'm asking you to do is to work a little less hard, a little less conscientiously, than usual. Nothing dishonest. Admit it – what I'm telling you is precisely what you dream of your boss telling you tomorrow morning.'

'I don't understand the logic behind your request at all. In any case, I'm not interested. You're barking up the wrong tree. I would ask you kindly, from now on, to leave me in peace,' I said, and got out of the car.

The man told me: 'If you continue to fail to understand the

logic behind my request, I would be happy to explain it to you more clearly one of these days . . .'

'Don't bet on it. My answer is no. Goodnight,' I replied, slamming the car door shut. I walked around the two men who were standing between the Audi Break and my Clio. 'Excuse me . . . thank you,' I said, then got behind the wheel and drove home.

On the A11, as I listened to the last pieces Franz Liszt wrote for piano, it occurred to me that – between the moment when I received Victoria's text and the moment when I drove out of the Madeleine underground car park – I had experienced the most intense day of my life. It was as if I'd travelled through three different countries, one after another, or as if I'd been three completely different people.

Because of the inertia of a number of the companies working on the tower, I decided to create a sign that I hung in the meeting room. It consisted of the word 'ANTICIPATION', followed by its dictionary definition: 'Thought process that imagines or sees an event ahead of time.' I was preaching in the desert. Nobody anticipated anything. It's our Latin spirit: tomorrow is another day.

I always succeeded on the construction site by getting involved at ground level. I put my boots and my helmet on, and decided to help the site's foremen by getting my hands dirty. I no longer had time to send emails and await replies; decisions had to be made there and then. I knew the only way we would get out of this hole was if I spent my days instantly rectifying problems and flushing out unacceptable behaviour (laxity, understaffing, unawareness of what was at stake).

Instinctively, I separated what was secondary and ought to be brushed aside ('For fuck's sake, don't waste my time with this shit – just get on with your job and stop messing around with this kind of bollocks') from what was essential and had to be looked into more closely ('Jesus, this is a mess! Call a quick meeting this afternoon – we need to deal with this urgently. Ask Dominique and Isabelle to come at four, and we'll sort this out straight away'), while at the same time ensuring that the neglected details didn't pile up into another problem that would catch us unawares later in the process. It was a question of dynamics, of thrust and drag, of angles of attack: I had to calculate when to accelerate and when to cruise as I walked around the site and investigated situations: this speed was responsible for the amount of precision and distance with which things would be analysed; this speed had to be constantly, instinctively adjusted, the way a composer – deep in his work, using only his ears – is constantly deciding on the internal dynamics of a symphony. It was the first time I'd dared to work so fully in this risky way – flying by the seat of my pants – as if the Jupiter Tower were my own personal property, a work I'd created, a place where I had freedom to act as I wished.

It was the only way we could possibly succeed. It was also the quickest route to disaster.

One of the suppliers called me: 'David, I've got a problem. Come and take a look.'

'Where are you?'

'Fourteenth floor, south side.'

'I'm on my way.'

When I got there, he said: 'Look, I've only got a 14 cm gap instead of 18 cm. What shall I do?'

'Close it up.'

'What do you mean, close it up? The gap isn't in compliance with regulations.'

'I told you to close it up. You know as well as I do that there's no risk.'

'Even so . . . I don't know. Will you put it in writing?'

'What are you talking about? What do you want me to put in writing?'

'That I should close it up.'

'Who told you to close it up?'

'You did. Just now.'

'Are you taking the piss? I told you to close it up?'

'David, stop messing around.'

'Nobody told you to close it up, you understand? Just do it. You're not going to stop construction just for this. I've got the wall guys coming tomorrow morning, and there's no chance you're going to get in their way.'

'I couldn't give a shit about the wall guys.'

'I could. And you ought to give a shit too, if you want my opinion.'

'They won't get it in the neck if we're caught by the inspectors.'

'Nor will I, mate, because to be perfectly honest I had no idea there was only a 14 cm gap. You'll take the rap for this on your own if we're caught. So at least close it up correctly. If you do it properly, I'll have a word with Dominique about your penalties. You do have a few million euros in penalties that you're trying to get rid of, don't you?'

'Fuck me, you're a real bastard.'

'I'm not a bastard. I understand the situation better than you do. We're all in the same boat, and I want to steer us clear of the rocks. You understand that, mate?'

The art of being a construction manager resides in knowing how much risk to take. The only instruction I received from the developer was to complete construction as quickly as possible – '*by any means necessary*', he'd emphasized at our last meeting. (And everyone knows what that italicized phrase, with its menacing subtext, might mean at a time like this.) One of the objectives of the site's regular meetings was, implicitly, to persuade the companies to be less strict about meeting regulatory standards, to adapt their procedures to the urgency of our schedule. In certain paroxysmal situations, when your bosses call you three times a day to find out if you're making progress at the pace they demanded of you four days earlier (having themselves been hauled over the coals by their own bosses, in the higher echelons of CAC 40), the dilemma you're left with as construction manager is either to hand in your resignation and go home to look after the children, or to make the companies and service providers understand that the site's immediate needs – in this case, increased speed – is sufficient reason for them to agree that meeting every regulation in the book is of secondary importance, even if – in order to pass the bank's methodical tests – it must be perfectly finished, at least on the surface. *On the surface*: to gain precious time, a whole mass of little malpractices and rule-bendings may be hidden behind this subtle nuance. You close up a false ceiling, knowing perfectly well that something inside it doesn't work.

But we can't change who we are, and I've always found it difficult to accept the need to do this kind of thing. So, sometimes I would use my own spare time to go back on the orders I'd given: the next day, during my lunch hour, instead of having a rest, I'd ask for the false ceiling to be reopened so that whatever didn't work could be repaired. In spite of my exhaustion and the disgust I felt at the developer's cynical attitude, I couldn't bear the idea that a building I'd spent four years of my life working on would be less than impeccable because we'd broken too many regulations, poured concrete over too many corpses and botched jobs.

Not only did we still have a large number of floors to complete, but Dominique had calculated that it would take us eleven months to deal with the 30,000 snags that had already been enumerated by mid-June. Some builders gave me the impression that they didn't even know where to begin tackling this appalling reality. Sometimes I saw them looking dazed at the apocalyptic state of certain areas of the building where they had to work, and I sensed that they were on the point of letting themselves sink silently into helplessness and despair – particularly builders from companies who were being worn down by financial difficulties. The delay on the Jupiter Tower prevented them from signing up for enough new site work to solve their cashflow problems. Dominique had let them off the penalties they owed us in return for their continued work (without extra pay) on the site, and that was why some of these companies were struggling so badly.

On 22 June, all of the contract managers and their site foremen were summoned at 6 a.m. to the tower's 18th floor. The dawn light revealed a skeleton floor, completely bare and unfinished, without even a doorframe in place. The weather was beautiful that day. The sky was pale blue, and you could see the first rays of sunlight – as gentle and innocent as the face of a just-waking child – coming through the rectangular openings. For a few seconds, as I waited for the meeting to begin, I felt myself propelled beyond this contentious atmosphere, and an impression of beauty filled my head. The hope of a better life rose up within me before being smashed to pieces by my boss's voice which boomed, solemn and masterful, in the silence of the cool daybreak: 'Good morning, gentlemen!'

I don't know whose idea it was to stage this meeting in such an intimidatingly dramatic way, but facing the group of builders were the boss of the property development company, the boss of the construction company, the boss of my company, my direct superiors, Dominique, myself, and all our closest colleagues – a fairly tight group of about twenty people all dressed strictly in black or grey, including a scary number of CAC 40 bigwigs and top-level decision-makers. The two groups were separated by a distance of a few metres: in that space, I could see dust particles dancing in the raking sunlight. This zone of pure springtime seemed to belong to another world, where you might hear the singing of nightingales, not to the world of conflict which set the decision-makers on one side of the divide and the craftsmen and builders on the other. This second group was made up of as many people as in the first group, but they seemed less solidly together. They were more spread out, and crumbling at the edges. Some of them coughed. There was something less sophisticated about their clothing, their poses, their movements and expressions. They wore jackets and jeans. Their faces were craggy and foreign-looking. The overall effect was less austere than that of the first group. The contrast between the two was glaring: the powerful were accusing and threatening the weak amid the first rays of sunlight, at a time when duels are held, in a place that resembled a misty field at dawn. It was a somewhat abstract duel, admittedly: fought with words not swords, over a question not of honour but of finance.

The objective of this gathering was to give electroshock therapy to the builders; to draw their attention to the extreme seriousness of the delay; to tell them about the pre-litigation we had entered into, not only with the bank but with all the investors. The boss of the property development company spoke slowly, emphasizing each word, as if it went without saying that some of the people to whom he spoke would soon pay dearly, and that he was already offering them his condolences. 'I would like to listen to you. I would like to hear you explain to me how you see things. I'd like to find out how aware you are of the situation; sometimes I think that you don't really understand what's at stake here. What's at stake for us, obviously – you know that, I'm sure – but also what's at stake for all of you. *What is at stake for all of you*,' he repeated, as slowly as it was possible to pronounce this sentence, like a torturer who takes pleasure from inserting a knitting needle into the bowels of his victim. 'You can see, in this place where we stand today, the state of progress of this construction site. I'll let you judge it for yourselves,' he continued, amid the silence of this vast plateau cluttered with stepladders, tools, ducts, cables and rolls of fibreglass. He enjoined them to intensify their efforts to significantly increase the number of workers at the site: 'The situation cannot remain as it is. The delay must be massively reduced in the coming weeks. We won't be the only ones who have to pick up the pieces if we fail; I will make you – all of you – pay part of the penalties too. You can be sure of that.'

In spite of this extraordinary intervention by the property developer (in fifteen years in the profession, this was the first time I had seen such important people get involved like this in order to increase productivity on a site), the delay on the Jupiter Tower only kept increasing. The day this meeting was held, there had been a delay of three months; two weeks later, on 10 July, the delay was three months and twenty days. Dominique's forecasts were thorough and damning: in almost every area (infrastructure, technical, architectural, floor layouts, spire, snag list), the progress curve kept moving further and further away from the forecast curve.

The only light in the darkness of my mind was the way my relationship with Victoria had taken off – the excitement I felt at the idea that we would soon be able to fulfil our fantasies. We had seen each other twice since that night at the Buddha Bar and the Louvre Hotel. We'd made love for a long time, whispering to each other the things we wanted to do. I spoke first, and she accepted and extended the images I hatched in her imagination. She questioned me; she asked how far she would be allowed to go. We spent hours describing detailed scenes in which Victoria took strangers in her mouth. We didn't dare act out our fantasies, though: we contented ourselves with making love through language, with promises to ourselves that we would go further next time. I had never felt such pleasure, nor seen such intense pleasure in a woman.

The exhaustion and disillusion that pervaded the construction site; the troubles that certain builders were experiencing; the laxity, incompetence, indifference and stupidity of certain others; the psychological resistance that, to varying degrees, we all had to overcome each morning in order to start work . . . this was what I had to try to eliminate, each Wednesday, during my long imprecations.

'We're starting the big clean-up on Saturday because next week there won't be a skip on the delivery dock any more. Why? Because we're building the final delivery dock. I'm going to say this calmly, and I'll repeat it three times if necessary; that's the point of today's meeting. Don't come crying to me next week with delivery problems. Don't knock on the door of my office every five minutes to ask me how you're going to manage. We have today, Thursday, Friday and Saturday to sort out these problems. Nothing can be delivered next week.'

'We can't bring in all the supplies we need before Friday! It's impossible!'

'I never said you had to bring in all the supplies.'

'I need twelve big bags of sand next week – and a dozen pallets of stones. When am I supposed to bring those in? On Thursday and Friday, they're pouring the concrete floor.'

'There's Saturday.'

'Saturday! Saturday!'

'Well, yeah, lads. I told you a week ago that we couldn't deliver anything!'

'Do they have to make the dock in one go? Can't they do it in two sections, to leave us half to work with?'

'He's right – do it in two stages!'

'What do you mean, two stages? We're not living in a book. How would you do it, technically, in two stages? How would you do the insulation in two parts? That's without even mentioning the concrete slab we're going to pour, with all the connectors, etc. A protective slab – in concrete!'

'Even so . . .'

'Even so, that's how it is. If you weren't behind schedule, there wouldn't be a problem. Don't force me to dwell on this subject, mate . . . don't force me to be unpleasant. It's time to stop all this bullshit now.' A pause. 'All right, so we're going to talk about something easier: cleaning the site. We're going to do a cleaning raid, and we need to be clear about this – that's why Fred is here. We've got a major emptying operation on Saturday. We've been in touch with Brossard, the skip guy, to organize the rotation. What are we cleaning? S2 is like Beirut – it's all over the place. There are still bits of scaffolding at the base that have been there for three months. The brick tiles I saw on S1 – we don't need those any more. In the skip! Servin: your cables, your cradles . . . I want it all out. So, tomorrow, you put your rubbish in a corner with 'FOR THE SKIP' written on paper and Sellotaped to it. Or you make big crosses in spray paint – something that means something – so that Aziz doesn't throw away stuff he's not supposed to. I won't be there on Saturday, I'm warning you now. For once, I'll be at home, not at the site, on Saturday. So, don't come crying to me on Monday morning, saying they've thrown all your stuff away. You've got three days to see Aziz and tell him exactly what he can and can't throw away. He's available now – go and see him. Understood? We need everything to be perfect next week. We need a clear vision of the building so we can get to work on it. Everything has to be clean. The site has to be spick and span. OK? Like that, when we get to late June, maybe we'll be able to say that we've landed a knockout blow. That's right, a knockout blow. I'm telling you, we can do it. All we have to do is get organized and motivated, and have a clear idea of what we're going to do. I advise you to go and see R1 – José's got started on the plastering. It looks good. It feels like it's close to being finished. We're going to start painting the car park next week, so anyone who's still messing around down there, if there are leaks or whatever . . . time's up: you sort out your problems and you get out of there. Come Monday morning, I don't want to see anyone in the car park – is that understood? The first person I catch in the car park gets landed with all the painting! I'm telling you: next week, we start again at scratch. I want everything in order. Don't kid your-selves: from now on, the Jupiter will be a rush job. I'll help you push your guys, but to be able to do that, we need to clear every-thing out first – we have to get the last supplies delivered. All right . . . everyone understood? Any questions? Don't start has-sling me on Monday morning! I've asked Fred to be there for this very reason – he'll listen to you. Talk to him. Fred, I really want you to help me with this. You're not there just to carry out my orders. You have to take the initiative if this is going to work. We need guys to work the lifts, and they need to be fit. And the lifts have to work properly. Understood, Pierrot? If you know there's something making funny noises in one of the lifts, change it now – don't wait for the lift to stop working on Saturday while you're enjoying a nice family barbecue at home. Check the lifts now – there's no room for error. We have a very small window of opportunity, we can't afford to miss it. That's why the electricians are going to be kind enough to make sure there's a current in the staircases, and to tell me why it keeps tripping out every five minutes. There must be a leak or something somewhere . . . The lighting needs sorting out at the base as well. So, as we're putting everything in order this week, I want it dealt with. There are still floors with no lighting at all. How are we supposed to work in those conditions? Behind the conference room, all we do is walk into walls – it's completely black in there. You need a miner's lamp! And you promised me you'd sort out the lighting six months ago! I don't know how we're even managing to work in those places. It's beyond belief.' A pause. 'We need to concentrate and get moving on this. Seriously. Please. Everyone. It's nearly finished – only a few months to go. We'll get there. So, today, let's prepare calmly and methodically for next week's work. And next week . . . the fun really begins.'

'But we can start deliveries again after the 30th?'

'What do you still need delivered? You're worrying me . . .'

'The door leafs. Either I deliver them today or . . . but you know how much space they take?'

'So? Put them on S4. I've told you a thousand times you should be using S4 as a place to store your stuff. We left the wall open; there's direct access to the goods lift. How many times do I have to repeat it? They'll have to send me to Sainte-Anne soon if you keep on like this . . .'

'But it's impossible to deliver the door leafs through the . . .'

'Why is it impossible?'

'Because each box weighs 350 kilos.'

'So? For fuck's sake, I don't believe this! You arrive at the base, you unpack the boxes, you get your doors ready, and we move them by hand! Well, yeah, that's how it is. Everyone wants their forklift, and four men to do the lifting. Everyone wants to do it in comfort . . . well, that's great! But, after a certain time, you can't do it like that any more. Things change – there's nothing we can do about it. So now we're in a situation where we have to think differently. From this point on . . . because we're intelligent people . . . Yes, it was all going really well: it was all nice and comfortable, a luxury five-star construction site, perfectly organized! But now, it's not going to be quite so nice. I know it's terribly upsetting, but you're going to have to get used to it being a pain in the arse for a little while . . . Why do you think there are men working at night, bringing in supplies at night? Servin, why's there so much going on at 4 a.m., in your opinion?'

'And what do you think we're doing at night?'

'I forgot Otis. You're right, I'm sorry. But Otis . . . there you go, maybe that's the solution? Think about it. Maybe we have to consider staggered hours? You deliver the stuff at 9 p.m., come in the small van, take your time, no rush, nobody hassling you . . . Because if we stick to your methods, we won't finish this tower till 15 December! That's where we are right now – that's the reality. Which we've known for a long time, but it seems like you're just waking up to it now. Because nobody in your company is doing what I'm doing today – these motivation meetings – and that's a shame. Project Jupiter is a joint effort: we're all in it together! Everything is connected: the bank, the investors, the city, elected officials, the security committee, the fire department, public transport, political institutions. So when you tell me you have problems with the big bags that are too heavy to transport, and that that's the reason why we're behind schedule, I can't help laughing. If you had any idea how hard we're trying to find solutions, to negotiate with the bank, with the city, with our neighbours, with the institutions in La Défense, to be given permission to spread out a little bit at the foot of the tower, to take up a small part of the boulevard . . . If you don't

help me; if you keep burdening me with your big-bag problems . . . then you can deliver them in half-big bags and transport
them on wheelbarrows like my dad used to do. Seriously, this has
to stop! Your problems with wheelbarrows and backache . . .
when I think about the shit we're dealing with every day . . . it's
a joke, frankly. You need to get motivated and get moving. You
need to find solutions – old-fashioned methods, manual methods –
to get us through the next month. You need to get organized and
show a bit of goodwill. And don't arrive every morning with a
coffee in your hand, starting your day without having any idea
what you have to do. For example, when I ask the Société
Labrousse when and how it's going to install its chimneys, I'm
stunned. I negotiated with Bouygues, which is developing access
to our neighbours. Yes, ME! On Friday, I NEGOTIATED the
possibility that we can work in their zone. You think they agreed
straight away? Hardly! It took a lot of talk. I had to get down on
my knees. I had to twist their arm to get that agreement! So there
is no chance that we're going to install the stuff while spreading
our mess over the boulevard. Every evening, Daniel, your lads
have to sweep up, they have to make everything clean. Every
morning, they have to say politely, "Good morning, gentlemen,
did you sleep well? We're going to be working in your zone
today, and I'm terribly sorry but that might mean we create a bit
of dust. But don't worry, because this evening we'll have everything cleaned and put back in order. Have a nice day!" That's
how it has to be – we have no choice. So, when Labrousse tells
me that he doesn't know if he'll be ready to install the chimneys
in this zone, I'm flabbergasted! I don't know what to do any
more. I feel like throwing in the towel. Because at some point,
Bouygues are going to give us shit. They're not going to run the
risk that we'll mess up their work just before they provide it.
They'll be out of here before you can blink. That's what you

don't seem to understand. It's completely insane! Bouygues's client is La Défense. And La Défense's client is the bank. And when Bouygues writes a letter, it sends it directly to Mr Autissier, head of the bank's property division – a two-page letter saying that we're a bunch of arseholes, and that because of our fuck-ups they can't do their jobs on time. You understand? You get it? You see the problem now? If you haven't installed your chimneys before we close that zone, we'll all be in the shit. We'll all get it up the arse. Everyone in this room – all of us will be fucked. We have to understand that we're all in this together. We're all in the shit! If someone doesn't do their job, the building won't be signed off and we'll all pay the price! We are all in the shit! That's what you have to understand! I keep telling you: we're a team! And what does that mean? It means that we help each other out. *Is that clear? Has everyone understood what I'm talking about?* I'm tired . . . so tired. I can't keep repeating the same things to you a thousand times over. You have to help me, lads. Seriously. You have to help me. I see the problems, I give out orders, but you have to show willing yourselves. Anticipate! Get there ahead of me. Take some of this load off my shoulders. I can't think of everything, of every detail, all the time. Please, I'm begging you: show a bit of willing. Help me get us out of this in one piece . . .'

I'd noticed that, if I stopped thinking about the building, if my mind turned away from the mass of operational data that constituted the reality of the construction site, if I relaxed the pressure for too long, suspended the spell cast by my words, the situation returned to its natural state of laxity and sluggishness. The lawyer I'd met in the Audi Break had been right: all I'd have to do is take two days off and the construction site would subside back into its immense torpor. The completion of the Jupiter Tower now depended entirely on my awareness of its needs – total, precise, panoramic – during each second of every day.

'I was almost blubbering this morning, listening to you. It was so poignant,' Dominique told me on one of these Wednesdays (it was the one after the 14 July weekend – I remember that perfectly) while we stood at the bar of the Valmy and quickly gobbled a sandwich.

'Yeah, right. What are you on about?'

'I swear it's true. Your voice was trembling. It was coming from the innermost depths of your being. I've never seen anyone talk like that before . . .'

'That's because they all make me want to cry. It's because I'm losing heart, and yet at the same time I have no other option but to try to get us out of this shit we're in. I'm close to imploding, Dominique. I'm on the very edge of exhaustion.'

'Are you sure you don't have another option?'

'I don't understand why I have to think for them all the time, tell them everything, repeat everything a thousand times, check everything, anticipate everything for them, organize everything so that work can move quickly and rationally. All the time. Constantly. For every single little thing that has to be done. I'm a bit like a parent, except I have fifty children instead of three: every morning I have to get them ready for school; it's 8.20 a.m. and I have to take them, but twenty-two of them are still in their pyjamas! They're driving me crazy, and I feel like I'm never going to get out of this. We're never going to get out of this, Dominique! I really don't see a way out for us.'

'After this morning's meeting, I think they understood that you can't carry this thing on your own. You gave them a shock. You pulverized them.'

'Today? Why? What did I do that was special?'

'You spilled your guts. They all saw it. It was like you opened up the insides of your body to show them a tumour. I've never heard a silence like that in a meeting room before. I've never heard anyone, except at the theatre, making such a powerful impression on other people . . . with their words, their presence. I had goose bumps at times. I think some of them were even a bit scared, seeing you in that state. In fact, I don't think it – I know it. They told me.'

'What state are you talking about? You're exaggerating, Dominique.'

'Such intensity, emotion, distress, tension . . . it's difficult to describe.'

'Are you saying I did a Sarah Bernhardt? That I was acting like a tragedian?'

'It wasn't far from that. I was scared too, David. I think you should . . .'

'What? What should I do?'

'Let go. Relax. You're going to have a genuine burn-out if you keep on like this.'

'A genuine burn-out? The way you talk . . .'

'You shouldn't be allowed to get into the kind of state I saw you in earlier. It's just a job, David! Think about it. The way you were talking, you'd have thought you'd lost your sister, or that one of your friend's children had been run over by a car! Jesus, come back to reality! What's the worst that could happen to you? The absolute worst-case scenario?'

'That this failure damages my reputation for the rest of my life.'

'Oh, stop it! You know perfectly well that's not true. Everyone knows you've given everything for this tower, that there was nothing you could do – we just didn't have enough time, or enough resources.'

'Actually, I've noticed for a while that you've been . . . Is that why . . . ?'

'That I've been what?'

'Working less hard. That's why I've had to intensify my own efforts. I noticed that you've started to let go. I understand – it's human nature. After a while, you can't take any more. But don't worry, I'll take up the strain.'

'I wanted to talk to you about this, actually. We need to think about it with cool heads, the two of us.' I was about to bite down on my ham sandwich when I heard this sentence. The expression 'with cool heads' surprised me, coming from a man like Dominique. I said, 'What do you want us to think about?' before moving the sandwich to my mouth. I looked at his face while I chewed: he was chewing his sandwich too. He seemed to hesitate before replying. Finally, he said: 'We need to talk about this in better conditions, when we're calmer and we have more time. We could eat dinner, for instance. What are you doing tonight?'

'We're not going to eat dinner, Dominique. We're going to talk about it now. If you've got something to tell me, tell me it straight away. If you need time to talk to me, we'll take as much time as it takes – here, at the bar. Even if you need all afternoon, I'll give you my afternoon. Do you want another beer?'

'Yeah, I'd love one.'

I ordered two more Carlsbergs. Dominique was sweating. He seemed preoccupied. Each time I looked at him, he struggled to muster a smile. When our beers arrived, I lifted my glass to his and we clinked them together. 'To your good health, Dominique.'

'And to yours, David.'

I stared at him. He wiped the foam from his upper lip with his fingers. Finally, I said: 'You've surrendered to the temptation of money, haven't you?'

Dominique gave me an embarrassed look, before replying: 'Are you talking about the lawyer . . .'

'The lawyer in the Audi Break, yeah.'

442

Dominique hesitated. I imagined him struggling with what was probably a feeling of shame, but I sensed that this would easily be replaced by the powerful temptation to escape. I understood that. Dominique's only problem was the damage he would cause for me if he distanced himself from the site. He ended up confessing: 'I basically decided to say yes to them.'

'You decided to say yes to them, or you said yes to them?'

'I said yes to them.'

'When?'

'This morning.' There was a brief pause. Then I said: 'But what's this all about? How much did they offer you?'

'Eighty thousand.'

'When did they first contact you?'

'Just over a month ago. And you?'

'About the same time. The day I thought there'd been an article about me in *Libération*, remember?'

'Yes, I remember it well. But you didn't give in?'

'I have no intention of giving in. And I have no intention of letting you give in.'

'It's too late, David. I said yes. It's too late. I can't run the risk of breaking my word – not with people like that.'

'But what is all this? Why are they offering us money to dump Jupiter?'

'They're not asking us to dump Jupiter. I won't do that, David. If that's what they wanted, I would have said no. All they're asking us to do is not to break our balls trying to reduce the delay; they want us to take our foot off the pedal; to ease up on the schedule. It's not the same thing at all.'

'OK, they're asking us to ease up on the schedule. Why?'

'Didn't they tell you? I don't understand . . .'

'I didn't leave them much time to explain themselves, unlike you.'

'The lawyer represents a foreign investor. A Russian, I believe, though I'm not sure about that. This man bought a quarter of the tower from the property developer. As he hasn't found anyone to take it until next April, and as he faces huge financial commitments in the meantime . . .'

'The delay suits him.'

'Exactly. The delay suits him. The property developer will have to pay him penalties if the delay is maintained. And the larger it grows, the bigger the penalties become. He wants the best of both worlds. If Jupiter is finished four months late, he'll receive a quarter of €20 million – in other words, €5 million. They're giving me €80,000, and they're giving you . . .'

'A hundred and fifty thousand euros.'

'. . . and they'll get €5 million from the developer.'

'And you decided to accept this deal, Dominique?'

'You'd better believe it.'

'And what does that mean? In concrete terms, how are you planning to sabotage the tower's completion, my friend?' I looked Dominique straight in the eyes. He turned his face towards the window, through which we could see the esplanade. Visibly embarrassed, he brought his gaze back to me. 'I'm not going to sabotage anything . . .' I interrupted him in a loud voice: 'Stop being so hypocritical. You're going to be paid €80,000 so that Jupiter won't be finished on time, while I'll get paid my salary so that it will be finished on time. How is that not sabotage?'

'I'm really sorry, David. But I think you also . . . I wanted to be able to . . .'

'Get to the point, please. I don't have time to lose. What are you going to do?'

'I wanted to talk to you about this, to invite you to dinner.'

'Dominique, I'm exhausted. Please don't say any more about that. Spare me your moods, and just give me the facts.'

'I'm going on holiday. I intend to leave on Friday evening . . .'

I was gutted. I said, 'This Friday? In two days' time?' Dominique nodded. 'Until when?'

'Early September.'

'What? Fucking hell, I can't believe I'm hearing this! You're pissing off, leaving me in the lurch, from mid-July to early September, while we finish Jupiter? You – Dominique, my friend, my brother. You're going to bugger off and leave me to sink or swim when I'm up to my neck in shit?'

'David . . .'

'What, "David"?' I was beginning to get angry now, and I had to force myself not to speak too loud.

'I'm not leaving you in the shit. I'm trying to persuade you. I'm forcing you to make the right decision. You should do the same thing.'

'I don't believe this!'

'David, what do you owe them? Why are you doing this work? Have they ever shown any gratitude? Have they ever really talked to you at all? Have you ever thought, when they were talking to you, that the property developer was actually speaking to you – the extraordinary David inside you?'

'Never, but that's not a reason to screw over the building. I don't want to complete this tower for the developer – I want to do it for myself. So I can look myself in the mirror and feel proud. Because it's my job – a job I love. Because I've wanted to build skyscrapers since I was six years old!'

'But everyone has their limits, David. This is going to end up killing you. You obviously don't realize the state you're in. You're digging your own grave!'

'I'm perfectly well aware of it, and I accept it.'

'David, we don't owe them anything. They've never given us

anything they didn't have to. All they care about is themselves, their stock options and dividends. These guys are slipping me €80,000 so I can go on holiday for a month. I'm not doing anything dishonest. All I'm doing is taking my foot off the pedal. I've given this a lot of thought, and I don't see any reason to refuse them.'

'You disappoint me, Dominique.'

'There's more.'

'What do you mean? You've got more news like this to tell me?'

'I'm getting married.'

'Who to?'

'Delphine.'

'Who's Delphine? The girl you took to the Louvre Hotel? Has she calmed down?'

'We're going on holiday together. First to New York – I'm going to book a room at the Plaza – and then I'm going to buy a big motorbike and we'll ride to San Francisco, Los Angeles, the Rockies. I've always dreamed of a trip like that. If I don't do it now, when will I ever do it? We want to get married in Las Vegas. We're going to cross the Nevada desert on a motorbike. I really don't see any reason why . . .'

'All right, that's enough. I get it . . .' I took a €20 note from my jacket pocket and tossed it on the counter, then left. As I moved away, I heard Dominique, his voice trembling, say: 'David, stop! Please, stay here . . . Fuck, shit, you have to understand . . .' But I didn't turn around.

We'd arranged to meet outside a café about 3 p.m. near the Saint-Augustin church, not far from Saint-Lazare. It was hot and the sky was blue; there was a slight breeze. I loved the atmosphere on the streets: it was as if the city had rid itself of all the people it didn't like. Between 14 July and 15 August, Paris reserves its charms for a fine few, becomes a more peaceful and intimate city, a slower city. This is precisely what was going through my mind when I saw Victoria arrive at the café where I'd spent the last twenty minutes waiting for her. She was coming from a meeting with the lawyers who were advising Kiloffer on the Lorraine case. She'd told me she would be busy with that until about 3 p.m., and afterwards she would be free. I'd replied that we could get together when her meeting ended: 'Don't worry if it drags on a bit,' I'd told her on the phone. 'I'll read in the sun while I'm waiting for you, like I used to in my student days.'

Victoria kissed me on the lips and sat down across from me. She was glowing with the pleasure of knowing that she had me to herself for such a long time. She was wearing a light dress that emphasized her body's curves, and high-heeled sandals. She'd put her folder about the Lorraine case on the table. They were in the process of finalizing the sale of the heavy industry subsidiary to the Brazilian corporation, which had offered to buy it while Victoria was still negotiating its spin-off with the unions.

'How did your meeting go?' I asked Victoria once she'd sat down. She turned her face to the sun and closed her eyes for a few seconds, her hand on mine, and said: 'Ah . . . God, this weather is beautiful . . .' Then, looking at me: 'It went very well. Everything's going to plan. I'm happy.'

'I'm thrilled for you,' I said ironically.

'All right, don't start!' she interrupted, laughing. 'But I don't understand . . . how come you're free in the middle of the afternoon? I thought you were up to your neck with the tower, and you felt like you'd never get it finished?'

'I'd had enough. I've taken a few days off. I love Paris at this time of year. See how calm it is – you'd think we were in a different city. When I was a student and I didn't have enough money to go anywhere, I spent the whole of July lounging around the parks and on the banks of the Seine. I drew sketches of monuments in my notebook, and in the evenings I read books outside cafés. Those summer months in Paris were the most beautiful I've ever known. It's funny: I was probably happiest during the part of my life I spent daydreaming.'

'You had to stop working, in any case. It was essential. I was worried you didn't realize this, but I can assure you that you would have ended up collapsing or losing it completely.' I looked at Victoria without replying. She said: 'So you're going on holiday, after all? I thought you told me you couldn't . . .'

'That was what I thought until quite recently. I'm going to see a travel agent tomorrow. I want to go somewhere far away.'

'When?'

'In August. Do you want to drink something?'

'Yes. I fancy a cold beer, like you. You're right to want to go somewhere far away. A change is as good as a rest.' Then: 'What happened to change your mind?'

'Nothing important. Something upset me.'

'What? What was it that upset you?'

'The boss of the property development company. But do you really want to talk about that?'

'Why not?'

'I bumped into him, two days ago, in the corridor of the office where I work – not at the site, but in the firm's head office in Issy-les-Moulineaux. I had a meeting with the managing director there. We were walking towards each other in a corridor. I was about to stop and shake his hand, so we could exchange a few words . . .'

'You're talking about the property developer?'

'Exactly. I was quite pleased to see him, as he'd be able to tell me to my face how happy he was with us. We've managed to reduce the delay recently: the progress curve has been getting closer and closer to the forecast curve.'

'So, what happened?'

'He walked past me without stopping or even replying when I said "Hello". He gave me a cold look; his face was closed; he was so aloof from me, I was appalled. You know when two high-speed trains move past each other, it's like an immaterial collision. It's as if two masses of air smash into each other, with extreme violence. For a short while afterwards, you see windows flash past, and then you see the landscape again. This was just like that: an icy face, the shock of my unanswered "Hello" . . . he brushed past me without even bothering to slow down. I saw his charcoal suit go past, and then I was left looking at the long, empty corridor again, unable to understand what had just happened.'

'I hate that kind of attitude. I'm constantly warning Kiloffer executives not to make that sort of mistake.' The waiter had stopped in front of our table, tray on hand, to ask what we wanted to order: we asked for two draught beers, a Heineken for me and a Leffe for Victoria. I stroked her thigh, then asked: 'What was I saying?'

'You were shocked.'

'Oh, yeah . . . When I reached the managing director's office, he told me: "Ah, this is good timing. Garrel just left me – he's furious!" I said I'd passed him in the corridor. The managing director asked if he'd spoken to me, and I said no, not a word. I looked the managing director in the eyes: he could see I was upset. He turned away, surprised and fearful, as if I were having a heart attack. I asked him why Garrel was furious with me. Tears ran down my cheeks . . . but not a child's tears: an adult's tears, full of hatred. It wouldn't have taken much to tip me over into destroying everything in the office. The managing director, looking scared, replied: "Don't. It'll pass. He could see that the progress curve was getting closer to the forecast curve; he just didn't think it was close enough. Clearly he was expecting more spectacular results." I replied: "We didn't reduce the delay enough? He's angry because he thinks our efforts didn't produce the miraculous results he had in mind?" The managing director was extremely embarrassed. "It's all right. Everything will be fine. Pretend I didn't say anything. Forget all that and go back to work. Would you like a quick pick-me-up? I should have a bottle of cognac somewhere in my office – present from a client, you know – let me look . . ." I left while he was opening a metal cabinet. He didn't see me leave. I got in my car and drove straight home. It must have been about 5 p.m. I hadn't made any decisions yet, but I was sure about one thing: that he would have to beg me if he wanted me to go back to the construction site. I would demand that the property developer offered me a personal apology. I wept constantly as I drove: the tears poured from me as if a dam had burst. I yelled that I didn't want anything more to do with their stupid fucking building, that they could all go to hell. Then I noticed, in my rear-view mirror, the car I'd seen following me on various occasions. It appeared on the horizon, approaching really fast, headlights on full beam. I put my indicator on. The nose of the Audi Break stuck to my brake lights. I took a right and exited the motorway. In fact, I parked in the same service station as I had the day you told me about Kiloffer's architectural projects – remember?'

'Of course.'

'Actually, where are we with that? I was supposed to have a meeting with Peter at the end of July. It's already the 20th . . .'

'It's going to be September now, I think. He's incredibly busy at the moment.'

'In any case, it doesn't really matter now . . .'

'Why do you say that?'

'Nothing.'

'What did you do, in the service-station car park?'

'I got out of my car and walked towards the Audi Break. One of the two men, the passenger, came out to meet me. I've told you about them – the two guys who were following me in the streets, back in May . . .' The waiter returned with the beers and placed them on the table. Victoria: 'So you weren't kidding then? Thank you,' she added to the waiter.

'No, I wasn't kidding. Thank you. To you, my dear and tender friend,' I said, lifting my glass to hers. 'You look very beautiful today.'

'To you. To your good health, and your holidays,' she replied, before taking a long swig. She reacted to my compliment by giving me a languorous look over the rim of her glass. Then: 'Ah, I needed that. It's so hot!'

'You've got a little foam moustache – hang on, I'll take care of it,' I said to Victoria, kissing her on the mouth. 'There, that's better . . .'

'What did they want, those two guys?'

'I'll tell you that in a minute. I told this man that I agreed to take a holiday and that I wished to meet his employer as soon as possible. He walked off towards the petrol pumps to phone him. He was kicking bits of gravel with the ends of his shoes, just like I did the day when you told me about the projects. He came back to me and said I had a meeting in the same underground car park in the Madeleine as when he made me the offer the first time.'

'What offer are you talking about?'

'They're giving me a bit of money so I'll work less hard. A generous man is paying for my holidays, but only on condition that I take them in August.'

'I have no idea what you're talking about.'

'You'll see. We went to the underground car park in Madeleine. I'd just parked my car when a Jaguar stopped next to me. I was invited to get in the back seat. I sat next to the same lawyer I'd talked to once before. I told him I'd given the matter some thought and that I now agreed to make sure that the Jupiter Tower would be completed four months late. The man welcomed this decision. He said he was happy I'd changed my mind. He said he'd never understood why I alone did not put my own personal interest first. He admitted he'd been fascinated by my integrity. He'd been amazed that I would reject such a large sum of money to help out people who thought only of their own profit and would undoubtedly have done everything they could to pocket the €150,000 that I'd refused. "I was stunned that you should be so contemptuous towards money. I didn't know whether to consider you a cretin, a hero or some kind of anachronistic idealist. Refusing such a large amount of money to protect your boss's interests . . ."'

'You met a lawyer who said that to you?'

'I replied that my idealism was clearly not as intact as I'd imagined. The proof being that I had not resisted his advances for very long. I, in turn, was succumbing to cynicism. I asked him if he'd brought the sum of money he'd promised me. He placed a leather briefcase on my knees, and I opened it.'

'You're getting money for finishing the Jupiter Tower behind schedule?'

'This is just between us, Victoria.'

'Of course it's just between us. But does this kind of thing happen a lot in your job?'

'It's the first time it's happened to me. You know, I'm so tired . . . you'd told me so many stories . . . you seemed to have so many different personas . . .'

I paused, and Victoria watched me in silence. 'And?' she said. 'What are you getting at?'

'At one point, I thought you were behind all this.'

'What do you mean? Behind what?'

'I wondered if Kiloffer was the secret investor. And all because I saw an Audi Break parked next to your 4WD in Kiloffer's car park.'

'That's Peter's car.'

'I know, it's absurd. It was just an association of ideas. The story wouldn't stand up for thirty seconds. But it's interesting in that it shows that my perception of reality has been completely infected by suspicion. I no longer believe what I see.'

'You no longer believe what you see?'

'Reality seems so misleading, so indefinable . . . I was going to say dishonest . . . It's such a mixture of information, issues, strategies and interests . . . things are never what they seem. The thought occurred to me that perhaps you'd been asked to slow down my work . . .'

'Oh, David! It really is time you took a holiday!'

'See? You're constantly advising me to take a break!'

'But, David, it's absurd!'

'I know it's absurd. I never thought it was true. All I'm saying is that I no longer believe in anything. Reality seems false to me, like some kind of *trompe-l'œil* maintained by a group of people who manipulate information about reality in their own interests. I no longer know, when I'm faced with a new situation, what the truth is, or even if the idea of truth has any meaning at all. Like you with your unions, when each story you tell them contains within it the story you will tell them next time . . . until the final story, the story at the centre of all the other stories – the sale of the heavy industry division. The reality is revealed only at the end, a bit like when you come out of the cinema, having watched a film, and find yourself on the street. The unions are waking up in front of the cinema, out on the street, having spent months watching the mirages of a film in three parts: at the end, they realize they've been fooled, that they've been sold to the Brazilians.'

'All right, David. Shall we stop talking about work?'

'Everything is like that. Half of what we believe to be true is invented by other people, or sometimes even by ourselves. Perhaps mostly by ourselves . . . I thought the property developer held me in great esteem, that he cared about me, that I would end up being rewarded for my efforts. I thought it was right that I should give everything to complete the Jupiter Tower on time. I thought that lawyer was the enemy of all I believed in and held dear. I thought I'd be able to start my own agency in September. And, all the time, I was fooling myself . . .'

'I told you, you'll meet Peter this autumn. I promise you that. I must admit I've lost all control of his schedule recently. But still, that's not a reason to doubt my word.'

'Nobody can say who's right – you or the unions – nor can they say where the truth lies in this conflict between you. Did you fool them in order to help them? Did they fool themselves by refusing to change? Or, on the contrary, did you really fuck them over, and now they're facing some dark and difficult times? Who's right, and who's wrong? Nobody, perhaps . . . Maybe this question no longer has any meaning. Maybe there is no longer any sense in wondering if people are right or wrong to do what they do, or to believe what they believe. Maybe the number of situations in which it's absurd to want to know who's right or who's wrong is going to keep rising. Perhaps, in the end, that's the definition of this capitalist world of ours, and it's why you embody it so perfectly . . . I'm probably just a bit exhausted, but

454

I feel like I no longer understand anything, that I no longer know what to think about anything relating to society or politics or economics. Here and now, I just don't know if you're horrible or wonderful, appalling or perfect.'

'Who knows! But I'd like you to find me perfect and wonderful . . .'

'Now I have this money, I feel satisfied, as if I've done the right thing – as if it were the logical conclusion to the months I've just endured. I don't feel any guilt whatsoever – quite the contrary, in fact. It's as if, finally, I've got the reward I deserved. Don't you find that strange? What happened to make me think like that?'

'You're right, it's very surprising. Anyway, what are we doing? Where shall we go?'

'I don't know. I want you. I find you ultra-sexy in that dress. All the men who walk past in the street are looking at you.'

'I want to make love too.' And, in a lower voice: 'I want you to fuck me.'

'Where shall we go?'

'To the Concorde Saint-Lazare.'

I took a €500 note from my jacket pocket and turned to wave at the waiter. Victoria gasped: 'Five hundred euros! My God, you really have become a rich man!'

'Tonight is on me. We'll make love, then I'll take you to an expensive restaurant.'

We walked towards the Concorde Saint-Lazare. As we were passing a porn cinema, Victoria said: 'Hey, that's where I went with Laurent.' We stopped, and I looked Victoria in the eyes. She trembled slightly, and I got hard. I asked her: 'Do you want to go in?'

'I don't know . . . Do you want to?'

'I think so. But we don't have to.'

'I'm a bit scared.'

'Me too. It's intimidating.'

'We've been talking about it for so long . . .'

'Come on, let's go. Just to look, not to do anything,' I said to Victoria. 'If it doesn't feel right, we'll leave.'

We bought two tickets and went in. There must have been about fifteen men in the cinema, scattered alone throughout. The audio crackled. The woman's orgasmic cries were somewhat distorted. The film itself was worn out, scratched, the images drained of colour; it must have been screened hundreds of times. To judge from the actors' clothes, the film had been made in the eighties.

We sat in the middle of an empty row. It was stiflingly hot. The sound was too loud, accentuating this oven-like, enclosed feeling. The poor quality of the dubbing made it seem like the dialogue had been tacked on to the images. The film was divided in two by the same barrier that separated actors from viewers, as if it were the spectator of its own squalor.

Up on the screen, a blonde woman was sucking a cock. I put my hand on Victoria's thigh and began caressing her skin, pushing back the fabric of her dress. She said: 'Touch my breasts.' I kissed her on the mouth, and slid my fingers into her cunt. It was soaking wet. I asked her: 'Do you want to make love, or do you want to leave?'

'No, go ahead. Make love to me. Let's do it now.'

'Here and now, in front of all these men?'

'Undress me. Show them my body. I want to be naked. I want them to touch me . . .' I removed her dress, her bra and her knickers: she was naked. There were men all around us: in front, behind, on each side. They came closer in the darkness – slowly, carefully, in order not to frighten us off. She held my cock in her hand. I saw that men's fingers had started to touch Victoria's skin – shyly and cautiously at first. As she hadn't tried to protect herself from these initial intrusions, the men's hands became increasingly bold. I even saw one trying to insert his fingers into Victoria's pussy. She was groaning in my ear. While she sucked my cock, I slid my middle finger deep into her anus. She lifted her head to tell me: 'Come on, let's make love. I really want it.'

I took Victoria from behind. She knelt on her seat, leaning towards the row behind, her breasts hanging over the top. I saw erect cocks all around her face. The men who were pressing close to us were masturbating while they watched us. My lips were close to her ear. While she moaned, I whispered: 'Victoria, have you seen all those cocks? You're making them hard. They all want to fuck you. Which one do you like best? Touch your favourite – I want to see you do it.' Victoria took a cock in her hand – quite a short cock, but thick and solid. She put it between her lips. I penetrated Victoria while I watched her go down on this stranger. My face was close to hers; the man's cock was a few centimetres from my lips. Victoria held it in her fingers and swallowed it. I watched the man's cock and fucked Victoria. I could feel myself close to coming. I pulled out before I could ejaculate.

I then watched as Victoria moved aside with two men. She held their cocks and kissed them passionately on the mouths. I asked Victoria to come and sit on me. We made love while she caressed the cocks of those two guys, whom she'd chosen above all the others.

I came. I told Victoria we had to leave. She was sucking the cock of one of those two men while the other one licked her pussy. She was sitting on a seat, legs spread wide and ankles resting on the tops of the seats in front. Groaning, she held the head of the man who was licking her while the short, thick cock moved in and out of her mouth. I leaned over her and said, 'Come on,

Victoria. We have to get out of here.' She replied: 'Not yet, please! We've just got started. Wait a bit longer.'

'No, now. Hurry up,' I said, pulling her by the arm.

'I've never seen such a beautiful cock. Hang on, I want him to fuck me. Do you have any condoms?'

'No, I don't have any condoms.'

'I want him to fuck me. Please, don't do this to me . . .'

'We have to go. Victoria, we can't stay here.'

'OK, we'll go. But they're coming with us.'

'Who?'

'These two.'

'Don't be ridiculous. Come on, that's enough. Get dressed.'

I searched in the darkness for Victoria's clothes – her dress, her bra and her knickers – and handed them to her. She was talking to one of the two men. She came out from between the seats to get dressed in the side aisle. The two men had followed her and were doing up their flies. The others were dispersing. A black man had moved to the edge of our group. One of the two men was helping Victoria zip up her dress. She smiled at him when she turned around, then kissed him on the mouth. They looked deep into each other's eyes. I waited for Victoria at the exit door, which I was holding ajar. I had her handbag and the folder about the Lorraine case.

I shouted: 'Victoria! What are you doing?'

One of the two men, hearing me, turned briefly to look at me.

The four of us left the cinema together, followed by the black guy who hung back a little bit. Once we got into the street, the two men led Victoria to the left. I couldn't get her attention any more. She wasn't speaking to me.

'Victoria, what are you doing? Stay here. Where are we going? Why are we following these guys? What did you say to them?'

We ended up in an underground car park. The two men stopped in front of a van. They helped Victoria inside, then got in themselves. She sat between them. I went to the passenger side and said to Victoria: 'What are you doing? You've lost your mind! Come here – stay with me!'

'Are you coming or not?'

'No, I'm not coming. And you're not going either, Victoria. You're staying here!'

'I should have guessed you'd be like this. If there's one thing I can't stand, it's being interrupted when I'm in the middle of something.'

'Victoria, I'm begging you. Please stay. Get out of there!'

'God, I don't believe this! You're such a pain!' The man closest to me said: 'All right, mate, so what are you doing? Are you coming with us? Answer your girlfriend.' I looked distractedly at Victoria while holding the handle of the van door so the man couldn't close it. She said: 'Jesus, you're such a prick. I'll be gone a couple of hours. I'll call you later.' And Victoria leaned forward to pull the door shut while the van reversed, then sped off. For what felt like a long time, I could hear the whine and screech of the van's tyres as it drove to the exit of that strange concrete world. I left the car park by climbing the stairs, the black man beside me.

'We're looking for him,' Christophe Keller told me during the first hours of custody. 'We're questioning the person who runs the phone shop you saw him enter when you went your separate ways. For your sake, I hope we find him and that he confirms your version of events while we search for the two men you mentioned. What I don't understand is why you took the van's registration number: if your girlfriend was in danger, you shouldn't have let her leave . . . and if she wasn't in danger, why take the registration number?'

'It all happened so fast. I didn't know how to react. We'd had a bit of a row . . .'

'But she'd been your mistress for almost a year! She'd only just met those two guys! How could a row justify . . .'

'I know. I don't understand how I could . . . It was only when I saw the van leave that I regretted not staying with her, and that's when I instinctively noted down the number. I don't know why exactly.'

'We found the van's owner. He's been in hospital for four days. We're questioning him to find out who he might have lent the van to. In the meantime, I'd like to try to understand something. How is it possible to let your lover go off with two strangers?'

'I told you, it all happened so quickly. I couldn't reason with her . . .'

'So why didn't you go with them?'

'I don't know.'

'Were you scared?'

'I don't think so.'

'You pick up two Polish guys in a porn cinema in Saint-Lazare. You watch them drive off at top speed with your girlfriend. And you tell me you weren't scared; that that's not why you didn't go with them! But, in that case, why didn't you go with them?'

'I don't know. I don't understand what happened. I was pathetic – is that what you want to hear me say?'

'I don't want to hear you say anything. All I want is the truth. What's to say you didn't kill this woman yesterday evening in the Sénart forest? What's to say you didn't take down a van's number at random and make up this entire story? We're going to try to get hold of the cinema cashier to see if he remembers seeing the four of you leave together – the five of you, counting the black guy. But we'll have to wait a while, given that it's only 10 a.m.

and that porn cinemas tend not to open so early. That's why, if your version is true, I'd like to understand why you let her go, why you took the registration number, why you didn't come to us straight away and make a statement. It would have won us some time. Who knows, maybe we might even have saved her?'

'I don't know.'

'You don't know, you don't know. You should have thought about this beforehand, rather than crying about it when it's too late. Here, have a tissue . . .'

'Thank you.'

'Do you do that often?'

'What are you talking about?'

'Oh, stop playing the innocent! It's getting on my nerves. You know perfectly well what I'm talking about.'

'It was the first time.'

'That's what they all say. It's funny: when something like this happens, it's always the first time.'

'Well, in this case, it really was the first time.'

'All right, let's say it was. So it was your fantasy for her to be screwed by strangers in a porn cinema?'

'For both of us.'

'Sorry, I didn't quite catch that. Could you speak a bit louder, and stop crying every five minutes?'

'It was a fantasy for both of us.'

'And yet you're telling me you'd never done it until yesterday?'

'No.'

'And what exactly was your relationship? How would you categorize it?'

'She was my mistress.'

'Were you in love with her?'

'I don't know.'

'What do you mean, you don't know?'

'It was complicated.'

'What was complicated?'

'Knowing if I was in love or not. We were both married. We both swore not to compromise our family lives.'

'Well, that was a great success.'

'. . .'

'Her too?'

'Her too what?'

'She didn't want to compromise her family life either?'

'No.'

'So she wasn't in love with you.'

'I don't think so.'

'You're sure or you don't think so?'

'I'm sure of it.'

'Of what?'

'That she wasn't in love with me.'

'Really? Seems to me you'd have to be really in love with someone to let them drag you into this kind of shit scenario.'

'She wanted it. She didn't do it to please me. The proof being that she continued without me.'

'You should have protected her.'

'I know. Charge me for not helping a person in danger, if that's what you want.'

'First we're trying to make sure you didn't kill her. We'll see about the consolation prizes later. So why didn't you?'

'Why didn't I what?'

'Protect her.'

'It went too fast. I didn't understand what was happening. She pushed me away and insulted me. It was violent.'

'Why did you let her leave, if it was violent? You must have guessed it would end badly.'

'I don't mean the two men were violent – she was. Her words were. The way she refused to stay with me, to listen to me. The way she wanted to go with them. That was what was violent. It was like she turned into someone else; I didn't recognize her any more. She was a stranger to me. Even the look in her eyes was different, her voice. I asked her not to go with them, but it was like banging my head against a brick wall. That's why I didn't get in the van. There was no place for me. She didn't need me to go with her.'

'She didn't need you to go with her.'

'She would rather have gone on her own than not gone. She was angry with me for interrupting her in the middle of something. That's how I felt, how she made me feel. She was wild. There was nothing she wanted except to do what she had in mind at that moment.'

'I can't believe that. It's just unbelievable.'

'And yet it's the truth.'

'It doesn't chime with what I've read in her private diary.'

'. . .'

'In her private diary, she seems completely in love.'

'I don't believe it. You're wrong.'

'When I read all these pages, I don't get the feeling they were written by a woman who would happily go off with two blokes she met in a Saint-Lazare porn cinema. I don't believe a word of your story.'

'And yet that's what happened.'

'Are you claiming she wasn't in love with you?'

'She never said or wrote to me that she loved me.'

'But I'm telling you she did. She was madly in love with you. So it's strange – I can't piece together your version of events with what she wrote about the two of you, about her desire to take things further.'

'I'm telling you it's the truth. I couldn't stop her leaving.'

'You still maintain you don't know if you loved her?'

'I don't know any more. Give me a break about that, will you?'

'No, I'm not going to give you a break. A woman is dead. The texts and emails I found on her BlackBerry indicate that you were the last person to have seen her alive. For now, you are the only suspect. So I'm going to continue questioning you, because something in your version of events doesn't stack up.'

'. . .'

'As far as she was concerned, things seemed pretty clear-cut. I'm talking about her feelings for you. On 16 July, for example – six days ago – there's this; I'll read it to you . . . "Each day, this man becomes a little more precious to me. Each day, he occupies more space, becomes more important in my life. I know we decided not to go too far: I have my life, he has his, and our being together is just one extra element in both. But I find it increasingly hard to accept this state of affairs. More and more, I imagine myself with David. More and more, I think about leaving my husband for him."' Silence. The policeman looks me in the eyes. I start to cry again. Then he asks: 'So, what do you think of that?' I can't reply. He watches me cry, not saying anything. Finally I mumble, 'I didn't know.'

'You should have made it your business to find out. You should have taken her to eat in a romantic restaurant instead of going to a porn cinema. Perhaps she would have told you about her feelings then . . .'

'She wasn't the type of woman who talked about her feelings.'

'Or what about this one, from two days ago . . . "Peter had told me he'd meet David, but I can sense he'd rather work with a major architecture agency. To win time, I let David think that

Margareth was going to phone him to arrange a date for the meeting. I lied to him, thinking I would manage to change Peter's mind, even if only for the head-office project. I don't know what to do now. I could tell David, but I'm afraid of losing him. I'm afraid he'll hold it against me, that he'll distance himself from me. I'm afraid of finding out that he's only staying with me because of the prospect of this position. Or I could hide from him the difficulties I'm having persuading Peter, but that seems dishonest. I know perfectly well that, if I insist, Peter will agree to meet David, but what's the point in both of them wasting their time? No matter how much I think about this situation, I always end up with the same irrational, absurd, utopian conclusion: that we should live together like true lovers; that we should dare to face the truth for a change; that he should leave his wife and I should leave my husband. However impossible it seems, I can't fight against this feeling. I'd help him start his own agency: I earn enough to provide for us both, and I have enough contacts in the business world to help him find work. Oh, my little diary, my only confidante, if you knew! How I would love to help him, to make him happy, to see him finally bloom! He seems so unhappy, so disillusioned. He would finally become an architect, even if, to begin with, it would probably be hard. But for both of us, it would be like a new life, a second youth . . . I need to summon the courage to talk to him about this one day . . . Maybe the day after tomorrow, because it seems like we'll be able to meet each other quite early, after my meeting with the lawyers . . . But we are reasonable, responsible adults, and such things are just not done. You can't ask a forty-two-year-old man with a wife and two children to throw up everything and start a new life with a woman he's never said he loves, not even once. Oh, how complicated life is! I don't even know if I love this man. I'm a bit lost.

We're so different, the two of us; sometimes I think it's just a whim. But we'll see the truth of that in September, when the summer is over. I'm dreading these holidays: I feel I've become a stranger for my husband, as he has for me. We've been living separate lives during the week for months now. We never make love any more. He is completely uninterested in my work. What do we have in common? Whereas with David, it's so intense, so addictive . . ."'

Forty-eight hours later, when I'd been released and I stood in front of Versailles police station holding my leather briefcase, I decided to drink a double espresso at the bar of a café.

I tried to call Sylvie's mobile, but it went straight to voicemail.

I went to the toilets so I could take a €500 note from my brief-case. I paid for my coffee with this, so I would have change, and then I took a taxi home.

I rang the bell, but nobody answered. I didn't have my keys. I walked around the house to make sure there wasn't an open door or window anywhere. Finally, I picked up a stone from the garden rockery and broke the kitchen window, at the back of the house.

The alarm sounded. I rushed inside to type in the secret code, and it went silent.

I collapsed on the living-room sofa.

There were dozens of paper aeroplanes on the carpet – aeroplanes of many different sizes, including some tiny ones – which had not been there the morning the police took me away. I assumed Vivienne had spent her time making them, alone, while her mum was unable to do anything but cry in her bedroom. The obsessive nature of this seemed to symbolize the madness that had taken over our lives. I started crying again. I stood up and

466

walked around the house. Nobody had left a note for me anywhere.

The doorbell rang.

I went to see who it was.

My neighbour, having heard the alarm, had wanted to make sure that everything was all right. I told him I didn't have the keys, so I'd had to break the kitchen window.

'Why didn't you come to us to get the keys?'

I told him I hadn't dared. He said he understood. He said I'd been mentioned on television and even in the newspapers. He asked if I'd been released.

'Did you think I'd escaped?'

I kept crying. He handed me a tissue.

'That's not what I meant. I'm going to leave you now.' He left.

I went to see if the suitcase was still in our bedroom wardrobe. It wasn't.

I wondered if Sylvie had left.

My only fear was seeing them return: having to face the looks in my daughters' eyes, unprepared.

I needed to hide out for a while, to run away so nobody would find me.

I wanted to die.

I walked around my house, not knowing what to do.

I imagined I would find a way to put an end to it all a bit later.

I had to leave before Sylvie came back with my daughters.

I threw a few things in a travel bag, picked up the leather briefcase, got in my car and drove away.

I took roads at random. I couldn't stop crying.

The direction I took was instinctive. I wanted to get away from the suburbs, to move as deeply into the centre of France as I could. I drove through towns and villages where I'd never been. I saw names on road signs – the kinds of names you see on the backs of plates.

I drove for hours.

Night fell. I hadn't slept for forty-eight hours. I stopped in front of a pink-walled hotel.

The sign was lit up. 'Hôtel de la Forêt'.

I switched off the engine and got out of my car.